Is he the man of her dreams?

Gorgeous
Grooms

Three dreamy and feel-good romances from
three beloved Mills & Boon authors!

Gorgeous Grooms

JACKIE BRAUN

LIZ FIELDING

NATASHA OAKLEY

MILLS & BOON

First published in Great Britain 2010
Harlequin Mills & Boon Limited,
Eton House, 18-24 Paradise Road, Richmond, Surrey TW9 1SR

GORGEOUS GROOMS © by Harlequin Enterprises II B.V./S.à.r.l 2010

Her Stand-In Groom, Her Wish-List Bridegroom and *Ordinary Girl, Society Groom* were first published in Great Britain by Harlequin Mills & Boon Limited in separate, single volumes.

Her Stand-In Groom © Jackie Braun Fridline 2004
Her Wish-List Bridegroom © Liz Fielding 2004
Ordinary Girl, Society Groom © Natasha Oakley 2005

ISBN: 978 0 263 88046 5

05-1010

Printed and bound in Spain
by Litografia Rosés S.A., Barcelona

HER STAND-IN GROOM

BY
JACKIE BRAUN

Jackie Braun is a three-time RITA® finalist, three-time National Readers Choice Award finalist and past winner of the Rising Star Award. She worked as a copy-editor and editorial writer for a daily newspaper before quitting her day job in 2004 to write fiction full time. She lives in Michigan with her family. She loves to hear from readers and can be reached through her website at www.jackiebraun.com

To Mom and Dad:
Thanks for passing on your love of reading.

CHAPTER ONE

THWACK!

Catherine Canton had made a career of opposing domestic violence, but that didn't keep her from using a bouquet of white roses to smack her prospective groom upside his philandering blond head.

Cursing amid a snowstorm of fragrant petals, Derek Danbury stopped his intimate exploration of the wedding planner's lacy black bra.

''What the—'' he began, before turning around completely. Once he had, his expression shifted from irritated to uh-oh.

In an instant he was slicking on the charm, as well as the boyish smile Catherine had once found so irresistible. How could she have been so naïve?

All but shoving the other woman aside, he said, ''Sweetheart, I can explain this.''

If she hadn't wanted to cry Catherine might have laughed at that absurd proposition. And if the situation hadn't been so wretchedly pathetic she might even have let him try, for the sheer entertainment value such an exercise would provide. Derek was a master at coming up with perfectly innocent reasons for doing the outrageous. She'd often found his justifications amusing, if exasperating. But this wasn't the same as showing up late for dinner with her parents or failing to meet her at some charity function.

No, he'd been helping another woman out of her clothes in the choir loft of a church. The same church where, in less than fifteen minutes, he was supposed to swear before God and their guests to forsake all others.

Catherine had never been blind to his flirtatious nature, but she had foolishly believed that flirtation was all he'd ever engaged in. Oh, there had been tabloid speculation to the contrary, but, as her mother had preached on more than one occasion, those rancid scandal sheets' attempts to sell more papers were hardly a valid enough reason for Catherine to question her engagement to one of the country's most eligible bachelors. This was especially the case, her mother had insisted, since she and Catherine's father had already plunked down so much of their dwindling fortune to give their daughter a memorable society wedding.

And so Catherine, ever the dutiful daughter, had brushed aside her nagging concerns as silly pre-wedding jitters. She didn't doubt for a minute her mother would be ruing the day she'd insisted on hiring a professional wedding planner.

"I don't need an explanation," Catherine said, as the wedding planner buttoned her blouse and wisely slinked away.

"It's really not what it looked like," Derek replied.

She might have been naïve to believe a notorious

playboy like Derek, heir to the venerable Danbury Department Store chain, was ready to settle down, but with the evidence of his infidelity now made so obvious she would not be thought stupid as well.

Holding up a hand, she said, "Please, don't insult my intelligence."

"Come on, Cath. You have to listen to me."

"Listen to you? What can you say to make this somehow less sordid than it actually is? I won't tolerate lies."

"I love you. That's not a lie." He reached out, caressed her arms through the white silk of her gown. Mere minutes ago she would have believed him. But how could he love her—truly love her—and do this?

She pulled away, her breath hitching. "Don't."

"I'm sorry," he repeated. "I made a mistake."

"Would you still think so if you hadn't gotten caught?" Her voice hiked up an octave, pushed there by pain and disbelief. "My God, Derek, you're in a church. It's our wedding day. And you were…" She shook her head, the image still revoltingly fresh.

"Let's keep our voices down, sweetheart," he urged, casting a nervous glance toward the railing, no doubt thinking about the multitude of guests already assembled below. "In fact, let's discuss this later."

"Later? When later? After we're married?" She crossed her arms and tapped the battered bouquet against one hip, her emotions swinging wildly from hurt to anger again. "I don't think so."

Alarm widened his eyes. "You're overreacting, Cath. Don't blow this out of proportion."

"Oh, that's rich. You almost had sex in the church with our wedding planner minutes before the ceremony. I don't see how I could blow this out of proportion. As offenses go, Derek, what you did is gargantuan already."

"You know, technically I didn't do anything."

Catherine closed her eyes and counted to ten, trying to summon up some of the control for which she was legendary. Ice Princess, some called her, but she was fuming now, a volcano ready to blow. She preferred that. Hurt and embarrassment could come later, and settle over her like suffocating ash. She dropped her hands to her sides. Her fingers fisted around the bouquet handle as if were a Louisville Slugger, and she was seriously thinking about taking another swing at him when someone said, "Excuse me, please."

Derek's cousin Stephen stood not five feet behind them in the choir loft. Despite similar heights and builds, and the fact their birthdays fell just one day apart, she couldn't imagine two men more different in either appearance or disposition. Derek was fair and always joking. Stephen was dark and brooding.

He stepped forward, his voice barely above a whisper. "Derek, your mother asked me to come and mention that the guests can hear this conversation. She suggests you move to a more discreet location."

Whatever he thought of the situation, none of it was reflected in the deep brown of his eyes.

Privacy. Catherine longed for it at this moment—
that and something far more comfortable than the
beaded pumps that were crushing the toes on each
foot into a single digit. But both would have to wait
until she'd dealt with the situation at hand. Picking
up the heavy train of the designer gown her mother
had insisted Catherine had to have, she walked to the
railing of the balcony.

"Can I have everyone's attention, please?"

"What are you doing?" Derek whispered, rushing
up from behind her. He grabbed her arm none too
gently, hauling her around. The act so surprised
Catherine that she dropped her bouquet over the rail's
edge. Its sterling silver handle struck the tiled aisle
below, echoing in the church like a shotgun blast.
Guests shifted in their seats to see what was going
on, some of them pointing, all of them murmuring.

Catherine gasped. "You're hurting me."

In an instant Stephen was beside them.

"Don't be an idiot, Derek. Let go of her arm." He
never raised his voice, in fact he lowered it, and he
seemed all the more menacing because of it.

"This isn't your concern, cousin. It's a simple misunderstanding between Catherine and me. We don't
require your interference."

"I'll be the one to decide that."

Stephen stepped between them, forcing Derek to
break his hold on her arm.

Catherine expelled a breath, still too stunned to believe what had just occurred. Over Stephen's shoulder

she stared at Derek, feeling as if she were truly seeing him for the first time. There was no denying he was a beautiful man, with sun-kissed hair and eyes a clear crystal-blue. Had all that physical perfection and his considerable charm somehow blinded her to the ugliness she now saw in his sneering visage?

He glared first at Stephen and then at her, and she could not help but recall the story of Dr. Jekyll and Mr. Hyde, for he seemed so different from the man who had swept her off her feet with words of love and eyes full of adoration.

At last something—manners? breeding?—resurrected itself. His tone hushed, he said, ''Have it your way, cousin. I don't really need her anyway.''

Need? What an odd way to put it. Before Catherine could puzzle through what he meant by that strange and hurtful statement, he was calling out, ''The wedding is off. Catherine and I regret the inconvenience to you all and thank you for your understanding. Please accept our apologies.''

The church erupted in full-fledged conversations now. The talk was no longer library-quiet but ball-game-loud, as guests traded speculation about the doomed couple.

Stephen lingered beside Catherine after Derek had stalked away, although he looked uncomfortable to be there.

''Are you all right?'' he asked.

She nodded stiffly, even as her heart seemed to shatter into a million jagged pieces.

"I got a note telling me to meet Derek here for a surprise. I thought maybe he'd bought me a gift, something he wanted me to wear down the aisle. Instead, I found him…"

She sucked in a breath, still not quite able to believe what she had witnessed. All that passion, and for a virtual stranger. Had she ever inspired that kind of excitement in her prospective groom? Had she ever felt it in return? Those questions as much as Derek's infidelity forced a sob from her lips. She covered her mouth, muffling another.

"Can I get someone for you? Your mother, perhaps?"

"Dear God!" It came out half-sob, half-hysterical laugh. "Why don't you just dump me over the rail along with my bouquet?"

Her mother was probably hyperventilating at this point. And her poor father had probably fainted dead away after realizing they'd just blown hundreds of thousands of dollars, much of it non-refundable, on a wedding that would never take place. At least he would have all that twelve-year-old Scotch to commiserate with. For a daughter who had spent a lifetime trying to please her difficult parents, she'd certainly made a mess of things.

"I'll take that as a no." A ghost of a smile hovered on his lips.

They were nice lips, a little fuller than most men's, softening the otherwise hard lines of his face. Catherine could only recall having half a dozen conversations with Stephen, all of them about polite, neutral topics. The cousins didn't share the same interests or circle of friends, but whenever she did spend time in his company, or whenever she ran into him while visiting Derek at the Danbury building, she found herself undeniably drawn to Stephen.

She sensed a sadness about him, a loneliness that she always assumed resulted from losing his mother and father as a boy and being raised by his stodgy grandparents. It was in Catherine's nature to soothe, to nurture, to comfort. That was the source of the odd attraction, she'd told herself when she'd first begun to feel it. Now, with her emotions reeling, she wasn't so sure. In fact, she wasn't sure of anything.

He cleared his throat, and she realized she had been staring at him.

Summoning up her manners, Catherine said, "Thank you for what you did just now. I don't know what came over Derek, grabbing my arm that way."

"Did he hurt you?"

Her arm ached, but she resisted the urge to rub it. "No, not really," she lied. "I hope there won't be a strain between the two of you because of this?"

Again that enigmatic smile lurked, although this time she thought he seemed a little resigned. "I'm sure this won't change a thing."

"Well, thank you anyway."

Stephen watched her leave, spilling out the train of white silk as she walked down the stairs. He knew from his aunt's endless chatter that the gown was an original, designed especially for this bride. The small pearl buttons that ran the length of Catherine's slender spine were the real thing, as were the tiny pearls that edged the neckline. He wondered if it disappointed Catherine that no one would see its beauty this day as she glided down the aisle on her father's arm. He knew it would most women of her sort.

Debutante. The word alone left a sour taste in his mouth. Admittedly, his opinion of Catherine was colored by his opinion of his cousin. Any woman who would consent to marry Derek surely had to be as shallow and self-centered as he. Still, Stephen was glad she'd discovered what kind of man her prospective groom really was before making a lifetime commitment. Stephen's regard for her had jumped several notches, watching her dump Derek just before the ''I dos'' were exchanged. She had literally lost a fortune by doing so, regardless of the prenuptial agreement she had signed.

Downstairs, people were already streaming from the pews, many of them heading straight for her, with pity pinching their mouths into thin smiles. Stephen felt a twinge of it for her as well. No one should be forced to listen graciously to trite and in some cases insincere condolences right after what Catherine had been through. But as he watched her summon up what he thought of as her serene society expression he knew she would handle this with her usual cool grace. That was what debs did, and Catherine Canton did it better than most.

Turning, he saw his aunt heading in his direction, high heels clicking on the tile floor. If not for the Botox injections Marguerite Bledsoe Danbury had had to reduce the wrinkles on her forehead and around her eyes, he knew she would be scowling. But the injections had frozen her face into an eerie mask of youthful blankness. Add to that the signature red hair, which she wore longer than most women her age, and a figure that had been liposuctioned and tucked to trimness, and she appeared a good fifteen years younger than her fifty-nine years.

"A word with you, please," she said when she reached him. Snagging Stephen's sleeve, she led him to a corner, which provided a modicum of privacy.

"Where is Derek?" Despite that bland expression, her eyes burned with fury.

"I haven't seen him since he left the choir loft," Stephen replied. He'd bet his inheritance his cousin was long gone, leaving it to others to clean up his latest mess. His aunt must have reached that conclusion, too.

"There are a dozen reporters and photographers, most of them tabloid, hanging around outside, waiting for a shot of the new Mrs. Danbury. I want Catherine out of here. Now."

Her first concern, as always, was herself. The young woman who would have become her daughter-in-law was now merely a liability to be dealt with.

"I'm sure her parents will take her home."

"See that they do."

It was not a request but a command. Marguerite never asked Stephen for anything. She made demands and expected her demands to be met without question or complaint. Stephen acceded to her wishes, even though he thought Catherine might have had enough of the Danburys for one day. Still, he'd rather she had to face him than his aunt.

He heard Catherine's voice as he approached the bride's room. The emotion he'd detected earlier, when he'd overheard her conversation with Derek, had been carefully edited out. "I'm fine, Mother, really."

"It's too bad about the wedding," her younger sister Felicity said. "You look stunning in that dress."

Stephen rapped his knuckles on the semi-open door. "Excuse me," he said. "May I come in?"

Catherine glanced over at him and he witnessed for a brief instant the strain she otherwise hid so well. She smiled, revealing an odd little dimple just to the left of her chin, a small bit of imperfection that somehow only enhanced the beauty of her classical Grace Kelly features.

"Of course."

He stepped into the room, closing the door.

"Stephen, dear, I was just telling Catherine not to let this little indiscretion ruin things," her mother said. "She and Derek can put this behind them."

In their social sphere, he knew, infidelity was often brushed under the rug. Wives weren't supposed to make waves, at least not publicly, and husbands were supposed to be discreet in their dalliances. Times might have changed, but obviously that was the pabulum still being force-fed to each new batch of old-money debs.

"I hope she doesn't share your opinion," he said, his gaze never leaving Catherine's.

"Well, I do," Felicity said. "I'd marry him, and keep this incident as leverage."

Catherine's sister was eighteen years old, and though he'd only met her on a couple of occasions just before the wedding, she appeared to be as spoiled as she was outspoken.

Catherine sent Stephen a bemused smile, but said nothing as her sister and mother continued to chatter on about the mistake she was making.

"My aunt sent me to tell you there is a limousine outside when you are ready to leave. The tabloid photographers are lining up, and surely more are on the way."

"Oh, dear," her mother said, fanning her face. "This is such an embarrassment."

Catherine looked embarrassed, all right, but Stephen didn't think it had anything to do with Derek at that moment. She reached up, as if to take off her veil.

"I wouldn't take the time to change," Stephen advised, knowing full well that a woman in shorts and a tank top could require half an hour. Who knew how long a woman in full wedding regalia would need to undress?

"He's right, Catherine. Gather up your things. You

can change at the house. Felicity, go find your father.''

''The house?'' A pair of finely arched brows shot up in question. ''I'd like to go back to my apartment, Mother. I hope you don't mind, but I'd like to be alone.''

''Nonsense. You'll come to the house.''

It was if she hadn't spoken at all, Stephen thought. Worse, it was as if she were a child, rather than a grown woman of twenty-eight. He watched as she turned and began to gather up her belongings, but then she dumped them back onto the vanity and marched to the door.

''Where are you going?'' Deirdra Canton called.

Catherine's gaze never strayed from Stephen's. ''I'm leaving. Now. I'll call you in the morning.''

Stephen didn't say a word. He simply opened the door, took Catherine by the arm and led her away.

''Thank you,'' she said a moment later. ''That's twice you've come to my rescue today.''

He shrugged off her appreciation. ''Don't thank me yet. We still have to outwit the paparazzi.''

He hustled her out the rectory door, but the photographers, as if scenting blood, were already there. Stephen blocked as much of their view of her as possible, holding her close and hovering around her like a bodyguard.

''Get in the limo,'' he said, all but pushing her inside the door he'd already opened. Behind them flashes popped and people shouted out their names.

Inside, even with the tinted windows, she huddled low on the seat opposite his, looking shell-shocked and shaken.

"I never dreamed this would be how I left the church on my wedding day. I feel like some hideous car crash, gawked at and then gossiped over."

"Hideous" was hardly the word that came to his mind as he looked at her lovely oval face, with its finely arched eyebrows and dark-fringed eyes the color of sapphires. A man could drown in those eyes. He glanced away. Perhaps Derek had, and that was why he'd considered trading in bachelorhood for permanent couple status when monogamy had never been his strong suit.

"Don't worry. It won't last forever. Next week some major star will go into rehab and that pack of vultures will be waiting outside the Betty Ford."

She let out a startled laugh. "Is that supposed to be the bright side?"

"Only if you're a desperate optimist. Where do you want to go? I don't suggest returning to your apartment for a while."

She shrugged. "I don't know. I'm open to ideas."

To the chauffeur he said, "Drive around for a while, but start heading toward the Belmont Yacht Club."

"The yacht club?"

"Trust me."

"Why not? What else have I got to do this evening?'' she said, her tone dry, her eyes suddenly starting to mist.

He fished a white handkerchief from one of his pockets and handed it to her. ''Here.''

''I'm not crying,'' she said, sounding slightly offended. But she didn't look at him, and even in profile he could see a tear slip down her pale cheek.

An hour later they arrived at the Belmont Yacht Club, a small and exclusive marina just north of the city. Catherine had been to the club a number of times with Derek, who docked his fifty-four-foot cabin cruiser there, and her own family retained a membership, even though their yacht had been sold when the stock market plummeted, taking a good portion of their heavily invested fortune with it. But she hadn't realized Stephen also boated. He corrected her immediately when she made the observation aloud.

''I sail.''

That surprised her even more. Of course, sailing would suit someone as quiet and self-contained as Stephen, but his parents, as well as Derek's father, had died in a sailing accident on this very lake when the boys were barely out of diapers.

He helped her from the limo, and then spoke to the driver as she tried to smooth out the crumpled silk of her dress.

''Meet us back here around one.'' Handing the man a sizable tip, he added, ''And if anyone asks, you never saw us.''

He grabbed the champagne that had been chilling in an ice bucket in the back of the limo and started for the waterfront, leaving her with little choice but to follow him. Along the way they passed a couple of bikini-clad young women, coming in from a lazy day spent out on the lake.

"Congratulations!" one called. To her companion she murmured, "I wonder which boat they're going to be rocking?"

And Catherine realized how it must look: Stephen in a tuxedo; she wearing her wedding finery. It was as if they were a couple, setting out for a romantic sunset cruise on Lake Michigan to toast their nuptials and kick off their honeymoon in style.

He must have realized it, too. His gaze swerved to hers, held for a lingering moment, but he said nothing.

Several slips down from Derek's luxurious cruiser, he swung aboard a graceful sailboat. It was much smaller than Derek's yacht, which took a five-man crew to operate. But at thirty-eight feet, it could hardly be considered little.

Standing on the dock, Catherine said, "What do you call her?"

"*La Libertad.*"

The foreign name rolled from his tongue, sounding like poetry, and he stared at her afterward. His gaze seemed defiant, although she couldn't have said why.

"That's Spanish for freedom, right?"

"Freedom." He nodded.

"She's a beauty. Do you take her out often?"

"As often as I can, which isn't as often as I like. And the season seems to get shorter every year."

"Are we going for a sail?"

"That's my plan."

"I'm afraid I don't know a mast from a jib."

"I've got it covered. Don't worry." He motioned for her to step closer. "Here, let me help you board. We wouldn't want you to wind up bobbing around in Lake Michigan in that gown."

He surprised her with a smile as he said it, reaching out for her waist to help her aboard. She rested her hands on his shoulders, transfixed by the rare smile and offering one of her own in return. Neither of them saw the photographer until they heard the unmistakable whirring of a camera's motor.

"Oh, no! Stop!" Catherine cried, bringing up her hands to shield her face.

Stephen's exclamation was far more graphic. And from his murderous expression she thought he might hop back onto the deck and dump the guy in Lake Michigan, camera and all.

"Get below," he called, pushing her in the direction of the cabin.

The man snapped off several more frames before Stephen managed to shove off from the dock. But Catherine had a feeling the first shot, the one of Stephen smiling as his hands spanned her waist, would be the one that graced the cover of whatever publication the guy worked for. She could only imagine what the accompanying copy would say, especially if the camera angle had also caught her smiling back.

Stephen might prefer sailing, but he used the boat's motor to take them out to open waters. Lake Michigan's vastness was the perfect place to hide in plain sight from the paparazzi. They could hear and see any approaching watercraft long before anyone aboard could click their picture.

She came above deck when she was sure they were safely out of range of even a telephoto lens, and settled onto one of the white padded benches near the wheel where Stephen stood. Just for a moment he reminded her of a pirate. He had shed his suit coat and black tie, and opened the collar of his white shirt, exposing more golden-brown skin. His cuffs were rolled to the forearm. The look on his face was one of relaxed satisfaction. Where he had looked debonair in a tuxedo, now he simply looked dangerous.

Arranging the folds of her gown around her on the bench, she thought it a pity that her own clothing was not so easily converted to casual. She had taken off the veil and tried to bustle her gown without much success. But at least she had finally shed those crippling shoes.

They were still using the boat's low-horsepower motor, which made their progress relatively slow. The motor was only intended for days when the wind failed to co-operate. That wasn't a problem on this evening. She had little doubt that if they had hoisted the sails they would have been halfway to Michigan by now. The wind was strong, breaking small white-caps in the water around them. It ruffled Stephen's dark hair, and it was probably wreaking havoc with the intricate style she'd spent the better part of the morning with a hairdresser to achieve.

"Ever sail before?" he asked.

"Once, as a child, in a small boat my uncle owned. I remember watching the sail tilt almost parallel to the water."

"Exciting, isn't it?"

She recalled only terror and an upset stomach. "I thought I was going to die."

"Well, it's not for everyone."

"But it suits you," she said. And it did. He didn't look quite so remote with the wind making his hair dance and excitement lighting up his dark eyes.

"I opened the champagne." He motioned to the small table in front of her. She couldn't imagine what they had to toast, and she said as much, but he merely shrugged. "There are glasses in the galley, first cup-board on the right, if you wouldn't mind getting them."

When she stood to fetch them she stumbled on her dress. Even as her fingers curled around the rail she felt his hands grip her waist, spanning it as he had when he'd helped her board. He turned her slowly and she caught the subtle scent of his aftershave.

"Steady now."

"If only Vera Wang would make a gown suitable for sailing," she quipped, suddenly ill at ease.

"If you want to take it off, I have something a little more comfortable you can wear."

Had the line come from Derek's mouth it would have been accompanied by a wolfish grin. Stephen merely waited patiently for her reply, no ulterior motive seeming to lurk in his steady gaze. Yet none of her discomfort left.

"That's probably a good idea."

He cut the motor and lowered the anchor before following her below deck, where he gave her the grand tour in under a minute. The cabin had two sleeping quarters, a tiny stall of a bathroom, and a main area that functioned as both kitchen and living room.

"It's small, but efficient," he said as if reading her mind. "And, unlike Derek, I don't need an entire crew to take her out."

That distinction would be important to him, she decided.

He opened the door to the bathroom and pulled a white terry-cloth robe from a hook on the wall. Handing it to her, he said, "I don't think my clothes will fit you. But this should do, even though it's bound to be too big, too."

When he started to leave, she cleared her throat. "Stephen. I…need your help."

He turned slowly, and her breath caught. Limned in the light that streamed from above deck, he seemed otherworldly. And she was about to ask him to help her out of her clothes.

"The buttons." She motioned over her shoulder. "I can't undo them by myself." With a rueful laugh that she hoped would lighten the mood, she admitted, "It took the assistance of two of my bridesmaids to get into this thing."

He said nothing, merely nodded. She turned as he approached, glad to present him with her back, since she felt suddenly awkward and shy. Perhaps that was because her groom should have been the one to help her out of the dress. Indeed, the exercise could have been considered foreplay.

Stephen obviously didn't consider it to be any such thing. He worked in silence, and swiftly, considering his hands were large and the pearls small and slippery.

At the base of her spine, however, he paused, lingered. And she thought she understood why.

"It's a birthmark." The words were barely above a whisper. With a self-conscious laugh, she admitted, "And the reason I've never worn a bikini in my life."

She could have sworn she felt a fingertip gently trace the large heart-shaped freckle that marred her lower back. But then he was handing her the robe.

"Come up when you're ready."

He stopped to retrieve two wineglasses from one of the cupboards in the small galley and then he was gone. Alone, Catherine expelled a breath and tried to find a rational explanation for her shaking hands and pounding heart.

He was sipping champagne when she came above

deck, wearing his robe. As he had predicted, it was much too large for her. At five-seven, she hardly considered herself petite, but it dwarfed her frame, hanging nearly to her ankles. Beneath its hem, her bare feet peeked out.

"I poured you a glass." He motioned to a seat across from his. On the small table between them sat the champagne bottle and an amber-filled flute. He raised his own and sipped again. She sat as well, pulling the robe tightly around her knees, and did the same.

"This can't be how you intended to spend your evening."

He shrugged. "The same could be said for you."

"No." She smiled sadly. "I thought I'd be Mrs. Derek Danbury by this time, listening to the musicians my mother hired slaughter 'We've Only Just Begun.' I can only imagine how upset she and my father are right now."

"I'll apologize for my cousin's poor behavior."

She sipped her champagne, enjoying the warmth it spread through her system. "Why should you? It's not your fault."

"No," he agreed. "But he's a fool. You made a beautiful bride, Catherine."

The compliment came as a surprise, as he didn't seem the sort to issue one easily. And so it warmed her, or perhaps that was just the champagne.

"Thank you. It was the dress. Who wouldn't look good wearing Vera Wang?"

"It was more than the dress," she thought he said, but the wind stole his words. Or maybe that was just what her bruised ego needed to hear.

The waves lapped against the boat's hull, rocking them gently. The rhythm and the wine made her sleepy, but she kept up her end of the conversation, even when he steered it to politics, business practices and current events. They were safe topics, and far more interesting than the usual polite small talk she'd encountered from men, who apparently thought because she wore a bra it meant she couldn't read a newspaper.

It was growing dark, and nearly half of the champagne was gone, but she held out her glass when he presented her with the bottle. After he'd filled it halfway, she said, "If we were at the reception you'd offer a toast."

He shook his head. "I wasn't the best man."

For some reason she wanted to dispute his words. In the end she said, "But as a Danbury surely you would have been expected to speak? What would you have said? I'd like to know."

"I would have wished you every happiness," he replied solemnly, dutifully. And she believed him.

"And now? What is there to toast now?"

She'd asked the question before, but this time Stephen had an answer. Holding up his glass, he said, *"La Libertad."*

The word rolled slowly from his tongue, the R a seductive purr that raised gooseflesh on her arms and left her to wonder whether he meant the sailboat that had spirited her away from reality or her near-brush with matrimony.

"*La Libertad*," she repeated, her accent not nearly as perfected. She swallowed the last of her champagne and settled her head back against the cushions. Closing her eyes, she said, "I like the sound of that."

CHAPTER TWO

FROM the window of his office, high in the Danbury Building, Stephen watched a sailboat slice through the choppy waves on Lake Michigan. He envied those on board, wishing he could be out there as well, harnessing the wind, outrunning old demons. Soon, too soon, August would give way to September, and then summer to autumn. Not long after that the world would become dormant, *La Libertad* would be put into storage, and ice would make Stephen's favorite place inaccessible for the next several months.

Unbidden came the memory of Catherine Canton, and the way she had looked wearing his bathrobe on that sultry July evening when they had hidden from the paparazzi aboard *La Libertad*.

They'd talked for a few hours, before he'd sailed the boat to port and taken her home. In that time they'd finished the bottle of champagne, and he'd glimpsed the woman beneath all the polish and panache. In addition to her dry sense of humor she possessed a quick wit. She was far smarter, far deeper, far more interesting than he had given her credit for being.

Debutante. The label no longer fit quite so neatly. Or perhaps his admittedly biased definition had changed. Before that night he'd written her off as beautiful, but shallow. But a shallow woman did not keep up on current events, or follow politics. Nor was she merely a fashionable woman, more interested in weekly manicures and facials than substantive issues. She knew designers and followed the latest clothing trends, he was sure, but she also understood branding, and in a brief conversation aboard a sailboat, relaxed by sparkling wine, she'd shown more insight into why Danbury's was losing customers to its competitors than many of the people in his own marketing department did.

He'd found himself on the verge of calling her more than once during the past several weeks, to pick that finely tuned brain. In the end he hadn't needed to. She'd called him.

Stephen glanced at his watch. Eleven-fifteen. He would be meeting her in less than an hour for lunch. The invitation had surprised him and left him intrigued. Business, she'd said. *What exactly did she want?* He shrugged into his suit coat. He would find out soon enough.

Catherine discreetly flipped open her compact and checked her appearance again as she waited in the restaurant for Stephen to arrive. Why she should be nervous about seeing him, she didn't know. This was business, after all. And yet she'd chosen a flowered silk dress rather than a conservatively cut suit. Okay, so maybe she had a little crush on her fiancé's—ex-fiancé's—cousin. It would never amount to anything, of course. They were too different. And yet, after spending that time with him aboard *La Libertad,* she couldn't help but wonder if, beneath it all, they might be very alike.

She dismissed that thought immediately as she watched him enter the restaurant. Stephen Danbury didn't walk so much as stalk, like a big black panther taking stock of his surroundings as he followed the hostess through the crowded dining room. Confident, powerful, in full command. He was a force to be reckoned with. His dark gaze panned the room before settling on her, and Catherine sucked in a breath which she held until he reached their table.

"Your waiter will be with you in a moment," the hostess said. "Can I get you anything to drink?"

"Coffee, black."

When they were alone, he said, "Hello, Catherine."

She held out a hand that was swallowed up in his and offered a smile.

"It's good to see you again, Stephen. And thank you for meeting with me. I know your schedule is very busy."

"I always have time for an intriguing offer."

He seemed to hold her hand a moment longer than was necessary, before finally releasing it and settling into the chair opposite hers.

"What is this business you'd like to discuss?"

No idle chit-chat for him. She'd counted on small

talk and pleasantries to carry them through at least the appetizer. By then she'd hoped to have sufficiently screwed up her courage. She pleated the linen napkin in her lap, a show of nerves she was grateful he could not see.

"Well, as you know, I am the executive director of the Safe Haven Women's Shelter. Our facility houses abused women and their children, helping them get back on their feet emotionally and financially once they've left an abusive relationship."

"A noble effort," he replied, but she couldn't tell from his expression if he meant the words or if he was just being polite.

"We can accommodate up to fifty women and their children. That might seem like a lot, but in a city the size of Chicago it's just a drop in the bucket. In fact, we're full at the moment and we have a waiting list."

"I'm familiar with the shelter and its work," he said.

"Oh." Catherine took a sip of water before continuing. "Then perhaps you are aware that the building we call home is old and in need of substantial repair. I've implemented a fund-raising plan that has helped tremendously. We encourage companies to 'adopt' different apartments in the facility and then refurbish them. Sometimes it's as simple as a fresh coat of paint, carpeting and new bedding. Other rooms need furniture, window treatments, plumbing right fixtures, rewiring, et cetera. It's a write-off for the companies that participate, and I try to make sure their efforts get adequate coverage in the local media.''

''That's a clever plan.''

''I can't take credit for it. Other communities are doing it with great success. I heard about it at a conference I attended.''

''It's still a good idea. And you were smart enough to recognize that.''

She smiled, ridiculously pleased with the compliment. ''Thank you.''

The waiter arrived with Stephen's coffee and took their lunch orders, giving Catherine time to mentally prepare the rest of her pitch.

''Recently we received a grant that will cover most of the repair costs for the boiler, so now the roof is our number one priority. It began leaking in the spring, and we had some patching done, but the contractor told us the entire thing should be replaced.''

''Roofs can be very expensive.''

Catherine cleared her throat and took a sip of her ice water. ''Yes, very. Especially on an old building whose structural integrity could be compromised if repairs aren't made soon.''

''Which brings us to the point of our lunch meeting, I presume?'' He smiled, but his eyes remained unreadable.

''We're hoping Danbury's can help us with a monetary donation that will cover part or all of the roof repairs. I'll personally make sure press releases are sent to the *Tribune* and *Sun-Times*, as well as local televisions stations. I've received three estimates from reputable contractors.'' She pulled papers from her slim leather case and handed them to him.

''You've done your homework.''

''I try to be prepared.''

He glanced up, his gaze steady. ''I enjoy a woman who's prepared.''

Nothing in his inscrutable expression revealed whether the double entendre was intentional, but Catherine felt her face grow warm.

''May I keep these?''

When she nodded, he folded the papers and tucked them into his breast pocket without another word.

''You don't need to make a decision right now,'' she said.

''I didn't plan to.'' He shifted forward in his seat, leaning over the small table. ''Can I ask you something personal, Catherine?''

Her pulse hitched. ''Yes.''

She realized that she had leaned forward as well when she felt his warm breath on her face as he said, ''Why didn't you ever ask Derek about this? He was your fiancé, after all. Talk about a trump card.''

She leaned back. ''I did. Twice.''

Stephen's dark eyebrows shot up. ''He never mentioned it to me.''

''He kept saying he'd get back to me.'' She gazed at the linen napkin that lay in twisted heap in her lap. ''I think he took my work seriously.''

''to,'' he muttered.

"If I'm remembering correctly from my high school Spanish class, you just called Derek a fool."

His use of the word surprised Catherine. Not many people resorted to a foreign language to issue an insult. Nonetheless, she enjoyed her first relaxed smile in more than an hour. Stephen, however, didn't smile. There was nothing teasing or relaxed about his dark gaze when it connected with hers.

"You're a woman to be taken seriously."

They were simple words, issued as a simple statement, and they left her simply staggered.

Late on Friday afternoon, Stephen studied the estimates Catherine had given him as he waited for his cousin to arrive. It was ten to five, and he planned to spend the weekend on his sailboat, so he hoped Derek wouldn't be late.

It surprised him that Derek had formally requested a meeting, and at this time of day besides. His cousin's weekend generally started on Thursday and lasted till Tuesday. And if he wanted to see Stephen he usually just barged into his office unannounced, flattering his way around his secretary if Stephen had asked not to be disturbed. But this time he'd sent word a day in advance, neatly typed on company stationary, no less, that he would like to meet in Stephen's office at five o'clock Friday. He had ensured Stephen's attendance by dangling this intriguing little carrot: he wanted to discuss the future of the company.

Stephen hadn't thought his cousin cared about the department store chain their grandfather's father had founded as much as he cared about the trust fund that kept him in designer suits and Swiss Alps ski vacations. When their grandfather had died two years earlier, he'd left Stephen at the helm of the faltering chain, with Derek second in command. Derek's title was officially vice president, but he generally left the day-to-day operations and all of the crucial decision-making to Stephen and the rest of the management team. He was no intellectual lightweight, but he'd made it clear he wanted the Danbury lifestyle far more than the burden of the legacy.

Stephen closed his eyes and pinched the bridge of his nose, hoping to ward off the headache that was already threatening. The truth was that the struggling department store chain might not be able to ensure Derek's lavish spending much longer without a major turnaround. Marguerite had been making noise about selling in recent months. So far Stephen had been able to block the move. Admittedly, it went beyond pure business for him. He was not about to give up the birthright he was still striving to prove to his dead grandfather he was entitled to.

He figured this meeting would probably be an attempt by Derek to wheedle him around to a sale, so he wasn't surprised when his cousin walked through the door followed by Marguerite. What did surprise him, though, was that they had brought with them the Danburys' longtime family attorney, Lyle Moore.

Stephen sent his aunt a polite smile and motioned toward the small conference table tucked into the corner of his office. Turning to Lyle, he said, ''This is unexpected. I didn't know you were coming by today.''

The man who had handled everything from Derek's prenuptial agreement to the cousins' trust funds barely spared him a glance. He seemed uncomfortable, nervous, even, and when he finally offered a hand its palm was damp and clammy.

''Can I get anyone a drink?'' Stephen asked.

The attorney shook his balding head, and Marguerite declined as well, but Derek flashed a cocky grin. ''I'll take one. To celebrate.''

Warning bells were going off in Stephen's head, though he couldn't figure out why. But the malicious amusement in Derek's light eyes made him wary.

''You know where it is.''

Derek poured himself a brandy at the bar discreetly tucked behind a door in the paneled wall. When he was lounging in his seat, swirling amber liquid in a snifter, Lyle unsnapped the flaps of the overstuffed leather case balanced on his knees and pulled out a document.

He cleared his throat and began, ''You've seen this before, of course.''

''Grandfather's will.'' Stephen's stomach knotted.

''Then you know what Sunday is.''

''Sunday?''

''It's your birthday,'' Derek supplied, his grin reminiscent of a shark's. "I never forget it because it comes just one day before mine."

The attorney cleared his throat a second time, and flipped through the papers he'd laid on the table before him.

"Um, as you know, since you are the oldest, your grandfather left you the controlling interest in Danbury's when he died two years ago, with Derek and his mother's portion totaling forty-nine percent of the assets."

"I believe we covered this at the time, Lyle."

"Yes, but the terms of the…um…codicil have not been met."

"Codicil? There was no codicil."

The lawyer ignored him and went on. "Your grandfather felt since you boys were born only one day apart—and you had come a few weeks premature, Stephen—he should make things a little more fair for Derek."

Stephen almost laughed aloud. Fair? His grandfather had always shown a preference for Derek, who looked so much like a Danbury should look, with his golden hair and sky-colored eyes. Stephen favored his mother, a sticking point with the old man, which was why Stephen had been surprised—shocked, even—when the will had been read two years earlier. Despite his obvious bias toward Derek, Maxwell had followed family tradition by giving the oldest Danbury heir control of the family empire. Stephen hadn't been the only one caught off guard. As he recalled his aunt had all but swooned at the time. Derek, however, had seemed to take it all in his stride.

"Your grandfather saw Danbury's as a family business, and he was troubled that neither of his grandsons was married and starting the next generation."

Stephen nearly smiled, remembering the arguments that had often occurred after Sunday dinner, at which some dreamy-eyed debutante or another would have turned up at the table.

"Yes, he believed it should remain a family enterprise, passed from one generation of Danburys to the next," Stephen agreed. Shooting Derek a look, he added, "He didn't want to see the company sold."

The lawyer pulled a pair of reading glasses from his breast pocket and settled them on his nose.

"Yes, well, your grandfather wanted to ensure its future through your and Derek's children. Unfortunately, neither of you has married and produced legitimate heirs at this point."

"So?"

Lyle glanced up nervously, but didn't maintain eye contact. "Well, you know how Maxwell could be. He thought perhaps a little incentive would move things along."

"Just cut to the chase, Lyle," Stephen said impatiently.

Derek's grin broadened. "Yes, Lyle, get to the good part."

"Well, as per the terms of the codicil, if by your thirty-fifth birthdays one of you was legally married, and hopefully but not necessarily on the way to fatherhood, he would inherit not just the controlling interest in Danbury's but all of it, with the exception of the five percent already willed to Marguerite.''

''What are you talking about?''

The lawyer ignored Stephen's outburst and continued.

''If both of you were married the terms of the original will would stand. But if neither of you were married, which is the case, you were to share the remaining ninety-five percent interest in Danbury's equally.''

''That's a lie!'' Stephen's fist pounded the tabletop, followed by an oath.

The lawyer jumped, but he continued in a shaky voice, ''You turn thirty-five on Sunday, Derek on Monday. The codicil states—''

''Let me clarify it for him, Lyle,'' Derek interrupted. He held up his glass of brandy, as if to offer a toast. ''As of Sunday, Mother and I own the controlling interest in Danbury's.''

''Shut up, Derek,'' Stephen said between gritted teeth.

Lyle blotted perspiration from his forehead with a neatly folded handkerchief. ''I'm sure Max didn't add this stipulation to create discord. He was just thinking about the company, and both of you, of course. He wanted to see you married and happy.''

''What Grandfather thought or didn't think is irrelevant. There's no codicil, Lyle, and you damn well know it.'' Standing, he faced the men sitting across from him. One was grinning smugly. The other was swallowing almost convulsively. Next to them his aunt smiled serenely, thanks to the Botox that had paralyzed a good portion of her facial muscles, but nothing could mask the triumph flashing in her eyes.

''It's there in black and white, dear, and signed by Maxwell. I can't believe you could have forgotten about it,'' she said with false sympathy.

''I didn't forget. I have a copy of the will in my safe at home, and there's no codicil. If that codicil is real I was never informed of its existence.''

''Three people in this room remember things differently,'' Derek said.

''I don't know what kind of game the two of you are playing.'' Turning to the attorney, he added, ''And I don't know how they managed to rope you into this. But I'll take this to court if need be.''

''Take it to court.'' Marguerite shrugged. ''Everyone who knows Max will find this to be just the type of thing that controlling old man would do. He was never above using a little high-handed pressure to get his way. Truthfully, I'm surprised you didn't bend to his will. You could easily have ensured a larger inheritance by getting married. You could have married the maid, even. Oh, but that's been done, hasn't it?''

''Leave my mother out of this,'' Stephen warned.

''So defensive.'' Marguerite tsked. ''I didn't mean to dredge up the past. It's just that you were always so pathetically eager to do Maxwell's bidding when he was alive, as if by jumping through all the hoops he set out you could somehow win his approval.'' She pursed a pair of pouty, collagen-filled lips. ''But all he had to do was look at you to know why you weren't an acceptable Danbury heir.''

Stephen pushed aside the old fury and struggled to concentrate on the matter at hand.

''Grandfather would have wanted the company to stay in the family, Lyle. Even assuming this codicil is real, surely you understand what these two barracudas are up to? And you know I was never informed.''

The attorney glanced up, and then away. But before he did, Stephen thought he saw regret and apology in his gaze.

''As Maxwell's attorney, it's not my place to question his motives or what results from them. I'm sorry things did not work out as you would have liked them to, but there's nothing I can do about it. Nothing,'' he repeated on a shaky sigh.

''Fine, this meeting is over, then.'' Stephen stalked to the door, yanked it open and glared back at his cousin and his aunt. ''Danbury's is still mine to run until a court of law says otherwise. And it's not for sale.''

''Don't be so sure. Fieldman's has made another offer,'' Derek replied, naming one of Danbury's most formidable competitors. For a man who rarely stumbled into the office for more than a few hours at a time he was suddenly very well versed in Danbury's financial status, the specifics of the federal bankruptcy code, and just how close Danbury's was coming to having to file for Chapter Eleven.

"Fieldman's wants a bigger slice of the market and it's in a position to pay handsomely to get it. We drag our feet much longer and there will just be bones for the scavengers to fight over. I don't intend to wait that long."

"Danbury's isn't dead yet. The name is solid. It resonates with consumers."

"It resonates with consumers sixty and older, so it might as well be dead. Among eighteen to thirty-five-year-olds we're not even on the radar. That goes double for the under-eighteen market and all their wonderful disposable income."

"We can turn it around. How can you even consider selling out?"

"Money," Derek said succinctly. "I've taken the liberty of setting up a meeting with Fieldman's people on Tuesday. I'm taking Monday off, since it's my birthday and I plan to be celebrating. They're coming to us, ten a.m. sharp. Get used to the idea, cousin. We're going to sell."

"We'll see about that," Stephen replied.

CHAPTER THREE

CATHERINE wasn't sure why she'd come. She could have called Stephen with the additional estimate she'd received on the shelter's roof. As for his robe, which she'd worn home from their evening on *La Libertad,* it could have been sent by messenger. But here she stood, in front of his home in one of Chicago's toniest suburbs, a good forty-minute commute from the city, so she couldn't possibly claim to have been "just in the neighborhood."

She'd been to Stephen's Tudor-style home only a few times, for company management parties he'd hosted while she and Derek were dating. Still, it surprised her to find that he lived on a quiet elm-lined drive where the estates were huge and ivy-covered but still managed to look homey and inviting. Derek lived in the city, in a penthouse apartment high above the throbbing nightlife and bustling streets. She called the city home as well, but she'd always hoped to again live someplace with a rolling green lawn and lush flower gardens to tend.

Catherine grinned when a yellow Labrador retriever streaked down the redbrick drive to greet her as she stepped from her car. She'd always believed she was a dog person at heart, even though her only pet as a child had been a finicky Persian cat her mother had named Cashmere.

"Hey, girl," she said, bending down to stroke the dog's wide head. The Lab instantly dropped to the ground and rolled over, eager for a belly rub. "Ah, boy," she amended. "Your master busy?"

Stephen's car was in the circular drive just ahead of hers. She straightened and started for the rounded steps of the front porch, noticing for the first time that that the door was wide open.

"Stephen?"

She got no answer, so she stepped inside. His suit coat lay crumpled on an oriental rug and it appeared his briefcase had been tossed onto the long-legged table in the foyer, knocking off a vase. Shards of glass littered the marble floor, and she stepped carefully around them.

Something was wrong, seriously wrong, but almost immediately she dismissed concern over a burglary or violent struggle. Surely the dog wouldn't have been running around outside if his master were in a fight for his life? From somewhere in the house she could hear Stephen's raised voice. He was shouting curses, some in English, some in what sounded like Spanish—all were vicious.

Catherine called out his name a second time. She got no answer, but followed his voice down a hallway and found him in a room she assumed was his home office. He was quiet now, too quiet, as he sat in a high-backed leather chair behind an ornately carved wooden desk, elbows propped on the edge of it, face buried in his hands.

"Stephen?"

He started at the sound of her voice and straightened in his seat. The naked pain in his eyes when he glanced up so surprised her that before she could ponder if he would appreciate her interference or not she was crossing the threshold and walking to him.

"My God, Stephen, what is it? What's wrong?"

"They did it."

"Did what? Who?"

He looked at her, seemed to look through her.

"I don't know how they did it, but they did it." His words clarified nothing. Nor did it help when he motioned to the papers scattered over his desktop and added, "Even my copy of the will, the codicil's there. They must have made the switch last month, when Derek volunteered to pick up some documents for me. I gave him the damn combination to my safe." He swore again. "I all but handed him my birthright."

She didn't know what he was talking about, but that didn't seem as important at that moment as offering comfort. She walked around the desk, laid a hand on his shoulder.

"How can I help? What can I do?"

"There's nothing you can do." He laughed harshly.

"There must be something."

He shook his head, as if realizing for the first time who she was. "Why are you here, Catherine?"

She decided against mentioning the shelter's roof. He obviously had more pressing concerns right now. So she pointed to the shopping bag she'd left just inside the door. "Your robe. I'm returning it."

"Leave it, then."

It was a dismissal, but she decided to ignore it.

"What can I do?" she asked again.

He didn't answer. Instead he stood, and with a violent sweep of his arm cleared the desk. A lamp crashed to the ground, followed by a telephone, and papers fluttered like snowflakes before finally settling on the hardwood floor.

Catherine jumped back a step, shocked by Stephen's uncharacteristic show of temper. In an instant he seemed to have gone from distraught to enraged. And in those dark eyes of his she saw fury, burning hot and lethal. And his gaze was now focused on her.

"It seems we have something in common, Catherine."

He rolled the R in her name, making it sound almost exotic. She backed up another step as he advanced, not sure what he meant to do. When he stood directly in front of her he raised a hand, and she held her breath. But his touch was gentle when he pushed the hair back from her face and tucked it behind her ear, his fingers sliding slowly down to the end of the strand before releasing it.

"What do we have in common?" she asked softly.

"Betrayal. Derek has betrayed us both."

He cursed again, before turning away from her and stalking to the window.

"I don't understand."

"Derek and his mother managed to either doctor our grandfather's will or conceal a key provision of it from me until today." He turned and pointed to the papers scattered over the floor. "There's a codicil that essentially gives them the controlling interest in Danbury's if certain conditions aren't met by my thirty-fifth birthday, which is Sunday."

"Any chance you can meet the conditions?"

He expelled a breath, ran one hand through his hair. Fury ebbed. He seemed resigned when he replied. "It's not likely."

"Okay, but surely you could go to court and challenge the will?"

"Perhaps. I'd need a new lawyer, since they seem to have bought off the one who's been doing our family's business for decades. It would get ugly," he said, as if thinking aloud. "And there's no guarantee I'd win, since I have no proof that they concealed the codicil. It's their word against mine. In the months or even years before the matter is finally settled the press would have a field day with the story, as would our competitors. I wonder what such a bitter battle would do to Danbury's already battered bottom line in the end?"

"I'd say your best option, then, is to try to meet the will's conditions."

He snorted. "Easier said than done."

"If you don't mind me asking, what are the conditions?"

"I have to be married," he announced. Glancing at his watch, he added, "And I have less than twenty-eight hours to do so."

"That's archaic—barbaric."

"That's my grandfather. Which is why I tend to think the codicil is authentic. Derek must have discovered it before Grandfather died and decided to make sure I didn't know about it until it was too late. I still can't figure out how he and his mother bought off Lyle. He's always seemed so by the book."

Something occurred to her then, a thought too hideous to even consider, and yet she had to know. "This condition, did it apply to Derek?"

He seemed to understand what she was asking. "I'm sorry, Catherine."

She acknowledged his apology with a brisk nod, as hurt and fury battled for dominance. Derek's words at the church came back to her. *I don't really need her anyway.* Had everything been a lie?

She recalled her first encounter with Derek, nearly two years earlier—just a month after his grandfather's death, she now realized. He'd bid an outrageous sum for a mediocre painting at a silent auction she'd organized to raise money for the shelter. She'd thanked him personally afterward, accepting his invitation to dinner the next day. She'd thought at last she'd found someone who shared her interests, respected her intellect and understood the importance of her work at the shelter and with other local charities that helped serve the city's neediest residents. Had his romantic pursuit really just been a means to an end?

"What would have happened if Derek had married me?" she asked in a quiet voice.

"That's not important."

"Don't try to spare my feelings, Stephen. I think I have a right to know. What would have happened?"

"He would have had it all."

"All of Danbury's?"

"Everything." His gaze skimmed her features in a way that made her breath catch. "And then some."

She thought about the prenuptial agreement she'd signed, ensuring a reasonable cash settlement but stipulating she would have no part of the family business. He would have had everything, all right.

"But without a wife he still wins, since you are unmarried as well?"

"Not as neatly. We'll technically have an equal interest in Danbury's. His mother's five percent, however, will mean they get to call the shots. And they intend to sell."

"So he would have married me just to get his hands on Danbury's." She shifted her gaze to Stephen. "Would you?"

"Excuse me?"

"Would you marry someone to keep the company?"

He snorted out a laugh. "I'm not even seeing anyone."

"That didn't stop Derek."

"No, but he had time on his side. I've got just over a day. I'm not a believer in love at first sight."

"You don't have to love her," she said, the cold truth settling in once and for all. "Derek didn't love me."

"He should have."

His tone was so matter-of-fact that she didn't doubt he believed it.

An idea began to take form, too outrageous to entertain, let alone voice, and yet she heard herself ask, "What kind of wife does the codicil state you need to have?"

He stared at her blankly for a moment, before shrugging. "The usual kind: female."

"Are there any restrictions? Do you have to…stay married?"

"No, I guess not." His brows pulled together. "But marriage should be permanent."

His tone sounded almost wistful, and the words surprised her. Stephen Danbury seemed too much of a realist to be a romantic. But then her judgment of men was hardly reliable. After all, she'd believed the lies Derek had packaged up and delivered. But he'd never loved her. He'd never intended to honor or cherish her. He hadn't even been capable of fidelity on their wedding day. And for his deceit he would have reaped huge rewards. Even having been caught he was still about to come out on top.

It wasn't fair. It wasn't right.

"You could marry me." Catherine laid a hand over her jack-hammering heart after she said it.

Stephen gaped at her, clearly as surprised as she by the suggestion. "Marry you?"

Self-conscious laughter bubbled to the surface. "You needn't look so horrified. It's just an idea."

Stephen came forward until he stood just in front of her. "I'm not horrified, just surprised. I know what I'd get out of a marriage between us," he said carefully, "but what about you? What would you get out of it?"

"I'm not expecting anything financially. I do earn a salary at the shelter, and I have some money from a small inheritance my grandmother left me."

"I didn't think you were after money, otherwise you would have married Derek even after finding him with the wedding planner. But why would you want to marry me?"

Helping people. That was what she did. She often put herself on the line for the underdog, albeit never quite so personally. And then there was the way her pulse hitched whenever he looked at her in that intense way of his. But attraction alone was no reason to marry. Why was she willing to do this? She had no answer for herself, certainly none for him. So she settled on, "It's for a good cause."

"The shelter?" he asked. "Is this your way to ensure you get that new roof?"

"Will it?"

Something flickered in his gaze, an emotion she couldn't quite read. "Consider it done."

"Thank you. But this isn't just about the shelter." She fussed with the mother-of-pearl buttons on her sweater set and admitted, "I'm afraid I'm not as altruistic as that."

His lips thinned into a smile. "Let me guess: this would be your way of paying Derek back? A little bit of revenge from the woman scorned?."

She nodded. "I suppose that's true. As much as I want the good guy in all of this to win, I'd also like to see the bad guy lose."

"Are you sure I'm the good guy, Catherine?"

His gaze locked with hers in seeming challenge.

"I want you to be," she whispered.

"Why?"

She gave a nervous laugh. "Yin and Yang, I suppose. One to balance out the other."

"So you'd marry me to keep the cosmic forces in order?"

She didn't reply. In a way it had to do with cosmic forces, all right, but not necessarily the ones he assumed. For the first time in her life Catherine was handing herself over to fate. This was the right thing to do. She could feel it, even if she couldn't articulate why.

"If we do this, we'll need to do it quickly and quietly," Stephen said.

"You'll marry me, then?"

Stephen studied Catherine's face. There was no denying her beauty. It had long beguiled him, even when he hadn't thought there was much else to her than physical perfection. Under other circumstances he might have been flattered by the proposal. Under other circumstances, however, he knew it would not have come. Women from Catherine's elite social sphere might condescend to take a dip in Stephen's gene pool, but they didn't want to swim there forever. Years of dating had told him so, despite his fortune.

"I'm desperate, Catherine," he said flatly.

He watched her wince and wondered was he so desperate he would take a wife, even if only on paper? He didn't have the luxury of time to clearly think things out. The one thing he knew without hesitation or question was that he did not want to see Danbury's sold. Marrying Catherine might be his only way to stop that from happening.

"Is that a yes?"

He nodded. "We'll need to move fast. Danbury's no longer has a company jet. The bottom line has been too thin in recent years to justify it. We'll have to catch a flight out of O'Hare."

"A flight?"

"Vegas." He shrugged. "It's quick and legal."

"Vegas," she repeated, looking as if she were sucking on a sour ball.

"You don't have to do this."

She moved forward, offering her hand as she came. "I do."

And it was with just those two words that she sealed the bargain.

It was nearly midnight when they arrived in Las Vegas. The city, however, seemed to have an abundance of energy and enthusiasm despite the late hour. Catherine had neither, especially since she was still working on Illinois time. She had never been to Vegas. She wasn't one for games of chance, which of course seemed ironic given the risk she would be taking with Stephen. For a woman who didn't believe in gambling, she'd certainly found herself in a high-stakes game.

What did she know about this man who would soon become her husband? Not much. Not nearly enough for the commitment she had agreed to make. He was private, but it was more than that. He hid something—not something evil, like Derek, of that she was sure. But those eyes that watched everything and rarely reflected anything told her that he found it easier—safer?—to tuck his feelings deep inside. She could appreciate that, she thought. She'd done it most of her life when it came to her parents.

"Tired?"

The softly spoken question startled her. She turned from the cab's window to find him staring at her. "No. Not really. I've never been to Las Vegas."

He studied her for a moment longer before replying, "It's not really your style."

"How can you be so sure?" She found herself a

little bothered that, while he seemed such an enigma to her, he should consider her such an open book.

"It's gaudy, flashy, at times crass and always greedy. You are conservative, traditional, sedate...generous."

"That's just how every woman wants to be described by her prospective groom. You might as well be talking about a station wagon," she said on a nervous laugh, but she wasn't really insulted.

He only raised one ebony eyebrow, and she found herself lost in those dark eyes. *How does he see me?*

"Try again," she said, turning in her seat so that she fully faced him.

"You have style," he said slowly.

"Hmm. Now I'm a Mercedes."

But she didn't laugh this time. She could scarcely breathe when he looked at her like that, his gaze so thorough, as if no detail could escape his notice.

"You're beautiful, but you know that."

"It's often an empty compliment," she replied.

"Which brings me to smart, but I suspect you know that, too."

She shrugged. "Well, it's not something I hear often from men."

Despite her outward nonchalance, genuine pleasure had her pulse spiking. Men so rarely complimented her on her intelligence. Oh, she was no genius, but neither was she a vapid member of the social elite. She had graduated *cum laude* from Stanford University, with a dual degree in business and social work. She put both disciplines to work in her job at the shelter. She enjoyed the work immensely, which was why she also volunteered her services at half a dozen other charities. She was a natural at fund-raising and organizing, and it made her feel useful rather than like some pretty ornament.

It also helped ease her guilt. Once upon a time she had been useless. Her best friend had paid the price. She pushed back that painful memory as the driver pulled the car to a stop in front of their hotel.

They had each only brought one small case to spare them from checking luggage, but Stephen insisted on carrying hers. Inside, it seemed ridiculous to request separate rooms when they were in town to be married, but Catherine wondered how she could sleep in the same proximity as Stephen, share a bathroom, when they had never so much as gone on a date. The dilemma was solved to a certain extent when he requested a suite. Their quarters were opulently decorated in navy and gold, and spacious enough with two bedrooms, each with its own bath.

"Which room do you want?" he asked politely as they stood in the living area and eyed one another with growing discomfort.

"Doesn't matter. I'm so tired I could sleep standing up." She laughed, hoping to lighten the mood. He didn't so much as blink.

"You can take that one." He pointed to the doorway nearest her. He hesitated at the threshold of the other bedroom, carry-on bag in hand. "Thank you, Catherine."

She nodded, not trusting herself to speak.

"Try to get some sleep. We have a big day ahead of us."

As Catherine settled between the cool sheets of the king-sized bed, she knew "big" was an understatement.

Early the next morning they picked a chapel within walking distance from their hotel, opting for what passed for understated in Las Vegas. Plastic blood-red roses dripped from a white trellis just outside the door, and inside the lobby guests could put a buck in a vending machine to buy a packet of birdseed to toss at the bride and groom.

Of course there were no guests: only Catherine, wearing a simple white A-line dress that flowed nearly to her ankles, and Stephen, dressed in a char-coal suit. She supposed it was silly to wear white for this farce of a wedding, but she believed in tradition.

A Vegas wedding, she soon realized, had traditions of its own, quirkiness being at the top of the list. They managed to bypass the Elvis impersonator, but to Catherine's horrified amusement, the I Do Chapel's minister bore a striking resemblance to Liberace.

"The standard wedding package includes your choice of song, a bouquet of white carnations for the bride and a snapshot to remember the happy occa-sion," Liberace droned. "For just a little more you can upgrade to the deluxe package and get the pretty little lady a bouquet of roses, three snapshots and these matching T-shirts.''

He pointed to the wall where the shirts were displayed. Emblazoned on the front of each were the words "We did it in Vegas at the I Do Chapel."

"Oh, my God," Catherine gasped, swallowing a bubble of hysterical laughter.

To her surprise, Stephen said dryly, "The deluxe package, by all means. We wouldn't want to miss out on those shirts."

The entire affair seemed so out of character for both of them, she supposed they would need the T-shirts to convince themselves they'd actually gone through with it. Of course, the marriage certificate would be real enough. That thought was sobering.

After filling out the necessary paperwork, they followed Liberace into the main room of the chapel.

"Are you expecting any guests?"

"No," Stephen said.

"Then I guess we'll get down to it."

Before Catherine could catch a breath, a woman shoved a bouquet of plastic white roses into her hands and snapped a hasty shot of her and Stephen as they stood before a makeshift altar. Liberace nodded to another woman, who cued up the music. "Greensleeves" filled the room.

"Dearly beloved," Liberace began, speaking to a room occupied by only five people, including the bride and groom. "We are gathered here today to unite this woman and this man in matrimony. Do you…?'' He glanced at the paper before him and then back at Stephen. ''I'm sorry. Could you pronounce your name for me, please?''

Stephen nodded, but his gaze never left Catherine's face as he replied, ''Stefano Anastasio Danbury.''

The name rolled from his tongue, a perfect complement to the dark hair and eyes—eyes that now stared in challenge, as if daring her to comment, and so she did.

''I wondered what the A stood for.''

Something like surprise flickered briefly in his expression. Clearly this was not the comment he was expecting.

''My grandparents—paternal grandparents—preferred it that way.''

Catherine had never met the elder Danburys, but she thought she understood what he was saying. Stefano would have been easy enough to Anglicize, but a name like Anastasio would have no English equivalent. She wasn't one to pay attention to the gossip, but she now recalled that she'd heard her mother talking to a friend once about a scandal of some sort, involving Stephen's father and the woman he'd married.

''Your mother was from Puerto Rico,'' she said, pleased with herself for finally remembering. It made sense to her now that he would have learned her native tongue.

"My mother was a maid," he said flatly. "No other comment?"

"Your initials spell SAD."

His brows tugged together.

"May I continue?" the minister asked.

"That's up to the lady," Stephen replied.

Did he expect her to call it off just because his name confirmed the heritage his looks hinted at?

"Is there suddenly a reason I shouldn't want to?" She lobbed the ball neatly back into his court. If he thought her a bigot, let him spell it out.

"You have every reason in the world not to want to."

"Those reasons were the same back in Chicago. Exactly the same," she enunciated. "I haven't changed my mind. Have you?"

"I'm beginning to wonder if I've lost my mind, but, no, I haven't changed it." He nodded to Liberace. "Proceed."

The ceremony was over in short order. A couple of "I dos," the exchange of two hastily purchased gold bands from chapel's display case—guaranteed not to tarnish for at least five years—and they were pronounced Mr. and Mrs. Stefano Danbury.

"You may kiss your bride."

Catherine hadn't allowed herself to think ahead to this part of the ceremony, or, for that matter, to the physical side of marriage. Of course their marriage would be in name only, a marriage of convenience. Wasn't that, to all intents and purposes, what her parents had? A useful and mutually beneficial union. They seemed content enough after twenty-nine years. Yoked together. Like a pair of oxen.

Of course she and Stephen were hardly in this for the long haul. They'd settled on a year, which seemed a reasonable enough length of time to silence the gossips and satisfy any lawyers Derek hired to fight the codicil or question their nuptials. Something told Catherine that her marriage to Derek would have ended much sooner and far less amicably than she predicted this one would.

Her gaze connected with Stephen's. For better or worse, literally, he was her husband now. She offered a smile, leaned forward for the kiss, expecting something brief and perfunctory. Then she caught the clean scent of aftershave on his warm skin, noted the sexy line of his mouth. Reaching up, she laid a palm against the hard plain of one of his cheeks, and, for no reason she could fathom, she sighed.

Stephen saw her eyelids flutter shut as his mouth touched hers, but he kept his own eyes open, watching this woman he barely knew, watching his wife. He deepened the kiss out of curiosity, sliding his tongue inside the pliant seam of her lips. She'd always seemed so cool, so in control. Once, a few months back, he'd walked into Derek's office and caught the pair of them kissing. Even with his cousin's hand on her nicely curved bottom and her arms twined around his neck she'd managed to look untouched. She didn't look untouched this time, though he'd so far managed to keep his hands to himself. And neither, he admitted, was he. Kissing Catherine was like sailing *La Libertad* in rough waters. He needed to hold on. He brought his hands up to frame her face, his fingers stretching into the soft gold of her hair.

"That's more like it," Liberace cracked. "Now, if you kids could just take this back to your hotel room, I've got another wedding to perform. Don't forget to pick up your T-shirts on the way out."

They sprung apart as if they had just been doused with a bucketful of freezing water. Her eyes, as big and blue as the deepest waters of Lake Michigan, reflected his own surprise and confusion. An electrical current of need had coursed through that kiss. It had carried with it a blast of heat that he hadn't felt in...ever. And it had come from the Ice Princess, Catherine Canton. The discovery, however, was not welcome. Business. That was what this was, Stephen reminded himself. Hormones didn't, *couldn't* factor into it. Even as he told himself this was so, he couldn't quite squelch the male satisfaction he felt when he noted the way her hand shook when she ran it through her hair. She'd worn her hair loose and long this day, a cascade of sunshine that haloed her face and flowed over her shoulders. He liked it this way the best, especially since the slightly mussed tendrils around her temples had been his doing.

The photographer handed Stephen the three Polaroids, which he stuffed into his pocket without bothering to look at them. They were nearly to the door, his equilibrium almost restored, when Liberace ruined it all by calling out, "Enjoy your wedding night."

CHAPTER FOUR

IN THE glaring sun, Las Vegas didn't have quite the high-voltage impact it did at night. But, sheened in a gaudy kind of glamour, it still throbbed with excitement.

Catherine wanted nothing more than a few minutes to herself, to try to put that searing kiss into perspective. She tried to be analytical about it. Could her reaction merely have been the desperate need for sexual validation by woman recently rejected? Perhaps, but that did little to cool her blood. This was the desert, but where had all that heat come from? She hadn't known a simple kiss could be like that, shooting a million flaming arrows of need through her system, each one of them unerringly finding its mark.

"What now?"

She hadn't meant to ask the question aloud, as it was more rhetorical than anything else, but Stephen answered.

"We can play tourist for a few hours, if you'd like. Our flight doesn't leave till this evening. Ever play poker?"

It seemed like such an outrageous thing to do just after getting married that she couldn't help but smile. "Once, at a Vegas night a literacy program held to raise money for supplies. Five-card stud, or something like that.''

''Well, your money wouldn't go for a good cause this time.''

''How do you know I'll lose?'' she asked, fascinated by the gold flecks the sun had teased out of his otherwise dark eyes.

''Odds favor the house.''

''I don't like those odds.''

He shrugged. ''Every now and then someone hits it big. That's gambling's allure, the potential for winning the jackpot. That's why some people bet their life savings and then some.''

''It makes sense that we're here, then.''

''Why do you say that?''

''You just bet on me, gambled with your legacy.''

''No, I'd already lost my legacy. I had nothing to lose. That's the first rule of gambling, by the way: don't bet more than you can afford to lose.''

''I guess Derek doesn't know that rule.''

''No. But then Derek doesn't care about his legacy either. He's about to lose. Big time.''

Catherine couldn't help but wonder if they had won or if they, too, would find themselves paying once everything was said and done.

Their flight home was the flight from hell. Delayed nearly two hours, and then rocked by turbulence, it seemed to last an eternity. A superstitious woman would have considered it a bad omen. White-knuckled and terrified, Catherine merely endured it as best she could. Beside her, Stephen slept like a baby.

To keep her mind off her nerves, she studied his features: the sensual line of his lips; the square jaw that was now shadowed and in need of a shave; the thick, dark hair that had fallen over his brow. In sleep he looked oddly vulnerable, and incredibly sexy. She recalled their kiss and felt her face grow warm. People called her an ice princess. She pressed her head back, stared at the ''fasten seatbelt'' sign and sucked in several calming breaths before closing her eyes. What would they say if they could read her mind just now?

''Penny for your thoughts?''

Her eyelids snapped open. Turning her head she found herself nearly nose to nose with Stephen.

They both straightened in their seats.

''I didn't mean to startle you. I just wondered what you were thinking. You looked so…intense.''

She forced a laugh. ''I don't care to fly.''

''Do the deep-breathing exercises help?'' he asked.

She met his dark gaze, felt her heart tremble, and said with conviction, ''Not one bit.''

It was well past midnight when they finally touched down at O'Hare. Glitzy Vegas had cocooned them in illusion. Gritty Chicago doused them in reality. They were husband and wife on what could still be called their wedding night, and yet they were stuck in all of the awkwardness of a first date.

"I'll take you home," he said, as if they had just gone to dinner and caught a movie.

"I can grab a cab," Catherine replied. "It's out of your way."

"I'll take you home. You can get your things."

"My things?"

"You're my wife, Catherine. You will live with me."

His tone offered no room for negotiation, let alone contradiction. Still, she heard herself say, "But I thought..." And then her voice trailed away.

Actually, she had not thought about their living arrangements at all. There simply hadn't been time during their mad dash to the altar.

"You'll have your own room, if that's your concern. I don't expect a physical relationship."

"I'll have my own room," she repeated, still feeling dazed. But Stephen must have taken her words to mean she was questioning his sincerity.

"I don't expect you to sleep with me, Catherine. We needn't consummate our marriage to make it look real to others. Living together should accomplish that."

Despite his assurances, her mind conjured up a vivid mental picture of them locked together in passion. She couldn't imagine where this inappropriate visual had come from, but at the moment the only question on her mind was: what kind of lover would Stephen be? That kiss made her wonder. Still waters, she thought. He'd be one to pay attention to detail.

To dot every i and cross every t. She licked her dry lips.

"There's no reason to be nervous," he said. "Despite my *hot Latin blood*, I can be a perfect gentleman when it is required."

His words were mocking, but she thought he sounded insulted as well.

"I'm not nervous, Stephen. I trust you."

He took the carry-on bag from her hand and started toward the exits. And she would have sworn she heard him reply, "Maybe you shouldn't."

The dog offered up a loud and enthusiastic greeting, his tail slicing through the air like a pirate's sword, when Stephen pushed open the door that led from the garage into the house. Stephen had asked a neighbor to come by to see to the dog's needs while he was away, but the Lab acted as if he'd been in solitary confinement for months.

"That's enough, Degas." He patted the dog's wide head. "Let's show some manners, shall we? There's someone I want you to meet. Sit."

The hound obediently plopped his hind end down on the floor, his tongue lolling out.

Turning to Catherine, Stephen said, "This is Degas. He's harmless enough, but he sheds a lot, so you might want to keep your distance. Or not," he added when Catherine, unmindful of her black linen pantsuit, bent down on one knee to give the dog an affectionate pat. Degas presented her with his paw, which she shook.

"We met the other day." When his eager tongue washed her face, she added, "I think he likes me."

She sounded as excited as a kid, and unbothered by the fact she'd just been slobbered on by a dog. *What's not to like?* he thought, and felt the same unmistakable surge of attraction he'd felt when he'd kissed her. Had that really only been mere hours ago? It seemed as if a lifetime had passed.

Need made his voice gruff when he said, "Come on, I'll show you to your room."

She followed him through the darkened house, wondering why he suddenly seemed so remote. Even the dog was more subdued as he walked beside her, as if he too sensed his master's sudden mood shift.

He flipped on a couple of lights as he walked, but their glow appeared to do nothing to brighten his mood. When he reached the staircase, he turned to take her carry-on case, even though he already had her suitcase. Then, without a word, he started up.

Their footsteps were muffled by a dark tapestry runner, and she wondered who had done his decorating. He'd hired it out, she was sure of it. It was certainly tasteful, with shades of navy and taupe carried throughout, but it seemed staid and lacking in warmth, just like the man himself at the moment.

Catherine missed the bright French country décor with which she'd decorated her apartment. When she and Derek had become engaged he'd persuaded her that they should live in his penthouse after their marriage and keep his modern furnishings, which complemented the high walls of windows and steeply angled ceilings. So she'd donated her sofa, chairs, coffee table, lamps, even her lovely Duncan Fife dining room set, to a charity auction. She'd come home on her non-wedding night to little more than a mattress on the floor, the sleigh bed having been disposed of as well.

"Is anything wrong?" Stephen asked.

"Nothing. It's not important."

He stopped at the top of the stairs. "Tell me."

"I just realized that it's a good thing I sold most of my furniture before my wed—in July. I don't have much to move now."

"Whatever you want to bring to my house I'll make room for. I'll hire movers first thing tomorrow."

Brisk, efficient, impersonal. They were discussing their living arrangements, and yet they might as well have been discussing the weather.

He turned to the right. The upstairs, she realized, was broken into two wings, separated by a long hall that offered a view of the great room below.

"I think you'll find this room acceptable. If you need more closet space, the room next to it also has a walk-in."

He opened the door, and all Catherine saw was the queen-sized bed. Liberace's words came back. This was their wedding night. Or it had been. Now, it was after midnight and they were back to being two strangers, albeit two strangers who shared a last name.

"Goodnight, Catherine."

"It's morning," she pointed out, and then smiled as a thought occurred to her. "And it's your birthday. Happy birthday, Stephen."

She reached out and squeezed his hand, but when she would have let go he held on, using it to draw her closer.

"You looked beautiful today, by the way."

Her heart fluttered ridiculously at the compliment.

"It wasn't a designer original this time."

"It didn't need to be."

He leaned down, hovered for a moment as if in indecision. Finally, he kissed her cheek.

"Should you need anything, my room is the first one to the left of the stairs."

"See you in the morning," she said.

She closed the door and then stood there with her hand on the knob, wondering about the man she had just married. Wondering if they would be friends when their year ended and they went their separate ways. Wondering how she was going to explain her hasty nuptials to her family, and what the press would have to say. Wondering if she'd just made the mistake of a lifetime.

And wondering why, despite all of her concerns, she felt an undeniable shimmer of excitement.

Stephen was not home when Catherine awoke the following morning. It was barely half past nine, and yet when she followed the scent of coffee to the kitchen she found only a note.

I'll contact the movers today. Coffee might be a little strong for your taste. There's cream in the fridge and sugar in the cupboard next to the stove. S.

Hardly a love letter, she thought, bemused.

After her first eye-opening sip of coffee, she decided to take him up on the offer of cream. Then, leaning back against the cupboard, she glanced around the kitchen. It was a generously proportioned room, with state-of-the-art stainless steel appliances, dark cherry cabinets, and a built-in nook with bench seating. A large window over the sink looked out into a beautifully landscaped yard. The room was functional and yet somehow looked cozy. She decided she liked it best of any room in the house.

"You must be Catherine."

Startled, she turned and found a woman of about sixty standing in the doorway. She wore a dark uniform dress that zipped up the front, and she held a couple of grocery bags, which she now set on the butcher-block island. Catherine had detected a lyrical cadence to her voice when she spoke and, based on her dark coloring, she decided the woman's native tongue was Spanish.

"Yes, hello. I didn't realize anyone was here."

"I'm Rosaria. I let myself in. Stephen called this morning and asked if I would pick up some groceries. I try to keep the kitchen stocked with good food." She winked. "Stephen, he likes…" She seemed to search for a word, then broke into a broad grin. "Junk."

"Junk?"

"You know." She pointed to the refrigerator. "Meals that come from a freezer. He says he doesn't have time to fuss with dinner."

Something seemed obscene about having a kitchen a gourmet would be proud to own and heating up pre-cooked dinners in the microwave.

"You're pretty." She made a little humming noise. "And so thin."

"Thank you," Catherine replied, not sure how else to respond to what might not have been a compliment.

"You're not Stephen's usual type."

"Oh?"

She motioned toward Catherine's hair. "Blonde. I don't know that I ever remember seeing him with a blonde woman before."

"I see." Which, of course, she didn't.

"Of course, I didn't think Stephen would ever marry. He used to say as much whenever I'd tell him that a woman would make good use of this kitchen and all the fancy appliances he had put in here. 'Men can cook, too,' he'd say. But he never bothered to. And no wonder. It's no fun cooking for one."

She put away the groceries as she spoke.

"You look hungry."

"I am, yes," Catherine agreed. "I was just trying to figure out what to make for breakfast."

"Dishes are in the those cabinets." Rosaria pointed. "I brought eggs, and a nice fresh loaf of bread. I could make you an omelet, if you'd like. I've got a few minutes before I have to leave."

"I can do it, but thanks."

"Well, I'll be going, then. Nice to have met you, Catherine." The woman stopped in the doorway. "It's not my place, I know, but Stephen is a good man. He deserves happiness, and there hasn't been a lot of it in his life. I hope you will make him happy."

It wasn't a lie when Catherine replied, "I hope we'll both be happy."

She spent the Sunday doing something she rarely did: puttering. She figured she would play it safe and stay out of sight for the day. Then she put away the belongings she had brought with her and walked around her new home, trying to picture spending all her evenings and weekends there with Stephen. Degas followed her every step.

"What does he do to unwind?" she asked the dog. The words seemed to echo from the vaulted ceilings. "Is he a night owl, a morning person? Does he work late? What does he do most weekends?"

The dog nuzzled her hand, looking for an ear-rub.

"You're about as talkative as your master."

There was a lot she didn't know about her husband, and his house, tastefully decorated as it was, revealed little. At the top of the stairs she turned left instead of right. One room remained to be explored. One room that might shed light on Stephen's personality.

Catherine hesitated only for a moment before turning the knob. This wasn't like her at all, invading someone's privacy, but she couldn't seem to stop herself from stepping over the threshold and into what was aptly named the master bedroom.

The walls were painted a vibrant red, set off by thick white trim at the windows and tall white baseboards. Other bits of color were splashed around the room, and she couldn't help but think he had saved all of it for this room, for so much of the rest of the house was done in less vivid hues.

She spied a photo on his nightstand and, though she had intended to venture no farther inside the room, she found herself crossing to it. It was his parents. She would stake her life on it. She sat on the edge of Stephen's unmade bed and studied the people in the picture. His father had certainly been handsome, with hair just a couple of shades darker than Catherine's and eyes as blue as a summer sky. But it was from his mother that Stephen had inherited his striking looks: the dark eyes, the fuller lips, the prominent cheekbones and slightly flared nose. His mother's eyes held secrets as well, but her smile was warm and inviting.

The dog whined from the doorway. She glanced over and her heart began to pound. Stephen stood there, his expression unreadable, although she had a good idea what he must be thinking.

"Curiosity satisfied, Catherine?"

"I'm sorry. I have no business being in here."

"None," he agreed. "Unless you'd care to change the rules of our marriage?"

He advanced, and she felt her mouth go dry.

"You'll find my bed comfortable and me... accommodating."

She stood. "I'm sorry. I think I should leave."

"Come now, don't tell me you've never wondered if all the talk about Latin men is true?"

"I'd like to think I'm above that kind of immature speculation," she replied stiffly.

"Does ice flow through your veins, Catherine?"

He rolled the R, and then he said something else in Spanish. The musical cadence of the foreign words made understanding them superfluous. And if there were ice in her veins it surely would have melted when he reached out to caress her cheek.

"Why are you doing this?"

"Doing what? Touching my wife?" He took another step forward and placed both hands on her hips.

"Stephen, I..."

"You're curious, Catherine. Admit it."

"All right, yes. I'll admit it. I'm curious about you. I don't think that should come as any surprise. We're married and we're going to be living together."

"I think it goes beyond that. I think you're curious about this."

Stephen intended the kiss to be punishing, but she responded to his boldness with surprising acceptance, shifting her position until their bodies touched from shoulder to thigh. He'd started out as the seducer and wound up feeling seduced, but his voice was steady when he said.

"I think you should go, *querida*. Before we do something that you'll regret."

CHAPTER FIVE

STEPHEN hadn't asked Catherine to attend the meeting Tuesday morning that Derek had scheduled with Fieldman's top brass. He'd mentioned it to her, of course, but not with the expectation that she would be there, especially after that fiasco in his bedroom. He simply wanted her prepared, in case Derek or some tabloid reporter called to confirm her marriage to Stephen. As of yet, word had not leaked out. So it shocked him tremendously when she walked through the door to his office fifteen minutes before nine o'clock. She looked fresh and lovely in a tailored silk suit the color of rich cream, her hair swept back and held in a pearl clip at the nape of her neck. He immediately wished she'd worn it loose.

"I hope I'm not late," she said, casting Stephen a rueful glance. Then she smiled brilliantly before adding, "I haven't been getting much sleep lately, so I'm afraid I didn't hear the alarm go off."

Derek and Marguerite had just settled into their chairs, sipping coffee, clearly pleased with themselves. At Catherine's arrival Derek bobbled his beverage, sending a good portion of it down the front of his snowy shirt.

"What are you doing here?" he asked, scowling

79

as he tried to mop up the mess. "We have an important meeting in just a few minutes. Anything you want to discuss with me will have to wait until later."

"Yes, dear," Marguerite said, trying to work up a look of sympathy on her frozen face. "It's really poor form to chase after a man, especially one who has made it pretty clear he doesn't want you."

Catherine ignored her, addressing Derek instead. "I'm not here to see you."

"You're here to see Stephen?" He laughed, as if she'd just delivered the punchline of a joke. "Well, that will have to wait until after our meeting, too."

"She stays," Stephen said, pulling out a seat for her.

"Stephen, really, whatever game you two have concocted, it's in poor taste," Marguerite replied. She motioned to their attorney, who had just entered the room, lugging his briefcase. "This is business, not an ice cream social. Fieldman's people will be here any moment."

"My wife stays," Stephen said succinctly, and had the pleasure of watching three mouths drop open.

Derek surged to his feet. "Wife? What do you mean, wife? When did this happen?"

"Saturday, in Las Vegas. You know, cousin, the place where fortunes are won…and lost?"

"You married her?" Marguerite looked suddenly pale.

"You won't get away with this," Derek said.

"I believe that was my line last week. Try to be original."

"Lyle, say something," Marguerite snapped.

The attorney smiled, relief flooding his expression, and offered a hand. "Congratulations, Stephen."

Marguerite swatted his arm. "Don't be a fool, Lyle. Congratulations aren't in order. Don't you see what he's doing? He only married Catherine out of spite. Surely there's something we can do."

"If the marriage is legal, there's nothing. Under the terms of the codicil, Stephen now owns ninety-five percent of Danbury's."

"But that's not fair," Marguerite had the gall to say.

"You still have your five percent," Lyle reminded her. "And Derek is hardly a pauper. He has other assets, although he may not be able to live quite so lavishly from now on."

"You haven't heard the last of this," Derek fumed, as he and Marguerite headed to the door.

When they were gone the room was silent for a moment, then Lyle sank into a chair and grinned. "I can't tell you how happy I am for you, Stephen."

"But last week you stood with them. You claimed I knew about the codicil."

"I never claimed that. Marguerite did. I just never corrected her, for which I'm sorry." His expression sobered. "They can be very persuasive, Stephen. My son had a little trouble a few years back, a gambling debt. A very large one to the wrong people, if you know what I mean. I engaged in some overbilling to gather enough to pay it off.''

"Why didn't you just come to me?"

"I should have. I was ashamed. Keith's not a bad kid, and he's turned his life around. But in trying to help him I broke the law. Derek found out about it somehow, and he used it to find out what Maxwell was planning in his will. When he learned about the codicil he blackmailed me to keep it from you until it was too late.''

"But it wasn't too late."

"No. Derek wanted to gloat." Lyle smiled again when he added, "His Achilles' heel."

"And I made the most of it."

"It obviously never occurred to him that you would beat him at his sleazy game."

The lawyer shifted uncomfortably after he said it, apparently realizing the unintentional insult his words contained. Glancing at Catherine, he said, "My apologies, Mrs. Danbury, that came out wrong.''

"An understandable mistake," she replied graciously, even as Stephen watched the color stain her cheeks.

"My congratulations and best wishes to both of you.''

"Thank you," she said.

The other man fiddled with the handle of his brief-case for a moment, then cleared his throat. To Stephen, he said, "I'll be resigning as your legal counsel, and I'll understand if you want to take action against me, legally or with the bar.''

Stephen was quiet for a moment, considering. ''I have no plans to do either. As you know, that pair tends to bring out the worst in people. I'd appreciate the name of a good firm, though.''

Lyle's face brightened. ''I know one of the senior partners at Rockwell, Martin, Stanwood. It's an old and respectable firm. I can have them brought up to speed in no time.''

Stephen nodded.

''Do you want me to stay for the meeting with Fieldman's?''

''No need.'' It was Stephen's turn to grin. ''I canceled it yesterday.''

''Of course you did.''

Lyle was chuckling as he walked out the door. When Stephen closed it behind the man and turned to face Catherine she swore the room got smaller.

''You didn't have to come.''

It didn't sound like a criticism, but the intense way in which he watched her made her uneasy, defensive.

''I felt I did.''

''Satisfied with the payback?''

''That's not why I'm here.''

''No?'' He'd walked forward as they spoke, and now he stood near enough that she was forced to look up, despite the stylish Italian pumps that added nearly three inches to her height.

''I thought you might need me.''

Something flickered briefly in his eyes and one side of his mouth lifted. "Worried about me?"

"I hear that's what wives do," she said lightly.

She thought of the other things wives did and nearly blushed. Just for a moment she was tempted to reach out, trail a fingertip over his chest and then use his very tasteful silk tie to pull him forward for a kiss. God, the man wore clothes well, which made her curious about what lay beneath them. They could lock the door, request that his secretary hold all calls. A vivid picture of what could come next filled her mind, shocking in all its sensuous detail.

She blinked and took a step back. What was wrong with her? She'd never entertained thoughts like this before. Indeed, she hadn't thought herself capable of sexual fantasies. But this one was a doozy, not to mention highly impractical. After all, a desktop *had* to be incredibly uncomfortable.

She was sleep-deprived; that was it. And there was no denying that Stephen was an attractive man. Stress. She filed the excuses away, satisfied that at least her brain still seemed capable of functioning. She'd wondered for a moment there.

"Everything okay?" he asked.

"Fine. I'd better be going."

"Busy day today?" He said it without the sneer that she now realized Derek had often used when referring to her work.

"Yes, I have a meeting at noon to discuss Project Christmas."

"Project Christmas? It's August."

"The end of August. And Danbury's has had wool sweaters on display for at least a month."

"Touché."

"Planning takes time if you want to do something right. I don't believe in doing things halfway."

She watched one dark eyebrow lift, but he said nothing. And again she thought about his desk and the sizzling fantasy that her sleep-deprived, stressed-out brain had manufactured. Catherine was not a woman known for her spontaneity, and yet she wondered if planning were required to do something like *that* right.

She had to clear her throat before she could reply. "We can count on Danbury's to host our drop boxes again this year, I hope?"

"Of course. Project Christmas is a great cause."

She nodded in agreement, grateful for the return of a steady heartbeat. "No child should have to go without gifts at Christmas, which is why I know Danbury's will also be generous with its corporate donation."

He smiled. "You're very smooth. I almost didn't feel you pick my pocket."

"Thanks." She pulled the thin strap of her purse over her shoulder. "Well, I should go."

"Yes."

They stood facing each other for an awkward moment.

"The move going okay?"

"Yes, fine."

She'd spent the better part of the previous evening unpacking the boxes the movers had brought, which had given her the perfect excuse to stay in her bedroom for the remainder of the night. Not that it had mattered. He'd left shortly before six and had not returned by the time she'd called it a night at ten o'clock. Where had he gone? For the first time she'd wondered if Stephen had a girlfriend. Rosaria had said Catherine wasn't his usual type. What or *who* was?

She found herself in an odd sort of conundrum. She didn't want to spend time alone with Stephen, and yet she liked even less the idea that he might be spending his time with someone else.

"I'm going to see my parents tonight. I have to tell them before a reporter calls for comment. I thought, if your schedule is clear, we could go over there this evening. That's if you want to go with me."

"I wouldn't expect you to go alone." He tucked his hands into the front pockets of his dark gray trousers and tilted his head to one side, looking oddly nervous. "How do you think they'll take it?"

You're a Danbury, she almost said. One Danbury would be as good as another to her mother. The connections, the social position, the prestige...the money.

"They'll be a little surprised." She offered a small smile.

He didn't smile. "I'll bet."

"What time do you think you'll be home?"

"Six."

And she would be there, she realized, in his big, quiet home, waiting for him.

"We'll just drop by my parents' house for drinks. I won't make you sit through an entire meal, I promise."

He walked her to the door of his office, opened it and then stood there for a moment, leaning against the jamb. "I wouldn't mind. They're bound to have questions."

Yes, Catherine thought. But she didn't have answers. At least not ones they would like hearing.

"Drinks only."

"Will you tell them about the codicil?" he asked.

"No."

"I didn't think so, but I just thought we should have our stories straight."

As she boarded the elevator, and hit the button marked "lobby", it saddened Catherine to realize that her parents would understand marriage as a business arrangement. After all, it was what they had. It was why they had thought her foolish for not marrying Derek even after his duplicity had been exposed. And not for the first time she wondered if the cool reserve for which she'd become well known was a byproduct of her parents' cold union.

Stephen was not home when Catherine arrived at his house late that afternoon, but the movers had dropped off another batch of boxes. Last night she had been grateful to immerse herself in the tedious chore of unpacking and assigning other boxes to storage in Stephen's attic. Now she was simply too tired to hunt through the boxes for the shoes she wanted to wear that evening.

Her cell phone rang as she contemplated where to start. She pulled it from her purse and sank onto her bed, grateful for the reprieve.

"Hello?"

"Cath, it's Felicity. Where are you?"

"I'm…home," she said, not quite ready to explain. She'd rather get it all over in one shot, which was why she'd asked Felicity, who still lived with their parents, to be sure to be there that evening.

"You're not home. I dropped by your apartment to borrow your diamond choker and the doorman said you had moved out. What's going on?"

Catherine sighed. "I'll explain tonight at the house. It's really not something I want to discuss over the phone."

"Are you in trouble?"

"Of course not."

She was touched by her self-centered little sister's concern until Felicity added, "That's a relief. You've already upset everyone enough by calling off the wedding. And then we've had to endure the tabloid stories. Mother's so embarrassed she hasn't been to the club in weeks, and I can hardly go out of the house without being laughed at."

"Yes, I know what a trial this has been for her, and for all of you," she said, somehow managing to keep sarcasm out of her voice. Just once, she thought, it would be nice to have someone in her family worry about her feelings and be supportive of her decisions. Perhaps she would get her wish later that night. "I've got to go. I'll see you around eight."

She hung up, even less enthusiastic about spending the next couple of hours unpacking than she had been before, so she decided to stall a little longer.

In the kitchen, she took a glass from the cupboard and went to the fridge for some orange juice. She noticed the cake right away. It was a double-layer with chocolate frosting. Not quite half of it was missing. Stephen's birthday cake. Much as it should have pleased her that he had had someone with whom he could celebrate, she couldn't suppress the spurt of jealousy that that someone had not been her.

Catherine chose a beige linen pantsuit to wear to her parents' house. Her mother would frown on the pants. Her mother often frowned, though, making pleasing her a virtual impossibility. Besides, Catherine figured by the time Deirdra Canton heard the word "married", she wouldn't be paying any mind to her daughter's wardrobe. She heard Stephen coming up the stairs as she put on her earrings. Sticking her head out the door, she watched him jog up the last few steps and turn in the opposite direction.

"Hello."

He turned, startled. "Hi."

She was surprised, too. The neat executive was nowhere to be found. In his place stood a sweaty man in gray cotton shorts and a T-shirt, hair windblown and skin glowing from exertion.

"You're ready."

She raised an eyebrow. "You're not."

"I heard the water running in your room when I got home. I figured I had time for a run and quick shower before you were ready. Most women…" He wisely let the thought go unfinished. "Give me fifteen minutes," he said.

She allowed her gaze to roam over the damp T-shirt that seemed molded to his powerful build. The fantasy she'd entertained in his office that morning came back to her in a breath-stealing rush. "Take twenty."

Catherine used the extra time to do some more unpacking, figuring the monotony would keep her mind off inappropriate thoughts. She had finally managed to reel in her pulse when, arms loaded with lingerie, she turned to find Stephen standing in her open doorway. His dark gaze lingered on the silky garments she clutched in her hands.

"I wondered…"

"Wondered what?" she asked, as she hastily stuffed the assorted unmentionables into the top drawer of the bureau without bothering to neatly fold and arrange them.

"I wondered…if this was appropriate attire for meeting the in-laws."

He wore a lightweight sport coat, crisp white shirt

and dark trousers. He'd forgone a tie, a definite no-no in her mother's book.

"Perfect."

The Cantons were already having drinks when Stephen and Catherine arrived. The economic downturn had decimated Deirdra and Russell Canton's once robust stock portfolio, but it had not changed the way they lived. They still insisted on having the best of everything, because keeping up appearances was more important than the fact their retirement funds were nearly gone, their savings obliterated and the house had been remortgaged twice.

Her parents and sister were seated in the room her mother insisted on calling the front parlor. They had no back parlor, so Catherine's practical mind had never understood the need for the distinction. As long as she could remember the room had been decorated the same, with spindly-legged antique chairs and a settee that had once belonged to her mother's mother. It was indeed a parlor, Catherine had thought more than once: a funeral parlor.

"Someday the furniture will be yours," Deirdra Canton had said often enough. Catherine considered the words a vague kind of threat, as if someday her own personality would be stamped out of existence and she would become her mother.

Not that she didn't love her mother, she just didn't believe they had much in common—whether it was their taste in furniture or their support for social causes for that matter. Deirdra Canton sat on beautification committees and raised funds for animal shelters. Worthy causes, certainly, but Catherine thought it more important to wade into the trenches to reach people who were too frightened and desperate to notice the lilies blooming in a downtown garden and too poor to afford food for their children, let alone their pets.

Her parents had objected to her having a career until she'd snagged a position at the shelter. It was close enough to charity work in their book so as not to raise eyebrows among their friends, whose debutante daughters had ensured their social standing by marrying well soon after college. Apparently her parents had entertained the same notion, expecting Catherine to earn a degree but not actually use it. Just as they had provided the scholarship that had allowed a young girl from one of Chicago's roughest neighborhoods to attend the same exclusive prep school Catherine had. Then they had objected strenuously when the girl had become Catherine's friend.

"We don't become involved with people like that on a personal level," her mother had chastised her more than once.

Catherine was still haunted by that lack of involvement, and what had happened to the young girl who, despite Deirdra's objections, had become Catherine's most treasured friend.

"Are you going to stand there staring at the furniture, dear?'' her mother asked with an embarrassed laugh.

''Sorry, my mind was elsewhere. Mother, Dad, Felicity—you remember Stephen Danbury?''

Her father stood, shook Stephen's hand. Her mother remained seated, smiling politely. Felicity offered a feline grin. At eighteen she had mastered flirtation. Indeed, she could have given Catherine lessons.

''It's nice to see you all again.''

''We didn't realize when you said you would be bringing someone that it would be Stephen. How is your cousin?'' Deirdra asked.

The inquiry was her mother's polite way of being rude.

''I'd imagine he has worked his way to irate right about now,'' Stephen said. Reaching for Catherine's hand, he added, ''Catherine and I have some news.''

''News?'' her mother and father asked in unison.

Felicity, glancing at their linked fingers, muttered, ''I have a feeling this is going to be bad.''

''We…married,'' Catherine said, deciding to just get it all out there at once. This discussion wasn't the sort that one could ease into anyway.

''M-married?'' Deirdra sputtered, her face a study in surprise, and not the good kind. What little hope Catherine had held that her parents would be pleased enough with her new status to overlook her serious breach in family etiquette faded away.

''When did this happen?'' her father asked.

"We were married over the weekend, sir," Stephen replied. "It was all very spur-of-the-moment."

"I'll say." Russell tossed back the last of his Scotch and scowled.

"But where?" Deirdra asked, as some of the color returned to her cheeks.

"In Las Vegas," Stephen said, and Catherine watched the color leak out again. In fact her mother's eyelids flickered delicately, as if she might faint dead away. At another time her mother's flair for drama might have been comical. But there was nothing funny about the tension snapping like an exposed electrical wire in the Cantons' staid front parlor.

"Great! Just great!" Felicity stormed. "The tabloids were just starting to forget about us. I leave for college in a week, Cath. One week! How could you do this to me?"

"I didn't do anything to you," Catherine said. "In fact, given the way the press has hovered since… Well, we just wanted something simple and private."

"And tacky, too, apparently," Deirdra harrumphed. Her near fainting spell had apparently passed.

"We wanted you all to be there, of course," Catherine said, as if her mother hadn't spoken. "It just seemed better this way."

"Well, then, by all means, let's pop out the bubbly," Felicity snarled. "We still have a few cases left over from Cath's other wedding, don't we, Daddy?"

"Felicity, there's no need for your editorial comment," Russell said.

''Yes, stop your annoying chatter,'' Deirdra added. ''You're giving me one of my migraines.''

Felicity sat down on the settee, outwardly subdued. This was quite the role reversal, Catherine thought. Usually Catherine toed the line that Felicity regularly stepped over. Catherine hadn't merely strayed a few inches into forbidden territory, though. With her unexpected marriage to Stephen she had taken one huge flying leap.

''I can't believe you did this,'' her mother said.

''We're very disappointed,'' her father added.

''I apologize for not including all of you in our plans or the ceremony,'' Stephen said. ''Catherine wanted to, but I insisted on secrecy. I felt it would be best to do this quickly and quietly.''

As he accepted the blame, he tucked her hand into the crook of his arm. The gesture seemed both chivalrous and protective. It seemed to say, *We are a unit*. And so it gave her strength.

Deirdra waved away his explanation. ''There's going to be plenty of talk now. Is *this*—'' she said the word ''this'' as if it referred to something vile ''—why things didn't work out with Derek?''

''This has nothing to do with Derek,'' Catherine replied, and then felt her face heat. In a way, it had *everything* to do with Derek.

''What were you thinking, Catherine?'' her father asked.

Anger rose to the surface, the source of which she could not determine. But it was there, bubbling hot, as impossible to hold back as steam from a boiling pot. "I was thinking you'd be happy for me. I was thinking that after the fiasco with Derek you might be wish me well."

"But *Stephen*?" Her mother sighed, as if the man were not standing in the room.

Beside her, Catherine felt him stiffen. "What's the problem, Mother? He's a good man, and I know it can't be his pedigree. He comes from the same family as Derek."

"But…" Deirdra let the thought go unfinished.

"But what?" Catherine persisted.

"I think I know where this is heading," Stephen said, his voice quiet, his features tight. "I'm not the right Danbury, am I, Mrs. Canton?"

"It's nothing like that."

"Like what? What's going on here?" Catherine asked, but she was afraid she knew. And it horrified her to think that her own mother could harbor the kind of prejudices that had already so wounded the man standing beside her.

"We're sure you're a fine man, Stephen. We just don't know you well," her father said.

"You can get to know him." You can get to know both of us, she almost said, because in that instant she realized there was more than one stranger in the room.

Perhaps it was her pleading stare, or the fact that her mother preferred entertaining to arguing, but her parents seemed to thaw a little. Resignation,

Catherine decided, would be a welcome substitute for acceptance at this point.

"I'd love some champagne," Deirdra said. "Fetch a bottle from the cellar, would you, Russell? Felicity can get the glasses."

She waved Catherine and Stephen toward the settee. "Come and sit."

Catherine had barely settled onto the brocade upholstery when her mother added, "One day, you know, that settee will be yours."

CHAPTER SIX

"THAT went well," Catherine said as they drove home after one of the most excruciatingly long and awkward hours of her life.

"Yeah. I'm sure they won't go into mourning when our marriage ends."

"Sorry about that."

"We are what we are, Catherine." And she knew he was talking about more than her parents.

Neither one spoke again until they arrived at the house. He parked the car in the garage and then held the back door for her.

As they passed through the kitchen, Catherine said, "Are you hungry?"

"Starving."

The way he looked at her when he said it had her mouth going dry. Something simmered in his dark eyes, and the memory of their last kiss stirred her blood.

"I could fix you a sandwich."

"A sandwich?" He smiled as if she'd told a joke. "Why not? But I'll fix it myself. Is there anything you want?"

His question went beyond cold cuts, she was sure.

She shook her head. "I'll keep you company, if you'd like?"

"I'd like."

She sat in the nook and watched him, the wealthy head of one of the most recognizable store chains in America, move around in the well-planned room in his stockinged feet.

When he was seated across from her, a huge sandwich and generous wedge of cake filling his plate, she said, "It looks like someone remembered your birthday."

"Rosaria made it."

Relief had her grinning. "I met her the other day."

"Yes. She mentioned it."

"She seems very nice. Does she just work for you the one day a week?"

Sandwich half way to his mouth, he paused. "Excuse me."

"She mentioned that she does the grocery shopping for you."

He dumped the sandwich back onto the plate. His tone angry, glacial, he said, "And you want to know what days she works for me?"

"I believe that's what I asked."

"Because someone who looks like her would of course be the hired help?"

"Stephen, did I miss something here? You're suddenly angry and I have no idea why."

"Of course you don't. I don't know why I expected

you to. We are what we are," he said, echoing his words from the drive home.

"If I've said something to offend you, please tell me so I can apologize."

"Drop it. It's not important."

"It seems important to you. I'd like to know—"

"Rosaria is my aunt," he interrupted. "You assumed she was the hired help."

It was her turn to be angry. "Yes, I assumed. I saw a woman, wearing a uniform, putting away groceries in your kitchen. I put two and two together and came up with four."

"Because that's the stereotype."

"Because no one told me differently."

"And it never occurred to you that I would have family?" His voice rose and he said something in Spanish that she decided was not at all pleasant. "I do. A family that looks a hell of a lot more like me than I look like the Danburys. It is because of them that I know how to speak my mother's language, even though my grandparents forbade me from doing so in their home. That only made me all the more determined to become fluent, which I was by the time I was thirteen."

"Did you see them regularly, then?"

"I saw my maternal grandmother every day. When the Danburys wouldn't allow her to visit me she offered to clean their house. She hired in as their maid so that she could be near me."

His voice shook with emotion—anger, and something else that caused Catherine's heart to ache for the little boy who had been denied so much.

"It's because of *mi abuelita* that I have pictures of my mother. My grandparents would not allow a single snapshot of her to be displayed. They were ashamed of her, ashamed that their Harvard-educated son had married a Puerto Rican maid who spoke broken English."

"Oh, Stephen. I'm sorry. I didn't know." She reached across the table to touch his hand. But he pulled away.

"Now you do."

The silence stretched, before she asked in a quiet voice, "Do they know about me? I know Rosaria does, but do the others?"

"I've told them about our arrangement, yes."

"Oh." He'd told them about their *arrangement*. She could only wonder what they must think of her.

"Will I meet them?"

"No. I see no point in that. You talk a good game when it comes to acceptance and equality, but the first time you run across a brown-skinned woman in a kitchen you automatically assume she's there because someone has paid her to tidy up. You disappoint me, Catherine. I didn't think you were so much like your mother."

Stephen said the words, and in his anger he meant the words, but then he watched her face pale and he wished he could snatch them back.

She scooted off the bench seat, eyes overly bright.

Her voice was a shaky whisper when she said, "I'm sorry."

And then she was gone.

Stephen's appetite fled as well, taking with it all his anger. Now he just felt like a heel. Catherine had had a stressful and not entirely pleasant day, and he'd just made it worse. He tossed his uneaten sandwich down the garbage disposal, along with the cake, and turned off the kitchen light. The house was quiet, and even though for the first time since he'd bought it six years earlier someone else was sharing it with him, it still felt empty.

And he still felt alone.

The rest of the week passed much as Stephen had expected it would. He and Catherine rarely saw one another, and yet they each managed to evade or else lie convincingly to the handful of persistent tabloid reporters who dogged their steps, hoping for confirmation of rumors of a Vegas wedding. An Oscar-winning star's brush with the law thinned the ranks of the vultures, but the speculation continued. *Celebrity Spyglass* featured the couple inside, along with a reprint of the photograph that had been taken of them aboard his sailboat in July and then been run prominently in the tabloid the following week, with the headline: *Is this why the wedding is off?* This time the headline asked, *Are they or aren't they?*

Even he wasn't sure he had an answer to that one.

At home each night, the only evidence that Stephen

shared his house with someone else was a small sliver of light from beneath Catherine's tightly closed bedroom door. She closeted herself inside before he arrived home and, to his surprise, was gone each morning before he left at seven.

Saturday morning, however, she was seated in the breakfast nook, enjoying a cup of coffee, when he walked into the room. An empty bowl sat on the table and she was reading the newspaper. Two things struck him immediately. She wasn't wearing any makeup and she was dressed in pajamas. She didn't need eyeliner and blusher to make her lovely. Those blue eyes needed no enhancing and neither did those high cheekbones. As for her clothing, he decided she could wear burlap and belt it with twine and still look classy enough to have tea with the Queen.

They had hardly spoken since the last time they'd been together in the kitchen, and his conscience nipped him hard. He owed her an apology.

"Good morning," she said.

"Good morning."

"I made coffee."

"Smells good."

"And tastes all right, too," she said, taking a sip. "I'm done with the paper." She folded up the *Tribune* and scooted it to the other side of the table.

He couldn't stand another minute of this polite, trite conversation.

"About Tuesday night. I'm sorry. I didn't mean to bite your head off."

"It's forgotten." She waved one delicate-looking hand. The cheap band on her ring finger somehow managed to catch and reflect the light. He'd have to do something about that, he decided.

He helped himself to some coffee and sat across from her. Something was on her mind. He could tell by the way she shifted in her seat. She didn't fidget, precisely. Someone who looked like Catherine didn't fidget. But she was ill at ease, apprehensive.

"What is it?"

"Excuse me?"

"Something's on your mind."

"I have a…function tonight. A ball and silent auction to raise funds for literacy. I didn't organize it, but the committee is hoping that I…that *we* will be there. If you're not free, I'll understand. It is rather short notice."

"Black tie?"

"Yes."

"What time?"

"Six."

"I'll be happy to escort you."

"We'll be the center of attention," she said, her tone apologetic. "They'll all be wondering about our marriage."

Stephen had long been the subject of gossip. This would be nothing new. But he meant it when he said, "Then we'll be sure to give them something good to talk about."

That evening, as he stood in his foyer and watched

Catherine walk down the stairs, he knew they would indeed be the talk of the town. His beautiful Ice Princess wore fiery red, an off-the shoulder sheath of curve-hugging material that reached to her ankles and shimmered with each step she took. She wore heels, the strappy kind that showed off neatly painted toenails the same color as her dress, and she'd left her hair loose.

"Encantador," he murmured.

"What does it mean?"

"Lovely."

"Thank you. And you look handsome. How would I say that?"

"Guapo."

"Muy guapo," she said, with a lift of her brows, adding the Spanish word for "very." Full lips bowed into a smile that was as red and tempting as her dress.

The ballroom at the Sheraton Towers was already jammed with several hundred of Chicago's wealthiest and most influential people when they arrived. Stephen recognized many people in the crowd. Some had even been frequent guests at his grandparents' home while Stephen was growing up. But he didn't consider any of them his friends, and the feeling was mutual. He nodded politely, as did they, and offered the standard greetings.

Catherine, however, worked the room like a veteran politician, shaking hands, air-kissing cheeks, chuckling in that reserved way of hers at every joke or even mildly humorous remark. He'd never seen this side of her at other social functions, but he should have guessed it was there. It was what made her such a good fund-raiser. She knew much of society thought her a vapid and wealthy woman who merely played at her job with the shelter, and she was smart enough to use it to her advantage, coaxing dollars from their pockets in much the same way a snake charmer coaxes a cobra from its basket.

The seating was assigned—each round, linen-covered table set with service for ten. No one was at Catherine and Stephen's table yet except for an older couple, Enid and Oscar Dersham. Stephen recognized them as contemporaries of his grandparents, although he didn't recall them coming to the house often, maybe just at Christmas for the annual party.

He snagged two glasses of champagne and headed in the direction of the table, content to wait there for Catherine. But he was waylaid before he could get there by a woman he had dated casually the summer before.

"I've heard a nasty rumor," Cherise Langston said.

She stood much too close to him as she spoke, and had the audacity to take one of the flutes of champagne he held and sip from it. Her forward behavior was just one of the reasons he'd broken things off with her long before they could become serious.

"Hello, Cherise."

"You're looking as tasty as ever, Stephen. So, is it true?"

He decided to play dumb. "True?"

"The rumor about you and Catherine Canton. The tabloids are claiming the two of you are married."

"Catherine is my wife," he said succinctly.

Her eyes widened, filled with malice, although her tone managed to stay light. "And you told me you weren't the marrying kind. I believe your exact words were, 'I don't plan to make that kind of commitment to anyone.'"

He had said that, and he'd meant it, but that had been long before he'd learned about the codicil. Long before Catherine.

"I changed my mind."

"Are you trying to tell me you fell in love with Catherine Canton?" She laughed, a grating noise that he'd found annoying even when he'd also found her attractive. Now it was truly offensive.

"I found it hard to believe when she snagged your cousin, but then Derek likes a challenge, and he's unencumbered by a conscience. I hear he was putting the moves on the wedding planner just minutes before their ceremony."

When he didn't dignify her speculation with a response, she continued. "What a waste of manhood." She held out her glass and clinked it against his in a toast. "Call me when you need some warming up. I'm not partial to playing second fiddle, but for you I'll make an exception. *Hasta luego*, sweetheart."

Catherine joined him at their table a few minutes later, already looking tired, though she camouflaged it well enough. She greeted the Dershams with her usual charm.

"You're looking well. Have you met my husband yet?"

"Your husband?" Enid Dersham glanced around the room. "We thought the wedding had been... No, dear, where is he?"

Catherine's laughter was mild and musical, taking the sting out of the awkward situation.

"He's right here. Stephen Danbury, may I present Mr. and Mrs. Dersham?" To Stephen, she said, "The Dershams have been incredibly generous to several children's charities, as well as avid supporters of the arts."

The Dershams eyed Stephen, clearly puzzled, but too polite to say so.

"We knew Stephen's grandparents. Very nice people," Enid said.

"Yes," Oscar chimed in, and, directing his comments to Stephen, added, "Your grandparents are sorely missed. They were true pillars of the community."

"Our grandparents were something," Derek said, causing all heads to turn in his direction. He stood just behind Catherine, bitterness making his eyes overly bright. "Catherine, you're looking well for someone who just stomped on my heart."

She didn't buy his words for a minute. His ego might have been bruised, but his heart had never been at risk.

"This is a surprise. I don't believe I ever had much success in talking you into coming to these functions."

She knew he considered it easier to write a check than to suffer through an evening of small talk.

"I'm only too happy to support a good cause," he replied smoothly, smiling for the Dershams' benefit. To Enid, he said in a stage whisper, "She broke my heart by marrying my cousin, you know, but life goes on."

"Office cleaned out yet?" Stephen asked. He draped an arm over the back of Catherine's chair, the move casual and yet proprietary.

Derek pretended not to hear him, but the tic in his cheek gave away his irritation. "All's fair in love and business. I came over here hoping to bury the hatchet."

Stephen snorted out a laugh. "Yes, which is why I'll be sure not to turn my back on you this evening."

People were starting to stare, as well as straining their ears to listen. No doubt word had already gotten around the massive ballroom that both Danbury heirs were present and a confrontation was ensuing. Catherine nearly groaned. As if there wasn't enough for the gossips to speculate on and twitter over. There would be no silencing the busybodies, but at least she could ensure the cousins were kept separate.

"Let's dance," she said, rising from her seat and forcing Stephen to stop glowering at Derek. "I love this song," she added, before realizing that the number the band was presently playing was the old Nat King Cole favorite "When I Fall in Love."

She took his hand and led him to the dance floor. The song was just ending as they turned to face one another.

Silvia Rathburn, one of the organizers of the event, rushed toward the stage.

"Don't go anywhere," she said as she passed Catherine and Stephen.

Silvia was a plump woman who considered pink her trademark color. She was wearing a shade just this side of shocking, and a gown whose cut was more suited to a prom-goer than a woman approaching her sixties. Catherine had worked with the woman on several projects, though, and knew her heart was far more generous than her fashion sense. At the microphone, the woman clapped her hands together as if to gain everyone's attention.

"I want to remind everyone that bidding on the silent auction will continue until we are seated for dinner. And I have an announcement to make. Would you all raise your glasses in a toast? It seems we have something else to celebrate this evening."

Catherine felt her mouth go dry as the woman winked at her, and she felt Stephen's arm tighten around her waist, as if he too were bracing himself for the inevitable.

"I know none of us likes to admit we read the tabloids, but sometimes, amid the stories of alien abductions and forty-five-pound newborns, they get things right. A little birdie just told me that Catherine Canton and Derek—'' She blushed, as embarrassed as they were by the unfortunate *faux pas*. ''Excuse me. My apologies. That is, Catherine and *Stephen* Danbury exchanged vows last weekend. Please join me in wishing the newlyweds every happiness.''

The noise level in the room immediately rose, along with the champagne glasses. Catherine and Stephen stood alone in the middle of the large dance floor, truly the center of attention.

''Well, I'd say our secret is out,'' Stephen said in a quiet voice. ''Are you okay?''

''They'd all have found out eventually,'' Catherine replied, somehow managing to keep a pleasant little smile curving her lips. The dimple winked and he admired her aplomb. And, though he rarely speculated about what others thought, he couldn't help wondering what was crossing the minds of this roomful of Chicago's elite.

The men would be jealous, he decided, looking at the lovely woman in his arms. The women? Envious that they didn't have Catherine's beauty or grace.

From the stage, Silvia continued, ''The tabloids say they got married in Las Vegas, so I'm sure they didn't have an opportunity to share a dance. I thought they could do that now.''

She motioned for the orchestra to begin playing, and the first strains of ''As Time Goes By'' filled the room.

Stephen couldn't resist teasing her with a famous

line from the movie that had made that song famous.
"Here's looking at you, kid."

He took her hand in his, raised it to his mouth and
kissed the back of it. The women in the room sighed
in unison, and Stephen told himself it had been entirely for show. She looked so lovely, a cross between
Ingrid Bergman and Grace Kelly with her classical
features and aloof mannerisms. As he rested his other
hand on her slender waist he was suddenly grateful
his grandmother had insisted on all those dance lessons he'd once considered a waste of time.

He led and she followed. She rested her cheek
against his jaw and he tightened his hand around her
waist, pulling her closer. Pulling them both in. The
music stopped, but he didn't release her.

"You dance beautifully," she said.

"Three years of lessons, courtesy of my grandmother."

"God bless her."

He laughed softly. "I cursed her at the time, but I
was just thinking the same thing."

She glanced around. "The music has stopped."

"So it has." He lowered his head.

"W-what are you doing?" she whispered.

"Satisfying their curiosity."

He'd said something similar that day in his bedroom. But that kiss hadn't been so much satisfying as
disturbing. The same thing, he realized, could be said
about this one. Need speared through him, welcome
and intrusive at the same time, taking as much as it

gave in return. Mere attraction? He wanted to think so. That would be so much tidier and more simple than anything else. But something nagged at him.

He mulled it over for the rest of the evening. Studied it, and Catherine, as he would any vexing problem found within Danbury's books. After all, at its core that was what this was: a business arrangement. And yet he could not honestly say his heart had ever pounded like a jackhammer when going over fourth-quarter earnings or market share data.

It was nearly midnight before they had inched their way toward the exits.

"I'll get your wrap," Stephen offered. "Why don't you say goodbye to whomever you need to say goodbye to, and I'll meet you by the coat check?"

Catherine smiled. "You read my mind. Give me ten minutes, and if I'm not there, send out a search party."

He was barely out of earshot when Derek sidled up next to her.

"Quite the cozy portrait of marital bliss you two painted tonight."

"Goodnight, Derek."

She turned to leave, but he grabbed her by the elbow. His grip was firm enough that extracting herself would have caused a scene. He, of course, knew this.

"What do you want?"

"Just wanted to wish you luck."

"Why would I require luck?"

"This is a game, isn't it?"

She didn't respond.

"A high-stakes game," he added. "Even a do-gooder of your caliber is in over her head, Catherine."

"I don't know what you're talking about. Now, please release me."

"Catherine, Catherine. He's using you."

"You would know all about that, wouldn't you?"

"Stephen likes to play chess."

His *non sequitur* threw her. "What?"

"You know—chess. The game where the object is to capture the other player's queen. You have to think carefully before each move. In fact, you have to think several moves ahead. It's about strategy."

"I'm familiar with the game."

"Ask yourself this: why did you come to the choir loft?"

"I received a note. And a good thing, I'd say."

"Who sent the note?"

She shrugged. "I thought it was you, but obviously not. Whoever sent it, I owe him or her a debt of gratitude."

"I'd say you're already paying it."

"Are you implying Stephen sent me the note?"

"Ah, now you're catching on. He set me up, Catherine. He knew about the will's codicil and he had to make sure I didn't get married."

"Even if that's the case, did you have to fall so neatly into his trap?"

"How do you know he didn't bribe the wedding planner to seduce me?"

"Because if you'd truly loved me you wouldn't have been seduced."

"Do you think Stephen loves you?"

She didn't answer. This wasn't about love.

"Just watch your back. He's using you." And with that he was gone, leaving unsettling questions in his wake.

Stephen walked Catherine to her door. Her bedroom door. It seemed silly and unnecessary and sweet all at once. Something fluttered insider her. Anticipation? Nerves?

Suspicion?

Derek's words echoed in her head. She pushed them aside, but her hammering heart was not so easily ignored.

"I had a good time tonight," he said.

"You sound surprised."

"Those things usually aren't very entertaining."

"Must have been the company," she replied.

His smile came slowly. "Must have been."

No one was present to fool, but he sounded so sincere. Suddenly she needed to know.

"Did you send me the note?"

"Note?"

"On my wedding day. At the church. Did you send me the note to meet Derek in the loft?"

His eyebrows lifted in…surprise? Dismay? But his voice held neither when he replied, ''I did.''

Her heart twisted. ''Why?''

He ran a hand through his hair, nearly turned away. But then he leveled that intense gaze at her instead. ''I thought you should know. It wasn't the first time I'd seen Derek with someone else. While you were dating there were…others.''

''Others?'' Now it was her stomach that felt knotted. ''But why didn't you tell me then, or after Derek proposed? Why did you wait until my wedding day?''

His gaze remained intense, but some other indecipherable emotion seemed to cloud his dark eyes. ''It wasn't any of my business. But you seemed nice and, well, I overheard him tell the wedding planner to meet him in the loft. I thought you could assess the situation for yourself, make your own decision.''

It seemed to make sense, not quite chivalrous, but close, and in keeping with Stephen's aloof nature. Still, doubts nibbled at her.

''You didn't know about the codicil then, though? Right?''

''Why the sudden questions?''

''I'm wondering, that's all.''

''That's not all. You could have asked these questions at any time. Why now? Did Derek say something to you tonight that has you suspicious of my motives?''

''No, nothing.'' She waved a hand, hoping to dispel the tension that had crept between them. Derek's doing, she realized, and hated herself for handing him so easy a victory.

"He must have said something."

"He just mentioned the note and said he thought you'd sent it. He said… It doesn't matter."

"Clearly it does."

He seemed irritated and cold once again, not at all the man who had danced with her in the ballroom and stolen her breath with a kiss.

"He just made sure to remind me that you had a lot to gain if he didn't get married that day."

"Yeah, well, I didn't know that, but he did. And he's right. I had a lot to gain. I had even more to gain when I married you. You knew that, and yet you still proposed. Remember that, Catherine. You popped the question, not me."

"Yes. I'm sorry. Let's forget about this. It doesn't matter. Derek is only trying to make trouble."

He shook his head, resignation edging his tone when he said, "I thought you would have figured it out by now. That's Derek's specialty. Goodnight, Catherine."

He turned away before she could say another word. At the other end of the long hallway she heard his bedroom door snap shut. With a heavy heart, she closed her own.

CHAPTER SEVEN

GIVEN his growing attraction to her, Stephen found living with Catherine a test of his will-power. Still, he rather enjoyed discovering her quirky habits and surprising interests. She was a good cook, better than he'd imagined a woman who grew up in a household where there was a hired professional to prepare the meals would be. He'd bet his last buck her mother didn't know how to boil water and had not encouraged Catherine's interest in the culinary arts.

And while she cooked she liked to sing. He found it amazing that a woman who looked like Catherine could be so tone deaf. He was surprised his Lab didn't start howling whenever she tried to hit a high note. Of course, the dog wasn't willing to bite that hand that fed him. And Catherine did a whole lot more than feed Degas. She'd barely been in the house a week when Stephen discovered his fickle hound camped outside her door. Now Degas was sharing her bed.

Lucky dog.

Stephen and Catherine had found some surprising common ground: old movies. He had long been a fan of black and white flicks. The genre didn't matter, although he was partial to Alfred Hitchcock and anything that starred Humphrey Bogart. They had that in common, except for her it was Cary Grant. She could recite entire scenes from *An Affair to Remember*. For him, it was *Rear Window* and *The Maltese Falcon*.

A few times a week they would spend a couple of hours in one another's company, suitably chaperoned by the work of some legendary Hollywood filmmaker. Then they would walk up the stairs together as the house grew dark and quiet around them, offer one another a stilted goodnight and turn their separate ways. Long afterward he'd lie awake on the cool sheets of his big bed, wondering if the same need that hummed through his blood was depriving her of sleep as well.

Most weekends they spent following their own pursuits. This weekend, however, they were expected at a tribute dinner Saturday night that the fire department was putting on to raise funds for the families of three firefighters who had died battling a warehouse blaze earlier in the year. The invitation had come to the house, addressed to the both of them, marking the first time they were invited to an event as Mr. and Mrs. Stephen Danbury. Stephen didn't really want to go. The gossip and speculation about their marriage had yet to quiet down. But he was just old-fashioned enough to believe that where his wife went he went, despite the particulars of their marriage.

Catherine plucked the square of ivory vellum off her bureau and tucked it into the small beaded clutch that was the same shade of emerald as the full-length gown she wore. The gown was new, a flirty Versace that left one shoulder bare and required her to skimp on dinner to wear it to its best possible advantage.

She was checking her reflection in the mirror a second time when Stephen tapped on her door.

"Catherine, we're already fashionably late," he called.

Even so, she reapplied her lipstick and fussed with her hair, which she'd left loose again, before opening the door, and was satisfied to see him suck in a breath.

"You do Versace proud," Stephen said. He took her by the hand, forcing her to turn a full three-hundred-and-sixty degrees.

"Thank you. And Armani looks good on you." She adjusted his bow tie, which was perfectly knotted, and used their close proximity as an excuse to brush non-existent lint from the lapels of his tuxedo jacket. "Have I ever told you that you wear clothes well?"

She was flirting, but she couldn't resist. He looked so handsome, so...interested.

"I can't say that you have." He leaned in, bringing with him the crisp scents of soap and aftershave. "Let's make this an early night."

She held her breath and tried not think about the double entendre when she replied, "Oh, is there something you want to do?"

Dark eyes seemed to smolder.

"As a matter of fact, there is."

The evening dragged, perhaps because the enigmatic answer Stephen had given before they left the house lingered in her mind, tantalizing her with its possible interpretations. It didn't help that as they ate, danced, or shared small talk with acquaintances she would look up to find him studying her in that intense way of his. She was in the middle of a conversation with the Mayor, pitching hard for more funds for youth activities, when he joined her.

"Ah, Stephen, I was just enjoying a conversation with your lovely wife," the Mayor said, offering a hand.

The two men shook, and it was obvious this was not a first meeting.

"Has she muscled some more money out of you yet?" he asked. There was pride in his voice, warmth in his smile, and heat in the hand he rested on the small of her back.

"The city's budget being what it is, not quite. But she's very persuasive."

"She is that. I'm afraid I'm going to have to steal her away now. We have another engagement."

She glanced at him in surprise and resisted the urge to ask what that engagement was.

"Of course. I understand. Newlyweds have all sorts of *engagements*," the Mayor remarked with a wink.

Stephen hustled Catherine out the door in record time, tipping the valet extra to bring his car around in a hurry. The teen took Stephen at his word, squealing the tires of his Jaguar as he maneuvered the sleek automobile over from the parking lot.

A lot of men would have gone into coronary arrest,

right after committing brutal, cold-blooded murder. Stephen surprised her by merely shaking his head and saying in a dry tone, "That's what I get for telling a kid to step on it when he's got the keys to my Jag."

Then he squealed the tires himself as the sleek sports coupé shot away from the curb and into night traffic. She figured out right away that they weren't going home, but he remained tight-lipped beside her, saying only, "You'll see," when she asked him their destination.

Then she saw the marquee and knew. *Charade* with Cary Grant and Audrey Hepburn was playing at an old theater that showed only vintage films, including the accompanying trailers and newsreels.

"We're going to the movies?" she asked needlessly, as he swerved to the curb and into a lucky parking space half a block from the theater. He hopped out, came around to her side of the car and all but yanked her to her feet.

"Yeah. Can you run in those heels?"

He didn't wait for her answer, but grabbed her by the hand and started off at a trot.

"Movie starts in less than a minute and I want to get popcorn." He sounded almost like a kid when he added, "They use real butter here. You like butter, right?"

Again, he didn't wait for her answer, but she didn't mind. She'd never seen Stephen like this, rushing as if his life depended on seeing a movie he'd probably already watched a dozen times. In fact, she didn't

doubt he owned a copy of it, either on video or DVD.
Perhaps both.

They were the only ones in the theater decked out
in formal wear, but he didn't seem to mind the dou-
ble-takes, raised eyebrows and whispers. He sent her
to the concession stand while he purchased the tick-
ets, and met her there just in time to pay for the king-
sized bucket of buttered popcorn, beverages and Milk
Duds he'd asked her to purchase.

The photograph caught her attention the moment
he opened his wallet. It was of the two of them, standing side by side in the I Do Chapel. She'd forgotten
about the pictures that had come with their deluxe
wedding package. Apparently Stephen had not. He'd
kept them, cut one down to fit the plastic protector in
his wallet and carried it with him. She was ridiculously touched.

"I didn't know you had these." She pointed to the
photograph.

He seemed uncomfortable when he replied, "Most
married men carry pictures of their wives."

"So, it's for effect?" she asked.

He didn't answer her question, instead he said,
"You looked beautiful that day." Dark eyes studied
her for a moment. Then he handed her one of the
drinks and a paper-covered straw. "You look beautiful every day."

Before she could respond, he hoisted the tub of
popcorn into his arms and grabbed the other drink.
"Don't forget the Milk Duds."

"I can't believe we're doing this," she whispered as they took their seats in the back of the theater.

"You have to admit it beats another two hours of small talk with the movers and shakers of Greater Chicago."

She dipped her hand into the tub and feasted on a mouthful of popcorn. When she was done she said, "I won't argue with a man when he's right. Do you have the napkins?"

"No, I thought you had them."

"Nope. Can I use your handkerchief, then."

"I have a better idea." As Cary Grant flirted with Audrey Hepburn on the screen, Stephen lifted Catherine's hand and one by one slowly licked the butter from her fingers.

He wasn't sure why'd he'd done it, although from the way she sucked in a breath and leaned toward him he didn't think Catherine minded. He rubbed his own buttery hands on his tuxedo pants, unmindful of the obscene price he'd paid for them. Then there was only the small matter of setting aside the popcorn tub so that he could take her face in his hands, bring it forward for the kiss. She tasted salty and incredibly sweet.

They were in the rear of a sparsely crowded theater, but they could have been front and center at a sold-out performance of a Broadway play and he doubted it would have kept him from trailing a hand down the slim column of her neck and then following it with his lips. He stopped at her collarbone and the cloth that covered it, and prayed for some sanity to return. He'd never wanted a woman the way he wanted Catherine.

"Sorry. I got carried away."

"I'll say," she whispered back.

But when he started to straighten she wound her arms around his neck. "Do you think you could get carried away again?"

His smile came slowly, despite his charging heart. "I'll see what I can do."

This time he was determined not to be deterred by clothing. He took Catherine's sexy little sigh as consent. His fingers were just starting to dip beneath the fabric of the gown's bodice when a beam of light all but blinded him. He kicked over the tub of popcorn in his haste to sit upright.

"Sir." It came out as squawk, so the teenager wielding the flashlight cleared his throat and tried again. "Sir, um, ma'am, we don't, um, you know, allow that kind of stuff in here. If you, like, keep it up, I'll have to ask you to leave."

When he was gone Catherine succumbed to a fit of laughter, and Stephen couldn't help but think that many of their acquaintances would have found it hard to reconcile this irrepressible and incredibly responsive woman with the overly regimented and cool image she often projected.

"Let's get out of here," he said.

"But the movie's not over. Don't you want to find out how it ends?"

He kissed her hard and let her go. "Oh, yeah. I want to find out how it ends."

They ran on the way back to his car, too.

On the way home they held hands, and it struck Stephen as absurd that he was essentially dating his own wife and wondering with all the hopeful anticipation of a teenager if the evening would end as well as he was imagining. He parked the Jag in the garage, but they didn't get out immediately. Both seemed to know that once they went inside everything would change.

"We're home," Catherine said needlessly after the silence had dragged and the light on the automatic garage door opener had gone dim.

"Yes." He opened the car door and the interior light popped on, haloing them in soft gold. "Shall we go inside?"

Catherine laid a hand on his arm. "Before we do, I need to know what's going on between us."

"I think it's this."

He leaned over and kissed her, and felt the jolt of that surprising attraction. His world had been careening and threatening to crash around him, but Catherine had saved him. And in the midst of chaos he'd found something special, something precious. He'd found... He rejected the thought before it was fully formed.

But it was she who ended the kiss.

"We shouldn't be doing this."

He couldn't help but smile. "We have more right than most. We are married."

"We're not really married." She straightened her clothing.

"Oh?" He arched an eyebrow. "I have a piece of paper that says otherwise."

"You know what I mean, Stephen. This isn't a love match."

"No, but I like you. I respect you. I think it's fairly obvious I'm incredibly attracted to you."

"I settled for attraction once," she whispered. "It's not enough. I like and respect you as well. And that's why I don't want to complicate things between us. My God, aren't they complicated enough?"

Much as he hated to admit it, she was right, but he wondered how long what was growing between them could be denied.

Once again he walked her to her bedroom door, leaving her there with Degas. The walk to his own room seemed as long and lonely as a walk to the gallows.

The next couple of weeks went by in a blur. Catherine didn't need to pretend to keep herself busy. Fall was always a hectic time for charities as they geared up for the holiday season, and long before she'd exchanged vows with Stephen she had committed to attend various events and fund-raisers.

She'd figured her full schedule would allow her and Stephen to give one another a wide berth, perhaps put some of their awkwardness behind them. But, to her utter amazement, Stephen always insisted on coming with her. He was a perfect gentleman, a perfect escort, with his impeccable manners and gorgeous dark looks. And, even though things remained strained between them, he never let it show when they were out in public. He would pull her close to dance, touch her shoulders a bit longer than necessary when he removed her wrap, tuck her hand into the crook of his elbow as they entered a room, and all evening he would watch her with those sizzling, sexy eyes that held too many secrets for her comfort.

Was it all just for show? Catherine didn't want to believe it was, but at home the byplay between them was limited to polite, if not awkward conversation. He'd told her that he liked and respected her. Was it possible that he could someday feel something more where she was concerned? For she feared that she was beginning to feel something much deeper for him.

She arrived home on Saturday, two grocery bags in tow, determined to try her hand at an Italian dish she'd seen in the gourmet cooking magazine to which she subscribed. When she opened the door from the garage, however, her eardrums were assaulted by Bob Seger's gritty voice. Stephen was apparently already home, even though it was barely four o'clock and he usually worked until six, even at weekends.

She followed the music until she found him. He was in a back room that he'd had converted to a weight room. Assorted sizes of dumbbells and free weights lined the walls. Stephen reclined on the slim bench, stripped to the waist in a pair of nylon shorts and pumping some serious iron. He didn't see her, so Catherine allowed herself a moment of pure ogling, and the hunger she felt had nothing to do with the fact she had skipped lunch.

So this was where he got the biceps she'd admired, not to mention the delts and pecs that did his tailored shirts proud. Oh, she would suffer some incredibly detailed fantasies in the future—and she did mean *suffer*—but it was worth it to be able to openly watch her handsome husband.

He stopped his reps and sat up, blotting the perspiration from his face with a towel he'd draped over the end of the bench. And then he saw her. He stood, switched off the blaring rock and faced her.

"Something I can help you with?"

"I didn't mean to interrupt." She motioned toward the bench. "Are you finished?"

"For now."

"They say that working out is a good way to relieve tension," she said, when he just continued to stare at her.

He stalked forward until he stood just in front of her, more than six feet of sweaty and seemingly angry male.

"I can think of better ways to relieve this kind of tension, Catherine."

He stepped around her and then he was gone.

Catherine burned dinner, but it didn't matter. Stephen had gone out shortly after their confrontation in the weight room. It was nearly midnight when Degas whined and she heard Stephen's muffled footsteps on the stairs. Again, she wondered where he'd been and whom he'd been with.

Catherine stumbled into the kitchen early the next morning, her system in need of some serious caffeine before she tackled the job of cleaning up the mess she'd made the night before. She'd been in no mood to scrub pots and pans after her disastrous dinner.

To her surprise, Stephen was already seated in the nook, dressed in casual tan pants and a cotton navy crewneck, munching on a slice of toast.

"You're up early today."

"I've decided to take *La Libertad* out for one last sail before dry-docking her for the winter."

"Hmm." She glanced toward the window and the patch of blue visible through it. "Should be a good day for it."

Sipping his coffee, he nodded. "If the weather forecast is to be believed it's going to be sunny and unseasonably warm."

She'd hoped for an invitation, but wasn't terribly surprised when one didn't come. If the man found it difficult to spend time with her in a six-thousand-square-foot house, surely a thirty-eight-foot sailboat would be sheer torture.

"Well, have a good time."

She turned and walked to the counter to pour herself a cup of coffee, and then nearly scalded her hand when he asked, ''Is it going to take you long to get ready?''

''You want me to go with you?''

''I want you…to go.'' He hesitated just long enough between the words to shroud his exact meaning.

''Stephen—''

He interrupted, his tone sounding sincere when he said, ''I want to spend the day with you, Catherine. Just the two of us.''

''I'd like that, too.''

''I figured we'd swing by a deli first, have a picnic lunch packed. We can make an entire day of it, if that suits you.''

An entire day aboard his sailboat, miles from shore, with no chaperones. Nothing good could come from it, her practical mind warned. Yet she found herself smiling with excitement, her blood humming with anticipation.

''It suits me.''

CHAPTER EIGHT

LAKE MICHIGAN proved a gentle hostess, her waters a calm and vibrant blue that reminded Catherine of satin. The sun warmed her face and allowed her to remain comfortable in the sweater and jeans she'd worn. And the breeze co-operated as well. It ruffled the sails and tugged the boat out to where the tall buildings on the shoreline looked so small they could be covered with one's thumb.

"Are you enjoying your sail?"

With her face turned to the sun, eyes closed, she smiled. "Very much. Thank you for asking me."

"I almost didn't."

She opened her eyes and turned to look at him, but said nothing.

"I remember what happened the last time we were aboard *La Libertad*."

She'd been sure he was going to mention the night at the movie theater, when needs and desires had beckoned...threatened to overtake them. His reference to that summer evening perplexed her.

"I don't understand. Nothing happened."

"Something happened. And it wasn't the first time. I've been attracted to you for a long time, even when I didn't want to be."

"When I was engaged to Derek?"

"Before that."

She sat upright. "But you never said a word."

"What was I going to say? I thought it would pass, especially after you became involved with my cousin. I thought I was just attracted to the pretty packaging. You're a very beautiful woman."

And so he had told her, on more than one occasion. Derek had told her that as well, which made the compliment seem hollow, almost an insult.

"I'd like to think I'm more than that."

"You are. That's what makes you so dangerous."

"Dangerous?" She laughed, sure he was joking, but his gaze remained intense, his mouth a taut line. "I'm not dangerous, Stephen. What you see is what you get."

"Oh, no, Catherine. You're much more than what one sees or what you choose to let people see. Why is that?"

"People make assumptions. You made them yourself."

"And you let them. Why?"

She shrugged.

"Last year, Project Christmas was falling short of its goal for the first time in fifteen years. It hadn't done that poorly since the last recession. I poured on the charm, made a few phone calls to some people who can be incredibly generous when they want to be or when they're talked into it. I'm good at talking people into doing things."

"Some might call that manipulation."

She nodded in agreement. "Maybe I do manipulate people, but not for my own gain. Surely that distinction counts for something?"

"What drives you?"

"I like to make a difference." It was her standard answer, but he didn't look convinced.

"It's more than that. You could make a difference by heading a beautification committee or simply writing a check."

His assessment was uncomfortably close to her parents' way of being community-minded. She thought of that lonely, frightened little girl who had reached out for help and received only money in the form of a scholarship in return.

"It's not enough."

Again he asked, "What drives you, Catherine?"

She'd never spoken to anyone about "the incident," as her parents referred to it. At first she had been too shocked and sad. Then had come the guilt, and so she had remained silent. But for some reason it seemed safe, easy to talk about the unspeakable with Stephen.

Her voice low, halting at first, she began. "I had a friend once, a little girl named Jenny. She came from the Projects, but attended my private school thanks to a scholarship my parents had set up. She was bright, vibrant, thankful for every crumb she received when everyone else I knew just expected everything they got and even then complained."

"What happened to her?"

"I knew she had a hard home life, even though I'd never been allowed to her home. My parents forbade it. But we hung out at school and I saw the bruises. No twelve-year-old is as clumsy as Jenny claimed to be."

"What did you do about it?"

"I told my parents I thought something was wrong. Jenny seemed to become more and more withdrawn at school. Her grades started to suffer."

"What did they say?"

"They told me it wasn't my concern. A couple of weeks later Jenny was dead. She'd been beaten to death by her mother's boyfriend." Once again, Catherine felt the stab of pain and accompanying guilt. "So, you see, writing a check isn't enough, Stephen."

"You can't blame yourself. You were a child. What could you have done?"

"More," she said simply.

He frowned. "How can you stand it?"

"What?"

"Having people think you're this cool, shallow woman when you are anything but?"

"I don't care what other people think of me. I know who I am."

He came forward and knelt in front of the bench on which she sat. Taking her face between his hands, he said, "I know who you are, too, Catherine."

"You do?"

"Yes, you're my wife."

This kiss was gentle, but persuasive. She had no choice but to give in to its seductive charm. And it really was no hardship to admit defeat. She took what he offered and then surprised them both by demanding more. Urgent now, the kiss had desire pounding through her veins. Every time she told herself the excitement of his touch would dim, he surprised new emotions from her, uncovering a reservoir of need she hadn't known existed. Was it just about physical attraction? She knew it wasn't for her, and surely Stephen had just as good as admitted that his feelings ran much deeper than what basic hormonal urges would manufacture?

A gamble. That was what this had been since the beginning. Even before their wedding in Las Vegas she'd taken a chance, bet on fate. Well, roll the dice.

"Make love to me, Stephen."

He stopped his exploration of her neck. Dark eyes regarded her intently.

"That night in the car you said—"

She placed her hand over his mouth. "What I said that night isn't important. Today is a new day, and I want my *husband* to make love to me."

He stood and reached for her hand, pulling her to her feet with a gentle tug. He whispered something in Spanish, beautiful, incomprehensible words that caused her breath to hitch, her heart to ache. *I will remember this moment always,* Catherine thought.

The moment when she first tumbled headlong into love.

He led her below deck, to the larger of the two staterooms, which was still small enough to be considered cozy. He didn't say a word as he began to undress her.

"You have nice hands."

She kissed the palm of one and then the other.

And Stephen was undone. Even if he could have ignored the passion stirring in her gaze, there was no mistaking the raw desire that had turned her demure voice into the smoky whisper of a siren.

"Catherine." He closed his eyes and said her name as reverently as he would a prayer.

Seemingly of their own volition, the hands she claimed to admire traveled down her torso and then back up, pulling the bulky sweater she wore with them. He pulled it over her head and then sucked in a breath at the pale perfection of her skin, which was in striking contrast to the lacy navy bra. Then, heaven help him, Stephen couldn't stop his fingers from inching aside the lace. He heard her echo the groan that tore from his own chest before she leaned forward and fused her mouth to his. This kiss, like the one they had shared in the car that night, was wild with need. His body responded instantly.

Stephen prided himself on his finesse as a lover, but just now he felt as desperate and out-of-control as a teenager. He didn't tease and tempt her with lingering caresses and sensuous nibbles. He wanted, so he took. His mouth plundered and devoured while his eager fingers grasped and clutched and tugged away the last barriers of her clothing.

Below him on the bed, Catherine gave a sexy little moan, her own hands making fast work of ridding him of the clothing he wore.

When he was naked, and straining over her, she ran her delicate hands up his chest and then fisted them in his hair, pulling him down for another hot kiss.

"Now." She breathed the word into his mouth. "Please, now."

"Say my name," he commanded, using every ounce of self-control to pull back just far enough so he could look at her. "I want to hear you say my name."

He watched her lips curve into a smile that was sensual and oddly shy. "Stephen," she whispered.

That was all it took. One word. His name. He brought their bodies together quickly, the need so fierce it astounded him. This kind of passion, this kind of emotional connection represented uncharted territory. Below him, Catherine responded, rhythm matching rhythm, need matching need, heat matching heat until they were both flung over the edge of sanity on a shattering climax. On the freefall back to earth he heard her call out his name again.

Then, using the language only those most dear spoke to him in, she whispered, *"Mi amor."*

Afterward, he rolled to his side and gathered her to

his chest, where she settled one hand over his still hammering heart. It felt for all the world as if she belonged there in the loose circle of his arms, her body limp from release, her head tucked trustingly beneath his chin. And the raging need he'd felt a moment earlier gentled into something far more disturbing.

The gulls woke him. Their irritating squawks blasted rudely through his dreams and had Stephen rolling onto his side, arm outstretched and seeking the warm, curved comfort of a woman's body. It came into contact with cool cotton and nothing more. He sat up and blinked in sleepy confusion at the rumpled sheets.

"Catherine?"

He found her puttering in the little kitchen, humming in that endearing off-key way of hers. She wore only his shirt, and he thought she looked sexier than a lingerie model. She had placed the sandwiches they'd bought at the deli on plates and was doling out pasta salad when he came up behind her and scooped her hair aside so he could kiss the back of her neck.

"Hmm. I like that."

"I've noticed," he replied, still amazed by what a responsive woman lurked beneath her quiet composure.

She turned, looped her arms around his neck and kissed him with a greedy passion that one would not suspect from such an otherwise generous woman.

"I seem to have worked up an appetite."

''Me, too,'' he agreed, as he began to unbutton his big shirt to reveal the feminine perfection beneath it.

It was another hour before they sat down in the cozy kitchen to eat their lunch.

The day was ending, Catherine knew. The magical, wonderful hours were drawing to a close. She wanted them to last, worried that once she and Stephen returned to dry land whatever spell the beautiful waters of Lake Michigan had cast would be broken, and if that happened she knew her heart would shatter as well.

The wind had picked up, making quick work of their sail back to the yacht club. Once there, she helped him unload their gear from the day. Then she waited in the car while he made arrangements for the boat to be stored for the winter.

''Are you tired?'' he asked as they drove home.

''Exhausted,'' she said with an exaggerated yawn. ''Can't imagine why.''

''There's someone I'd like you to meet.''

She straightened in her seat. ''Now?''

''It's on the way home.''

''Who?''

''My grandmother.''

Catherine wanted to meet his family. She knew what his grandmother meant to him. The woman had been like a surrogate mother, giving him the love and encouragement the Danburys had withheld, filling in the blanks of his rich heritage. Oh, yes, she wanted to meet her. But right now?

"Oh, Stephen. My hair is a mess and I..." she flipped down the visor to check her reflection in the mirror. Tilting her head to one side, she blanched. "Oh, my God! Is that a whisker burn?"

He chuckled. "My grandmother is near-sighted. Don't worry."

"Oh, but look how I'm dressed." Her clothes were rumpled from an afternoon spent on the floor of the stateroom.

"My grandmother won't be offended. There's no need to dress for dinner at her house. It's a casual affair, believe me."

"Dinner? She's having us for dinner and you never said a word about the invitation before now?"

"It's a standing invitation. She makes enough for an army every Sunday. Whoever stops by is welcome."

"Who else stops by?"

"My aunts, cousins, their families." He shrugged.

"They'll all be there?"

"Some of them, sure."

"You said before that they knew about our arrangement. I'll feel...awkward in their presence."

"They know about our arrangement," he acknowledged. "They also know I would never bring someone I didn't care about to dinner." He took her hand, kissed the back of it. "I want you to meet my family, Catherine. Will you do me the honor?"

When he put it like that, she couldn't refuse.

"It's me who is honored, Stephen."

His grandmother's house was not especially large, nor was it in an exclusive neighborhood. But there was no denying its charm. With its stone façade, it reminded her of a fairy-tale cottage. Chrysanthemums bloomed like pots of gold in the flower beds, where other perennials had already enjoyed their glory and had now been cut back in preparation for winter.

The instant they stepped across the threshold they were surrounded by boisterous, enthusiastic relatives of varying ages and sizes, all chattering excitedly. Some spoke in English, some in Spanish. All with the kind of welcoming fondness that Catherine had thought only Hollywood could manufacture. She was kissed and hugged by people she had never met before and whose names had already become confused.

"Welcome, welcome," a plump older woman said, wiping her hands on an apron as she crossed the room to where they stood just inside the door. It was as far as they had gotten before being surrounded by family members.

"*Abuelita*," Stephen said with a grin. "I'd like you to meet Catherine. Catherine, this is my grandmother, Consuela Fuentes."

"It's nice to meet you, Señora Fuentes," Catherine said. She had barely gotten the words out when she was wrapped in a pair of surprisingly strong arms and soundly kissed on both cheeks.

"You will call me *Abuelita*, yes?"

"*Abuelita*." She tried out the word, liking the way it sounded. Stephen's family nodded their approval.

Throughout their visit it became clear to Catherine that while Stephen had grown up in privilege, surrounded by servants and wealthy grandparents who had been miserly with their affection, here he had known generous helpings of love. There was no sign of the aloof, intense man in Consuela Fuentes's homey living room. He wrestled on the floor with his cousins' children, joked with his uncles, complimented his aunts.

Dinner was a casual affair, the food not as spicy as Catherine had thought it would be, but filling and delicious and made in massive quantities. People laughed and talked, sometimes over one another, passing serving bowls or even hopping up to walk down to the far end of the table for what they wanted. It was informal, bordering on chaotic. It was fantastic.

From all of the chatter Catherine deduced that the evenings when Stephen had slipped away, not to return till late, had been spent here.

Afterward, when the last bit of dessert had been eaten, Catherine helped Stephen's three aunts and grandmother clear the table. They wouldn't let her help wash the dishes, but she sat on a stool at the counter in the kitchen and listened to them chatter happily about babies and bargains, the lyrical cadence of their voices making even the mundane seem magical. And she knew if not for her presence much of the conversation would have been conducted in Spanish and more than likely would have centered on her.

"Christina and Miguel are expecting again. They are hoping for a boy this time." For Catherine's benefit Rosaria added, "They already have four daughters."

Miguel was Stephen's cousin and Rosaria's oldest son. From the introductions, and from listening to the conversations, Catherine thought she had all the relationships down.

Stephen's grandmother had four daughters, including Stephen's mother, Galena, who had been the oldest. Rosaria was the second oldest, then came Rita and Selena. All of the daughters, with the exception of Galena, had married men from their native Puerto Rico or men who were Hispanic. Most of their children were grown now, with families of their own.

"When will you and Stephen start a family?" Rosaria asked.

The question startled Catherine enough that she spilt her tea. A family? They had not planned to start a family. They had not planned to remain married. But surely after today, after that wonderful afternoon of making love, things had changed?

CHAPTER NINE

A BITTER wind whipped through downtown Chicago, stealing pedestrians' breath and turning their cheeks more ruddy red than rosy. It was barely November, but the chilly temperatures heralded the long winter to come. Even so, Stephen was whistling as he entered the Danbury Building and headed to the elevators. It had been an incredible month, and now another weekend was drawing near. An absolutely free weekend. He and Catherine had no charity functions to attend, nothing that required their presence.

Since the afternoon on *La Libertad*, she had spent every night in his bed, and he figured this weekend would be as good a time as any to move the rest of her things into the master suite. That was where she belonged. Near him. Next to him. In his bed just as surely as she was in his heart.

It still frightened him, this need, this…love. He'd never felt anything quite so overpowering, quite so consuming. Or, he admitted, quite so fulfilling.

His fingers closed around the small velvet box in the pocket of his overcoat. Inside it was the ring he planned to give Catherine that night, to replace the cheap one they'd bought in Las Vegas. This was not just any ring, but the one his father had given his mother: a flawless two-carat marquis-cut diamond surrounded by sapphires. He'd just come from the jewelers, where it had been cleaned and resized based on another ring he'd found in Catherine's jewelry box.

He would give it to her after dinner, maybe even get down on one knee and propose. They could renew their vows, maybe even have a real wedding this time, complete with all the trimmings she'd missed out on in Las Vegas. She'd like that. She was such a romantic.

Life was good, he decided, and then nearly took it back when Derek stepped into the elevator just before the doors closed.

"What are you doing here?"

"It is the Danbury Building, and I am a Danbury. More of a Danbury, I might add, than you'll ever be, *Stefano.*"

"You have no business here. You're no longer an executive with the company. The new vice president starts next week."

"Yes, Sam Maxwell from the Hartford store. As by-the-book as they come," he sneered.

"Which means he'll actually do some work to earn his keep," Stephen countered.

"What's Catherine doing to earn her keep?"

"Don't go there," Stephen warned, as fury vibrated through his system.

"So touchy."

"I won't discuss my wife with you."

"Well, a word to the wise, *cousin*, her family's broke."

"The economy has been hard on a lot of people, Derek. That's no newsflash."

"It's been harder on the Cantons than most. Your in-laws are mortgaged to the hilt. And you know how Catherine likes to help people out."

"Catherine's family is no concern of yours."

"Yes, you're right. In fact even if we had married they would have been none of my concern. They might have thought I was going to be their meal ticket, but I knew better. And I was smart enough to make Catherine sign a prenuptial agreement. Somehow I doubt that in your rush to the altar you got around to that," Derek drawled.

"Again, it's none of your concern."

Derek laughed. "I thought as much. No prenup." He tsked. "You are a fool. What if you wind up losing Danbury's anyway? Or at least half of it to her in a divorce settlement?"

"You're wrong about her. Catherine's no gold-digger. She's not like that."

"*All* women are like that," Derek replied. "And Catherine has more reason to be than most. After all, by marrying you she's already proved the old adage about hell having no fury like a woman scorned."

"You don't know anything about our marriage."

"Come now, don't tell me you have feelings for her? You were never more than a rebound to

Catherine, a way for her to get even with me. And, I'll admit it, she has. You both have.''

''This is no longer about you.'' Maybe it never was, Stephen thought now.

The elevator doors opened and he stepped out. But before the doors could slide shut again Derek held out a hand to stop them and said, ''Don't tell me you think she loves you? A few months ago she loved me. She probably still does.''

''You don't love her. You never loved her.''

''I love the half of the company a shrewd lawyer could help her take from you in a divorce.''

Again he laughed, setting Stephen's teeth on edge, and, worse, introducing a niggling seed of doubt. Could Catherine still have feelings for Derek?

''Even if she left me she'd never take you back. Not after what she witnessed in the church.''

''We'll see. But in the meantime she's in a very good position to take you to the cleaners. And, should that happen, I'll be only too happy to begin seeing her again.''

''You're delusional.''

''I don't know.'' Derek offered a dazzling smile. ''I've been told I can be very charming. I believe Cherise Langston told me that just last night. You remember Cherise?''

Stephen shook his head in disgust. The pair of them deserved one another.

''If you're attempting to make me jealous it won't work. Cherise was a lovely distraction for a brief time, but nothing more. If you want to talk about gold-diggers, I think she qualifies.''

Derek merely shrugged.

''Give Catherine my best.''

He let the doors slide shut, whistling the same tune Stephen had been just moments before, and taking with him a good portion of the joy Stephen had been feeling.

Catherine was in the kitchen when Stephen got home. He offered her a smile as he absently patted Degas's broad head. She knew him well enough after these past several weeks to know when something was wrong. He seemed distracted—edgy, even.

She had planned a romantic and intimate dinner, and had spent the better part of three hours preparing and cooking it. The sautéed scallops with leeks and lemon butter sauce were already on the dining room table, along with a salad of mixed greens and fresh rolls she'd picked up at the bakery. A glance at the clock told her the pork loin was ready.

''You're just in time for dinner. I thought we'd eat in the dining room tonight.''

''Hmm? Uh, sure. That's fine.''

''Why don't you change your clothes and pour yourself a drink? I'll put this on a serving tray and join you in a moment.''

He nodded.

A few minutes later Stephen entered the dining room, clad in casual trousers and an oxford. He'd been only too glad to shed his suit and tie. If only his mood were as easy to change. He glanced at the flickering candles in the middle of the dining room table. He thought about the romantic evening he'd had planned, and the ring he'd stashed away in a drawer upstairs. He hated to let his cousin ruin his plans. Indeed, he'd once admonished Catherine for allowing Derek to raise suspicions and stir up trouble. But the doubt was there, as well as the old insecurity.

Maybe it was too soon to talk about love and life-long commitments. After all, under normal circumstances they would just be in the beginning stages of dating. So far they'd gotten everything backward. They'd married and then begun a courtship. They knew each other's living habits without knowing each other's hearts. Perhaps if things moved more slowly, built up more gradually, as they would in a normal relationship. The ring could wait, he decided.

"What's bothering you?" Catherine asked when she joined him in the dining room.

He shrugged. "Why do you think something is bothering me?"

"You just seem like you've got a lot on your mind. Work going okay?"

"The same." He rubbed a hand across his brow. "Profits look to be down again this quarter."

"It's the economy. Everyone is feeling the pinch. People are scaling back on purchases. But Thanksgiving is right around the corner, and then the

Christmas shopping season will kick into high gear. Things will turn around.''

He smiled and reached out to take her hand.

''Is this a pep talk?''

''Is it working?''

''I'll let you know.'' He tugged on her hand, pulling until she left her seat and settled sideways on his lap. He tried to keep the urgency out of his kiss, but the desperate need he felt for validation must have slipped in.

''Are you sure everything is all right?'' she asked.

''It's…been a long day, and what I really want right now is you.''

She smiled, that odd little dimple denting in her cheek. ''Well, you have me.''

Do I? The question went unspoken, though. He kissed her instead, deeply, passionately, until they were both breathless and more than a little aroused.

''This chair isn't adequate for what I have in mind.'' He tilted her head to the side, nibbled her neck. ''What do you say we go upstairs?''

''What about dinner? You haven't even sampled my scallops yet.''

''I'd rather sample you.''

Her blouse was a wrap style and he had no trouble removing it. Before Catherine could fathom what he meant to do she found herself divested of it, and the silk camisole underneath, and perched on the edge of the dining room table in the exact spot where Stephen's place setting had been. The china had been pushed back, along with her skirt. Its hem now rode the tops of thighs, offering a glimpse of the lacy white garters that held up her sheer stockings.

He hooked an index finger beneath one of the fasteners and said, "What have we here?"

He hadn't seemed hungry a minute ago, but now he looked absolutely ravenous, and Catherine rather doubted her well-seasoned pork loin had anything to do with it. Indeed, the culinary feast she had painstakingly prepared had been crossed off her own list of priorities.

"I was planning to buy a cheesecake for dessert, but I splurged on some new lingerie instead. Do you like it?"

"I haven't seen it. Not all of it, anyway."

"Let's go upstairs."

"Uh-uh." One side of his mouth lifted in a smile. "I've changed my mind. Let's stay here."

He reached behind her and undid the hook on her skirt, then pulled the zipper as low as the table would allow. She scooted off the edge and stood. The skirt slid down her legs and puddled at her feet. She should have been embarrassed to be standing in the dining room wearing nothing but a snowy white thong, garter belt, sheer stockings and black high heels, but the look on Stephen's face made her feel empowered instead.

Catherine thought about the many fantasies she'd entertained since their marriage. And, even though she had no complaints about their lovemaking, she couldn't dismiss the excitement she felt just now.

"I've never made love in a dining room before."

"I can't say that I ever have either. Is that an invitation?"

She smiled, only too glad to give the order. "Take off your clothes."

Dinner grew cold even as the temperature in the room spiked to sizzling.

Later that night, as Catherine slept beside him, Stephen thought about Derek's allegations. He wouldn't believe them, he decided. Even as he made this vow, however, he couldn't quite escape the worry that somehow his cousin would manage to best him again. All their lives Derek—the golden boy with the classic Danbury looks—had come out ahead. He had been doted on by their grandparents and eyed by debutantes' mothers as Stephen had stood on the sidelines and watched.

Derek claimed to be charming, and indeed he was. His smooth manners, charismatic smile and good looks hid his egocentric nature. Could his cousin persuade Catherine that he still loved her? She had fallen under the spell of his charm once. Could she again?

When morning broke he still wasn't sure he knew the answers.

Catherine stared at the small stick and reread the instructions that had come with the test kit. There was no mistake. She was pregnant. She laid her hands on her flat stomach, stared at her reflection in the bathroom mirror and grinned, happier than she could ever remember being.

She didn't have to wonder when she had conceived. That day aboard *La Libertad* had been the only time they'd made love without protection. After that they'd always had something nearby. Even a week earlier in the dining room they'd shown admirable restraint until a condom could be slipped on.

She chuckled at the care they had taken during the past several weeks. As it turned out none of it had mattered after that magical sailing trip on Lake Michigan. A baby was growing inside of her. Stephen's baby.

She would tell him that night. Maybe light a few candles, pour some champagne. Champagne? She laughed out loud. No, no, not champagne. She was expecting a child now. She couldn't be drinking alcohol. They would toast this new life with sparkling grape juice. Then Stephen would take her in his arms, kiss her and tell her how much he loved her.

Her smile faltered and the fantasy dissolved. He had yet to say the words. And, oh, how Catherine wanted the words. Now more than ever she needed to hear them, especially since he had seemed so preoccupied in recent days. Sometimes she would catch him looking at her, as if trying to decipher the answer to something that puzzled and troubled him greatly. Whenever she asked what was wrong his answer was always the same: nothing. But something was bothering him. Could it be he regretted that their relationship had changed? Maybe as much as he enjoyed her company he still wanted his freedom at the end of the year.

No, he loved her, her heart insisted. Surely he had told her so in dozens of other ways—with searing kisses, gentle caresses, thoughtful comments and quiet conversations in the dark as they cuddled in his bed after making love. All of those things mattered more than the actual words. Even so, she decided she would wait to hear him declare his feelings before telling him about the baby.

''Want to watch a movie tonight?'' she asked as they ate dinner that night.

''*The Maltese Falcon?*''

She wrinkled her nose. That wasn't what she had in mind at all.

''I was thinking *Sabrina*, the original version.''

She wanted moonlight and yearning, passion and romance. She wanted a happy ending. Not only for Audrey Hepburn's character, but for herself.

He shrugged. ''I guess I can sit through it.''

''Ah, chivalry. Who says it's dead?''

He helped her clear the table and load the dishwasher. She was humming a popular ballad when she glanced over and caught him smiling.

''What's so funny?''

''I enjoy hearing you sing.''

"I know I don't have a good voice. Felicity says I couldn't carry a tune if it came with handles."

He kissed the tip of her nose. "I enjoy hearing you sing," he said again.

And he did, Stephen decided. Off-key as could be, and yet there was something perfect about the way she slaughtered a song as she puttered in their kitchen. *It had to be love.* Why else would such an assault on his ears also be endearing?

Again, he knew a moment of panic. What if she didn't feel it, too? The signs were there that she did. The glances, the way she casually touched the back of his hand during conversation. She tucked her body close to his in sleep, called his office during the day for no reason at all. Still Derek's words haunted him. For the first time in his life Stephen had opened his heart, and he couldn't bear the thought that the woman he loved might not love him in return.

Catherine was still humming, oblivious to his concerns. But he needed a moment to put his old demons back where they belonged.

"I'll go get the movie ready while you finish up in here."

Catherine settled onto the couch in what Stephen had dubbed the entertainment room. It had a large flat-screen television, with movie-theater-quality picture and sound, and everything from dimming the lights to controlling the room's temperature could done with the push of a button on a large remote control. The room had its own refrigerator, stocked with soft drinks, beer and mixers, a liquor cabinet, and a microwave for making popcorn, even though Stephen always insisted that the best popcorn was made in a pot on the stove and then smothered in real melted butter.

''Popcorn tonight?'' he asked, as he slid the movie into the VCR—he didn't have this one on DVD yet—and began to fast-forward through the trailers and credits.

''No, thanks. I'm too full from dinner to eat anything else.''

''Wine, then? I picked up a nice Merlot on the way home from work.''

''I'll pass.''

''It's that Merlot you told me you wanted to try last week.''

''Oh. Well, the fact is I've decided to give it up wine altogether. It, um, makes me too sleepy.''

Stephen couldn't have said why, but he didn't think she was telling the truth. But why would she lie over something as insignificant as not wanting a glass of wine?

As the weeks passed, though, it seemed to Stephen that Catherine was using all sorts of small lies and evasions. He swore she was hiding something. And, whatever it was, it seemed to be taking its toll on her health. She was often tired—nodding off as they watched a movie, yawning through dinner.

Sometimes he arrived home from work to find her napping. And her appetite had fled as well. Food she had once loved seemed to hold no appeal for her, and sometimes she looked positively green.

"Must be the flu," she told him.

She'd had the "flu" four times that week.

He worried that she could be seriously ill, but she insisted she was fine, just busy because of the holiday season. But then he came home one day to find a message on their answering machine from a doctor's office, reminding her of an appointment the next day. He waited for her to mention it, to confide in him about whatever was going on. But she merely picked at her dinner that evening and then went to bed early.

Stephen sat up with a glass of Scotch and Humphrey Bogart for company.

Catherine felt the strain of keeping her secret. She longed to tell Stephen about this new life growing inside her, to share her excitement and first pregnancy trepidation. But as one day passed into the next Stephen seemed no closer to expressing his feelings. Worse than that, he seemed to be pulling back. Oh, he was courteous and polite. She could never fault his manners. But he was killing her with each reserved please and thank you that he uttered. Their relationship seemed to be spinning back in time, instead of progressing forward.

As the icy winds of December battered Chicago, she despaired. Would she ever be able to thaw her husband's heart?

CHAPTER TEN

WITH her doctor's approval—indeed, encouragement—Catherine continued to visit the health spa three times a week, eschewing weights and high-impact aerobics for walking the track or swimming laps in the pool. She usually went in the mornings, before heading to the office, so it surprised her to run into Marguerite on this particular Monday morning. The other woman was not known for rising before ten, and even though they had both belonged to the club for years they only rarely ran across one another. It was just Catherine's luck they would have to run across one another on this day.

She was just finishing up five miles on the indoor track when she heard her name come over the public address system.

"Will Mrs. Danbury please come to the front desk?"

Catherine blotted her face with the white towel she had draped around her neck and headed downstairs from the elevated track that ringed the interior of the building and afforded members a pleasantly distracting view of most of the facility.

Turning the corner, she nearly collided with Marguerite, who was coming from one of the aerobics rooms.

The two women eyed one another warily.

"Catherine."

"Hello, Marguerite."

"Here trying to keep your figure?" She didn't wait for an answer. "Smart girl. Men soon lose interest in a woman who lets herself go after saying 'I do.' And it looks like you've put on a few pounds."

Catherine dismissed the nasty remark. She had not gained so much as a pound, despite her pregnancy. "I haven't heard Stephen complain."

"Not yet. But he will, dear. Trust me. You should talk to Len. He's the club's most requested personal trainer. He's a real taskmaster, but he does get results."

Marguerite put her hands on her own trim waist and offered a smile made no less catty by the fact her tight face barely moved.

"Oh, I thought you owed your figure to Dr. Redmond?" Catherine replied innocently, noting the name of a well-known plastic surgeon whose specialties were tummy tucks and breast augmentation.

Marguerite's gaze turned glacial. "Excuse me, I was paged."

Catherine smiled. She felt small but somehow satisfied to point out, "Or it could be me. I'm Mrs. Danbury as well."

She let Marguerite stalk off ahead of her, humming as she followed. When they reached the desk, a harried young woman glanced up. Brittney, her name tag read, and she looked to be fresh from high school.

New to the job, no doubt, and left for the first time to cover the front desk on her own.

"Can I help you?"

"I was paged," Marguerite said, raising her chin just enough to look down her professionally sculpted nose at the young woman.

"One of us was paged." Catherine offered a warm smile. "I am Catherine Danbury and this is Marguerite Danbury."

"Oh." The young woman frowned for a moment before her expression brightened. "It must be the younger Mrs. Danbury."

But Catherine didn't have long to enjoy Marguerite's irritation at the unintentional slight. Brittney held out a video. *"Yoga for Mothers-to-Be.* Tanya said to give this to you," she added, offering the name of the club's yoga instructor.

"Thanks." She was sure her face was flaming, even as the speculation burned in Marguerite's eyes.

"Expecting, are we?"

"That's really none of your business."

"No reason to be so touchy. When does the blessed event occur?"

"Again, none of your business."

"I wonder…"

"What's that supposed to mean?" she asked, but she knew what was going through the other woman's shrewd mind.

"Nothing, my dear. Not a thing."

*   *   *

Marguerite left the health club with a plot already hatching. She and Derek might never get their hands on Danbury's, as they had once schemed to do, but neither Stephen nor Catherine deserved to be happy after ruining their well-laid plans.

Revenge was sweetest when you shared it with someone. So she told her driver to take her to her son's apartment building. She didn't bother to have the doorman announce her. She used her key to access the penthouse elevator and let herself up, not bothering to wonder if Derek would be home or in the mood for unexpected visitors.

It was not quite nine in the morning when she stepped off the elevator. She headed straight for her son's bedroom, barging in on a scene that most mothers hoped to avoid.

A naked woman shrieked, diving for the sheets. Derek covered himself as well, but his expression was one of irritation rather than mortification.

"Is it too much to ask that you at least call first, Mother? I have my own home for a reason."

"Yes, well, this couldn't wait." She turned her attention to the quivering woman. "Get up, child, and get out. I need to speak to my son in private."

The woman emerged from the bed, wearing the top sheet like a toga.

"I'll call you later, Cherise," Derek said.

Cherise glared at him over her shoulder as she made her way to the bathroom, scooping up her clothing as she went. "I don't think I'll be home."

"Touchy," Marguerite commented as the bathroom door slammed shut.

"I wonder why?" Derek drawled. He pointed toward the living room. "Give me a minute, Mother."

Five minutes after an indignant Cherise had stalked out Derek emerged, freshly showered and fully clothed.

Marguerite forgave him for keeping her waiting. She was in too good a mood to let anything spoil it. She'd even made coffee, a chore she preferred to leave to the domestics. But Derek didn't employ any on a full-time basis.

"Now, what is so important that you had to roust me out of bed?"

"It's not as if you were sleeping."

"That's precisely my point."

"I ran into Catherine at the health spa this morning."

She sipped her coffee and Derek waited, knowing his mother would get to the point in her own good time.

"It seems your ex is going to have a baby."

"Are you expecting me to offer my congratulations to the happy couple?"

Unable to properly frown, she shook her head. "You disappointment me, Derek. For someone who has been looking for a way to cause problems, you should be able to see the golden opportunity presented here."

"How far along is she?"

"She wouldn't say. Very tight-lipped about the whole thing, which makes a person wonder." She managed something akin to a smile.

"Sorry to disappoint you, Mother, but you're not going to be a grandma yet. Catherine and I didn't enjoy much of a physical relationship, and when we did I was very careful—as always."

"Whether the child is yours or not doesn't matter. What Stephen thinks, however, does."

Derek grinned as her meaning apparently sank in. Setting his coffee aside, he stood.

"I trust you'll let yourself out when you're done with your coffee?"

"Where are you going?"

"I thought I would pay my dear cousin a visit."

Stephen was in a foul mood. He shuffled through the report on his desk, hoping for better news, better numbers. The holiday shopping season was in full swing, but sales were still sluggish thanks to a soft economy. Danbury's had already been running huge sales and promotions just to lure in price-conscious consumers. At this point they might as well be giving the merchandise away. Other retailers were in the same boat, but there was little comfort in having company to share the misery. He'd hoped for a profitable season. Danbury's future might well depend on it.

Just when he thought the day could not get worse,

Derek walked through the door unannounced. Stephen's harried-looking secretary scurried in behind him and offered an apologetic smile.

"It's all right, Lottie. Come in, Derek." As his cousin plopped down into one of the chairs and crossed an ankle over one knee, Stephen added sarcastically, "Have a seat and make yourself comfortable."

When they were alone, Stephen asked, "So, what brings you out at—" he consulted his watch "—ten-forty on a Monday morning? You didn't believe in rising before noon when you worked here."

"This is social. A friendly little family visit."

Stephen snorted. "We're not friends, Derek. And you don't even like to admit we're family. Why are you here? Trust fund run out already?"

"Actually, I came by to congratulate you."

Stephen eyed him suspiciously. "For what?"

"The baby, of course. You and Catherine must be thrilled."

Baby? Stephen somehow managed to keep his expression neutral, despite the throbbing in his temples. His cousin had to be wrong. This had to be one of his petty little mind games.

"And you heard about this how?"

"Mother told me. She ran into Catherine at the health club this morning and learned about it then."

He didn't buy it for a moment. It couldn't be true. Catherine would have told him. She wouldn't have kept something this monumental to herself.

Even as he told himself this he realized it all made sense. The queasiness. The fatigue. Her sudden objection to drinking wine. He knew a moment of pure joy. A baby. A family. But then the wariness returned, accompanied by the doubts that pecked at him like a flock of hostile crows.

"And you're just here to congratulate me?" His mind was reeling, but he decided to play along until he knew exactly what Derek was after. "That's very big of you."

"I'll admit when I heard about it I wondered if it could be mine. We weren't always careful, if you know what I mean. You never know..." Derek let the thought hang out there as he smiled his serpentine smile. "Of course I'm sure Catherine would never have agreed to marry you if she thought she was pregnant with my child."

Derek watched his cousin's face pale. Direct hit. Oh, to be a fly on the wall in the Stephen Danbury domicile that night. If it went as he hoped, accusations would fly and hateful things would be said. And when it was all done Derek would be there to pick up the pieces.

Deciding not to overplay his advantage, he rose. "Well, I won't keep you. I know how busy you are. Kiss the mother-to-be for me, will you?" Then he couldn't resist adding, "On that cute little mole of hers."

When he had gone Stephen slouched back in his

chair, his mind busily trying to process all the information and the not so subtle accusation his cousin had made. Was Catherine really pregnant? She didn't look it, but then they hadn't been very intimate lately. Why hadn't she told him? Could it be, as Derek insinuated, that Stephen was not the father? He didn't want to believe that, but the more he thought about it the more it seemed to make sense. What other reason would she have for keeping something like that secret?

Stephen was waiting when she got home, sitting on the living room couch, nursing his fourth Scotch. His mood had grown more volatile with each sip, shifting from melancholy to simmering rage. Norah Jones sang a haunting melody in the background. And, since he hadn't bothered with the lights, the room had grown dim along with winter's short day.

"You're home." She smiled warily, gaze sliding to the glass he held. "Bad day?"

"I've had better."

"I'm sorry to hear that. I thought we could try that new Greek restaurant tonight. I have a craving for feta cheese."

"I'll bet," he muttered.

"Excuse me?"

He took another sip and said nothing.

Her expression turned uncertain. "I guess we don't need to go out, but I didn't plan anything for dinner.

Give me an hour, though, and I can probably whip up something. Anything in particular you want?"

She walked to him and bent to kiss his mouth. He turned his head and her lips brushed his cheek instead.

Catherine knew something was seriously wrong even before he grabbed her wrist as she started to straighten and in a glacial voice demanded, "You can tell me the truth."

She pulled her hand free and backed up a step. "I don't know what you mean."

But of course she did, and her heart squeezed most painfully at this glowering expression. This was not how she wanted to tell him about the life they had created together that one wonderful afternoon aboard *La Libertad*. Not when he looked so remote, so cold, so far removed from the love she had wanted to believe had begun to blossom in his heart.

"Come now, Catherine." His voice was low, dangerous, and the rolling of the R caused her to shiver, as if the frosty wind pressing insistently against the windowpane had somehow won entry into the room.

"Tell me about the *happy* event that should be taking place in a matter of months."

He drained his glass, setting it down none too gently on the coffee table. Catherine jumped, surprised by the anger he barely managed to suppress. She had never dreamed he would be furious about his impending fatherhood.

"Stephen, I—"

"Tell me!"

''We're having a baby,'' she whispered, as the tears blurred her vision.

''We?'' His tone was mocking, and it tore at her already battered heart.

''I know it wasn't part of our…arrangement.'' The word tasted bitter in her mouth. She'd been so sure there was more to their relationship than an impersonal business deal set to expire the following summer.

''It wasn't. It changes nothing,'' he said. As he stood, he repeated, ''Nothing.''

Catherine fell back a step, grateful for the overstuffed chair she sank into when her knees grew weak.

''Nothing?''

''That's what I said and that's what you'll get when the year is up. Nothing. I won't change the terms of our deal now.''

''You think this is about money, Stephen? You think I planned this baby?''

''I'm sure you didn't plan it, or you probably would have gone ahead with your wedding to Derek.''

''Derek? What has Derek got to do with—?''

But then she understood, and what hope she'd had that she could win her husband's heart withered like an orchid struck by frost.

The tears came, and she let them course unchecked down her cheeks. She cried for herself and for her baby, but she also cried for him. Would he never learn to trust, to love?

"Oh, Stephen, no. You think this baby is Derek's?"

"Why else wouldn't you tell me, Catherine? Why else would you keep something this important so secret that the person from whom I had to find out was my own cousin?"

She closed her eyes, imagining just how much Derek would have relished his role as messenger. "I'm sorry for that."

"I don't want your apology. I want to know why."

Talking about love seemed pointless now. He'd made up his mind not to believe her. That much was clear. "My reason doesn't matter anymore."

"I think I'm entitled to an explanation. You owe me that much." He said something in Spanish, and, given his harsh tone, she was grateful her knowledge of the language was limited. "I thought I knew you, Catherine."

"Yes, and I thought I knew you as well. I guess we were both wrong." She stood, wiped away the tears as she came to the only decision she could under the circumstances. "I'll be leaving in the morning."

"The year's not up, Catherine."

"I can't stay here. Not when you think so little of me. You once admonished me for letting Derek stir up doubts and suspicions. You're nothing but a hypocrite. The first time he hisses some venom into your ear about me you believe it."

"Give me a reason not to," he said quietly. And she didn't doubt his sincerity.

"The thing is, Stephen, I shouldn't have to."

Stephen watched her walk up the stairs with that quiet grace and dignity he had long admired. He was the wronged party here, and yet her tears had seemed real, the heartache shimmering in her sapphire eyes authentic.

He wanted to go to her. Plead with her to stay, to love him. But pride kept him planted in his seat. He'd long ago learned that you could not force people to have feelings for you. He watched her turn to the right at the top of the stairs. They seemed to have come full circle, from strangers to lovers to lovers estranged.

When he heard her bedroom door snap shut he stood, picked up his glass, and, palming it like a baseball, threw it at the fireplace. It crashed against the marble surround, shattering into dangerous jagged pieces that mocked his heart and matched his mood.

"Why?"

Stephen wasn't asleep when he heard his door open. Light from the hallway spilled inside, silhouetting Catherine's image for a moment before she stepped over the threshold. He rolled to his side and switched on the bedside lamp. If she had come to try to seduce him into changing his mind about her she wasn't dressed for the part. The conservative robe she wore was tightly belted and pulled closed at the lapels. Her expression, he noted, was pinched, pained, as if she could no longer hide her distaste for him and what she was about to do.

Even as his body made a liar of him he opened his mouth to tell her he didn't want her. But halfway to the bed she doubled over.

"Stephen!" she cried.

He shot from beneath the sheets, scooping her up into his arms before she could crumple onto the floor.

Heart hammering, he asked, "My God, what is it? What's wrong?"

"The baby." Catherine squeezed her eyes shut, the pain in her heart much greater than the pain radiating through her abdomen. She couldn't lose this baby. She just couldn't. It would be all she had of the man she loved.

He laid her gently on the bed they had shared for the past several weeks. She rolled to her side, pulling her legs up close to her body.

"I'm bleeding," she whispered, the horror as fresh as the crimson blood she'd discovered an hour earlier.

"I'll take you to the hospital."

"No."

But he was already pulling on a pair of pants. As he shoved his arms through the sleeves of a shirt he said, "Maybe I should call an ambulance?"

"No."

Shirt unbuttoned, hands falling to the side, he said, "Tell me what to do and I'll do it."

His voice was soft, pleading, and for a moment she

almost gave in to his request. Love me, she thought. Just love me. But even in her agony she could not beg him. It wasn't about pride, for if stripping herself of pride were the answer she would have done so without hesitation. But love had to be given freely, without prompting, without limitations, for it to mean anything.

The telephone rang.

"That will be the doctor," she told him. "I had his service page him."

Stephen snapped up the phone. "Hello!"

Catherine held out her hand for the receiver, but he shook his head and sat down on the edge of the bed.

"The doctor wants to know when the bleeding started."

"About an hour ago."

He relayed the information and then asked, "Is it heavy? Are you experiencing any cramping?"

"It's not too heavy, but I'm having some cramping."

He told the doctor that as well. It seemed absurd to keep up this three-way conversation, but she was too frightened to insist he hand her the telephone. She didn't want to go through this alone. If this were the only way he would be involved in her pregnancy, she would let him.

"I see," Stephen said. And then, "Yes, I'll have her in your office first thing in the morning. Thank you, Doctor."

"There's nothing we can do, is there?" Catherine

slumped back against the pillow, her eyes filling with tears.

"I'm sorry, Catherine."

His hand was gentle as it brushed the hair back from her face. He wiped away a teardrop and caressed her cheek.

"I worked out today. The doctor said I could. He said I was perfectly healthy. Maybe I did too much?"

He wiped away another tear, and then reached for her hand. Giving it a squeeze, he said, "Don't blame yourself, Catherine. You did nothing to cause this."

"Why, then?" More tears leaked from her eyes.

Stephen had uttered the same question just hours earlier, his emotional pain as acute as hers was now. As much as he wanted to hate her, he couldn't. And he didn't want to see her like this—devastated over the prospect of losing his cousin's child. Still, he had to know.

"Do you still love him?"

When she just looked at him blankly, he said, "Derek. Even after everything he did, do you still love him?"

"I don't love him, Stephen. After these past several months with you I realize I never loved him, not the way I should have. Love isn't a tepid emotion, and that's all I felt when I was with him."

Left unsaid was what they both knew: nothing that had transpired between them could be considered merely tepid.

"I'll take you back to your room."

''No, please.'' She clutched his hand. ''Let me stay with you. I don't want to be alone right now.''

''Catherine—''

''Just hold me, Stephen. Tomorrow will come soon enough. Just give me tonight. Let me pretend everything is going to be all right. That's all I'm asking of you. Please.''

He was not cold-hearted enough to deny her request. And so he slipped into bed beside her, wrapped his arms around her slender body and let himself pretend as well.

CHAPTER ELEVEN

THEY didn't speak as they sat in the doctor's waiting room. Words seemed unnecessary, and what was there to say, really? Stephen had made his feelings well known to her the night before. He didn't love her. He didn't trust her.

The bleeding had stopped early that morning, and the cramping had subsided as well, but Catherine's nerves remained taut. Her world seemed to have been turned upside down in the past twenty-four hours, and she was still reeling.

A door opened and a pastel-coated nurse emerged.

"Catherine Danbury?" the nurse called out.

Catherine stood.

"Come on back to examination room one."

When Stephen remained seated, the nurse said, "Your husband can come, too."

"I'll wait here."

She wanted him with her, just as she had last night. But the sun had risen, and with the new day he'd apparently taken her at her word that she would ask nothing else of him.

The examination room was small and cold, especially since Catherine was dressed in nothing but an aqua paper gown that afforded her no warmth and little modesty. The nurse rolled a machine into the room, explaining that it would allow the doctor to perform an ultrasound to better determine the baby's status.

"We don't do this for everybody, since it can be quite costly. But with a last name like Danbury..." The nurse winked. "Well, we know you're not worried about whether or not your health insurer will cover it."

The test wasn't particularly comfortable, but she focused on the doctor, trying to read her diagnosis in his expression.

Finally, Catherine could stand the silence no longer. "Is my baby going to be okay?"

"I can't make any guarantees, Mrs. Danbury. But everything looks normal right now."

"What about the bleeding? The cramps?"

"It's not uncommon for women to experience spotting and cramping in their first trimester; sometimes it's nothing to worry about, and sometimes..." He shrugged. "Nature has a way of taking care of itself, and there is nothing medical science can do about it, I'm afraid. But try not to worry about that. As I said, things look fine."

"Is there anything I can do?"

He took off his glasses and stuffed them into the pocket of his white coat. "Take it easy. Stay off your feet for the next few days. Above all, try to relax. I'll see you in another month."

As the doctor left the nurse winked at Catherine.

"My advice, honey, is to make your husband wait on you for a change. I've got four kids, and let me tell you I milked every pregnancy for all it was worth. I even got a remodeled kitchen out of the last one."

Catherine tried to smile, but couldn't. Hormones, combined with worry and heartbreak, had tears blurring her vision.

"Come on, sweetie, there's no reason to cry," the nurse said, giving Catherine's hand a reassuring squeeze. "Just take a look at this."

She turned the screen so that Catherine could see, and pointed.

"There he—or she—is. Too soon to determine the sex, but you can make out the arms and legs."

"Oh, my." Wonder filled her. The image showed tiny arms and legs, completely out of proportion with the rest of the body, but the baby was beautiful, perfect, and the love she'd felt since she'd first learned about this new life swelled until she couldn't contain it any longer.

"Get my husband, please. I want him to see this."

Stephen didn't know what to expect when he walked into the examination room. It certainly wasn't Catherine, sitting on the edge of the table in a flimsy paper gown, crying and smiling at the same time.

"Look." She pointed at the screen. "Just look how perfect."

He studied the image and tried to be as enthusiastic as she was, but his heart was too heavy. Even so, he was happy for her.

"Everything's okay, then?"

"The doctor said to take it easy for a few days, but…yes, everything is okay."

"I'm glad. I don't wish you ill. I know how much this baby means to you."

Her smile dimmed, turned sad. "I know. I'll…I'll be making arrangements to move out today."

"It doesn't have to be done today. Wait until you're feeling better. There's no rush."

"Thank you, but I think we both need space right now."

She reached for his hand and threaded her fingers through his. Part of him never wanted to let her go.

"No matter what happens between us, Stephen, I will always love you."

He stumbled back a step, stared at her, sure he had not heard right.

"I love you," she repeated. "I had hoped, but… Well, it doesn't matter what I'd hoped. Still, it doesn't change what I feel, what I will always feel. And I wanted you to know."

He didn't respond. He couldn't. He returned to the waiting room and sank into one of the stiff-backed chairs, flummoxed. She loved him. Even though she was carrying his cousin's child, her heart belonged to Stephen. She had declared her feelings and he found he couldn't doubt her. Not when she was also determined to make arrangements to walk out of his life.

Looping a piece of tinsel from the Christmas tree that had been set up in the waiting room's corner around his finger, he recalled the past several months with Catherine. Even if she had already been pregnant when they married, he hadn't imagined the sparks that had ignited between them. Something was pressing at him now, a pressure building until it overwhelmed him, forcing him to see the truth once and for all. She loved him, and, despite her baby's paternity, he loved her in return. He had had the good fortune to stumble upon something rare, precious, and he had to do something quickly to keep from letting it slip away.

Tucking the strand of tinsel into his pocket, he came to a decision.

Their car was parked on the sixth floor of the adjacent parking structure. He waited until the elevator's other occupants exited before he hit the emergency stop button between floors five and six. The alarm sounded and Catherine gaped at him.

"What are you doing?"

"What I should have done weeks ago, when I first planned it." He bent down on one knee, pulled the strand of tinsel from his pocket. She offered no resistance when he took her left hand and tied the silver strand around her fourth finger.

"I have a real ring at home, I promise. It was my mother's. I had planned to give it to you a while ago, but then…" He shook his head. "I've been a fool, Catherine. A first-class fool. I don't deserve you, but I do love you."

He watched her lips quiver with what he hoped was the beginnings of a smile.

"I want you to be my wife. I want the vows we exchanged in Vegas to be for real. I promise to honor and cherish you. I promise to love you in sickness and in health, for richer and poorer. And I promise to love your baby as much as I love you."

"Oh, Stephen." She covered her mouth with one hand and began to cry in earnest.

"Don't cry, *querida*. I'll make a good father. Give me a chance." He squeezed her hand, kissed the back of it. "Please, please, give me a chance."

When she just continued to cry, he lowered his head. Too late, he thought. I am too late.

Catherine stared down at Stephen's bent head and then reached out to stroke his cheek. Hearing the words was sweeter than she could have imagined.

"It's a very good thing I love you so much," she said on a watery sigh.

"Why is that?"

"Because that's the only way I can forgive you for believing, even now, that this child is Derek's."

The elevator began to move, but Catherine doubted that was why her husband fell back until he was sitting on the floor.

"Mine? I'm...? We're...?"

"That's right. And now to answer your earlier question, yes, I want to stay married to you, too."

He was still holding her hand, so she used it to help pull him to his feet.

"Kiss me."

When the elevator doors swung open on the sixth floor a dozen people were waiting to board, but Catherine and Stephen were too busy renewing their vows to notice.

EPILOGUE

"ANOTHER deep breath," Stephen coached. "That's it, Catherine, you're doing great."

She watched him wince slightly as she gave his hand another vise-like squeeze. But he didn't pull away. He stayed where he was, fingers caught in her white-knuckled grip, something solid to hold on to as a fierce pain lanced her abdomen.

Her hold slackened as the contraction ebbed. His grew firmer.

He bent near and whispered in her ear. *"Te amo, querida."*

She found the energy to smile. "I love you, too."

"It will be over soon," the nurse promised. "You'll welcome you new baby into the world and all this pain will be forgotten."

Truer words…Catherine mused. She and Stephen had weathered enough turbulent seas even before she'd learned of her pregnancy. But soon all the confusion and doubt, as well as the past two months of doctor-ordered bedrest, would be worth it.

The pain began again, gathering like a storm cloud on the horizon before moving in with all the intensity of a hurricane breaking shore.

"It's time to push, Catherine," the doctor said.

Caught up as she was in the mission at hand, she heard Stephen's words of encouragement, felt him stroking the hair back from her damp forehead. She did the work, pushing and straining as her muscles protested and continued their merciless contraction. But there was no doubt in Catherine's mind that she and Stephen brought their child into the world together. They were a team, a unit. Made so not by the vows they'd exchanged in Las Vegas those many months ago, but by the love they shared, which grew stronger, grander and more encompassing each day.

"It's a girl," the doctor said, holding the squalling infant up for Catherine and Stephen to see.

"A girl," Stephen repeated, his voice a hoarse whisper. "We have a daughter."

A couple of hours later Catherine lay in bed in her hospital room, watching Stephen pace from the bassinet to the window. He'd been doing so for the past forty-five minutes.

"Have you decided on a name yet?" she asked. She'd left the choice up to him, although she'd long had something in mind.

He stopped, gently picked up their daughter. Cradling the baby in his arms, he said, "I'd like to name her Galena Rosaria, after my mother and aunt."

"It's a lovely name," Catherine replied, resisting the urge to smile smugly. Not long after she'd discovered she was pregnant she'd decided they should name their child after Stephen's mother if it was a girl or his father if it was a boy.

"Of course we can call her Gail," Stephen said.

"No."

"No?"

"I won't have all the poetry removed from her name. We will call her Galena. Galena Rosaria Danbury."

The names rolled from her tongue. Her accent had improved dramatically in the past several months, thanks to Stephen's grandmother and aunts. After Sunday dinners, as they washed dishes in the kitchen, they taught Catherine various words and phrases. She was far from fluent, but determined to get there. Determined that their daughter would someday be proud of her diverse heritage and conversant in her paternal relatives' native tongue.

Sitting on the edge of the bed, sleeping infant snug in the crook of his arm, Stephen gazed down at his wife.

"I never thought I'd say this, but I owe Derek a huge debt of gratitude. Thanks to his scheming, I have you."

She pulled him toward her for a kiss, and then said, "I'll save my gratitude for my mother."

"Your mother?"

"Well, she is the one who hired the wedding planner."

HER WISH-LIST
BRIDEGROOM

BY
LIZ FIELDING

PROLOGUE

'JULIET? Time to go.'

Glancing up from the figures she was checking, Juliet Howard smiled at the man framed in the doorway. Paul Graham was dressed in the standard executive uniform—dark suit, white shirt, discreetly striped tie—but on him they looked anything but standard. The man had the smouldering, chiselled good looks of a male model or an actor. Every office should have one, she thought as he closed the door and walked towards her.

Fortunately, this one was all hers—or at least he would be at the end of the month when his temporary secondment from the bank finished and her self-imposed rule of no relationships within the office would be over. Something that Paul had respected, with only the occasional—and flattering—display of impatience.

'I've told you not to do that in the office,' she chided as he leaned across her desk and kissed her, well aware that her attempt to appear stern was wasted on him.

He solemnly crossed his heart with his thumb. 'I swear I'll never do it again.'

That hadn't been quite the response she'd anticipated, but she waved him away with a, 'Make sure you don't.'

Instead of leaving, he reached out and wiped the edge of his thumb along her lip. 'I've smudged your lipstick. You'd better run along and fix it before you

5

come to the boardroom. Our newly ennobled chairman wouldn't approve of messy lips.'

Their newly ennobled chairman made no secret of the fact that he believed women were useful only for breeding and the tedious work that men were too important to bother with. He did not like her and made no secret of the fact. Fortunately, she was too good at her job for him to find an excuse to be rid of her. She hoped he enjoyed his day, because once she'd delivered her plan for streamlining the transport arrangements of the company he was going to be seeing a lot more of her. 'Messy lipstick is going to be the least of his worries next week, but you're right, there's no point in aggravating the miserable old devil unnecessarily.' And she smiled.

She'd been smiling a lot lately. She'd arrived at Markham and Ridley, clutching her degree in business administration, seven years ago with one ambition. A seat on the board of one of the most old-fashioned and male dominated industries in the country. Stone, aggregates and all the products made from the hard stuff. The company had been coasting for years, relying on old licences to extract giving them a virtual monopoly in certain areas.

She'd done her research before joining them, had seen the possibilities and given herself ten years to achieve her goal.

Three months ago John Ridley had asked her to put together a paper, lay out her long-term plans for cutting costs, improving productivity. It was a recognised precursor to the offer of a directorship. On Monday she was going to deliver it.

She was within a whisker of having it all.

And not just the directorship—which proved she was

the equal of any man in the company. She had Paul, too—the most thoughtful, charming and attentive of men—proving that she was equal to any woman.

She had every right to smile. But this would not be a good day to be late. 'I'll just go and powder my nose. Grab a glass of champagne for me.'

'Yes, ma'am.'

She slipped a comb through her sleek, neat, conservative hairstyle—this was a very conservative company—and refreshed her lipstick. Tugged her jacket into place. Then the smile broke out again. It had been a tough journey, hard work, but it had paid off. She'd finally arrived.

The boardroom was already crowded when she opened the door and she couldn't immediately see Paul. She took a glass of champagne from the tray as she squeezed in, apparently the last to arrive, clearly having spent rather more time daydreaming about the success to come than she'd realised.

She had no time to think about it as the managing director tapped a glass for attention and raised a toast to their chairman. She took a sip and waited for the inevitable speech.

It was shorter than expected. But not nearly short enough.

'While I'm obviously delighted to have been honoured in this way, my greatest pleasure comes from an announcement I've been planning from the time I stood as his godfather thirty years ago.' He extended a hand and rested it on the shoulder of the man standing at his side. She craned around the person in front to see who it was.

Paul.

The expectant silence was only disturbed by a discreet rustle as two or three people glanced back to look at her.

Paul was Markham's godson? But why hadn't he told her?

'You all know Paul Graham,' he continued. 'He joined us a few months ago and has put that time to good use, studying how we do things. Now he's going to tell us how we can do it better. He'll be joining the board with immediate effect and will assume responsibility for implementing his plans to streamline the organisation and cut transport costs. A year from now Markham and Ridley will be fitter and leaner. A greyhound of a company that will leave the competition standing.'

The pause that followed this announcement went on just a little too long. And this time no one was looking at her. Not that she was noticing anything. She had eyes only for Paul.

His plan? Greyhound? That was a direct lift from her own paper...

What the devil was going on? What was Paul doing standing up there where she should be? Why wasn't he looking at her? This was a joke... It had to be a joke...

'Please raise your glasses and join me in a toast to Paul and to a bright future for all of us.'

No joke. Paul was Markham's godson. As he raised his glass, his lordship looked straight at her. He wasn't just smiling. He was positively smirking.

They both were, she realised.

As she stepped forward a path seemed to open in front of her and, for the first time in her life, Juliet Howard, the most careful girl in the world, the girl who'd planned her life down to the last comma and full stop, did something without thinking through the consequences.

There was no space in her mind to think. It was too busy fast-forwarding through every moment she'd spent in Paul's company. How he'd wooed her, how he'd made her feel safe and wanted without ever pressuring her. But had always been there from the first day she'd been asked to allow him to shadow her.

Right down to the Judas kiss he'd bestowed minutes earlier to delay her.

There was only one word to describe him and she used it, then flung the contents of her glass in his face.

CHAPTER ONE

'GET up, Jools.'

Juliet Howard heard her mother's voice but she didn't move. Packing her things—or rather watching her mother pack them—and the drive home to Melchester slumped in the passenger seat, had taken every scrap of energy she'd possessed. Getting out of bed was beyond her. It had been beyond her for weeks. Even the effort of opening her eyes was too much.

The sound of the curtains being drawn back heralded an implosion of light into the room. She turned away, burying her face in her pillow, trying to ignore the rattle of coat-hangers as her mother pulled out some clothes for her. Tossed them on the bed.

'I've written a shopping list. I didn't have time to shop this weekend so I've got nothing in. You might not care whether you eat or not, but I do. Put a move on and I'll drop you in town on my way to work. You can sign on at that job agency near the bus station after you've picked up my book from the Prior's Lane book-shop. Tell Maggie Crawford that I'll see her at bingo tonight.'

Her briskness was relentless.

Then, 'You should come, too.'

'To bingo?'

'Hallelujah! It speaks...'

Oh, right. She rolled over. Her mother wasn't serious about the bingo. She'd just thrown it in to get a response. 'Mum, you don't have to do this.'

10

'Convince me. Get up, take a shower, while I make some coffee.'

'You'll be late for work.'

'I will if you don't get a move on.'

'No…' But her mother, who had never been late for work in her entire life, didn't linger to argue. But then she never had. She'd never had the time for that. Had never allowed the fact that she was a single mother to give an employer the opportunity to say that she was unreliable. Had never once given in to self-pity, at least not when anyone was around to see. How many tears had she shed in the dark, lonely hours of the night?

Disgusted with herself, Juliet rolled over, allowing gravity to take her feet to the floor. The same technique that had got her out of bed on days when going to school had seemed like another day in purgatory.

The sun shining in at the window was an affront to her misery, the smell of coffee from the kitchen was making her feel sick, but her mother had surrendered her entire life, given all she knew and more to make sure her daughter had a chance of something better. Even now she was the one picking up the pieces. She had taken precious time off to go to London, had put her flat in the hands of a letting agent so that the mortgage would get paid, so that she'd have something to go back to. Had packed up and then brought her home and tucked her up in her childhood bed.

Even the teenager had been strong enough to get up, face the misery, counting each day she'd survived without attracting the attention of the school bullies a small bonus.

It wasn't strength now but guilt that propelled her into the shower, got her into the clothes laid out for her and, shivering, into the car. The sun was shining but it was still March and the wind was the lazy kind that didn't take the long way around but went right through you.

Her mother decanted her onto the pavement. 'Don't forget my book. And buy a bunch of daffodils from the market.'

She called at the job agency first, filled in the form they produced, sat while the woman behind the desk glanced over her qualifications, the steady advancement with her only employer since university.

'You haven't answered the question about why you left your last employer.'

'No.' Well, that was a tricky one. 'Sorry.' She took the form and wrote 'Bridget Jones Syndrome' and pushed it back across the desk.

'You shagged your boss?'

'No, I was the boss, but you know how it is with men. They always want to be on top.' It wasn't strictly true but it short-circuited the difficult questions. And she was sure that Paul would have made the sacrifice if she'd been less scrupulous, less careful of her career and reputation, less gullible...

'Oh, right.' She got a sympathetic look, but precious little else. 'You're a bit over-qualified for us, to be honest. The highest we go is junior execs. You really need a London agency.'

'I just want something temporary while I reassess my career options,' she said. Something the last specialist executive recruitment agency she'd contacted had suggested. They hadn't gone as far as asking her if it was true that she'd had a breakdown; they'd taken one look and drawn their own conclusions.

* * *

'What on earth persuaded you to buy this dump, Mac?'

Gregor McLeod looked around his latest acquisition with a certain amount of satisfaction. As a builder's yard it had had its day. Small places like this couldn't compete with the massive combined trade and DIY superstores that had sprung up on the business park at the edge of the city, but owning it had been high on his 'want' list for a long time.

'Just put it down to pure sentimentality, Neil. Once, in the dim and distant past, I worked here. Not for long, but I've never forgotten the experience.'

His deputy glanced around. 'I didn't know that.'

'Yes, well, you were away at university while I was sweating my guts out for Marty Duke, shifting loads that would have had Health and Safety screaming blue murder if they'd known.'

'Not exactly fond memories, then.'

'It wasn't all bad. There was a classy temp in the office. Long shiny hair, legs to the stratosphere and a voice as rich, smooth and expensive as Swiss chocolate. She had a smile that made coming to work a really worthwhile experience.'

Neil shook his head. 'What is it with you and posh birds, Mac? I'd have thought once bitten even you would have been twice shy.'

'Yes, well, in her case I wasn't on my own. She couldn't type in a straight line but Duke paid her well above the hourly rate because the builders used to line up to drool as she took their orders.'

'Why do I anticipate a sorry ending to this story?'

'Because you know me?' Greg shrugged. 'When I saw Duke with his hands where no employer should have them, I didn't bother to point out that sexual harassment in the workplace was inappropriate, I just decked him. He fired me while he was still lying flat on his back.'

'I hope the goddess with the expensive voice was suitably grateful.'

'Not noticeably, but then she was too busy playing Florence Nightingale to the boss. She must have made a really good job of it because he offered her a full-time position.'

'As his secretary?'

'No. His wife. I clearly misread the signals. She might have been up for a little hot necking in the stationery cupboard, but she had bigger ambitions than hooking up with a nineteen-year-old labourer with no prospects.'

Neil grinned as he looked around at the derelict yard. 'Her mistake.'

'You think so? I had nothing to offer her. She, on the other hand, did me a real favour. She taught me that when it comes to a choice between money and muscles women will choose money every time. And she showed me that I wasn't cut out to work for someone else.'

'So you bought a yard you don't need, saved Duke from going under, out of sheer gratitude to his wife? The woman to whom you owe your fortune?'

'I owe my fortune to hard work, a sharp eye for a good deal and a large measure of luck. I bought the yard for a number of reasons, the most pleasurable of which, I have to admit, was the fact that Duke had to look me in the eye and call me Mr McLeod.'

'What about his wife? Was she there?'

'She's still his secretary, would you believe?'

'I told you. It was a poor career move. What did she have to say?'

'Not much until she showed me to the door.' He pulled a face. 'Then she said, "Call me…"'

Juliet left the agency with the promise that 'if anything suitable came up' they'd call her. She'd done her best. Or the best that she was capable of right now. Tick one thing off the list, she thought, heading for the shops. The sooner she got the shopping done, the sooner she could go home.

She'd picked up her mother's basket without looking at the notebook lying in the bottom. Most women recycled old envelopes for shopping lists, but not her mother. She'd always used a notebook, not just for shopping lists, but for everything, maintaining that it freed the mind to think of more important things. And it made her feel good when she actually managed to tick an item off, especially the ones that began with the word 'pay…'

It was a habit she'd fostered in her daughter, encouraging her to write down not just the must-do everyday items such as prompts for handing in school projects, but developing one-year, five-year, ten-year plans.

And she'd told her she shouldn't just write down the big stuff because it got downright depressing when there were no new ticks. The thing was to write down absolutely everything because a person needed to see that she was achieving things, even if it was only remembering to buy a loaf of bread.

Picking up the ring-bound notebook, she realised it was an old one of hers. She'd had it in her stocking the Christmas she was twelve or thirteen. She remembered her pleasure in the glossy black cover with its bright red rings. Until then she'd had notebooks with cute cats or hamsters or cartoon characters, but this one seemed very grown up and so she'd carefully made a label.

JULIET HOWARD
A MASTER PLAN FOR HER LIFE

The label was barely legible now and the gloss had been rubbed off the cover from always being tucked away at the bottom of her school bag safe from the vicious prying of the school bullies.

She swallowed, aching for the lonely little girl she'd been, and then, as someone pushed past her muttering irritably about people with 'nothing better to do than block the pavement,' she took refuge in a nearby café, ordering coffee she didn't want in return for a quiet space, somewhere to think.

What had that child yearned for?

She remembered the big plans, the ones that had never altered. A place at a good university, a first class honours degree, to one day be as successful as the woman she'd seen opening a branch of her chain of aromatherapy shops in the city.

Some things never changed.

Flipping through the pages as her coffee cooled, she saw that she'd dutifully started her goals with getting an A in maths, turning in her projects on time, keeping her room tidy. But after that came the heartfelt goals— the painful desire to have her hair cut really short so that she could spike it up with gel like the 'cool' girls at school. The yearning for impossibly expensive sports shoes so that she would fit in. And then there was the holiday at Disneyworld in Paris. Had she really wanted to go, or was it on the list because it had seemed as if it was something everyone else in her year had done? Even the ones from single parent homes, like her. Because not going marked her out as a 'loser' in the eyes of the other girls.

Whatever, like so many of the dreams, it had never been ticked.

There was nothing to stop her packing her bags and going right now, of course. But really, it was too pathetic to go to Disneyworld without children of her own with whom to share the magic.

She saw she'd planned on four of her own—a reflection of her 'only child' desire for brothers and sisters, no doubt. She hadn't specified who would be their father at the time.

That was the last item on the list. Just before the book had been abandoned. That was the problem with having a master plan. It was an upwards progression. Life, on the other hand, was a game of Snakes and Ladders.

She turned the page. The shopping list had not been written in the notebook, but was on a yellow peel-off note. Clearly the notebook had been her mother's not entirely subtle way of reminding her that her life hadn't come to an end simply because the goal she'd set herself had shifted from the 'achievable' to the 'downright impossible' level.

You just had to start a fresh list. Write a new five-year plan. As for those impossible dreams…

'One step at a time, Mother,' she muttered to herself, dropping the book back into the basket.

There was nothing too taxing on the shopping list. Nothing that she couldn't have got from the eight-till-late on the corner. Except the book—which could easily have waited until another day. And the daffodils—specified, no doubt, because of their hideously cheerful yellowness.

She compromised by buying some paper-white narcissi from a stallholder in the little market at the bottom of Prior's Lane and then headed in the direction of the bookshop.

The sooner she got everything the sooner she could go home.

And then what? Stare at four walls and feel sorry for herself? Had her mother ever behaved so pitifully? Why on earth was she being so kind? Why wasn't she telling her to pull herself together and get over it?

She glanced at the notebook lying in the bottom of the basket. Okay. Her mother was. Or at least suggesting that it was time she wrote herself a new list. Item one would be easy enough. Stop feeling sorry for herself.

Except that wasn't how it worked. They had to be real things that you could tick off. Okay. Item one. Find a job.

Then she'd be too busy to feel sorry for herself.

Unfortunately no one in their right mind was going to employ a senior manager who'd ruined the chairman's big day by drowning him and his protégé in champagne.

Stress! That wasn't stress. It was a lot simpler than that…

After that it got a bit silly. While mentally compiling a list of all the terrible things she wanted to do to Lord Markham and his wretched godson had a certain cathartic effect, they were downright impossible. The whole point was to be able to cross things off so that you felt as if you'd achieved something. Felt better.

Which put a stop to her list making. Feeling better was not going to happen anytime soon.

She stopped, looked around to check where she was. Prior's Lane curved up the hill from the river to the cathedral. It wasn't just one street but a network of narrow lanes and alleys that had once been the medieval heart of the city, a world away from the sterile, traffic-free shopping area in the city centre where look-alike chain stores meant you could be in any town, anywhere.

It had once provided shopping on a human scale with exciting little shops and smart boutiques and the air had been redolent with the scent of freshly roasted coffee. Now the predominance of charity shops was a sure indication of an area past its use-by date. Even the shops that were clinging on were in dire need of a coat of paint.

She felt a jag of irritation at such a waste of a resource. What was the City Council thinking of? She'd been to other cities where places like this were thriving tourist haunts making a valuable contribution to the style and financial well-being of the area.

It wasn't all bad news. Maybe it was the unaccustomed exercise, the surge of healthy anger, but the scent of freshly baked bread sparked a sudden hunger and once she'd bought a crusty French loaf, still warm from the oven, it seemed perfectly natural to add a small piece of Dolcelatte and some fat olives—her mother loved them and she deserved a treat—from an old-fashioned Italian mama-and-papa grocer's.

In the part of London where she'd lived—until she'd tossed away her career along with the contents of her champagne glass—shops like these would have been packed out with foodie fanatics fighting over the freshly made pasta and virgin olive oil. Here everyone seemed to be hanging on by the skin of their teeth.

A bell jangled as she opened the bookshop door. It was exactly as she remembered it. No concessions to the new age of book selling. No coffee, no snacks, no armchairs, no incentive to linger.

She did, however, find the Cornwell her mother had put on the list and a Paretsky that she hadn't—her mother preferred crime novels with strong female heroines—and she picked that up too. Then, since no one had appeared to take her money, she called out. 'Hello?'

There was no answer so she made her way around some shelves dividing the front from the back of the shop and blinked at the array of sofas and armchairs, the fact that back here the shelves were stacked with used books.

Then, approaching the small office at the rear, 'Hello? Mrs Crawford? Is there anyone…'

And that was when she saw Maggie Crawford stretched out on the floor, an overturned chair lying nearby telling its own story.

She was so pale that for one terrible moment Juliet thought she was dead and her first reaction was fear. Panic. The shaming impulse to bolt and leave someone else to find her, deal with it.

An overwhelming 'I can't' and 'Why me?' response.

Then, dropping everything, she ran to help. 'Mrs Crawford? Can you hear me?'

She opened her eyes, looking vaguely surprised and said, 'Oh, hello, dear. It's Juliet, isn't it? Your mother said you might drop in…' Her voice was weak, but at least she was making sense. Then she said, 'What on earth am I doing down here?'

'No!' Juliet put her hand on the woman's shoulder as she moved to sit up. 'No, you just stay there. You've had a fall.' And she dug her phone out of her pocket and dialled the emergency services, unfastening her coat, switching hands so that she could slip her arms through the sleeves and lay it over the woman to keep her warm, as she explained what had happened to the dispatcher.

'It's Mrs Crawford. Mrs Margaret Crawford. The bookshop, Prior's Lane…'

'Oh, dear. What a nuisance I'm being.'

'Nonsense, Maggie.' She replaced the receiver and knelt at her side, taking her hands, chafing them between her own. 'Just hold on, help is on its way. How long have you been lying here?'

'I don't know, dear. I just wanted to fix a piece of card in the window,' she said. 'To block the draught. I was reaching up and then I felt dizzy and the next thing—'

'Shh—'

'No. You don't understand. I can't leave it like that…'

She was beginning to get fractious and Juliet, looking up, saw that one of the panes was broken near the catch. It had all the hallmarks of an attempted burglary. At least she assumed it was just an attempted burglary. The office didn't look as if it had been ransacked.

She saw a small electric fire and turned it on to counteract the cold air coming through the window, then, in an effort to reassure her, keep her still, said, 'Don't worry. I'll sort something out, get it fixed, just as soon as—' She heard the shop door open.

'Hello? Did someone call for help?'

'Through here.' It was with considerable relief that she handed responsibility for the patient over to the paramedics. First aid had never been one of her strong points.

The window, on the other hand, was something she could fix. Or at least she could find someone who could do the job for her. There was a hardware shop across the way. The sign outside boasted that it was an 'old-fashioned store with old-fashioned service' and in truth it looked like something out of a working museum. It seemed like a good moment to put that 'old-fashioned service' ethic to the test. 'It'll be a few minutes before you can move her, won't it?' she asked the paramedic. 'I want to organise someone to fix the window. She's fretting—'

'Maybe you could do it after we've gone, Miss. We need a few details, if you don't mind.'

'But...' No. Obviously someone had to stay until the window was fixed, and there wasn't a queue forming. Just her. 'Of course.' She gave them her name, answered what questions she could, while one of them made Maggie more comfortable.

The shop doorbell jingled again. When she didn't move, the one asking the questions smiled and said, 'Okay, I think that's all we need from you, Miss. You can see to your customer if you like.'

About to say, *No... I'm the customer,* she let it go. Someone had to go and explain that the shop was temporarily shut, put up the Closed sign.

'I'm sorry,' she began as she approached the woman who was standing by the cash desk and searching through her bag for something. 'I'm afraid there's no one here to serve you just at the moment—'

'I don't need serving. I've just come to pick up a book I ordered. It's paid for,' she said, handing over a receipt as proof. Then, when she was clearly at a loss, 'Maggie usually keeps special orders under the desk.'

'Does she? Oh, right. Is this it?' She held up a thick paperback, a historical romance. There were several more copies obviously waiting to be picked up. 'It seems to be a popular book.'

'It's the romance reading group choice for next month. Maggie always orders them in for us.'

'Oh, I see.' She placed it in a carrier bag and handed it to her, making a note of what she'd done on the notepad beside the phone.

'Been taken poorly, has she?' the woman asked, in no great hurry to leave. 'Maggie?'

Pointless to deny it with the ambulance blocking the lane in front of the shop. 'She's had a fall.'

'Nasty.' She shook her head. 'She's not a young woman and it shakes you up, something like that. You lose your confidence. If she's broken something I imagine it'll be the end of another Prior's Lane shop.'

'Surely not?'

'Who's going to take it on? These little shops can't compete, can they? It's cheaper to buy the bestsellers in the supermarket, which is okay if all you want to read is bestsellers.' She patted the carrier with the paperback in it. 'You won't find anything like this on their shelves at three for the price of two.'

'No, I suppose not.'

She could probably have bought the Cornwell at the supermarket but it was unlikely they'd stock the Paretsky...

'Okay, Miss Howard, we're bringing her through. If

you ring Melchester General in a couple of hours there should be some news for you.'

'Oh, but—' She let it go. Her own concerns were unimportant. 'Maggie, is there someone you'd like me to contact for you?'

'You will take care of the window?' she asked, her mind apparently fixed on that. 'They will keep breaking them…' It was clearly an effort for her to speak and Juliet didn't press it. It wouldn't be any trouble to get the window fixed and she'd probably be able to find a contact number for someone in the office.

'I'll see to it, then I'll lock up and come in to see you later.'

'Poor dear,' her customer said, as she was loaded into the ambulance. 'She's only got her son and he's working out in the Middle East somewhere.' *Oh, great!* And having dropped that little bombshell, 'Well, I must get on. Good luck.'

'But—'

It occurred to her that she'd said 'but' more times in the last half an hour than she had in the last seven years. Her usual response to a problem was to say, *No problem.*

Angry with herself for being so pathetic, she turned the sign on the door to Closed and slipped the catch. There was 'no problem.' All she had to do was find a glazier for the window, find someone who could take responsibility for the shop and then go to the hospital to reassure Maggie that everything was taken care of.

That was all. A piece of cake for someone with her experience and ability. She sank down on to a stool behind the counter. Window… Glazier…

She pulled herself together. The hardware shop.

First she had to find the shop keys. She could hardly

walk out and leave it unlocked and, if she locked the door behind her, she wouldn't be able to let the glazier in to do the work.

She finally found the shop keys in the desk drawer at the back of the shop but, halfway to the door, she changed her mind and decided to phone them in case whoever had tried to break in had simply been disturbed and, having seen Maggie carried out, was hanging around, waiting for another chance at the till.

Pulling the telephone directory towards her, she realised that she'd have to do something about the till, too. Secure the money. She reached for a pen and, with a certain sense of irony, she fished her notebook out of the basket and began to make a list.

'So what *are* you going to do with the yard?'

Greg looked out of the filthy office windows at the deserted builder's yard, wondering what had happened to the men who'd worked there. 'It's not just this dump. The deal included the freehold on some retail property in the old part of the city.'

'Oh, great. Low rents, high maintenance.' The phone began to ring and as he reached for it Neil said, 'Leave it. Duke's Yard is no longer trading—'

'Duke's Yard,' Greg answered.

'And besides,' Neil continued, but with the resignation of a man who knew he was talking to himself, 'it's lunchtime.'

'Oh, thank goodness. I got your number from the hardware shop in Prior's Lane, but they weren't sure you were still…'

Greg, his attention suddenly wholly engaged on the voice in his ear, ignored Neil, instead propping himself on the edge of the desk. Some days weren't just good—

'Still what?' he prompted.

'In business.' When he didn't confirm or deny it she said, 'Obviously he was mistaken.' Greg said nothing. 'Fortunately.' Then, 'Look, this is an emergency. Can you help?'

'Try me,' he offered.

There was the slightest pause before she said, 'Right, well, I have a small window-pane that needs replacing as a matter of urgency. Is there any chance of you sending 'round someone to do it today?'

—some days were perfect, he decided.

'What time today?'

'The sooner the better. I'm in Prior's Lane. The bookshop?'

'I know it. And your name?'

'Howard.'

'Really? You don't sound like a Howard. You sound more like an Emma or a Sophie or—'

'Juliet Howard.'

'Or a Juliet.' There was the slightest sound that might just have been a choked off suggestion of disbelief. 'I'm sorry, did you say something?'

'No. Look, can you do it because if you can't—'

She sounded as if she was at, or at least very near, the end of her tether. 'And your telephone number, Juliet?'

'Why do you need my telephone number?'

'Because, oddly enough, some people think it's amusing to call out workmen on completely phoney jobs. I make a point of calling back to double check.'

She obviously decided that she had no choice because, after a momentary hesitation, she gave him the number.

He made a note of it and said, 'I'll be with you in ten minutes.'

'Really?' She sounded as if she was torn between incredulity and relief, with incredulity winning by a nose.

Neil frantically shook his head, pointing at his watch as he mouthed the word, 'Lunch.'

Greg grinned and mouthed back, 'Swiss chocolate.' Then, into the phone, 'Is that a problem?' he asked.

'No, I'll be here,' she replied, but he got the distinct impression that she wouldn't be holding her breath.

'So,' Neil grumbled as he replaced the receiver, 'she's got a voice like expensive chocolate. She's probably got a blue rinse, twin set and pearls to go with it.'

Greg shrugged. 'If you're right I'll have done my good deed for the day. If you're wrong...'

'If I'm wrong?'

There had been a crisp edge to her voice, exactly like the snap of the finest chocolate, along with a just a touch of melting vulnerability as she'd uttered that disbelieving, 'Really?'

Irresistible.

'You know me, Neil. I believe in playing my luck while it's running with me.'

'Luck! First you land us with an expensive waste of space and then you decide to abandon a working lunch on the off chance that this bird's face fits her voice.'

'Faint heart...' he replied. 'And it's my expensive waste of space, not yours.'

Neil's response was short and scatological.

'Okay, make that my expensive space that's going to be included in the new development zone.'

'You—' Then, 'Duke didn't know about that, did he?'

'I certainly didn't tell him.' Then, 'Since you won't be having a long lunch at my expense you can use the time to find out what happened to his workforce. If any of them are out of work, see what we can do for them.'

'Oh, for heaven's sake!' Juliet flipped her mobile shut and tossed it on the desk. *Try me*... Not in this lifetime. The very last thing she needed was some jack-the-lad who thought he was the answer to every woman's prayer.

Not that she could afford to be fussy.

Duke's Yard had been the last number on her list and 'jack' was the only one who could do it this week, let alone today. She wouldn't tick it off her list just yet though. Despite his promise, he hadn't called back.

And, even if he did turn up, she was firmly crossing her fingers that his availability meant he had a brief window in his busy schedule, not that he was so useless no one would employ him. Fortunately it wasn't anything cerebrally demanding, such as electrical wiring or plumbing, that needed doing. How difficult could it be to replace a small pane of glass in a window? She could probably do it herself if she knew where to go for the glass, had the tools, the putty...

She realised that her hands were shaking. There was a tiny kitchenette next to the office and she found the kettle, filled it at the sink and switched it on before looking around for a jar of coffee.

She was spooning some into a mug when there was another in a long series of knocks and rattles as, ignoring the Closed sign, hopeful customers still tried the front door. The shop might not be warm and well-lit with the inviting scent of coffee, but it didn't seem to be short of people trying to get in.

Whether they were actually desperate to purchase a book or just curious about why the ambulance had been there she didn't know and didn't have much trouble resisting the temptation to find out.

Then, as she poured the boiling water on to the coffee, it occurred to her that it might—however unlikely it might seem—possibly be 'jack' coming to fix the window. A whole minute early. How likely was that?

She went to check anyway.

By the time she'd walked through to the front of the shop whoever it was had given up. On the point of unlocking the door to check outside, she heard another knock, this time at the back door. Unlike the shop door it was made of solid wood rather than glass and before she opened up caution prompted her to call out, 'Who's there?'

'Knight Errant Incorporated. Damsels in distress a speciality.'

Oh, great. Not just a jack-the-lad who believed he was irresistible but one who thought he was funny, too. She supposed she should be thankful that he'd resisted the more obvious 'Romeo' she decided as she opened the door to be confronted with six feet two inches of toned manhood wearing a worn leather bomber jacket and a pair of jeans that appeared to have been moulded to his body.

His thick, dark hair was too long, his grin too knowing and his eyes a totally impossible shade of blue. The effect was aggressively male. Cocksure. Arrogant. And behind him, propped on a stand, was a motorbike to match.

Gregor McLeod, she realised, hadn't changed one bit.

CHAPTER TWO

JULIET'S mouth dried and for a moment she couldn't think of a thing to say. All she could think, hope, pray, was that he wouldn't remember her.

'I am in the right place?' he prompted finally, breaking the long silence. How could she not have recognised his voice? Soft, gravelly and far too sexy for common decency... 'The bookshop? You did call Duke's Yard about a broken window?' And he glanced up at the window as if to say, *Well, one of us knows what they're talking about.*

So that was all right.

There wasn't the slightest sign of recognition.

As far as she knew he'd never known her name; he'd always called her 'princess,' for which she'd been teased mercilessly, although never in his hearing.

And back then she'd been a skinny thirteen-year-old in charity shop clothes, metal-framed glasses—years before Harry Potter made them fashionable—and with her long hair in a childish plait, quietly shadowing her hero around the school.

Except, of course, he hadn't been a hero.

A hero wouldn't have just disappeared from her life without a word.

'Yes.' She pulled herself together, ignoring the little tug of disappointment that while he'd made such a major impact on her, she hadn't even dented his memory. Refusing to regret that she hadn't made more effort with her appearance. Put on a little make-up. Done more than twist her hair up and impale it with a few pins. 'Yes, this is the bookshop. But I don't need a knight errant,' she said, at last finding her tongue and having no difficulty in resisting the 'irresistible rogue' look now she was old enough to recognise it for what it was. 'I need a glazier, or at least someone who can replace the glass in that.' She stepped out into the access lane that ran along the back of the shops to indicate the broken pane, bending down to pick up a piece of jagged glass, rather than continue staring at him.

She'd already seen enough.

'Leave that.' He bent beside her, taking the glass from her fingers.

Startled, she looked up.

'You'll cut yourself.'

'Oh, right. Thank you.' No. He hadn't changed at all. He was heavier, of course, but all of it was muscle and there were lines carved into his cheeks, fanning out from his eyes, adding character to his youthful good looks. But he was still the same Gregor McLeod and she had the weirdest feeling that, by looking at her list of goals, ambitions, she had conjured him up out of her past.

'I'd like it done today,' she said, standing up and brushing the dust of the lane from her fingers.

'If you're hinting that I didn't get here in the ten minutes I promised,' he replied, ignoring her snippy tone, 'then blame yourself. If you'd bothered to open the shop door when I knocked I'd have been a full thirty seconds early.'

'Oh, was that you?' She hadn't asked him in, hadn't actually been aware of standing back to let him past, but he was, nevertheless, inside the office and making it feel uncomfortably small. His closeness raising the hair on the nape of her neck, goosing her skin... 'I assumed—'

'You assumed that when I said "ten minutes" I was being over-optimistic?'

'Well, yes.' Then, realising that might not have been the wisest thing to have said, 'No! You were very prompt. I meant that I assumed you were a customer.'

'So you ignored it? I don't want to tell you how to run your business, Juliet, but you won't sell many books that way.'

'You're absolutely right,' she replied, straining for politeness. 'But then I don't sell books.'

'Well, there you are. Point made,' he said, the grin deepening as he made himself at home, propping his perfectly formed backside on the corner of the desk.

Oh, puh-lease...

Some men couldn't help it. They looked at a woman and whether they fancied her or not—and she was quite sure that she was no more his 'type' than he was hers now she knew better—they just had to flex their 'pulling' muscles.

Well, he was wasting his time on her.

Working her way to the top in a man's world, she'd quickly learned that the only way to deal with his kind was to remain calm and businesslike. Never to show by even the smallest twitch that she was aware of any sexual overture.

You might get the reputation for being a frigid cow, but there were worse things.

Stupidity, for instance.

Gullibility...

Mercifully his kind had a very short attention span; they knew that if one woman didn't respond to the muscle-flexing and chest-beating there'd be another one along in a minute.

It was the quiet men, the ones with brains, that you had to watch.

'I was waiting for you to call and check back that I wasn't some teenager playing a stupid prank,' she said.

'No teenager ever sounded like you, princess.'

She swallowed. Clamped down hard on her jaw to cut off the ridiculous stinging at the back of her eyes. Clearly he called every woman he met 'princess.' So much easier than all that bother of having to remember their names.

'Can you handle the job?' she demanded. Then, realising that probably sounded sharper than was entirely prudent, 'I mean can you handle it today?'

'That's what I'm here for.'

'Right,' she said. 'Good.' Then, 'How long will it take?'

'Well, let's see. I'll measure the window, go and get a piece of glass cut and then, while I clean this out and fit it, you can make me a cup of tea—top of the milk, two sugars—and tell me the story of your life.'

'How long?' she repeated, in the same even tone.

He seemed to find that amusing. At least she assumed that was why he was grinning.

'An hour should do it. Depending on how interesting your life has been until now.'

Oh, joy. A whole hour of flirtatious backchat. 'And how much will an hour of your time cost?'

'Why don't you just buy me lunch and we'll call it quits?'

And he had the nerve to criticise her lack of business sense?

'I'll fetch you a steak from the butcher on the corner, shall I? I imagine you do eat it raw?'

He took a steel tape from his pocket and reached up to measure the window—and he didn't need to stand on a chair. 'You know,' he said, his back to her, 'I had a date this lunchtime. I was just on my way out when you rang. I could have told you I was busy.'

'Why didn't you?' she asked. 'Everyone else did.'

'You sounded as if you needed help.'

She refused to be seduced by his apparent empathy. 'I did. I do. But I need a glazier not a chat-up line so why don't you save time by leaving out the tea and the life story? Call your date.' She refused to succumb to the flutter of jealousy, the 'Who?' and 'Where?' that flashed through her brain. 'I'm sure she'd wait for half an hour.'

'Would you?' he asked, glancing back over his shoulder. 'Wait?'

Ignoring the disconcerting way her pulse kicked into overdrive, she said, 'I wouldn't have agreed to have lunch with you in the first place so the occasion would never arise.'

'Consider the question hypothetically.'

This was her fault. She'd broken the cardinal rule— never get involved with someone in the office. Six months ago, three months even, and she could have handled this kind of conversation without losing her cool. Even with Gregor McLeod.

But her cool had been permanently blown by Paul's callous pretence and no matter how much she tried to keep it pinned down, anger would keep breaking through the miasma of misery like little puffs of sulphurous smoke warning that a volcano is about to blow.

'Hypothetically?' she repeated.

Ice cool. Mill pond calm. Duchess polite—no, *princess* polite. She could do it if she tried.

'That's what I said.'

'Then, hypothetically,' she replied, 'I'd say that if I had agreed to have lunch with you and you called to explain that you'd be late because you were helping a damsel in distress…' She stopped, seeing the trap a fraction of a second too late.

'Go on,' he said, but not making much of an effort to hide his amusement.

'I'm sure you'll think of something.'

'You wouldn't be suggesting that I've had a lot of practice in making excuses, would you?'

'You can't help it,' she said, deciding that since cool, calm and polite weren't doing the trick, she might as well go for natural. Whatever that was these days. 'You're a man. The excuse mechanism comes ready packaged with the chromosomes.' She listened to the words coming out of her mouth with a certain amount of horrified fascination. For a woman who, until a few months ago, hadn't taken a single risk in her life, had kept her emotions locked up for so long that she'd forgotten where she'd put the key, she seemed to have suddenly lost the plot.

Fortunately her knight errant was fully occupied writing down the window measurements in the notebook he'd taken from the buttoned down pocket of his cream wool shirt. It looked just like her notebook. The shiny black cover worn dull with use. It would be warm from his body, she thought. Full of his thoughts…

'Please accept that I'm deeply appreciative of your sacrifice,' she went on quickly in an effort to distract herself.

That did provoke a reaction. Nothing excessive. Just some slight movement of an eyebrow suggesting he wasn't totally impressed by her declaration of appreciation, no matter how deep.

'I would, however, be grateful if you'd get on with the job so that we can both get on with our lives,' she concluded, primly. 'I assume you do have one.'

'Do you?'

He looked up, regarded her thoughtfully, and it occurred to her that it would be a lot wiser to stick to the job. Personal remarks simply gave him an open invitation to develop his chat-up technique.

When she didn't answer, he said, 'The thing is, I like to show an interest in my customers. Get to know them. Build up a rapport.'

'Very commendable.' That was better. Suitably distant. 'I promise that if I should ever need someone to fix a pane of glass in the future, Duke's Yard is the first name that will come into my head.'

'Sarcasm is not attractive in a woman, Juliet.'

Sarcasm? That wasn't sarcasm. 'Well, thank you—'

She pulled herself up short. He was using her name in an attempt to get her to ask his. The truth was that she'd just come very close to using it without thinking. If she did that he'd want to know how she knew it and, while it probably wouldn't embarrass him one bit that he didn't remember her—and why should it?—she'd be embarrassed beyond bearing if he discovered that she'd never forgotten him. Because he wouldn't need the reason spelled out in words of one syllable. He'd know why.

'I'll be sure and make a note of that useful advice,' she continued, 'and stick it up somewhere I'll see it every day.'

Now *that* was sarcasm, she congratulated herself. Then, in the moment of silence that followed this pronouncement, when her words seemed to echo around the room, she realised that he was right.

It was not attractive.

Not that it deterred him.

'So, what happened to Maggie Crawford?' he asked. 'Have you taken over the shop?'

'No.'

'You're working for her?'

'Not even that.'

'Pity. This place could do with something to brighten it up.'

On that she agreed with him, but she wasn't about to admit it. As for her brightening anything...

'Maggie fell off a chair this morning. She was trying to stuff a piece of cardboard into the window to keep out the draught. She's been taken to the hospital.'

'I'm sorry to hear that.' He was deeply convincing. She almost believed him. 'So, what's your connection?'

He just wouldn't quit. 'Don't you have to go and fetch some glass?' she enquired.

'You know, I'm feeling distinctly peckish. Maybe you're right. I could still catch...'

'No!'

'No?'

'Look, I'm sorry, but it's been a trying morning. I just came in here to pick up a book for my mother. I found Maggie lying on the floor.'

'And you stayed to sort out the window?' he asked, looking around and catching her watching him. 'For someone you don't know?' And without warning the blue eyes looked dangerous rather than laddish.

'She was concerned. Agitated. And I do know her. At least, my mother does. I used to come in here when I was at school. She used to let me sit quietly out the back and read the books I couldn't afford to buy.'

'I see. I'm sorry. It's just occurred to me that you probably need to get back to work.'

'No, you're all right. I'm between jobs.'

'There's going to be a vacancy here, by the look of things. A temporary one, anyway.'

'Yes, well, I'll ask Mrs Crawford what she wants me to do about that when she's fit enough to talk about it. In the meantime I could hardly leave the shop open to the elements. Or any passing felon hoping to find a rare first edition of that popular classic, *The Beginners Guide to Successful Breaking and Entering,*' she added.

He was *supposed* to grin at that. Laddish she could deal with. Instead he looked thoughtful, glancing back up at the window.

'I doubt this was done by someone hoping to brush up on his lock-picking skills. More likely it was some-one attempting to break in to the pharmacy next door.'

'An out-of-his-mind junkie looking for a fix?' Maggie had said it kept happening… 'Oh, great. That makes me feel so much easier in my mind.'

'You could stick a notice on the window,' he of-fered. 'Something along the lines of "This is a book-shop. Please break in next door…"'

'I'm sure the pharmacist would really appreciate that.'

'He'll have much better security,' he said, heading for the door. 'I'll go and fetch the glass. Why don't you see if you can round up a couple of chocolate Hobnobs to go with the tea since lunch has been can-celled? It's been a long time since breakfast.'

'This is a bookshop not a grocery store…' But once he'd decided to go he hadn't hung around and she was talking to herself, with nothing but the pheromone-laden atmosphere and the throaty roar of a motorbike to account for her raised pulse rate.

Gregor McLeod was a throw-back to the Dark Ages, she decided. Positively Neanderthal. How she could ever have thought he was… Well, it didn't matter what she'd thought. He did at least appear to know what he was doing. And he had come when he'd said he would. Maybe she shouldn't have been quite so hard on him.

On the other hand, he clearly didn't need any encouragement and, making sure the door was not just shut but locked, she settled at the desk with her lukewarm coffee and flicked through Maggie's Rolodex looking, without success, for her son's address.

She went through the desk diary, too, but that didn't prove any more illuminating and there was no sign of Maggie's handbag. It would have to wait until she went up to the hospital. She must have a neighbour or friend who could take in some personal things.

Someone who could take responsibility for the bookshop.

Then, when her stomach reminded her that it had indeed been a long time since breakfast—not that she'd actually eaten any breakfast—she looked at her watch and realised just how much time had passed since her knight errant had departed. Terrific. He'd probably had a better offer. Or he'd decided to put his lunch date before her cry for help. She could hardly blame him when she'd been so…sarcastic.

She sighed. She really shouldn't have let him get to her. He wasn't responsible for her childish hero-worship of him. Well, he was, but all he'd done was pick her up when she'd been pushed over. Had set her on her feet. Picked up her things, and by that one act of kindness, kept the bullies at bay for months. They'd only returned to bait her when he'd disappeared…

She glanced at the window. If he didn't return soon she'd be the one climbing on that decidedly wobbly chair and trying to jam a piece of cardboard into the gap.

What joy…

She left it while she rang the hospital, pretending to be a relative of Maggie's. There was no news beyond the fact that Mrs Crawford had been admitted and was 'comfortable.'

Her coffee had gone cold so she made another cup. Then, realising that she was hungrier than she'd been in weeks, she tore a lump off the end of the French bread, found a knife in the minuscule kitchen and slathered it with the creamy Dolcelatte.

She'd just bitten into it when there was a sharp rap on the back door. Bearing in mind the fact that there might still be a junkie in pain out there she didn't leap to open it but, mouth full of bread and cheese, managed a fairly fierce, 'Whooth at…?'

'Juliet?'

She opened the door. 'Thorry,' she said, gesturing with the bread she was still holding. 'Unch.'

'Thanks,' he said, taking it from her as if she'd offered it to him. 'I'm starving. You know, for a minute there I thought your burglar had returned and gagged you to blunt your sharp tongue.'

'My thung isn'th tharp…' she declared in an outraged shower of crumbs.

His response was to bite into the bread and cheese. Oh, terrific…

She stopped, chewed, swallowed. 'What took you so long?' she demanded when she could speak properly.

He'd used the time to finish her lunch and, after sucking some cheese from his thumb, said, 'Since that window is so easily accessible I had a look around the yard for something a bit more substantial than a pane of glass as a deterrent. Hold the door will you, while I bring the stuff in?'

Stuff?

'What stuff?'

He didn't answer, just opened the rear doors of a small scruffy van with Duke's Yard painted on the side and handed her a box that according to the label contained a burglar alarm kit.

'No. Wait...' He glanced at her. 'I can't...'

'Can't what?'

What on earth was the matter with her? She was dithering like a girl on her first day at work. Not that she'd dithered even then. She'd known exactly what she wanted—it was all on the list—and had been determined to get there.

No, she was dithering like a girl who'd been set on her feet by the sexiest boy in school. The boy every girl wanted to be noticed by. Even skinny girls with glasses...

'Look, I'm sorry Mr... Knight.' Oh, that felt so *good.* 'Mr...Errant. Or are you Mr Duke?' she enquired innocently.

'Now you're just being insulting,' he said. 'My name—since you're asking—is McLeod. Gregor McLeod,' he elaborated when she took rather longer than usual to respond.

'Really?' she said, snapping back to the present. 'I must have misheard you before.' Then, 'I'm sorry, Mr

McLeod, but I'm not in a position to sanction that amount of expense on Mrs Crawford's behalf.'

'Greg or Mac,' he said. 'Only people I don't like are required to call me Mister. And who said anything about expense? Buy me dinner and we'll call it even.'

Well, he had his priorities sorted. One pane of glass equalled lunch. A burglar alarm was worth dinner. She didn't want to know what she'd be expected to barter for the metal window grille he was lifting out of the van.

'On the other hand, I'm sure it would make her mind easier if she knew her premises were safely secured,' she said.

'Dinner would be cheaper,' he said, following her inside.

Not in her experience.

'I'm really not interested, Mr McLeod.'

'Women usually call me Greg,' he said, elaborating on the name thing. 'Or Gregor.'

'I only call people I like by their first name,' she replied, 'but I'm happy to drop the Mister if it offends you.' And, just to show him that it wasn't anything personal, she smiled and said, 'I'll make you that cup of tea now, McLeod.'

'You're all heart,' he said, reaching into his jacket, 'but I have the feeling I was well advised to bring my own chocolate biscuits.'

He handed her the packet, warm from his body.

'Lovely,' she said, holding the packet unenthusiastically at arm's length, as if it might bite. She just knew the chocolate was going to stick to her fingers when she opened it and that she wouldn't be able to resist licking them. Once she'd done that…

No. She'd done the night of shame with chocolate

and she dropped the packet on the desk out of harm's way. If he wanted them, he'd have to open it himself.

'I'm a really cheap date,' he assured her.

'I'll bear that in mind.' Realising that he was looking at her expectantly, that her heart lifted in response to his steady flax-blue gaze in just the same way as it had done all those years ago, she added cruelly, 'If I should ever need a cheap date.'

She left him to it and went into the little kitchenette to fill the kettle at the sink indicating that as far as she was concerned the exchange was at an end and she'd appreciate him getting on with the job.

Not that she expected him to be put off that easily. Surprised—and if she was honest just the tiniest bit disappointed—when he didn't come back with some outrageous comment, she glanced back over her shoulder.

He'd taken off his jacket and, as she looked, he peeled off his shirt to reveal a T-shirt that clung like a second skin. Only a man who wanted to display his Tarzan credentials would wear such a garment, even to work, she thought. Or a man who didn't understand the temperature control on his washing machine. Pathetic on both counts. But his lack of repartee was explained by the fact that he was concentrating on removing the broken pieces of glass from the window.

As he reached up the muscles on his shoulders bunched and rippled and the T-shirt rode up, threatening to expose an inch or two of flesh at his waist.

Realising that she was holding her breath in anticipation—she might be off the entire male half of the population but she wasn't dead—she quickly turned away and switched on the kettle before going through to the shop where she made herself useful tidying the books on the 'new titles' table. Flipping through the unopened post to see if there was anything that looked urgent and giving herself a moment to recover from the unexpected rush of mindless lust that had caught her by surprise.

She didn't do mindless anything, but even she had to admit that the sheer physicality of a man in close-fitting jeans made a refreshing change from the Paul Smith suits, handmade shirts and indecently expensive haircuts favoured by the men in what, until very recently, had been her everyday life.

Actually, despite the fact that it brushed his collar, she had to admit that whoever cut Gregor McLeod's hair knew what he—or more probably she—was doing.

'You might want to do something about this kettle,' he called out, breaking into her idle musings.

On the other hand, in the politically correct world of corporate management no one would have expected her to make the tea. Not that it made a whit of difference when it came to the crunch.

To make it to the top at Markham and Ridley, you still had to pee standing up.

'You could do with one of those kettles that switch themselves off,' he said, as she returned to a kitchenette filled with steam. Not bothering to acknowledge him, she flipped it off, dumped a tea bag in a mug and poured on the boiling water.

It *was* supposed to switch itself off. Clearly it was past its use-by date. Along with the rest of the store. The whole street.

'I think Maggie might have other things on her mind,' she said, as she added some milk and a pile of sugar to the mug before placing it on the desk behind him.

'So who will be taking care of things?' He eased the glass into the opening and set to work with the putty. 'While she's in hospital.'

'Um? Oh, I've no idea,' she said, dragging her eyes away from the swift, deft movements as he pushed it in place with a broad thumb. She might have added that it wasn't his either, but had no wish to prolong the conversation. 'Maybe her son will come home and sort something out.'

'Jimmy? I doubt it. He couldn't get away fast enough.'

'You know him?'

'We went to the same school. What about you?'

'Did I go to the same school as you and Jimmy Crawford?' she asked, more as a delaying tactic than because she hadn't understood what he meant.

He laughed. 'You've got to be kidding. You have the kind of voice that goes with the panama hats, blazers and privilege of St Mary's Ladies College. Or somewhere very like it.'

And obviously, Juliet thought, if the rumours that had flown around after his disappearance were true, he would know all about that.

'I just wondered if you knew Jimmy Crawford,' he persisted.

'Oh, I see. Well, I suppose I might have seen him in the bookshop but I've never spoken to him.' He didn't look as if he believed that her motive was totally altruistic. 'I haven't lived in Melchester since I left for university.'

He shrugged. 'If you say so. It's just that I'm still trying to get my head around why you'd go to all this trouble. You could have just slipped the lock on the door and left once the ambulance had taken Maggie to hospital.'

'I'm a caring and responsible citizen,' she replied, trying not to think about her initial panicky response. That split second when she'd nearly bolted.

'Oh, right. Well, that would be it. So where have you been living? London?' She didn't give him any encouragement. He didn't need any, taking her silence for assent. 'And now you're home. What was it? Marriage break up?'

He was relentless. Another five minutes of this and he'd have her entire life history including the whole sorry story of her return home to lick her wounds.

A sharp and continuous rapping on the front door saved her. 'Actually, I think I'll get that. Since I seem to be stuck here for a while I might as well do something useful. Like sell some books. If you'll excuse me?'

She didn't wait to discover whether he did or not. She might not have much of a clue about the retail book trade, but it had to be a lot less trouble than Gregor McLeod.

Greg watched her go. The woman had class written all over her and it wasn't just the voice. She was prickly, though, and definitely on the run from something. No make-up, hair like a bird's nest, his first impression had been one of disappointment. But then she'd bent down to pick up that piece of glass and when she'd looked up at him it was as if he'd been there before.

Something about her silvery-grey eyes had been so familiar, the wisp of streaky fair hair that had worked its way free of pins, and he'd found himself on the brink of saying, 'Haven't we met somewhere before?'

Fortunately, he'd managed to stop himself. She couldn't have made her lack of interest plainer and it didn't take much imagination to work out what her response would have been to an old chestnut like that.

CHAPTER THREE

'WHAT are you doing?'

Juliet stopped struggling with the heavy table and looked around. McLeod was leaning against the nearest bookshelf watching her. He'd replaced his shirt and looked as if he might have been there for some time, which seriously irritated her for some reason.

'I'm moving this table,' she explained, as if speaking to a very small child.

His look suggested that he was considering a rerun of his 'sarcasm' comment. Obviously he thought better of it because he said, 'I'll rephrase the question. What are you doing struggling with that table—'

'Because it's in the way,' she snapped. Three times she'd had to squeeze around it to reach a book for a customer, three times she'd banged her shin. Enough was enough. It hadn't taken her ten minutes to see that the whole shop needed reorganising... 'What's the point of having books on display if no one can reach them?' she demanded.

'—when all you had to do was call me and I'd have helped,' he finished, moving to the other side of the table and gripping it in a pair of strong, capable hands. 'So, Juliet, where do you want it?'

He was facing her, arms wide, shoulders like an iron girder for heaven's sake. So...in her face. So... physical. Worse, he had a look in his eye that appeared to tempt her to take his question any way she wanted. She cleared her throat and stepped back.

'Nowhere.'

'Really?'

He put a world of meaning into that word. Mostly disbelief. She suspected that the answer he expected, the one he usually got, was 'anywhere.' She had been wrong when she'd thought she could handle his type. Gregor McLeod wasn't a 'type.' He was unique.

A long time ago she'd thought he was uniquely kind…

'Really,' she said, ignoring the fact that she was considerably warmer than she should be considering the chilly March weather and the poor heating in the shop, but nothing on earth would tempt her to take off her sweater.

Now she understood that he was just uniquely provoking…

'In that case you'd better clear the books off it first. If the legs come off I should be able to get it in the van.'

Uniquely irritating…

'The van?'

'You want it out of the way, don't you? There's a skip at the yard, I'll dump it in that.'

'You can't!'

'It's no bother.' And he did something with his mouth, one corner lifting up in something that wasn't a grin, it wasn't even a smile, but it was definitely…something. 'I'll just add it to the bill.'

A bead of sweat trickled down the back of her neck.

Uniquely sexy.

'No!' Oh, good grief. 'I mean…' She hadn't a clue what she meant. 'Forget it.' Then, 'Are you done?'

'All ready for inspection, ma'am.'

'Good. That means I can go.'

She turned her back on the table and crossed to the front door, flipped the lock, shot a bolt near the floor, then jumped as she straightened and turned to find Greg blocking her way.

'You missed one,' he said, reaching above her to slide home a bolt at the top, giving her a close-up of his broad chest and a whiff of mingled masculine scents—leather, some illusively subtle aftershave, linseed oil from the putty...

'You're quite sure about the table?' he enquired, stepping back to let her escape.

'What? Oh, yes.' She was nearly thirty years old, for heaven's sake. She did not drool. Not even Paul had reduced her to that. Had not even come close, but it was as if having once let down her guard she was now vulnerable... 'I just got carried away for a moment.' She retrieved an untidy strand of hair that had escaped the pins and tucked it behind her ear. 'It's one of the pitfalls of the job.'

'You're in furniture removals?'

She managed a smile. 'No, McLeod. I am, or least I was until very recently, in corporate management.' Although how anyone so good at 'managing' could have made quite such a pathetically bad job of her life was hard to see. Paul, unlike Gregor McLeod, hadn't even been on her list...

'Really? And that involves shifting furniture, does it?'

'It involves dealing with problems,' she said.

'And the table is a problem. Tell me, princess, if I told you I had a problem would you be overcome with an almost irresistible urge to fix it for me?'

She could not believe he'd said that.

She really could not believe that she was blushing...

'I'm afraid you're going to have to stand in line. Right now I'm the one with all the problems and until I've found a job and somewhere to live…' She stopped. That was more than he needed to know. 'What I don't need is the encumbrance of a bookshop that's going downhill fast. Just like everything else around here. What's the matter with these people? With a little imagination—and a fresh coat of paint—this area could be a real attraction.'

'Your imagination must be taking regular workouts. This area needs levelling so that we can start again from scratch.'

'You're kidding, surely? Prior's Lane is full of character. Full of history. The cathedral and castle are real magnets to visitors and this used to be the place where those people came to spend their money.'

'Not since the new shopping centre was built.'

'The new shopping centre's just a carbon copy of a dozen others all over the country. This is different.'

'It's certainly that.'

'All it needs are some decent places to eat, a bit of a face-lift and the right publicity to attract retailers back into the area. Like the Portobello Road. Or The Lanes in Brighton.'

'Isn't the antiques trade a little over-subscribed?'

'Forget antiques. There used to be lovely little shops down here. There still are a few, although you have to look for them. A good baker's, a terrific Italian delicatessen—you've already tried their products—and there's a hardware shop like something out of the nineteen-fifties. A real showpiece. You can still buy individual screws in there. Nails by weight.' She could see that he didn't get it. 'What Prior's Lane needs is the kind of shops you don't see anywhere else. There used to be a wonderful haberdasher's, and a hat shop…'

'A hat shop?'

'Well, okay, but when I was a little girl I used to stand and gaze in the window just dreaming…' Realising from his expression that she might just be getting a bit carried away, she shrugged and said, 'It's shopping as recreation.'

'Obviously it's a girl thing,' he said. Then, with the kind of grin that should be an arrestable offence, 'Although I like the sound of the loose screws.'

She considered responding with 'innuendo is very unattractive in a man' but decided that ignoring him would be infinitely wiser and simply said, 'Not that it's any of my concern, of course.'

'I can see that you haven't given it a moment's consideration.'

'It didn't need a moment. One look was all it took.' It would make an interesting project, something really worthwhile. If she didn't have more pressing problems to worry about. 'I haven't got time for more. Or to start shifting furniture about on a whim.' No matter how much it needed doing. 'And presumably Maggie likes it this way.'

'Maybe. Or maybe she just doesn't have anyone to help her shift this stuff. Maybe you'd be doing her a favour.'

'Possibly, but really it's none of my business. How much do I owe you?'

He shrugged. 'As you so rightly pointed out, it's none of your business.'

'I called you. I'll pay the bill.'

'Why don't I just send it to the landlord?'

'But I don't know who that is.'

'I do.'

'Right.' Then she frowned. 'Would he be responsible for the replacement of a broken window?'

'If he's difficult about it I'll give you a call and you can buy me that dinner you promised me.'

She ignored the little shiver of anticipation that rippled through her. She'd made enough mistakes for one year and it wasn't even Easter yet.

'I didn't promise you anything, McLeod. What about the security grille and burglar alarm?'

His eyes creased to a roguish smile. 'Ah, well, that's another story. But I'm open to negotiation.'

Refusing to rise to yet another innuendo, she said, 'Won't Mr Duke object to you moonlighting? Using his van, his old stock, for your jobs on the side?'

'Duke will never know.'

'I see.'

'Do you, Juliet?'

She saw that he was involving her in ripping off his employer. 'Maybe I'd better call him. Settle the bill direct.'

That dealt with the smile.

'Are you trying to get me into trouble? When I gave up my lunch date for you?'

'No. No of course not,' she said, totally out of her depth now and with the shoreline fast disappearing... 'I'm sure you'd prefer cash in hand for the alarm,' she said, trying to gather her wits and remember where she'd left her handbag.

'I've already told you, I don't want your money.'

She had never had so much difficulty outgunning a man's gaze, or found it quite so difficult to look away. 'That's really very generous of you,' she managed through a mouth that was suddenly bone-dry. 'I'm sure Maggie will be very grateful when I tell her.'

His smile returned. It wasn't the full-blown version, but rather more thoughtful, leaving her with the uncomfortable feeling that he knew something that she didn't. But all he said was, 'I'd better show you how this alarm works before I go.'

Go? That was it?

He turned and led the way to the office. 'Do you want to check the window?'

Apparently it was.

She picked up the cup of cold coffee she'd abandoned and took a sip to moisten her lips. 'It looks fine.' Then, belatedly, 'Thank you.'

'That sounded as if it very nearly choked you.'

'Did it? I'm sorry. Maybe I'm coming down with a cold or something. I'm really very grateful. You've done a good job.'

'Are you saying that you'd recommend me to your friends?'

Friends? She didn't have any friends. She'd been working too hard to make friends. She had colleagues, business acquaintances and a cheating ex. None of whom wanted to talk to her right now. Or possibly ever.

'Of course.'

'Just a fraction too long before you answered there, Juliet, but thanks for the effort.' He turned to the switch he'd fitted to the wall. 'This is very simple. Just turn it on when you leave. Down for on, up for off. There's a ten second delay before it wakes the dead.'

'That's it? Isn't there a code I need to know?'

'No. This isn't anything fancy, just a simple contact wire connected to the back door and window,' he said as he showed her how to set it, 'but it's loud, which is usually enough to deter the opportunist thief.' Then, 'Are you sure you don't want me to help you move that table before I leave?'

'Quite sure.'

'Okay. I'll be going, then.' He took a card from his shirt pocket and handed it to her. 'That's my mobile number in case you have any more little jobs that need doing.'

He was going? Just like that? She'd expected him to repeat the offer of dinner at the very least. He'd implied she owed him as much. But no, he climbed into the seat of that tired old van, started her up and with a casual wave was gone.

Right. Well, okay. That was good. She'd wanted him to go.

She closed the door.

Now she could leave too.

First she printed a note to inform customers that the shop would be closed temporarily and stuck it on the front door. Then, after paying for the books she'd bought, counting the money in the till and leaving a note to say exactly how much it was, she put them all in one of the shop carriers and tucked it away in the bottom of her basket under her mother's shopping. Then she picked up her flowers, flipped the alarm switch and let herself out of the rear of the shop, making sure that the door was firmly shut behind her.

Juliet put the narcissi on the bedside cabinet and leaned over the bed.

'Maggie?'

'Hello, dear,' she said, looking very small in the high hospital bed. Very fragile. 'They're pretty.'

'Mum sent them. She said to tell you that she'll play your bingo cards for you. Split the winnings.'

Maggie laughed. 'That's the way we do it. She's such a dear. And so are you. I don't know what would have happened to me if you hadn't come to find me.'

'I just did what anyone would have,' she said guiltily. 'How are you feeling?'

'Very stupid. I keep telling them that there's nothing wrong with me except for a few bruises. I just came over a bit dizzy, that's all.'

'Well, I won't disturb you for long. I'm sure that rest is the very best thing for you right now, but I thought you might be worrying about the shop.'

'No, dear, you said you'd take care of it and I believed you.'

A trusting soul, too...

'I've had the window fixed and locked everything up.' There didn't seem to be much point in bothering her with the details of the rudimentary burglar alarm fixed up by McLeod.

'You have been good.'

'It was no bother and the man who dealt with it said he'd send the bill to the landlord.'

'The landlord?' She tried to laugh, but it was obviously too much effort. 'He'll be lucky. He won't even fix the things he's supposed to take care of.'

Juliet offered her water, settled her back against the pillows, then said, 'Don't worry about that for now.' She'd have to go down to Duke's Yard and see if she could find McLeod. Sort things out. 'What I really need to know, Maggie, is what you want me to do with the money from the till. I've got it safe, but it should be in the bank. And there's the key, too. What do you want me to do with that?'

'Money? There was only the float.'

'Well, I stayed while the window was fixed and people kept coming in. And of course I bought two books, so there's quite a bit...'

Realising that Maggie's eyes had drifted shut and that she was talking to herself, Juliet picked up the flowers and went in search of something to put them in.

On her return she was waylaid by a nurse. 'Did you call earlier? Mrs Crawford's relative?'

Oh, good grief. She'd forgotten all about her little white lie.

'Yes,' she said. 'And then again, no. I'm Juliet Howard and I did call, but I'm not actually related. I knew you wouldn't tell me how she was unless I said I was family.'

'So who are you?'

'No one. Well, obviously I'm *someone*...' She stopped. 'My mother knows her. I found Mrs Crawford this morning and called the ambulance.' She gave an apologetic little shrug. 'Sorry.'

The nurse frowned. 'So you're a neighbour, then?'

'Not even that, I'm afraid. Just a customer in her bookshop. Is there a problem?'

'Nothing that a relative—or a neighbour—couldn't have fixed. The thing is Maggie could do with some personal things. Nightwear, toothbrush?' she offered hopefully.

'No one else has been to see her? Didn't she ask you to call anyone?'

'She told us her son is overseas and she refused to give us a contact number. Said there was nothing he could do so there was no point in worrying him.'

McLeod had more or less suggested he wouldn't

want to be bothered. She had told the truth when she'd said she didn't remember Jimmy Crawford. It was possible that he was older than McLeod, of course.

'I don't suppose you have any idea how to get hold of him?'

'I'm afraid not and Mrs Crawford is right about one thing, he can't do anything about the toothbrush.' Then, because there didn't seem anything else she could say, 'Actually I've got her keys. I'll ask her if she'd like me to fetch some things for her if that will help.' And hopefully find a neighbour willing to take over. 'How long is she likely to be in hospital?'

'It's difficult to say. Mrs Crawford said she had a dizzy spell. We'll be running some tests, but it's likely she's had a mild stroke.'

'In that case someone will have to get hold of her son and let him know what's happened so that he can make whatever arrangements are needed.'

Quite early in this sentence Juliet realised that no matter how concerned she was about Maggie the staff nurse had caught sight of something behind her that was claiming her whole attention and she turned to see what it was.

Not a what. A who.

'McLeod.'

The jeans had gone. He was wearing a pair of good looking casual trousers, a soft shirt and a fine suede blouson jacket. And he was carrying a bunch of flowers that made the narcissi she was holding look totally inadequate although she was too busy being grateful that she'd taken the trouble to wash her hair, coat her washed-out complexion with a little make-up, to care about that.

It wasn't that she'd anticipated seeing McLeod

again, but there had been the possibility that she'd run into someone else from school. Someone who might remember her. At least that was what she'd told herself...

Her mother hadn't said a word, but had looked well pleased as she'd handed over the keys to the rust-bucket she laughingly called her car to save Juliet a three-bus journey to the hospital.

'It's nice to see you, too, princess.'

'Please don't call me that.'

He shrugged. 'How's Maggie doing?'

'As well as can be expected.' Then, seeing the nurse's hopeful expression, 'Sorry, he's not Maggie's son. He's just the odd job man.' She turned to him. 'Why are you here? Oh, no, don't tell me. Maggie said that the landlord would refuse to pay for the glass.'

His eyes momentarily darkened and she felt the heat from a flash of pure anger. 'I'm sure that when you've had time to think about it, you'll wish you hadn't said that.'

She didn't need time to think, she was already sorry. But there was just something about all that unbridled testosterone that irritated the life out of her. But at least she was feeling something. Even irritation was better than the low grade depression she'd been enduring for the last few weeks.

'She's through here, McLeod,' she said, turning abruptly on her heel and leading the way to the small bay with half a dozen or so beds where Maggie was being cared for. She didn't look back to see if he was following. It wasn't necessary. The whiplash ripple of turning heads as she passed assured her that he was on her heels.

'She's asleep,' McLeod said.

'Please don't feel you have to linger if you have a more pressing appointment,' she said, putting the vase she was holding on the locker. 'I'll be happy to tell her you called when she wakes up.'

'I'm in no hurry.' He smiled at a young nurse and handed her his flowers. 'Can you find a vase for these, sweetheart?' The girl blushed and took them without a murmur.

'Why didn't you ask her for a cup of tea, top of the milk, two sugars?' Juliet asked. 'While you'd got the smile turned on.'

'You remembered.' And he regarded her from beneath heavy lids for a moment, his look so thoughtful that her own cheeks began to heat a little. Then, apparently satisfied, he turned to Maggie, whose eyes were now open.

'Hello, Maggie,' he said, dropping a kiss on her forehead. 'I heard you'd been in the wars.'

'Gregor…' She smiled. 'How lovely to see you. Are you visiting someone?'

'Just you. I heard what happened and came to see if there's anything you need. Do you want me to try and get hold of Jimmy? Let him know what's happened?'

'Oh, no, you mustn't bother him. He's far too busy to come running home every five minutes,' she said.

'Someone has to take care of the shop,' he pointed out. 'Juliet's been doing a fine job—'

'Maggie,' Juliet interjected. The last thing Maggie Crawford needed just now was to be bothered about the shop. 'You're going to need some things. I'll be happy to go and fetch them for you.' Then, 'Or if you've a friend or neighbour you'd prefer me to call?'

'Oh, heavens, that would be difficult. There aren't many neighbours now. People used to live above the shops but no one wants to do that anymore. It's all offices these days.'

'Offices?' Juliet glanced at McLeod, hoping for some explanation.

'Maggie lives above the shop,' he said. 'I assumed you knew.'

She stared at him. Was that why he'd fixed the alarm? Of course it was. Damn it, now she *did* feel bad.

'No,' she said. 'I wish you'd mentioned it. I could have brought some of her things with me.' And once again she wished she'd kept her mouth shut. Getting ratty with him wouldn't help. None of this was his fault. 'Never mind, I can go and fetch them now. Is there anything in particular you want, Maggie?'

'That's very sweet of you, dear, but there's no need to worry yourself. I keep telling them I'm not stopping. If they'd just bring me my clothes—'

'You can't go home just yet, Maggie,' Juliet said gently. 'You'll have to stay just for a while, while they run some tests.'

'Oh, no, that's quite impossible. As Gregor said, there's no one to look after the shop.'

Juliet glared at him. Thoughtless, stupid man. Worrying the poor woman. Who could say when she'd be fit to work in the shop. On her feet all day.

He smiled back in a manner that suggested she was about to deeply regret that 'odd job man' remark, then said, 'As I was saying, Juliet did a very good job today. In fact she was all ready to start moving furniture around—'

'Not before time. I keep meaning to get someone in to move that table. I'm always banging my leg against it.'

'Then she's your girl. She's in management—'

'Not retail management—'

'And, by good luck, she's looking for a job, too. Why don't you ask her to take over until you're back on your feet?' he continued as if she hadn't spoken.

'Oh, I couldn't bother her,' Maggie said, saving her the embarrassment of explaining how impossible it would be.

'It wouldn't be a bother, would it, Juliet?' McLeod persisted. 'You've a lot in common, you know. She's very keen on restoring the Prior's Lane area to the way it used to be.'

'Oh, don't get me started on that,' Maggie began.

'No, really, I'd love to help, but—'

'And there's the top floor flat. It is still empty, isn't it? Juliet's looking for somewhere to live, too.'

'Are you? Well, I suppose staying with your mother is a little restricting for both of you. It'll need a good seeing to, I'm afraid. All those stairs are a bit much for me these days.'

'McLeod!' Juliet snapped. 'Maggie, take no notice of him. The last thing you want is someone you scarcely know running your shop or moving in upstairs.'

'Oh, I've known you all your life, Juliet. And your mother is the kind of woman I'd trust with my life. But it's not just the shop. I have to go home because of Archie.'

'Archie?'

'Archie?' McLeod echoed.

Who or what was Archie?

'He can't be left on his own, poor thing,' Maggie said, oblivious of their horrified exchange of glances over her bed as she struggled with whatever drugs she'd been given to stay awake. 'He pines so when he's on his own. And of course he has to be fed.' Then, 'You did find his food, didn't you, dear?'

Well, that wiped the smile off McLeod's face. Not that she had anything to look pleased about.

'Of course she did,' McLeod said quickly before she could own up. Then, 'Will you be all right for a while if I run Juliet into the city to collect some things for you?'

'I don't need a lift.' Especially not on the back of that motorbike. 'I've got transport.' After a fashion. The BMW that had gone with the job had, well, gone—with the job. 'Is there anything special you need, Maggie? Or will you leave it to me?'

'Don't you bother about it, dear. I told you, I'm going home—' She made an effort to sit up, just to show them that she meant it, before subsiding weakly against the pillows. 'Well, maybe you're right. I should stay in for tonight. But only if you'll promise to stay with Archie.'

'Of course she will,' McLeod promised for her. 'It won't be a problem, will it, Juliet?'

'No problem,' she repeated after the barest hesitation. 'We'll talk about it when I get back, but right now I need to go and fetch your things. McLeod will stay and keep you company until I get back.' She glanced up at him pointedly. 'That's if you don't have a dinner date?'

He smiled lazily, not in the least fazed by her barely concealed hostility. 'Well, now. That rather depends on you, Juliet.'

CHAPTER FOUR

GREG allowed her to escape, if only to enjoy the grandstand view of her departing rear encased in a pair of softly draped trousers as she walked away as quickly as she could—short, that was, of breaking into a run and betraying the fact that Archie not only hadn't been fed, his very existence was news to her.

Whatever she'd been doing in London, he decided, she must have been very good at it if the quality of her clothes was anything to judge by. Which begged the question, What was she doing back in Melchester? Fine city though it undoubtedly was, and expanding fast, London seemed the obvious milieu for anyone in 'corporate management.'

'What a lovely girl,' Maggie said as he turned back to her.

'Exactly what I was thinking.'

'I doubt that, Gregor.' Her laughter subsided into a fit of coughing, then, letting her eyes drift close, 'Why don't you go with her? The city is no place for a young woman on her own at night.'

'Exactly what I was thinking,' he repeated. But she was already asleep. He stopped at the nurses' station to explain that they'd be returning later and then walked out into the car park.

The first thing he saw was an aged car with the bonnet up and the unmistakable figure of Juliet Howard bent over it. He'd have recognised that pretty *derrière* anywhere. 'You know I'd have put you down as the owner of something sensible and smart,' he said.

'Really?' She straightened. 'Well, you can't always be right.'

'True. But I can always be useful.'

'Prove it by making this start.'

'The only useful thing I'm prepared to do for this pathetic excuse for a car is call a scrapyard and have them put it out of its misery.'

'No good with engines, huh?'

'That tactic won't work with me, princess. I've got nothing to prove, especially when my trusty steed is eagerly waiting to gallop off with a damsel in distress.'

'You're offering to lend me your motorbike?'

'Not in this lifetime. What I'm offering is to drive you to the shop. In my car.'

'I'm sorry, McLeod, but my mother told me never to take lifts from strange men.'

'I'm not strange.'

'That's a matter of—'

'I'm not even a stranger.'

She started, as if he'd touched a nerve, and the feeling that he knew her intensified. Had she worked in one of his offices? But, if that were the case, she'd have recognised him too. And if she had? Why wouldn't she say so?

'McLeod—'

Anticipating further argument, he brushed his concerns aside—he could run a check later—and said, 'Before you say another word I should warn you that you'll have to wait twenty minutes for a taxi, minimum, and although I suspect you think it might be worth it, just give a thought to poor, starving Archie.'

'I'm trying very hard not to,' she declared, slamming

down the bonnet lid before she extracted her bag from the car and locked it. 'I promise you, nothing else would persuade me to accept a lift from you.'

'Take my word for it,' he said, 'nothing else would persuade me to offer you one.'

And finally he got a smile. 'I guess I deserved that.'

'Without a doubt, but we'll discuss your unaccountably hostile attitude towards me some other time,' he said, not returning the smile or suggesting that over dinner would be a good time. She would be expecting that and have her snappy little refusal all ready for him. It was time to move the game up a gear and stop being so predictable. 'Come on, I'm parked over there.'

She paused as he approached the long, low bulk of his immaculate midnight-blue vintage E-type Jaguar and opened the door for her.

'This is yours?' she asked, the barest catch in her throat. She definitely hadn't expected something like that.

'Odd job men get good tips,' he said.

'No…'

First the smile and now she was just a little bit flustered. As flustered as when she'd turned from locking the shop door and had found herself standing too close to him. There was something very appealing about a self-possessed woman losing her cool. The extra touch of colour in her cheeks emphasized by the lighting that leached all other colour from her skin…

'I just meant…' Her gesture indicated that she wasn't quite sure what she'd meant. He could take a pretty good guess.

'You meant, have I borrowed it? And, more importantly, did I get the owner's permission before I did?'

'Yes...' Then, 'No! I'm sorry. I don't know what I meant.'

And an apology. The full set. He was finally getting somewhere.

'It's a beautiful car, McLeod,' she said, sliding into the seat with the easy grace of a woman who knew how to climb into low sports cars. Rear end first, then legs. 'She's a real classic.'

'She is,' he agreed. Then, referring to the car, 'And you can rest assured that I have the owner's full permission to use it.'

She looked up at him. 'It's yours, isn't it?'

'Every last cog and piston,' he assured her, closing the door on her before sliding behind the wheel and starting her up.

He never got tired of the soft, throaty roar of the engine, the way people turned to look as he passed them in the street. He could have driven any car he wanted, the fastest sports car, any of those symbols of wealth that poor-boys-made-good drove to demonstrate to the world that they'd arrived. He'd got half a dozen to choose from in the underground garage beneath his Thames-side apartment in London, at the rambling cottage he'd just bought in a village within driving distance of Melchester. But this forty-year-old beauty was his favourite.

It never failed to make women—even cool, totally self-possessed women like Juliet Howard—catch their breath.

'Did you restore it yourself, McLeod?' Juliet asked, carefully polite, her breath apparently well under control as he took the ring road, heading for the old part of the city. 'The Jaguar?'

He could do polite, but he wasn't letting her get

away with that. 'Surely you aren't suggesting that a simple odd job man could restore a car like this to museum condition?'

'I don't believe I ever suggested that you were simple. And I'm aware that in the pursuit of their passions people are capable of extraordinary things.'

'Restoring cars is not my passion.' He stopped for traffic lights and glanced at her. 'I've got more interesting things to do lying on my back than getting covered with grease.'

If he'd anticipated some sparky response to such blatant innuendo he would have been disappointed. She said nothing and, with her profile backlit by street lighting, it was impossible to see her expression. Instead she lifted her hand and tucked back a smooth wing of silky hair behind her ear with slender fingers in a gesture that was nervous, he decided, rather than flirtatious.

It gave him the uneasy feeling that her confidence was all on the surface. That there was fragility beneath the poise and the self-assurance was nothing more than a surface mask—well polished, but very thin. It brought out all his most protective feelings and he found himself wishing he'd offered her reassurance rather than provocation. Wanting to reach for her hand and say, *Don't worry. It'll be all right. I'll make it all right.*

Madness.

Neil was right. Women like Juliet Howard had always caused him trouble. He was a lot safer with women he understood. Straightforward women who knew exactly what he was offering, knew he'd give them a good time, mutually enjoyable sex and absolutely no commitment.

But when had 'safe' ever appealed to him?

He pulled smoothly away from the traffic lights—this was not a woman to be impressed with boy-racer starts—and said, 'Look, I wasn't trying to manipulate you back there.'

She glanced at him. 'I'm sorry?'

He didn't believe that 'sorry.' She was far too quick not to know exactly what he was talking about. But then he was being a touch economical with the truth himself. Not about the flat. Although it would be perfect. For him. If she moved in he'd be able to take all the time in the world playing her at this game they'd embarked upon. And he'd have the perfect get out clause the minute he felt his independence was threatened…

But he played along anyway.

'About the flat,' he said. 'It'll probably need decorating—I seem to remember a lot of black and red and I don't suppose Maggie's changed it since Jimmy left. But there's plenty of room up there. You said you needed a job and somewhere to live. This would mean all your problems were solved at a single stroke.'

'The only problem I have is you,' she snapped.

'And Archie,' he reminded her.

She raised her hands in a helpless gesture. 'All right. And Archie. But that's just temporary. I can't possibly take responsibility for Maggie. Or the shop. Who knows how long it will be before she's back on her feet? The nurse said it was probably a mild stroke. It's possible she'll have another.'

'And if someone doesn't take over straight away, someone competent, the shop will close, you know that, don't you?'

'You're the second person to say that to me today.'

'Well, you know that I'm not just saying it, then. And obviously it won't be a long-term thing. She's a bit confused at the moment, but once she realises what's going on Maggie will take steps to organise someone permanent.'

'She'll need home help too. She won't be able to live alone in a first floor flat. Suppose she has another stroke. It could be thirty-six hours before anyone even missed her.'

'Given that kind of ammunition, Jimmy'll have her in a nursing home quicker than you can say the words.'

'You seem to know him pretty well.'

'Well enough. He takes after his father. The only person he's interested in is himself.' Then, catching her curious look, 'Maggie was very good to me when I was in trouble and needed someone. Buy me dinner and I'll tell you all about it.'

'I've got a better idea. Why don't you move into the flat above the shop yourself? That way you'll be on hand if she needs anything.'

'I'm not the one who needs somewhere to live,' he pointed out. 'And I've got a job.'

'What as? A snake oil salesman?'

'Excuse me?'

'You're giving it the hard sell, McLeod.'

'Me? What have I got to gain?' He struggled to keep his grin under control. *Snake oil salesman.* If Neil had heard that he'd never live it down... 'I'm simply trying to help everyone. It's your decision, Juliet. Take a look before you decide.' He'd been easing the long car through the narrow lanes near the cathedral and finally pulled up at the rear of the shop. 'But first we have to take care of Archie. What do you reckon he is?' he asked as she unlocked the door and turned off the alarm.

'Your friend Jimmy didn't have a taste for exotic pets, did he?' she asked.

'You really don't want to know the answer to that one.' She raised her eyebrows as if to suggest he needed to grow up. Obviously she thought he was kidding. 'How long do wolf spiders live, do you think?' he asked. 'And pythons?'

'Oh, please...' she muttered contemptuously. But she couldn't quite repress a shiver.

'Yes, well, it was a long time ago. Archie's probably nothing more interesting than a neurotic budgie.'

'Probably. Even so, I'm beginning to wish we'd owned up and asked Maggie who or what Archie is before we left the hospital,' she said, bending down to peer under the desk.

'We? You're the one she left in charge. I'm just here out of the goodness of my heart,' he said. 'And I don't think you're likely to find Archie there, Juliet, or we'd have seen him this morning.'

'Not me,' she replied. 'I wasn't looking.' Then, straightening, 'But you're right, there's nothing here.'

'Time to brave the unknown, then.'

'You are such a comfort.'

He extended his hand. 'Take my hand if you're scared.'

'Keep your hands to yourself, McLeod,' she said, opening the door that led upstairs, then leaping back with a shriek as something soft and furry flew out of the dark.

And suddenly she wasn't so keen to reject him. No objections now as he caught her, held her close.

She really was trembling and he knew he should feel

bad about teasing her, but holding her felt much too good to indulge in sham regret.

Her hair, scented faintly with shampoo, brushed against his cheek, the soft cowl neck of her sweater had the unmistakable touch of cashmere and her body, even through her jacket, was enticingly curvy. With considerable difficulty he kept his hands still, resisting the hot rush of desire that urged him to go for it, pull her closer, turn her in his arms and kiss her. His treacherous body said, *It'll be all right. She wants it as much as you do.*

Maybe she did. But he wasn't taking any chances. When he kissed her he wanted to be able to see her face. Wanted to know that she'd die if she had to wait another moment.

'It's okay,' he said, easing back a little. It didn't come out quite as authoritatively as he'd intended and he was forced to clear his throat before he said again, 'It's okay, Juliet. It's just a cat.'

'I knew that...'

Juliet gave a little shudder. She hadn't believed in the spider or the snake, but just the thought had been enough to lift the hairs on the back of her neck and although she pulled free it was with considerable reluctance. After the kind of day she'd had the temptation to lean into a pair of strong arms, no matter how annoying the man they belonged to might be, was almost overwhelming.

But she'd fallen for that once when she'd been trapped in a lift just long enough to feel claustrophobic. Had that all been planned, too? No matter, it had been her mistake, why she was back at square one, starting again from scratch, and she'd always made a virtue of learning from her mistakes.

Never repeating them.

And, stepping away from the invitation in his too husky voice, she stooped to stroke the cat, murmuring softly to reassure him that she wasn't a threat.

'I was really hoping Archie would be a budgie,' she said, her smile rueful as she picked him up. He was comfortingly large and cuddly, ginger with a white bib and paws. A storybook cat. She had longed for one just like him when she was little. 'I could have taken a budgie home with me.'

'You couldn't take a cat?'

'My mother has already got me back home disturbing her peace. I suspect a cat might just be one lodger too many. Even supposing she wasn't allergic to them. Come on, Archie,' she said. 'Let's go and find you something to eat.'

He butted her chin with his head, purring loudly.

McLeod dealt with the litter tray while she fed Archie and filled his water bowl.

'Thanks for doing that,' she said.

'It's what an odd job man's for.'

'Oh, look, I'm really sorry I said that. It's just—'

'I know. You've had a rotten day.'

'I've had worse,' she admitted. 'In fact this one could have been a great deal worse without your help.'

'Before you start getting too nice, I think I should make it clear that Archie is not coming home with me.'

'You can't say your mother's allergic,' she replied. 'I've already bagged that excuse.'

'I haven't seen my mother for years, so that isn't the problem.'

'Oh…' She bit off the expletive. 'I'm really sorry.'

'It was her choice. I've learned to live with it. But I

still can't take Archie off your hands. I'll be away tomorrow night.'

'Oh. That's convenient.' Then, 'Holiday or work?'
As if it mattered. Before he could answer, she said,
'Sorry, none of my business. I'd better go and put to-
gether some things for Maggie.'

'Actually, it's my daughter's eighteenth birthday.
Her stepfather is throwing her a party.'

'Oh.' *He had an eighteen-year-old daughter?* She
did a rapid calculation and realised that she must have
been born just before he disappeared from school... 'I
didn't know. I'm sorry.' Then, 'Not about the daughter.
About the stepfather.'

'It's okay. We're all being very civilised. He's allowing me to pay for it.' Then, 'While you're looking
around for Maggie's stuff, don't forget to check out the
sofa.'

Still trying to get her head around the fact that
Gregor McLeod had a grown-up daughter, she said,
'The sofa?'

'You promised that you'd be stopping. Remember?'

There were so many questions she wanted to ask
him. Had he been married? How long had it lasted?
What was his daughter's name? If she'd been honest,
owned up to recognising him, she could have done
that...

'Actually,' she managed, looking away, 'I believe
you were the one making free with the promises.'

But she had gone along with it. She looked down at
Archie who, having made short work of the food she'd
given him, was now stropping himself against her legs,
purring desperately, wanting to be picked up and cuddled.

He was missing Maggie, undoubtedly. And was

probably afraid he was going to be left for more long hours by himself.

'I don't seem to have much choice,' she said, giving Archie a reassuring hug. 'But it's just for tonight. I'll sort out something long-term tomorrow.'

Sorting out stuff was what she did best, after all. How difficult could it be to organise care for one bookshop, cat included? It wasn't as if she had something more interesting, exciting, important to do. The alternative was sinking back into the pit of self-pity.

'That's the spirit and, just to show that I'm not leaving you to cope unaided, I'll do my best to sort out your car for you when we get back to the hospital.'

To suggest that McLeod looked smug would have been a gross understatement but, despite an almost overwhelming urge to kick his shins, she just about managed to restrain herself. Men offering to fix her mother's car were pretty thin on the ground. Nonexistent, unless they were being paid an exorbitant hourly rate for the job, actually. Nevertheless she refused to appear entirely helpless when faced with the complexities of the internal combustion engine.

'It's probably just the spark plugs,' she assured him. 'It usually is. I had my emery board out to give them a quick clean when you turned up and did your Sir Galahad act.'

'I think you're confusing me with some other knight errant,' he said, 'but if I need to borrow it I'll let you know.' He took a mobile phone from his pocket. 'I have to make a phone call. Can you manage the packing?'

'First lunch, now dinner? Whatever you do, don't tell her the truth, McLeod, she'll never believe it,' she warned, firmly quelling the ridiculous sense of disappointment, annoyance that while he was flirting outrageously with her some other poor woman was waiting for him to turn up.

The wretch just grinned at her and, leaving him to it, she went in search of Maggie's bedroom.

What else had she expected? He was the youth who'd picked her up, dusted her off, called her 'princess,' when all the time he was making out with some sixth form 'queen' from St Mary's.

She'd been a kid. He'd been kind when she'd been hurt, but apart from that he'd scarcely been aware of her existence. The fact that she'd adored him, that her heart had nearly broken when he'd just disappeared off the face of the earth, was not his fault.

She was hurt now, a little subconscious voice prompted. Why not let him pick her up again, dust her off…

Because she was all grown up, that was why. Big enough to fight her own battles. And maybe it was time she started doing just that.

Then, pushing him firmly out of her mind, she looked around. Despite its city centre location, the flat had all the chintzy cosiness of a country cottage. Smoke-darkened oak beams added to the illusion, although the original open fire in the sitting room had been replaced with a gas fire that looked pretty much like the real thing.

Staying overnight certainly wouldn't be any kind of a hardship. In fact, babysitting a bookshop—cat included—suddenly sounded a very attractive proposition. It didn't exactly fit her job description. It was, however, useful if unpaid employment that would help out someone who'd been kind to her when she was a little girl. Whom her mother considered, if not exactly a close friend, then a cherished acquaintance.

She might even bring her laptop and start a major overhaul of that fine work, Juliet Howard's Master Plan for Her Life.

Then, as she opened bedroom drawers, found nighties, slippers, a dressing gown, and piled them into a small holdall, she decided that she might think about reorganising the shop too.

It would be a small project but at least there wouldn't be a glass ceiling keeping her firmly in her place.

She moved on to the bathroom, found a bathrobe, towels in the airing cupboard. Tossed in a tin of talc.

'A penny for them?'

She jumped at the sound of McLeod's voice, turning to see him standing in the doorway watching her as she scanned the bathroom shelves, checking for anything vital that she'd missed.

'A penny?'

'For your thoughts. You were miles away.'

'I wasn't questioning what you meant, it was your grasp—or lack of it—of inflation that I was querying.'

'If you don't want to tell me, princess, you just have to say so.'

'Actually, I was simply trying to decide what I'd want if I was in hospital.'

'To go home.'

She smiled. 'That sounds heartfelt.'

'I had my appendix removed when I was six.' He straightened. 'Come on. You can always take in anything else she needs tomorrow.'

'Yes, I suppose so.'

He held out his hand for the bag she'd packed. She

was quite capable of carrying it herself, but saying so would provoke another of those edgy little exchanges so she surrendered it without a murmur and gave Archie—who'd stuck to her heels like glue all the time she'd been packing Maggie's bits and pieces—a big cuddle and assured him she'd be back very soon before shutting him inside the flat. She didn't want a repeat of that furry rush out of the dark. Not when she was on her own.

At the hospital McLeod dropped her off at the entrance and, taking her car keys, left her to settle Maggie. When she returned half an hour later the car engine was running. He turned it off, climbed out. 'Try it,' he said.

It fired first time. 'Good grief. You're a genius.'

He made a slight bow, then said, 'It will have to be a very good dinner.'

'Sorry?'

'The one you owe me.'

'Actually, this one is down to my mother, McLeod. It's her car.'

'I did it for you, Juliet. I'll look to you to settle the account.'

'Oh, look—'

'Don't panic. I've cancelled the table reservation for tonight.'

'Excuse me?'

'What else did you have planned? Once you'd done your duty visiting the sick?'

So that was why he'd turned up. He knew she'd be there…

She firmly quashed any inclination to be flattered by his persistence and said, 'My plan was to scour the local paper in the hope of finding a flat I can afford to rent,' she lied.

He grinned. 'Well, that's sorted, so we can concentrate on food. By the time you've picked up what you need it'll be too late for anything but a carry-out. What's your preference? Since you're paying. Chinese, Indian? Or there's a very good Thai—'

'Back off, McLeod. I never agreed to buy you dinner and even if I had done...'

No, no, no! Now she'd given him an opening.

'Yes?' he prompted, taking it.

'I prefer to do the asking. Decide the where. And when.'

'I think we both know that if I leave it to you it will be the first cold day in hell.'

It would if she'd any sense... 'Half the pleasure is in the anticipation,' she said sweetly.

'Half? I think someone's been short-changing you, princess.'

'Really? I was referring to good food, fine wine and excellent company. Maybe you had something else in mind?' And finally she had something to smile about. 'Fast food, perhaps?'

'Ouch.'

'Anytime.'

'Okay. I'm prepared to spend a little time anticipating good food, fine wine and excellent company. Let's say until Saturday. After that be prepared to turn up and pay at my convenience.' And he didn't give her an opportunity to tell him what to do with his convenience but carried straight on with, 'In the meantime you're going to need a lift back to Maggie's. Unless your mother is prepared to offer you her car on a full-time basis?'

'No, she needs it for work but you don't have to play chauffeur. I was planning on calling a taxi.'

He didn't argue, just said, 'Please—let's not have that conversation again. I'll follow you.' And he closed her car door before climbing into the Jaguar.

By the time he'd started it she was out of the car park. She wasn't exactly keen on returning to the dark access lane behind the shop on her own, but she certainly wasn't going to allow McLeod to believe she was incapable of managing without him. Not that she imagined she'd have to and, sure enough, the next time she looked in her mirror she could see the Jaguar following at a safe distance.

It was ridiculous to feel irritated by his certainty that, sooner or later, she'd fall for his undoubted charm. She'd be the first to admit that he had every reason for his self-confidence; he had no way of knowing that she'd just had a booster shot against manipulative men with blue eyes and charming smiles and was now totally immune.

She just wished he'd go and find someone more appreciative to flirt with. Someone who didn't object to being called 'princess.' The girl he'd stood up at lunchtime, for instance.

'I won't be long,' she said when he pulled up outside what had once been quite a grand old house but had long ago been divided into small flats.

For one awful moment she'd thought he was going to insist on seeing her to the front door and that she'd be faced with the prospect of explaining who he was. She might be rising thirty, but her mother would take one look and put two and two together and believe she knew exactly why she'd taken so much trouble with her hair and make-up for the first time since she'd lost

her job: she'd feel like a teenager bringing home the
school bad boy. Not that she ever had. She wasn't *that*
stupid. Her mother had drilled into her the necessity of
having a proper education, a good career. All she'd
ever brought home from school was homework and
more homework.

Until now.

'I just need to explain where I'll be,' she said dis-
couragingly. 'And pack an overnight bag. I'll be ten
minutes tops.'

'Take your time. I'll stay here.'

On second thought, as the archetypal bad boy, he'd
probably spent a lifetime avoiding tight-lipped mothers,
she realised.

He needn't have worried. Her mother hadn't returned from her weekly game of bingo and she quickly
dashed off a note explaining where she was, leaving it
with the car keys.

He was leaning against the Jaguar when she
emerged, talking into his cellphone. He straightened
when he saw her and, flipping it shut, slipped it into
his pocket.

'Is she getting impatient?' she asked.

'He,' McLeod replied, taking her laptop and the
overnight bag and opening the door for her. 'It was
work.'

'Oh.' Then, 'It's rather late for that, isn't it?'

'You know how it is, Juliet.' His smile was slow,
starting at one corner of his mouth and working its way
up until his whole face joined in. 'An odd job man's
work is never done.'

She got into the car without saying another word.
He was still grinning when he slid in beside her. Let

him laugh. She'd already apologised. She wasn't about to grovel.

'Did you decide what you'd like to eat?' He glanced at her. 'You *are* hungry?'

She was starving. For the first time in weeks she could have eaten the proverbial horse but she wasn't about to admit it. Maggie would undoubtedly have a can of baked beans that she could heat up and have on toast.

'Thanks all the same, but I think I'll just hold myself in anticipation until Saturday.'

'Saturday?'

'That was the deadline you set, wasn't it? Shall we say eight o'clock at the Ferryside?'

'The Ferryside?'

'Is there an echo in here?'

'Can you afford the Ferryside?' he asked.

Probably not, but it had been worth it just to see him momentarily lost for words.

'I told you, McLeod. I don't do cheap dates.'

CHAPTER FIVE

GREG forced himself to resist all kinds of urges, not least of them the urge to kiss Juliet Howard and hang the consequences. He'd learned a lot over the years, especially patience, how to wait for what he wanted, and he'd wanted her from the moment he'd picked up the telephone and her cool, touch-me-not voice had jarred loose something primitive in him.

It was the same impulse to reach beyond his grasp that had got him into so much trouble as a youth. The same drive that had pushed him to take so many risks and, finally, come home ready to stamp his mark on a city that had once disowned him.

But time and experience had tempered his impetuosity. Had taught him that hurling himself against a closed drawbridge brought him nothing but pain. That with sufficient patience—and enough money to oil the hinges—almost any door would open to him.

Almost.

All his instincts warned him that Juliet Howard would need a subtler approach. In fact they were suggesting, quite strongly, that he'd be wise to take those 'hands off' warnings she'd been flashing him all day very seriously indeed. It was probably no bad thing that he'd be spending a couple of days at the other end of the country where temptation couldn't get the better of his best intentions because, for the first time in as long as he could remember, he felt like tugging against the restraints, kicking over the traces and letting the consequences go hang.

He climbed out of the car before he could forget himself—he'd have opened her door too and helped her to her feet, but she didn't give him the chance—and set her bag inside the back door of the shop once she'd unlocked it, remaining outside, well out of harm's way.

'Are you going to be all right here on your own?' he asked.

'It's rather late to be getting a conscience about pushing me into it, don't you think? Or was that a prelude to the suggestion that you should come upstairs to check for burglars under the bed?'

'No, you're safe,' he said, raising a grin. It didn't come easily, but he felt certain she'd expect it. 'I checked earlier. Make sure you reset the alarm before you go upstairs.'

'I won't forget. Goodnight, McLeod.'

As she moved to close the door he blocked it with his shoulder. There was a moment of resistance, her eyes widening slightly as he took her arm and pushed back her sleeve. Then, without taking his eyes from her face, he reached into his jacket and took out a ballpoint pen.

'Call me and tell me where you'd like me to pick you up on Saturday,' he said.

The smooth white skin of her forearm was warm and faintly scented with vanilla, a temptation to the senses. It took every bit of will-power to stick to his original purpose and use it as a blank sheet on which to write his telephone number.

'I already have your number.'

'You do?'

Of course she did.

He'd given her his card, but this had been about more than giving her his number. It had been much more primitive than that. It had been about touching her, putting his mark on her, and the momentary stillness before she pulled free suggested that she knew it too.

'And I was so certain you would have thrown it in the bin the minute my back was turned.'

'Why would I do that?' she asked, her silvery eyes gleaming in the reflected security lights of the pharmacy next door. 'Good odd job men are such... treasures.'

Her sarcasm was oddly reassuring; she was using it to keep her distance, suggesting she was fighting herself as well as him. Which was promising.

'Thank you for the "good,"' he said.

'Credit where it's due.' Then, 'Besides, I thought you were confident that I'd be here...' and the unspoken 'waiting for you' hovered between them for a moment before she continued '...seduced by the top floor flat into taking care of Archie and the shop.'

He shook his head. 'I suspect that any response I make to that is only going to cause me grief. Shall we just say that I'm taking nothing for granted other than good food, good wine and excellent company?'

His reward was an unforced smile.

'Oh, that's good, McLeod. You're really good.'

For a moment he was transfixed by the fleeting glimpse of a dimple just above the corner of her mouth as a synapse connected and something stirred in his memory.

Why couldn't he remember?

'McLeod?'

'Sorry, I was speechless there for a moment,' he said. 'I'm so happy you appreciate how hard I'm trying.'

'Trying,' she replied, 'is a very good word, but be sure that's all you'll be getting. And, since this is just dinner and not a date, I'll meet you at the restaurant.' Then, 'If you don't turn up, I'll just assume you've been distracted by some woman needing her stopcock fixed.'

'Damn it...' But before he could tell her that it would be no more than she deserved if he stood her up, he found himself facing a closed door. 'Trouble,' he muttered, recalling Neil's warning. 'Definitely trouble.'

But as he stepped back, looking up at the first floor, waiting for a light to reassure him that she'd made it upstairs without disaster, he discovered he couldn't do a thing about the wide grin spreading all over his face.

Of course he couldn't possibly let her have the last word...

Juliet made herself some supper, then, with Archie sitting at her feet purring loudly, she spent an hour surfing the Web, looking at recruitment sites, each of them urging her to sign up and let them find her the job of her dreams. Yes, well, she'd already signed up with the major players and they weren't beating a path to her door.

It drove home the painful fact that the job she'd always wanted, the one she'd worked for, was no longer remotely attainable.

The truth of the matter was that no job would satisfy her other than the one she'd earned with hard work, long hours and sheer dogged effort when the 'boys' were having a good time doing whatever it was that 'boys' did after work. She was forced to admit that nothing would satisfy her but the sight of Lord Markham on her doorstep admitting that he'd made a mistake. Telling her that Markham and Ridley needed *her* to implement the plan—the culmination of all her ideas, all her experience, put together over so many years as she'd slow-stepped her way up the ladder to the top—and begging her to come back on her own terms.

Now that *was* stupid.

The first rule of management was that no one was indispensable but she called up the file anyway. The one that she had kept so safe, determined that no one should see it until it was finished. Except Paul. She'd been vain enough to want his opinion. His praise. Wanting to impress him with her cleverness...

Archie butted her ankle. As she bent obediently to rub his ear she saw the number that Gregor McLeod had written on her arm.

Safe? Oh, right. Inviting McLeod out to dinner had scarcely been the act of a woman hooked on safety.

But exactly where had keeping her mind on business, playing safe, got her?

She'd fallen for Paul simply because he'd appeared the very opposite of the kind of predatory male that any woman determined on a career avoided like the plague. Despite his boyish good looks, perfect grooming, he'd seemed so... She struggled for a word to describe him and all she could come up with was *harmless*. Not much of a reference for a lover. But she'd felt in control with him. He'd never pushed her, had let her set the pace. She'd thought it was because he was her temporary shadow. That he was taking care not to overstep any invisible line while they worked together. She'd liked him for that. She'd felt *safe* with him.

So safe that she'd talked through her ideas with him, flattered by his interest, calling him in the middle of the night to tell him when her opus was finished. He'd arrived twenty minutes later bearing champagne, insisting that they must celebrate.

Was that when he'd copied it, downloading it in seconds on to the little memory stick that he carried on his key ring, while she'd been fetching the glasses? She'd expected him to make a push to stay that night...and knew that she wouldn't have resisted. Instead he'd made some excuse about a family get-together that weekend, an early start.

He hadn't touched her at all, until that Judas kiss that had mussed her lipstick and delayed her just long enough to put some distance between them.

What had he done? Closed his eyes and thought of the directorship?

'Make that stupid times two, Archie,' she said.

His soft burble, somewhere between a purr and a mew, was comforting. Maybe, when she found somewhere of her own, she would visit the animal rescue centre and offer a home to some other lost soul.

'Oh, for heaven's sake, Juliet Howard,' she exclaimed. 'Stop feeling so damned sorry for yourself. You're not the first person this has happened to and you won't be the last. Get over it. Move on...'

Or at the very least *move*.

Living at home, being cared for by her mother like a needy child, was no way for an adult to behave. She was done with self-pity. And, carrying Archie with her for company, she climbed the stairs to the top floor to take a look at the flat beneath the eaves.

It had the same floor area as Maggie's flat but the living space was smaller because of the sloping ceilings. And the dark walls didn't help. McLeod had not been kidding about the black and red. Very Gothic. But it was nothing that couldn't be fixed with a few cans of paint.

Maybe, she thought, he'd fix it for her. It would cost a lot more than dinner, she was certain, even dinner at the Ferryside, and she found herself smiling at the prospect of haggling over the price.

Irritatingly full of himself the man might be, but he had reminded her how to smile…

Then, slightly shocked at the wave of pleasurable anticipation evoked by the thought, she went back downstairs, settled down on the sofa for the night and with Archie at her feet lay awake thinking about how easy it would be to turn that large, if awkwardly shaped, entrance hall into a workspace with an L-shaped desk under the sloping ceiling. Pale buttermilk walls would make it so much lighter, and there would probably be good floorboards beneath the nasty carpet…

Pure fantasy, of course. She didn't need a workspace.

But it was rather more interesting than counting sheep.

And a lot more effective in distracting her from the undoubted pleasure to be obtained from getting up close and personal with McLeod. That was somewhere which, despite the very real temptation, she had no intention of going…

*   *   *

The postman woke her, ringing on the shop doorbell with a package from America that had to be signed for.

'How's Maggie? I heard she had a fall. Nothing too serious, I hope.' He handed her a pen and held out the clipboard for her to sign. 'Are you taking care of things while she's in hospital?'

'It looks that way,' she said as she handed him back his pen before taking the package and a pile of letters and closing the door.

She sifted through the mail as she walked to the back of the shop, leaving the package—which, according to the shipping label, contained books—on the desk. There were a couple of bills but the rest of the mail looked personal, so she put it to one side to take to the hospital with her before heading back upstairs to take a shower.

She'd just reached the half-landing when there was another knock, this time on the back door. A quick glance out of the small window confirmed that it was the Duke's Yard van standing in the lane at the rear of the shop.

The hippity-hop leap that her heart gave was a dead giveaway; she might, in theory, know that Gregor McLeod was not the kind of man a sensible woman would ever get involved with, but reality had a way of creeping up and catching you on the blind side. 'Bad boys' didn't get their reputations for nothing. It took more than a pair of blue eyes and a smile that could reduce the knees of the most determinedly 'good girls' to jelly if they had a mind. Men like Gregor McLeod exuded an almost irresistible air of danger. A Pied Piper magnetism.

Maybe it had been her good fortune that none of them had ever so much as noticed her.

Or maybe not.

'Safe' could get to be a habit.

'Couldn't stay away, hmm?' she asked as she slipped the locks, then felt a total idiot when she opened the door to discover that it wasn't McLeod standing on the step, but a middle-aged man she'd never set eyes on before. He was wearing painting overalls, carrying a tool-box, and had the confident smile of someone who was sure that his arrival was good news.

'Miss Howard?'

She nodded.

'Dave Potter. Mac sent me.'

Crushing a disappointment so intense that she could almost taste it, she said, 'Did he leave something behind yesterday?'

'Sorry?'

'When he fixed the window?'

Startled out of his smile, Dave Potter glanced up, then said, 'Mac fixed your window?'

Concerned that his good deed might have got him into trouble, she said, 'In his lunchtime. Maggie Crawford is an old friend.'

'Oh, right.' Then, 'I don't know anything about that, he just asked me to redecorate the top flat. He said it was urgent. I've got some colour cards so that you can choose the paint,' he said, handing her a large envelope. 'Or if you'd rather have wallpaper Mac said to pick out whatever you want and leave the rest to me.'

Paint? Wallpaper…

'No rush,' he went on when she didn't reply. 'I've got plenty to do making good and preparing surfaces before we get to the good stuff. Do you want to give me the key to the outside entrance?' he prompted, presumably taking her goldfish impression for wordless appreciation. 'That way I won't have to disturb you with my comings and goings.'

Any number of responses to this question flickered through her brain, each one more scathing than its predecessor, but this poor man was innocent and didn't deserve any of them.

There was only one person she wanted to talk to and by a stroke of luck his number was faintly printed on her arm despite her best efforts to remove it. But then there had only been cold water last night.

'Can you give me a minute, Mr Potter?' she said as she reached for the phone and dialled.

She didn't give the wretch a chance to speak. 'McLeod,' she declared furiously the minute they were connected. 'I have to tell you that you are without doubt the most—'

A voicemail prompt cut in and she stared furiously at the phone for a moment as it invited her to leave a message, unsure whether to bang it, or her head, against the nearest wall.

'Mac's on his way to Scotland,' Dave said kindly, 'so he'll probably have his phone switched off, but he said to tell you not to worry about paying me. He'll put it on the bill.'

'He said *what?*'

'Maybe I misunderstood him,' he said, backing off as she turned to glare at him.

'No. No, I'm sorry. It's not your fault.' She lifted a hand to push back her hair, then, realising that it was shaking, tucked it under her arm. 'Scotland?' she repeated.

'Some family do, I think. All kilts and bagpipes.' Then, 'I'll, um, get on, shall I?'

Kilts and bagpipes?

Why was she surprised? He might not have a Scottish accent, had certainly been brought up in Melchester, but with a name like Gregor McLeod he clearly had deep roots in the Highlands…

Replacing the telephone on the cradle with great care, she took a deep breath and then said, 'Wait here. I'll get the key.'

If he wanted to splash out on redecorating the flat for Maggie to rent out that was entirely his business, whatever hopes he might harbour to the contrary. But since she'd spent half the night thinking about colour schemes, there was no reason why he shouldn't have the benefit of her advice.

She fetched the key and then quickly marked rooms to colours on the shade cards so thoughtfully provided.

'You might want to take up the revolting carpet in the hall too. A rug will look much better once the floor's been sanded and polished,' she said, handing them back.

Well, it would.

'That was unexpectedly painless,' Dave said, clearly impressed by her ability to make a decision without a single dither. 'That part usually takes longer than the work.' Then, 'What about the rest of the flat? Do you want the floors stripped everywhere?'

'I don't want anything, Mr Potter. This has nothing to do with me,' she informed him, ignoring all that middle-of-the-night planning. Deciding what furniture she'd throw out. What she'd keep and where to put it.

That had been all so much pie in the sky.

The flat came with strings and she refused to be manipulated by Gregor McLeod. She might be out of a job, but it was a temporary blip on the 'master plan.'

She wasn't going to run a bookshop. The minute she found someone to take over, she was out of here.

She certainly wasn't going to hold Maggie to her offer of the flat in return for a simple good turn.

Then, 'Actually, bare wood would be a bit noisy, don't you think? With someone living below. Every time you dropped something it would sound as if the ceiling was coming in.' She'd once had an upstairs neighbour with stripped floors and she knew what she was talking about. 'The rest of the carpet isn't bad. It just needs cleaning.' She gave a little shrug, attempting to distance herself from any decision. 'Probably.'

Dave just said, 'Yes, Miss Howard.'

She had the uncomfortable feeling that he was taking whatever she said as an order and, having a belated attack of guilt, said, 'You'd better clear it with Mr McLeod first. It might be rather expensive.'

For a moment he looked as if he might be about to say something, but in the end left it at, 'Yes, Miss Howard.'

'I'll bring you a cup of tea as soon as I've sorted myself out.' And she went downstairs, found the switch for the water heater and put the kettle on to boil.

Her mother was her next visitor, ringing the bell and banging on the shop door until she went downstairs and opened it.

'Hello, Mum,' she said, not particularly surprised to see her, although she'd thought she'd have left it until lunchtime. 'Won't you be late for work? Second time this week.'

'Second time in twenty years,' she corrected, 'but I phoned to say I wouldn't be in until ten. I just wanted to make sure that you were okay. Are you going to take care of the shop while Maggie's in hospital?'

'It's just temporary but she was fretting about it. And her cat. Not that I know the first thing about running a bookshop.'

Her mother shrugged. 'It isn't rocket science,' she said. 'How is Maggie?'

'Mild stroke, they think. They're doing tests. I suspect at some point she's going to have to rethink living here on her own. Maybe even let the shop go.'

'Maybe, but she'll do better if she thinks she got something to come back to. I'll pop up and see her this evening. We had a little win at bingo last night, that'll cheer her up.' Then, 'Have you had breakfast?'

'No. I thought I'd pop over to the bakery as soon as I get a minute.'

'You put the kettle on, I'll go fetch a couple of Danish.' She took a book from the new titles table and turned it over to check the jacket before looking around. 'You'd never know it from outside, but this is a great bookshop. Maggie always stocks crime books you can't get anywhere else, but it could do with bringing up to date. Most of them serve coffee these days, don't they? And snacks. But there's not much point in doing it up, I suppose. Not now it's all going to come down.'

'Come down? What are you talking about?'

'This part of the city. It's all very run-down now.'

'But it's the historic heart of Melchester. Surely it's listed? Protected? Where did you hear that?'

Her mother shrugged. 'Someone mentioned it at bingo last night. She heard from someone who knows a girl who worked as a temp in the planning department that it's going to be included in the new development plan.'

'Oh, right, just Chinese whispers. You had me worried there for a minute. Can you bring an extra pastry? There's a decorator working upstairs on the flat and I'm sure he'll enjoy one with a cup of tea.'

'Flat?'

'Maggie has offered me the top floor flat. It's rather nice, at least it will be once it's decorated. If I was going to stay in Melchester. I'd invite you upstairs to look around but Archie will have you sneezing all morning.'

'Archie?'

'Large, ginger and neutered.'

'That's a pity. Men are a bit like bicycles. You take a tumble, you need to get back on as quickly as possible before you lose your confidence.'

Slightly shocked, Juliet said, 'I thought that was horses.'

'Horses, bicycles…what's the difference? It's all just transport.'

'I haven't noticed any inclination on your part to take a trip. Was my father such a turn-off?'

'Your father…' She stopped. 'I'll go and get that Danish.'

That was two words more than her mother could usually be coaxed into and Juliet let it go. 'I could do with a loaf of bread too. And could you get some decent ground coffee and milk from the deli? Hold on, I'll give you some money.'

'Don't worry about that. You can pay me later. Tell me, this flat, is it tied to the job?'

'There isn't a job. I'm just helping out in an emergency, but if I've outworn my welcome you just have to say.'

The shop door opened. 'Are you open? I heard Maggie was in hospital, but I hoped to collect a book.'

'Come in,' Juliet said, ignoring her mother's grin as she left for the bakery. 'Let's see if we can find it for you.'

She had a flurry of customers who'd heard about the accident and were anxious to collect their orders. It took time to reassure them that the shop wasn't closing—at least not in the immediate future—and she still hadn't made it to the kitchen to put on the kettle by the time her mother returned.

'Don't worry, I'll get a cup at work,' she said, placing a carrier on the desk. 'Is there anything you need from home?'

'You don't have to run around after me, Mum.'

'You're going to be very tied on your own here.'

'That's true. I'd hoped to get up to see Maggie this afternoon, get some things settled. I'd be a lot happier if she'd let me get in touch with her son so that he can take responsibility for the business. But I suppose it'll have to wait until this evening.'

'What you need is a capable girl to help out. School broke up for Easter at the weekend and one of the women at work has a sixth former who might be interested in earning a few pounds. She's a nice girl. Reliable. Shall I ask her to come and see you?'

She scarcely hesitated. Maggie was getting her for free, after all. 'Please. The sooner the better.'

'Right. And I'll come and cover for you at lunchtime if you like. You can borrow my car to run up to the hospital.'

'You know you are a really terrific mother. I don't tell you that often enough.'

'Yes, well, just be kind to the poor old dear. She started first time for me this morning.'

'Did she?'

Her memory supplied an instant playback of McLeod demonstrating this trick. The self-satisfied pleased-with-himself smile men were so good at. The one that said, *Don't you think I deserve a great big…*

'Well, excellent!' she declared. 'Let's hope the old girl's still in a good mood at lunchtime.'

Her mother's quizzical look suggested she'd gone slightly over the top in her effort to shut him out.

'Are you all right, Juliet? You look a bit flushed.'

'Fine,' she declared, grateful to her mobile phone for ringing and giving her an opportunity to cut short the conversation. 'Absolutely great. I should be there and back in under an hour, traffic permitting,' she said, waiting until her mother had gone before flipping open the phone.

'Juliet Howard.'

'Hello, princess.'

McLeod. Why on earth hadn't she checked to see who was calling before she'd answered? Given herself time to catch her breath…

'I had a missed call and thought it might be you.'

'Think again.'

He tutted. Just how annoying was that? The arrogance of the man, assuming it was her. Implying that she was lying.

Why would she lie?

Why *had* she lied…?

'So, how are you?' he asked, breaking into the confused babble in her head. 'Did you manage to get any sleep last night?'

Sleep?

Breathe, breathe, she told herself as her brain scrambled to formulate a reply. Something sufficiently distant, cool enough to indicate that she hadn't spent one second of the night awake and thinking about him.

'Sleep?' she repeated, playing for time.

'You know, you lie down, close your eyes, and if you're lucky the next thing you know it's morning. You were supposed to be doing it on Maggie's sofa. So how was it? Were you warm enough?'

'Oh, *sleep*. Yes, I was fine, thanks. Archie made a great hot water bottle.'

'I'd have made a better one.'

There was no answer to that—or at least not one that she was prepared to contemplate—so she said, 'I do hope you're not using your phone while you're driving, McLeod. Even "hands off," it's terribly dangerous.'

CHAPTER SIX

THERE was nothing in Gregor McLeod's expression to betray the fact that he'd just had one of those 'light-bulb' moments—the flashes of insight that had made him so successful.

Safety.

Despite her apparent strength, her in-your-face, I'm-my-own-woman attitude, Juliet Howard—whether she was aware of it or not—was hooked on safety.

'Has Dave started on the flat?' he asked, making no effort to reassure her despite the fact that he was doing nothing more dangerous than sitting in the rear of the Rolls transporting him from the airfield; it wasn't his personal taste in transport, but it did such a good job of irritating his daughter's maternal grandparents that he was prepared to suffer.

Besides, if Juliet was worrying about him, it meant she was thinking about him. Since he couldn't get her out of his mind it seemed eminently fair that she should be similarly burdened.

'He's been at it since just after eight o'clock,' she replied. 'I'm sure Maggie will be very grateful.'

'I'm not doing it for Maggie,' he said. 'But then, unless you're not nearly as smart as I took you for, you already know that.'

'You think I'm smart?' Her ironic turn of phrase prevented that from sounding less like a plea for a compliment than an invitation to offer a put-down.

'Either that,' he said, happy to oblige, 'or so wilfully

pigheaded that you'll turn it down rather than risk being further in my debt.'

'Paint away, Gregor McLeod, if it pleases you. I owe you nothing.'

'Is that right? Then why are you taking me out to dinner on Saturday?'

There was a sharp intake of outraged breath before she said, 'Oh, go have a Highland fling, McLeod.'

And then he was listening to the dialling tone.

'Damn...'

'Is the bird with the posh voice giving you a hard time?' Neil enquired without looking up from the papers he appeared to be engrossed in.

'You could do with an update on politically incorrect labels for women, Neil, although I doubt that even in the dark ages of your youth Juliet would ever have been described as a "bird."'

Far from it. He might not have been overwhelmed by his first impression of her, but he was always ready to admit a mistake. His reward was her appearance at the hospital where, from the top of her glossy dark blonde hair to the tips of her designer shoes she'd carried the unmistakable aura of a successful career woman. He'd known enough of them to recognize the real thing when he saw it. So just what was she doing, out of work and with sufficient time on her hands to help out in a bookshop that was past its sell-by date?

Realising that Neil had looked up, was evidently waiting for something more, he said, 'She's an educated, elegant woman.'

'Then you really are in trouble. Don't say I didn't warn you.'

Just a touch too smugly, Greg thought, as he tossed the phone down beside him on the soft leather upholstery and picked up the architect's impression of the revamped river frontage that he'd been perusing when he'd been overcome with the need to hear her voice again.

That was one of the drawbacks of employing someone who'd known you since you were in nappies. They just had no respect...

'I'll bear that in mind when she's buying me dinner at the Ferryside on Saturday night,' he replied.

'She's buying *you* dinner?'

Well, that dealt with the smugness...

'You should pay closer attention when you eavesdrop.'

Neil shrugged. 'If it was a private conversation you wanted, you should have waited until we reached the hotel.' Then, 'You're not really going to let her pay, are you?'

'This is the twenty-first century, Neil. It's an equal opportunities dating world out there.'

And, having allowed himself a momentary smile of anticipation, he studied the mixture of conversions and new buildings that would front on to the marina development around the old dock. It wasn't, he discovered, quite enough to distract him from the thought of partnering Juliet in any kind of a 'fling.' Scottish country dancing had never been high on his list of enjoyable pastimes but suddenly he could see the attraction of the boisterous, body-clashing rush of an eightsome reel. The charge in having the waist of a flushed beauty beneath his hand as he whirled her around.

And he wished she was with him instead of his cynical right hand man.

But the city father's decision to announce the development area ahead of schedule meant he'd had to bring Neil along with him so that they could work around Chloe's party and he forced himself to concentrate. 'Mark Hilliard has done a good job. I don't see too many problems.'

'For the fee he's charging he should have the city lay down the red carpet for you.'

He allowed himself the smallest smile. 'That, Neil, is the general idea.'

'Well, don't count your chickens. Once your scheme becomes general knowledge there'll be objections from action groups dedicated to propping up every decrepit pile of old bricks in the country.'

'Pity none of them were taking an interest when Duke was letting the Prior's Lane area fall into disrepair even while he was hiking up the rents.'

'Talking of the blot on your bright new landscape, what are you planning to do with it?'

'The City would love us if we gave them some more parking spaces.'

Neil pulled a face. 'You could pave over half of Melchester and there still wouldn't be enough of those. They should be working on reducing the need for people to use their cars to come into the city.'

'Yes, well, Hilliard's having a look at how he can include it in the scheme. I'm seeing him on Friday afternoon.'

Juliet, still feeling a little shaky, went through to the little kitchen at the back of the shop and set about making a pot of coffee, tearing into the package of books that had arrived while she was waiting for the kettle to boil.

She couldn't believe she'd been so stupid. What on earth had she been thinking of, inviting McLeod to dinner at the most romantic restaurant in the county? Possibly in the entire country...

She looked at the cover of the book she was holding—a breathless and well-endowed beauty clasped in the embrace of a masterful Highlander wearing only a kilt and a plaid tossed over his naked shoulder—and dropped it on the desk as if burned.

A difficult customer proved a welcome distraction and by the time she got around to unpacking the remainder of the books she was calm enough to remember to hunt down the list of books that had been ordered and put some of them aside for the readers' group. It appeared to be good business and she wondered where they got together to discuss the books they'd been reading.

And suddenly the sofas and armchairs made sense.

Taking advantage of a quiet spell, she buckled down to work, going through the paperwork to see how the shop ran. Automatically making notes of what sold, bringing the cash in over the counter. What stayed on the shelves for months. Puzzling over the high postage costs. Letting her mind drift as she realised just how easy it would be to convert the rear of the shop into a proper lounge area where the buyers could stay to browse while they indulged in the high profit items of coffee and cake.

Was there a crime readers' discussion group? Surely, if there had been, her mother would have been a member.

If Maggie had been a client, paying good money for her expertise, she'd advise starting one, making a virtue of the fact that she concentrated on romance and crime. Shout it out loud by giving the place a makeover and turn it into the kind of specialist bookshop which fans of those genres would go out of their way to visit.

Dave's time would be much more valuably spent down here repainting the walls, brightening the place up. Or perhaps McLeod might be persuaded to put in some time for a good cause...

Her drifting thoughts were brought back into line by the arrival of Saffy, the student despatched by her mother. She had a nose stud, too much make-up and a miniskirt that displayed a yard of leg—just an average seventeen-year-old, in other words.

'My Mum said you needed some help,' she said.

'I do.' And, having laid down the ground rules and established the terms of engagement, Juliet—having banished the thought of having her rearrange the window display so that she could attract passing males as shockingly unPC—set about teaching her how the till worked.

'How're you doing, Maggie?'

'I'll be all right once they stop sticking needles in me and taking blood for tests. That nurse is worse than Dracula.'

'Well, you sound a lot better,' Juliet said, putting a carton of orange juice on the locker.

'I'll survive. How are you coping? Who's looking after the shop?'

'My mother's standing in so that I could come and see you. She'll call in herself this evening. I've taken on a girl, too, just temporarily in the school holidays. I hope you don't mind.'

'You do whatever you have to. I don't know what came over me asking you to step into the breach this way. But I'm very glad you did.'

'Blame Gregor McLeod, he put the idea in your head. He could see how worried you were. And it's fine, honestly. We curled up on your sofa and were cosy as anything.'

'You and Gregor?' Maggie enquired, with just the suspicion of a twinkle in her eye.

'Me and Archie,' she said firmly. 'I've brought your post—at least I've brought the personal stuff. The bills can wait a few days.'

'Better bring them with the cheque-book next time you come,' Maggie said, apparently resigned to staying put for the present. 'And these aren't personal letters—they're orders for books.'

'Orders? You sell by post? Is that usual?'

'Probably not, but I've been doing it for years. There was an American woman living locally who couldn't get books by her favourite authors and she asked me if there was any way I could order them for her. When she moved away she continued to order by post and it just grew from there. She told her friends about me and how great the service was and before I knew it people were writing and phoning from all over the place. Even Americans wanting books by English authors. Some people don't trust the Internet.' She handed back the envelopes. 'Can you deal with them?' she asked, leaning back against the pillows, clearly tired by the effort of talking. 'You'll find the special padded envelopes I use in the cupboard under the stairs.'

That explained the postage, then.

'Maggie, do you remember saying that you'd let me move things around? Make some changes in the shop?'

Maggie frowned, then said, 'Was it something to do with that wretched table?'

'Well, yes, but I was thinking of doing a little more

than that.' And she quickly laid out her ideas. 'I don't want to rush you into anything. Just think about it. We can talk about it in a day or two.'

'No, you're right. I've let things slip terribly. Maybe I am getting past it.'

'You're nothing of the sort. But you could do with some proper help, I think. You'll have the rent of the flat coming in to boost your income, so I'm sure you can cope with the cost of a temporary student.'

'What about you? I can't expect you to work for nothing.'

'It's okay. It's in the nature of a holiday for me.'

'It's not what I'd call a holiday.'

Juliet grinned. 'Well, maybe it's something of a bus-man's holiday,' she agreed, 'but I think it's doing me rather more good than lying on a beach somewhere.'

'Well, if you say so. But you'll need some money to pay this girl. You'd better ask the nurse for the phone trolley on your way out. I'll get my accountant to come in and see you.'

'Right.' Then, 'Oh, by the way, Gregor McLeod has sent someone to paint the upstairs flat.'

'Dear boy. He was a bit wild, you know, when he was young. Got himself into a lot of bother over a girl. But he's good at heart.' Then she smiled. 'And very easy to look at.'

'It's all right, then?' Juliet said, refusing to be drawn on whether or not she enjoyed looking at McLeod. Refusing to give in to her curiosity and ask what kind of 'bother'—the fact that he had a daughter suggested the answer. That 'girl.' 'I let the painter get started because you said yourself that it needed decorating but then afterwards I did wonder if I was doing the right thing.'

'From what I've seen of you, Juliet, I'd say you made a habit of doing the right thing, but you needn't have worried. Gregor popped in here at some unearthly hour before he flew off to Scotland to let me know what he'd done. He said he'd left you to choose whatever colours you wanted.'

'He did, but...'

But Maggie had closed her eyes. Whether she was really tired, or just wanted to avoid talking about the flat, Juliet would have been hard put to say. But it felt suspiciously like a conspiracy to her. They both wanted her to move in for their own reasons. Maggie, so that the shop remained open.

As for Gregor McLeod...

No. She wasn't even going to think about what he might want.

But he was right about one thing. The only reason she wasn't grabbing it with both hands was a pigheaded resistance to being manipulated. Or maybe she was just clinging to the pathetic hope that she'd be back in London very soon.

She had to accept that it wasn't going to happen. At least not in the short term. She'd already put her flat in the hands of an agent—well, her mother had—and she might just as well withdraw her name from the agencies she was registered with for all the good they were doing her. Give her whole energy to revitalising the bookshop. There was just one thing...

'Before I'm prepared to think about moving in, Maggie,' she said firmly, ignoring the closed eyes, 'we're going to have to discuss rent. And draw up a proper agreement to protect us both.' Getting no response, she gathered up the post and stood up. 'But

don't worry, if you don't feel up to it I can always get
in touch with your son and ask him to sort it out.'

'Don't you dare!' Maggie declared, her eyes open in
a blink. 'He'll have me into a retirement home before
I can whistle Dixie.'

'Not if I've got anything to do with it,' Juliet said.
'You're too young to put out to pasture and don't let
anyone tell you otherwise. But when you're home and
it won't disturb the other patients, I'd really like to hear
you whistle Dixie.'

Maggie chuckled. 'I wish I could oblige. I can't even
whistle a dog, but it's what my husband used to say.
He lived in America for a while and I guess some of
the phrases must have stuck.'

'You must miss him.'

'Not as much as I should, but then he wasn't the
world's best husband. It was hard on Jimmy when he
left, though. A boy needs a father.'

Girls need them too, Juliet thought.

McLeod might have been a 'bit wild' but at least
he'd made the effort to keep in touch with his daughter,
even though he couldn't have been more than eighteen
or nineteen when she was born.

Maybe she had been a bit hard on him.

Later, as she walked up Prior's Lane on her way to the
post office with a pile of padded envelopes, she found
herself stopping to look along the curve of the narrow
street, imagining how it would look with fresh, glossy
black paintwork all picked out in gold with every shop
decorated with hanging baskets of flowers.

What the area needed was some kind of traders' as-
sociation, she decided. An action group to regenerate
it. But those things didn't just happen. It took hard

work and effort from someone who wasn't working all the hours in the day to simply survive. Someone with the know-how to seek out grants from the government, from historical groups.

She did her best to ignore the little voice in her head that chipped in with *someone like you*, but by the time she'd joined the queue in the post office she was into full list-making mode.

A meeting venue was the first requirement. Leaflets to lay out the objectives and get everyone there, with a personal follow-up call to rally the apathetic. And then, once it had become clear who was prepared to help and who was prepared to nod through anything so long as they didn't have to do anything themselves, a very small committee…

Her train of thought was abruptly interrupted by the headline on the evening paper being read by a man ahead of her in the queue.

New City Development Area Announced

There was a photograph of the abandoned warehouses by the riverside docks. A sketch plan of the area involved. Frustratingly, he'd got the paper folded so that she could only see half of it. The half she wasn't interested in.

Surely, though, the rumour that her mother had heard had been blown out of all proportion in the telling. No one could seriously be thinking of levelling the historic heart of the city and replacing it with an office block or a car park? Could they?

The minute she'd despatched the books she dashed

across to the newsagent's to buy her own copy before heading back to the bookshop. It took just one look to discover that 'they' could.

The editorial described Prior's Lane as a 'shock' inclusion in the plan and, while welcoming the regeneration of the docks, the money and jobs brought into the city by the new office complex, the proposed marina, it anticipated considerable resistance to this further erosion of the 'city's historic past.'

'You can bet on that,' Juliet said.

Saffy looked up from a book she'd picked up and begun reading. 'Sorry?'

'They will be. If some get-rich-quick developer thinks he's going to walk all over us, he can think again.' Then, realising that Saffy hadn't a clue what she was talking about, she handed her the newspaper so that she could read it for herself. 'It's scandalous.'

'Why? They're just going to knock down a lot of horrible old buildings.'

'Not just a lot of horrible old buildings. Prior's Lane is included.'

'So?' Then, realising that this wasn't quite what she'd hoped to hear, 'I mean, it's a bit of a dump, isn't it? Who'd come out here in the cold and wet when you can buy everything you want in the shopping centre? And those cobbles are a nightmare to walk on in high heels.'

'Maybe, but they're prettier than paving slabs and a lot harder wearing.' But the girl's reaction made her think. She'd assumed everyone remembered it the way she did, but maybe not. 'I suppose you've got a point. There's not a lot to bring people out of the warmth of the new shopping centre. It's a real shame. There used to be some lovely shops here,' she said, describing the way it had been when she was Saffy's age. And sounding, she realised, uncomfortably like her mother when that same new shopping centre had wiped out the old High Street.

The girl didn't look convinced. 'So, if they were such neat shops, why did they close?'

'Yes, well, that's a very good question.'

Definitely one for the agenda. And, aware of the value of striking while the problem was fresh in everyone's mind, she wrote out an invitation to a meeting which, since she didn't have time to find a proper venue, she'd hold in the bookshop. Then, once Saffy had been to the library to get photocopies made, she despatched her along the lane to deliver them.

Her mother arrived as she was shutting up shop.

'How did it go?'

'Fine,' she said as she bolted the door, stretching to reach the one at the top. 'My feet ache, my back aches...actually just about everything aches, but apart from that I've had a good day.'

'In that case you can't have seen the paper.'

'I've seen it. I've already organised a meeting for tomorrow night.'

'Good grief, you don't waste much time.'

'No. From being unemployed and unemployable yesterday, I now appear to have two major projects on hand. Revitalising the bookshop and saving Prior's Lane.'

'You've got the work. Have you got a client?'

'Someone to pay, you mean? No, but there'll be plenty of publicity in the Prior's Lane cause. If I handle it properly it will demonstrate that I'm not the gibbering wreck that my former employers are implying.'

'Good thinking. And there's no reason why the re-

generation of the bookshop shouldn't do you some
good too. It's the sort of thing that the *Country
Chronicle* likes to feature. Combined with the fight to
save Prior's Lane, you might even get some interest
from the Sunday newspapers.'

It was rather lowering to discover that management
skills she'd always assumed were the result of hard
years of study and experience had probably been
learned at her mother's knee. A woman who'd never
had any kind of career. Pregnant and on her own by
the time she was seventeen, she hadn't had much
chance of that; she'd just had to take jobs that would
pay the bills and fit around child care. All the while
making very sure that her daughter had a better start
than she had had. That her life wasn't messed up before
it began.

Had her father been like McLeod? Young, scared,
running as fast as he could from the mess he'd helped
make? Except that McLeod hadn't run.

On an impulse she gave her mother a hug.

'Hey, what was that for?'

'Everything.' Then, 'Are you going to be home this
evening? I'm going to need some of my stuff. My
putting-on-a-front clothes among other things.'

'Come home with me now. We'll pick up some take-
out on the way and I'll help you pack while you tell
me what you've got planned.'

'How was the party?'

'Lavish,' Greg replied as he climbed into the car.
'Chloe's stepfather spared no expense.'

'Really?' Neil frowned. 'I thought you were footing
the bill.'

'As I said, he spared no expense. Not that I begrudged a penny of it. She's all I've got and I see precious little of her.'

'Well, that'll change once she comes south to university, won't it?'

'Reality check, Neil. Unlike you, I never made it to university, but I'm sure you didn't waste too much time hanging out with your dad.' Then, 'Tell me what's been happening on the Melchester front. Did the announcement go ahead as planned?'

'It did.'

'And?'

He handed him a sheet of paper. 'I took this off the Internet this morning.'

Greg found himself gazing at a picture of Juliet Howard with Prior's Lane in the background. It looked quaint rather than tired in the spring sunshine. And he noticed that someone had placed tubs of daffodils outside the bookshop to add some colour. Nice touch.

'You know who this is?' he asked.

'Yes. It's "trouble." The girl with the chocolate voice has used it to good effect, organising the Prior's Lane traders into a pressure group before the ink was dry on Wednesday's final edition. They will not, according to the editorial, be moved.'

'No?' Greg grinned. 'Damn it, Neil, doesn't she look amazing? I love that suit. It shows exactly the right amount of leg. Just enough to make you want to see more—'

'I fail to see why you find it so amusing.'

'I'm not laughing. Frankly, I'm lost in admiration.' Then, 'Come on, you've got to be impressed. How long did it take her to organise all this?'

'You're the genius, you do the maths. The development plan was in the Wednesday evening edition of the *Chronicle*. This was in today's first edition. Friday.'

'Less than forty-eight hours.'

'And she was on local radio this morning too.'

She didn't just look amazing. She was amazing. What on earth was she doing messing around in Melchester? Why wasn't she running some corporation? He'd give her a job tomorrow. Today. If she wasn't doing such a brilliant one for him in directing the professional agitators' attention away from the main development.

'What are you going to do, Mac?'

'Nothing. At least nothing directly.' He'd already run a check through personnel and made certain that she'd never worked for him in any capacity. But clearly she'd worked for someone. 'I want you to get on to one of those executive head-hunting agencies. Tell them that we're in the market for an experienced, well-qualified woman for a senior line management post. Late twenties, early thirties. Someone with a strong organisational background. See if her name crops up.'

'And if it does?'

'Email me everything they've got. And in the meantime get someone to check and see if the radio interview is online. I'd like to hear what she had to say.'

He just wanted to hear her.

'But—' Neil shrugged. 'Okay, Mac. I'll get on to it.'

'And remind everyone in the office that if the gentlemen of the press try to corner them their only comment is "no comment." The same goes for any nice people who suddenly want to buy them a drink in the pub. I've gone to a lot of trouble to see that my name isn't linked in any way with this project but now it's in the public domain there'll be people very keen to find out who's behind Melchester Holdings.'

'What about Marty Duke? He's just sold you the freehold on land that he didn't know was going to be included in the development plan. He must be spitting feathers.'

Greg grimaced. The same thought had occurred to him. 'According to my information he was ready to leave the country the minute the bank transfer went through, no doubt with a pack of creditors at his heels. Let's hope they haven't caught him. Yet.' Then, 'Is there anything else that needs my immediate attention?'

'Nothing that I can't handle.'

'Good. In that case I'm going home to take a shower and change before I drive down for my meeting with Mark Hilliard. I'll be at the cottage all weekend if you want me, but please don't call unless it's a real emergency. I've got a date with a beautiful woman.'

'You're still planning on having dinner with Miss Howard? Now that she's—she's…'

Neil made a vague gesture, apparently unwilling, in the face of his obvious interest in her, to suggest exactly what Juliet Howard might be.

'Leader of the opposition?' he offered. 'Tell me, my friend, why would I pass on the prospect of hearing from her own lips what plans she has for thwarting my ambitions?'

Neil was clearly shocked. 'Well, yes, but it's hardly ethical, is it? Especially since she's the one paying the bill.'

'Hey, can I help it if she thinks I'm just an odd job man?'

'She's going to kill you when she finds out and you know what? I'm on her side.'

CHAPTER SEVEN

JULIET paused in the entrance of the pretty riverside restaurant to catch her breath. The day had started early, long before the shop opened for business, and the queries, phone calls and offers of help from people who'd seen the paper had come in at such a rate that she'd scarcely had time to think, let alone breathe.

Half a dozen times she'd picked up the phone to call McLeod and put off dinner, pleading pressure of work. If he'd seen the newspaper he must know how crazy her life had become.

Even if he hadn't seen the paper, he would want to check up on Dave's progress. Wouldn't he?

Every time the shop door had opened she'd looked up, half hoping, half dreading it would be him, coming to see for himself what was happening. Offering to take a rain check on dinner. Or at least letting her off the hook to the extent of suggesting she relax, put her feet up in front of the fire with a glass of wine, while he went and fetched the finest Chinese take-out that Melchester could offer.

On her, of course.

She'd been torn between a completely irrational desire to see him standing there and the desperate hope that he'd keep well away until Dave had finished in the bookshop so he could see for himself how great it was looking. Then, no matter how mad he was, he'd have to admit that she'd got her priorities right.

Finally, just mad that he hadn't even bothered to ring

and confirm their 'date,' she'd gone completely over-board and was now standing in the doorway of the Ferryside in her highest heels, with her lashes extended courtesy of the latest technology in mascara and wear-ing the kind of little black dress that in London had been the height of sophistication but which, on a Saturday night in the provinces suddenly felt just a lit-tle too low in the neckline, just a little too short in the skirt.

And she knew she should have made that call.

What on earth had made her pick this particular res-taurant from all the hundreds there were to choose from in the area?

Because you wanted to impress him, stupid, that smug little internal voice that seemed to know all the answers offered far too readily. Demonstrate that you are a woman in control. A woman who can take de-cisions, follow them through…

No, no!

Okay, well, maybe just a little. But mostly it was the need to convince herself. Restore her self-confidence.

But the voice refused to shut up.

You wanted to dress to kill, it continued, to slay Gregor McLeod, to have him look at you and want you. To prove to yourself that you weren't still the pathetic little girl who'd trailed him around at break time, hop-ing to be noticed. Who'd walked on air for a week when he'd winked at you…

She put her hands over her ears to shut it up.

'Juliet? Are you all right?'

She jumped at the soft, gravelly voice, so close that she dropped her evening bag. McLeod stepped from the shadows beside the door, picking it up, his fingers touching hers as he handed it to her.

The dangerous thrill of excitement that rippled through her found a betraying echo in her voice. 'M-McLeod.'

'You sound surprised.'

'N-no. I didn't see you there. In fact I didn't expect you to be here yet. I came a little early to make sure…' He waited. 'Well, you know.'

'Have the maître d' take your card details to avoid any embarrassment over the bill?'

'It's how I've always handled business lunches… dinners…in the past.'

And this was business, she reminded herself. Buying him dinner at the Ferryside would cover all outstanding debts. At least until he'd seen the shop…

'And I came a little early because, since you rejected my offer of a ride, I wanted to be sure that you weren't sitting in the bar on your own.'

She swallowed, wishing she hadn't made that remark about 'business.' 'That's very thoughtful of you.'

'I'm a nice guy, Juliet.'

'Always ready to help out a damsel in distress. Kind to old ladies…' *Protective of little girls who were being bullied…* 'Tell me, do you take in stray dogs too?'

'It has been known. I even feed the birds in my garden,' he said, helping her from her coat and handing it to a hovering waiter as if it was something he'd done a hundred times. Completely at home in the quiet luxury of their surroundings. 'Is it politically acceptable these days to say that you look lovely? Since this *is* business?'

'Perfectly acceptable, thank you, McLeod. And so do you.' And it was true. He looked good enough to eat. His dark hair curled into his collar, sleek and glossy, the jacket of his suit sat across his broad shoulders as if it had been made for him, his tie was undoubtedly silk. He looked exactly *right*. Standing out, attracting attention only because he was the kind of man who would turn heads wherever he went, whatever he was wearing.

And yet…and yet… Despite the civilising clothes, he seemed, somehow, infinitely more threatening than he ever had in a pair of jeans and a leather jacket.

Then, blushing as she realised what she'd said, 'I meant you look smart. In a suit.'

There was nothing different about his grin, though. It still raised her heartbeat so that she could feel her pulse hammering in her throat.

'They won't let you in here wearing jeans.'

'No. Sorry. I hope you didn't have to buy it specially.'

'You slay me, princess.'

Well, mission accomplished, then. Easier than she'd imagined…

'You have a garden?' she enquired, firmly changing the subject.

'I sense just a hint of disbelief in your voice. You don't see me as a horny-handed son of the soil?'

There were some conversational gambits that were better avoided, she decided, offering no response other than slightly raised eyebrows.

He laughed. 'You're right, of course. A ride-on mower to keep the grass low enough so I can find the beer and a hammock slung between a couple of handily placed trees does it for me. We're over here.' And with his hand at her back he guided her in the direction of the bar.

She was not wearing enough dress.

She'd been concerned about the length of the skirt,

the neckline; she hadn't given a thought to the low cut of the back. Not that McLeod was being heavy-handed. On the contrary, his hand was barely grazing her skin; it was scarcely more than the transference of warmth raising the down on her back, cutting off all connection between her brain and her senses. Only touch was making it through; he had to be leaving scorch marks...

'Did you come in your mother's car? Juliet?'

'What?' Then, 'Sorry, it's rather warm in here.' She waved the little clutch bag she was carrying as if it were a fan. 'My mother's car?'

'That candidate for the scrapyard you were driving the other day,' he prompted. 'Or did you decide to play safe?'

Safe? This was *safe?*

'No. Yes...'

The truth was that she hadn't even asked. She felt too unsure of herself to risk the third degree on her 'date'; as far as her mother was concerned, she was tucked up in bed having an early night.

But she was beginning to sound like a complete idiot.

'That is, no,' she clarified with determined briskness. 'I didn't come in my mother's car. And yes, I decided not to risk the chance of having to fiddle with its innards and ruin my manicure. This was definitely an occasion for a taxi.'

'Well, I'm glad we've finally got that established. It means that we can have a drink while you tell me all about your plans to save the world from big bad property developers.'

'You saw the newspaper then,' she said, thankful to change the subject as he ushered her towards a secluded table. A waiter instantly appeared and began to open a bottle of champagne that was chilling nearby and she jumped even though he deftly twisted the bottle so that the cork made the most discreet of pops.

'You seem a little on edge,' McLeod said as he sat beside her. 'You're not nervous, are you?'

'Should I be?' Then, before he could answer, 'Are we celebrating something?'

'It isn't every day you appear on the front page of the *Melchester Chronicle* raising a standard to rally the troops against the onslaught of heathen developers. Definitely a champagne moment.'

'I don't think so.' She'd had it with champagne moments...

'Don't worry, this is on me,' he said, handing her a glass then clinking his own against it. 'To the heroine of the hour.'

'Oh, please. I'm just the traders' spokesman.'

'A little more than that, I suspect. I thought the daffodils were a nice touch.'

'Did you?' she said, taking just a sip of champagne before quickly putting her glass down so that he wouldn't notice how much her hands were shaking. It was a kind thought. A generous thought. He wasn't to know that it was her least favourite drink...

Daffodils, she thought. Just stick with the daffodils. They were a nice safe subject.

'Yes, well, I wanted to show Prior's Lane off at its best. Some really lush hanging baskets would have looked better, but it's the wrong time of year.'

'No, truly, I hardly recognised the place, but then the photographer did a really good job of keeping the background slightly out of focus so that the peeling paintwork didn't show.'

'It took a while to get it exactly right,' she admitted. 'Thank goodness for digital cameras.'

'And helpful newspaper photographers who respond to flattery?'

She began to relax. Even managed a smile. 'You are such a cynic, McLeod,' she said, risking another sip of her drink.

'Am I? Really?'

It was okay. After all, it wasn't the champagne that had ruined her life...

'I promise you, he was as shocked as I was to think such a historic area might disappear under twenty storeys of steel and concrete. And it was in both our interests to get a really good photograph.'

'Please don't tell me you talked him into providing the daffodils too.'

'What? Oh, no. Dave found me a couple of half barrels...' Damn! She hadn't meant to let it slip that he wasn't hard at work painting the flat. 'And I haggled with one of the market traders for a job lot of flowers. They were a bit past their best,' she added quickly, hoping he wouldn't query it. 'I got them for next to nothing. But then they're not sure where they're going to be shifted to either.'

'He's doing a good job? Dave?'

Obviously not quickly enough.

'He's been great. I meant to thank you.'

'I'm sure you would have done if we hadn't been cut off in the middle of our conversation.'

'We weren't cut—'

She stopped, took a breath—she was not doing at all well here—and caught the waiter's eye.

He stepped forward instantly, refilling their glasses

before rescuing her with, 'Are you ready to look at the menu, madam? Sir?'

'Thank you.'

'That was heartfelt, princess,' Greg said, even while admiring her diversionary tactics. Indicating that the man should leave the menus on the table—he wasn't ready to let her hide behind one of the huge leather-bound folders just yet—he continued, 'Anyone would think you hadn't eaten for a week.' Instead of doing her best to change the subject. And with good reason.

But then she had no way of knowing that Dave Potter had checked with him before allowing himself to be diverted from painting the flat. That he'd had chapter and verse on the work that was being done in the shop.

'Well, maybe not a week,' she said with a rueful smile, 'but the truth is that I've been rushed off my feet all day. I don't believe I've had more than a cup of tea since breakfast.' She paused as if to think about it. 'Actually, I don't remember having any breakfast.' Then, just to toss in a further change-the-subject conversational grenade, 'And, on the subject of political correctness, didn't I ask you not to call me "princess"? It gives the impression you can't remember my name.'

'No danger of that, Juliet.'

She was right, though, he was casual enough in the use of the standard endearments—'sweetheart,' 'darling,' 'babe'—and mostly for the reason she gave. Never 'princess,' though. That had come from somewhere deep inside his head...

'But don't wear yourself out over this,' he said, letting it go. It would come to him. 'At the end of the day you're going to walk away from Prior's Lane and the bookshop, go back to your real life.'

'My *real* life? It doesn't get much more real than this.' Then, looking around the beautiful restaurant, 'Okay, not *this*. But you know what I mean.'

'I know that if the people whose livelihoods are bound up with Prior's Lane don't care enough to fight for it, then nothing you do can save them.'

'But they do care. Most of them.' He raised his brows, suggesting she was being a touch optimistic. 'Obviously I'm not going to get too much support from the charity shops who are simply there on short leases. If the area becomes desirable again, they'll lose their sites.'

'In the cause of progress someone always loses.'

'If the place disappears under a megaton of concrete, everyone loses. They just need an outsider, someone with a fresh eye and time to organise the resistance.'

Or someone, Greg thought, who needed a cause to rekindle her enthusiasm, to restore her self-confidence, although seeing her sitting there, a picture of poise in a dress that would be responsible for an epidemic of cricked necks in the morning, it was hard to imagine what could possibly have brought her running back to Melchester with her tail between her legs. She certainly wasn't looking for another job...

'It's really hard for them,' she went on, when he didn't offer her any encouragement. 'They all work really long hours, you know.'

'Yes, I do know. I just hope they know how lucky they are to have you looking out for their interests.' And he finally picked up the menus, handing one to her.

It was her turn to stall as, clutching it against her, she said, 'Does that mean I can rely on you to help?

We've formed an action group and I've enlisted the aid of the historical society—'

'Thanks, but I've got a lot on right now.' And somehow he didn't think her 'action group' would take it at all kindly when they discovered she'd invited the enemy into their war room.

'Don't you care what happens? We know, more or less, what they're planning to do with the rest of the development site, but apparently the Priory area is a last minute addition. If you don't care about Maggie and the rest of them, try a touch of self-interest. Duke's Yard is included too, you know.'

'I saw the paper.'

'Oh, right.' She sat back, clearly disappointed that this tactic had failed. 'I thought it would affect you. What about your job?'

'I don't work there. I work for myself.'

'But I thought...' He could see what she thought. 'You answered the phone. You were driving one of their vans.'

'I bought it,' he said, leaving her to interpret his answer as she chose.

'The van?'

He was vaguely disappointed. If she'd called him he'd have owned up—had, in fact, done nothing to hide the truth—but it had just never occurred to her to see what was plainly before her eyes. You acted like an odd job man, you got treated like one...

'Among other things. You were right, Juliet. Marty Duke has gone out of business. I just happened to be there when you rang. The phone was cut off minutes after your call.'

'But what about the stuff you brought? The security grille, the alarm?'

'It would have gone into the skip. Forget about it.'

'Right,' she said, but she was frowning, clearly trying to puzzle something through that didn't quite make sense. There was hope for her yet.

'What did you think of the rest of the plan?' he asked. 'For the dock area of the city.'

'What? Oh, well, it sounds good on paper. I don't suppose it'll please everyone, but there's no point in clinging on to the past just for the sake of it.'

'No.'

She caught the wry edge in his voice and her eyes narrowed.

'I'm not a Luddite, McLeod. But there's a big difference between revitalising an area with exciting new buildings and burying the past under a multi-storey car park.'

'A multi-storey car park? Is that what's going to happen to it?'

'Well, it's just a rumour but you know how desperate the city is for more parking spaces and Prior's Lane is in exactly the right place for a new multi-storey. Right next to the shopping centre and all those new offices.'

'It looked to me as if the developer had made adequate provision for parking.'

As she shrugged the light gleamed off her creamy shoulders and it took all his concentration not to give in to the demands of his body and reach out, touch.

'Can't the planning office tell you what's happening?'

'They don't seem to have a clue. Or maybe that's just the impression they want us to have. And all the anonymous holding company that's fronting the development company is saying is "no comment."'

'Maybe you should consider picketing them,' he suggested.

'Oh, please. Me, my mother and Archie. That would really worry them.'

He began to laugh. Then, seeing that she was serious, quickly straightened his face and said, 'What you need is some sort of blocking mechanism to force them to talk to you. Maybe the history people will come up with some antique statute granting trading rights in the lane to the citizens of Melchester in perpetuity.'

'They're looking into it.'

'Good for them. In the meantime you seem to have got your hands rather full. How are you coping with the shop? I suppose you've had to forget about making changes for the time being.'

'Well…'

Juliet knew this was the moment to own up, tell him the truth. That she'd taken Dave away from painting the flat and set him to work painting the shop as fast as she and Saffy could shift books, reorganise the shelving. But it would all be so much easier when it was finished and he could see for himself that she'd done the right thing.

And even if he was angry with her, it would be too late for him to do anything about it. Other than send in the bill…

So she fudged it with, 'Maggie thinks the world of you, McLeod.'

He responded with a smile so lazy that it never reached his eyes, leaving her with the feeling that he knew exactly what she was doing. But all he said was, 'The feeling's mutual.'

'Then won't you help us? For her?'

'You don't quit, do you, princess?'

'Not when it's something this important,' she assured him, furious that he wouldn't get involved. And that he'd apparently forgotten her name again.

The casual nickname had charmed her as a little girl when she'd known no better, but obviously he used the same catch-all pet name for every girl he'd ever met. So much easier than having to make an effort. So much less trouble than getting a name wrong.

'And I hate to be the one to tell you this, McLeod, but your short term memory could do with some work. The name is Juliet.'

'And mine,' he replied, 'is Gregor. Use it and I promise you won't be able to keep me away from Prior's Lane.'

That wasn't what she'd asked him and he knew it.

'Really? You'd be prepared to spend all your free time envelope stuffing, making posters, organising petitions?' she pressed.

'Just say the word, princess,' he replied, deliberately baiting her with the meaningless endearment.

His face was shadowed in the subdued lighting, but his eyes gleamed with a touch of recklessness that made the heat rise to her cheeks as his voice, soft and low, issued a challenge to take the smart-mouthed flirting beyond words.

He only had one thing on his mind, she knew, and it wasn't Prior's Lane...

Maybe he wasn't alone.

Gregor...

She wanted to feel his name grate over her tongue. Whisper it softly, hear the sound...

'No. You're all right,' she said abruptly, hoping that the low lighting would conceal her colour. 'It wouldn't be fair to involve you. Not when you've, um, got a lot on.'

'Your decision. You can change your mind any time,' he said, his smile as slow as his voice. 'But maybe it's time we ordered. I suspect the maître d' would get seriously annoyed if you were to pass out from hunger. Very bad form.'

It was like the heat from a briefly opened oven door, she thought. That glimpse of something unexpected, the temptation to get her fingers burned.

The moment passed as quickly as it had come, but as she opened the menu Juliet knew that in laying out the possibilities, inviting her to take a gamble and put herself in his hands, their relationship had changed subtly and forever. Not because he would try and push her into something she wasn't ready for, but because he hadn't. He'd left it entirely up to her. And now every time she looked at him, called him McLeod, they would both know that she was thinking about what he'd said.

All she had to do was say the word.

Gregor…

She glanced over the top of the menu, hoping to steal a peek at him, and found herself looking straight into his clear blue eyes. It was a moment when she could so easily have abandoned all thought of food, grabbed him by the hand and simply run for the dark in a rip-your-clothes-off moment of naked passion.

And she knew why a girl could so easily have forgotten all her mother's wise words, her father's warnings and walked on the wild side.

Then he grinned, breaking the spell. 'Do you want to help me with this?' he asked as, abandoning his own menu, he moved closer and with his arm around the back of her chair, said, 'Us odd job men don't get taken out to French restaurants very often.'

She didn't believe for a minute that he was fazed by the menu, but she didn't actually care. The smooth cloth of his jacket felt good against her shoulder. His arm felt solid and protective at her back.

So what if it was an illusion? As long as she recognised it for what it was, straightforward sexual attraction between two adults with no pretence, no lies…

She shivered a little.

'Are you cold?'

He was looking at her, but suddenly she couldn't meet his gaze. 'No, it was just…' It was just as if a goose had walked on her grave. 'Well, maybe I should have worn something rather less…' The only word that came into her mind was 'revealing.'

Taking advantage of her hesitation, McLeod said, 'Less? Is that possible?'

'I think perhaps the word I was struggling for is "more" rather than "less." Something warmer.' And she managed a laugh. 'It's crazy, isn't it? Men go out for the evening properly dressed in a suit and a shirt, with a silk tie around their necks to keep out the draught. Women, on the other hand, seem to take it as some kind of challenge to wear as little as they can get away with.'

'Well, speaking for the men,' he said, bending to plant the gentlest of kisses on her shoulder, 'I think it's a really good system.'

CHAPTER EIGHT

'WARMER?' Greg asked, looking up, meeting her wide-eyed gaze as she struggled to find words to convey exactly how she was feeling, but the fact that she was finding it so difficult told him enough. 'You don't have to thank me,' he said. 'Central heating is all part of the service.'

It was cruel to tease, but it was just so easy to make her blush. Juliet Howard was such a muddle of contradictions. Cool, businesslike one moment. Floundering in confusion the next. And she was the one who'd insisted that this wasn't a date, something her dress denied with every clinging fibre, every inch of skin it left exposed.

She pressed her lips together firmly, refusing to be tempted into indiscretion and, ignoring him, gave her full attention to the menu, leaving him free to give his total attention to the way her hair slid over her elegant neck and fell forward to hide her face. The satiny skin of her back...

She glanced back, saw where his gaze had wandered and said, 'Keep up, McLeod. I want to eat tonight.'

'Yes, ma'am.'

For a while the conversation concentrated on nothing more disturbing than the merits of fish versus fowl, the remembered pleasures of good meals, sharing experience, getting to know one another. Easy, relaxing conversation. Relaxing enough, once the waiter had departed with their orders, for Juliet, back in control following that outrageous kiss, to venture into danger-ous, personal territory.

'So, McLeod,' she began, 'how was your trip to Scotland? Did your daughter's party go well?'

'Very well, if your idea of a good time is a crush of people eating too much, drinking too much and danc-ing to music of ear-damaging loudness.'

'To be honest, it's not.'

'Nor mine.' He smiled as if they were a couple of misunderstood grown-ups, in it together. 'But Chloe appeared to have a good time, which is all I care about.'

'Such a doting father,' she said, the unexpected wob-ble to her voice catching her unawares. Not entirely in control, then... 'I don't suppose for one minute you have a photograph of her?'

'You wouldn't be making fun of me, would you?' he asked, reaching into his jacket pocket and taking a snapshot from his wallet.

The young woman smiling out of the photograph reminded Juliet so much of McLeod at the same age that instead of answering him she caught her breath. She had that same heavy, dark hair with a wayward inclination to curl. The same vivid blue eyes. But none of her father's dangerous edge. Or maybe the formal, girls-in-pearls portrait with its innocent smile disguised deeper feelings. She would, after all, have inherited a streak of recklessness from her father. And perhaps her mother, too.

'You are in deep trouble, McLeod,' she said, hand-ing the photograph back.

For the first time since they'd met she saw him dis-concerted. 'I am?' He looked at the photograph, clearly wondering what she'd seen in it that he'd missed.

'Unless she joins a convent she's going to leave a trail of broken hearts in her wake wherever she goes.' Then, 'Obviously she takes after her mother.'

'Her mother has red hair, green eyes and freckles,' he said.

'Freckles? I thought you were a gentleman!'

He grinned. 'Okay, not freckles. Just a sprinkle of gold fairy dust.'

'Oh, for goodness' sake,' she said, slapping down a nasty little green spike of jealousy that wanted to be told that Chloe's mother had big ginger freckles all over her face. That yearned to be told that she, too, had fairy dust... 'It must be tough for you, her living so far away.'

'Not nearly far enough for her grandparents. They did everything they could to keep me away from her. And Fiona, of course.'

'The freckly redhead?' she asked, as he stowed the photograph carefully away. 'Obviously they didn't succeed.'

'Not for want of trying. You know, it's strange. I hated them for years, Fiona's parents. Never forgave them for what they did. But then, at the party, I saw Chloe in a clinch with some loutish youth and I finally understood what they went through all those years ago. Understood that all they wanted to do was protect her from the likes of me.' He looked up, smiled. 'It would seem that it's my turn to suffer.'

'You're a parent. It goes with the territory.'

'Yes, well, I've had it easy so far. Turning up once a month with some new toy she'd asked for, never having to play the heavy at bedtime, be the bad guy over homework, is a piece of cake compared with the real work of being there.'

'I'm sorry. It must have been so hard for you,' Juliet said, reaching out instinctively to lay her hand on his arm. Knowing that there had been another man his little girl had run to when she'd fallen and hurt herself. Who had been there all the time to read her stories. Who had just been…there. 'You did what you could. More than a lot of men in your position.'

'It wasn't enough.'

'No.' It wasn't just his little girl he wanted. It was her mother.

She carefully lifted her hand away and then, punishing herself, said, 'Fiona's parents stopped you from being together? Getting married? Or is that terribly old-fashioned of me?'

'If it is then I'm with you, but the only thing we had in common was that we were both eighteen and ready to have a good time. She was in her last year at St Mary's Ladies College with a place at Oxford hers for the asking. I was just finishing my first year of sixth form at Melchester Comp. Totally different worlds. She was all glossy hair, polished vowels and panama hats.' He glanced at her. 'Well, I don't have to tell you.'

She remembered his assumption that she'd come from the same privileged background. 'No,' she said. 'You don't have to tell me.'

It had been on her 'list.' Part of her master plan for life. To be one of those confident, always smiling girls with identical uniforms so that old or new they were all the same…

'I was the kind of boy that she'd been warned about all her life.'

'Bad boys, especially ones with motorcycles, have an apparently irresistible attraction for well brought up young ladies.'

'How did you know I had a motorbike?'

'I'd have bet my shirt on it,' she said, covering her slip with what she hoped was a serene smile. 'My best silk shirt,' she added.

'Yes, well, her parents clearly believed that I was entirely responsible. If they could have, they'd have had me arrested for the despoliation of a virgin. Not that she was. Those clean-cut, blazer-wearing good boys from St Dominic's apparently considered it their duty to relieve the St Mary's girls of that particular burden as soon after their sixteenth birthdays as...' He stopped, clearly thinking he was telling her something that she already knew. 'Yes, well, at least I was bright enough not to tell them that.'

'So, if not quite a Galahad,' she said softly, 'very close.'

He glanced at her, his brows drawn together in a frown. Then, 'If one of her friends hadn't gone out of her way to tell me, I'd never have known about Chloe.'

'You weren't still seeing her?'

'I was never part of her long-term plans, just a summer fling to celebrate the end of school, fill in the time before she went to Tuscany for the summer. The morning sickness must have really messed up her holiday.'

'I'm so sorry.'

'It's okay, princess,' he said, reaching out and retrieving the hand that she'd so briefly used to offer some comfort, his thumb absently rubbing across the back of her fingers. 'I'd like you to believe that I was broken-hearted, but in all honesty it wasn't anything more than a case of juvenile lust at first sight. Careless lust at that.'

She tried to obliterate the image of two young people in too much of a hurry to make sure they were properly protected. A sudden yearning to know how it would feel to be so utterly lost in desire…

'Why didn't she tell you herself? About the baby.'

'She always maintained it was because she was afraid what her father would do to me. I suspect there was an element of self-preservation mixed in with that. She was in enough disgrace without admitting she'd been playing on the wrong side of the tracks. She wasn't noticeably overjoyed when I turned up, demanding my rights. But I wasn't going to allow her, or her family, to airbrush me from the family tree.'

'It does you credit,' she said.

'Yes, well, my parents thought I was crazy. Told me I should be grateful for being let off the hook, run not walk away. They just didn't understand, refused to help. In the end it was Maggie who found out what I had to do, helped me get a court order for a blood test to prove paternity. Then, before it could be served, there was a For Sale sign outside the house. No one home.'

'So *that's* where you went.'

'What?'

She realised that her stress was all wrong. That she'd said it as if she'd missed him.

'You went after them. To Scotland,' she said quickly.

Then, 'Oh, no. That would have been easy.' He shrugged. 'Easier. I have family in Scotland, would have had somewhere to stay at least. But Fi only moved there when she married her laird, years later. No, I finally tracked them down to Ireland, where I had to start the legal process all over again. Maybe that's when they realised that they couldn't pretend I didn't exist. That I wasn't going to conveniently disappear.'

'You dropped out of school to pursue her? Gave up your own chance of a place at university?'

He shrugged. 'Some things are more important.'

'I doubt many eighteen-year-old boys would have thought so.'

'Maybe I wasn't cut out for an academic career. Anyway, I was eventually conceded visiting rights, allowed to spend one afternoon a month with Chloe in the presence of her nanny.'

'Once a month! That's monstrous.'

'Maybe. Maybe they thought I'd lose interest, that it would be harder for Chloe if she really knew me. Anyway, when they discovered to their undoubted surprise that I wasn't totally uncivilised, that despite my working class background I bathed regularly, knew how to use a knife and fork, things got a little easier. I was even invited to Chloe's birthday parties.'

'With faces as stiff as the frosting on the cake, I'll bet.'

'Only the adult faces. Especially the time I arrived with a bouncy castle in the trailer. But the kids loved it.' He grinned briefly at the memory. 'And I'm a stubborn bastard. No matter how chilly the welcome, I just kept going back.'

'And now they don't just invite you to the parties, they let you pay for them too.' She couldn't believe how much she disliked them all, sight unseen. 'I hope the welcome is warmer.'

'To be honest, I've never been able to quite work out if the bagpipes are to welcome me or are an attempt to drive me away.' And then, when she laughed, 'Maybe there were faults on both sides, but she's my daughter and I'd give her the moon if she asked for it.'

'She's a lucky girl.'

'Yes, she is. She has a family who love her and a father who'd...' He shrugged.

Die for her, she thought, filling in the gap.

'What about Fiona?' Juliet asked. 'How does she feel about having you around?'

'I didn't see much of her. She took a gap year to cover having Chloe, before going to Oxford as planned. Then she met Angus and maybe because they wanted to make a point, or maybe it was just because Chloe was bridesmaid, her parents invited me to the wedding. Now they have three little Rob Roys of their own.'

'A happy ending for everyone except you, then.'

'I'm working on it. What about you? I know you have a mother who drives a wreck of a car. What happened to your father?'

'A good question. Unlike you, McLeod, he didn't make a virtue of his paternity.' She glanced up as the waiter approached them, for a moment planning to snatch the chance to walk away from a pain she'd never shared with anyone. 'The truth is, I've never met him.'

McLeod waited until they were seated at their table and they were alone before he asked the question that had seemed to hang in the air for the long minutes while they were settled.

'Do you want to? Meet him? Get to know him?'

'It's difficult,' she said, picking up a fork, toying with the seared scallops she'd ordered. 'He abandoned my mother. Ran away. I can understand how scared he was, but she had the courage to defy her parents, insist on keeping me even though they refused to support her.'

'Brave woman.'

'Hardly a woman. She was even younger than Fiona.

I saw how she had to struggle, how hard she had to work, not just to support me, but to give me the kind of chance that she'd been denied. I could never feel anything for him but contempt.'

'But?'

'But...' She sighed. 'There are these great gaps in my life and no one to ask. If she doesn't already, you can be sure that Chloe will one day realise just how lucky she is that you're the man you are.'

'Thank you. I have sometimes wondered if my welcome would be quite as warm if my appearance wasn't always accompanied by toys.'

'Toys?' She laughed. 'I'd take a bet than you aren't getting away with Barbie doll accessories these days.'

'Your best silk shirt would be safe with that one. This year the car wasn't made out of pink plastic.' Then, 'I thought you were hungry. This is really good.' He offered her a sliver of smoked duck. 'Try it.'

It seemed the most natural thing in the world, taking food from his fork. 'Mmm...'

She caught his eye and realised how close he was, how intimate the gesture. Paul had never been so warm, so spontaneous, but then, he'd never wanted anything from her but the contents of her laptop. He'd gone through the motions, but in comparison with Gregor McLeod he was completely wooden. Which was bad enough. It was the fact that she hadn't had the wit to realise it that really hurt.

McLeod, on the other hand, made it clear with every look, every gesture that he only wanted her.

And she found herself struggling for breath.

'It's so subtle,' she managed, easing back a little, going for thoughtful. 'What is that flavour?'

'I've no idea. But then I don't actually care beyond

the fact that it does the job. I'm not going to rush home and try to replicate this dish in my kitchen.'

'You don't cook?'

'Not unless the alternative is going hungry,' he admitted. 'What about you?'

She gave a little shrug. 'Maybe women are used to cooking for themselves.'

'Just for yourself?'

She smiled. 'The chef could teach you a thing or two about subtlety, McLeod. But yes, just for myself. I was involved with someone rather briefly. It's over now.'

'That's why you came back to Melchester?'

'Who says I ''came back''?'

'You did. You told me that you haven't lived in Melchester since you left for university. You're looking for a job, somewhere to live. *Were* looking for somewhere to live.'

'I seem to have found myself plenty of work. Not that any of it's salaried.'

'Maggie's not paying you?'

'We're at something of a stand-off on the issue of finances. She won't even discuss a proper rent, so I won't let her pay me for helping out. And her accountant is practically blowing a gasket at the changes I'm making. He seems to think Maggie should shut up shop altogether.'

'Funny way to do business.'

'Well, I can't say I took to him, but he's got a point. My mother partners her at bingo, but she hasn't seen me for years. I could be anyone. I could be robbing her blind.'

'You should have told him how much a pane of glass

in that back window is costing you, that would shut him up.'

'He'd probably have had a heart attack right there and, believe me, I've taxed my first aid skills to the limit this week. He calmed down a bit once he'd run my name by a credit agency and checked out a couple of references I gave him, but he's still not happy.'

'He's an accountant, he's not supposed to be happy. What he should be doing is making sure the shop continues to trade. Whatever it takes.'

'Maybe he thinks that it's not worth it,' she said, 'since, unless we *all* make a huge effort to protect the area it's going to be under a car park by this time next year.'

He shook his head, a wry grin lining his face. 'Nice one. I wondered how long it would be before you got back to your favourite subject. So, tell me, what are you offering the planning committee?'

'Offering?'

'You want to save your precious little street, but you must see that it can't be left as it is?'

'Oh, no. Well, obviously it needs a total make-over. A fresh coat of paint, flowers...' Even as she said it, she realised it was nowhere near enough. 'Actually, I have worked out why it became sidelined as a shopping street. Shoppers used to have to use the old car park by the station and walk up to the town centre through Prior's Lane. The new shopping centre has its own car park that delivers the shoppers right to the door. And Saffy said something interesting—'

'Saffy?'

'A student I've got working in the shop. She wanted to know why anyone would bother to go out into the rain and cold when they could get everything they wanted in the mall.'

'So? Are you saying that it should be covered in some way?'

'I haven't a clue if it's even possible. We could really do with an architect or a structural engineer on board.'

'They cost money.'

'This is a community project. We're all volunteers.' She ignored his choked response. 'And of course we'd have to interest retailers in moving back. I've been doing some research...' She ran on for a while, full of ideas. Then, realising that he hadn't said a word in ten minutes, she stopped abruptly. 'I'm sorry. You're clearly bored to tears. It's just that I've been living this since I saw the newspaper.'

'I'll admit, retail trade is not on my conversational top of the pops when I'm in a romantic restaurant with a beautiful woman, even if it is just dinner and not a date. But you're right about one thing. Getting a few potential retailers interested will do more good than all the petitions in the world.'

'You're only saying that because you're scared I'll ask you to stand outside the bookshop with a clipboard.'

'I'm not scared. You can ask me to do anything, princess. If I don't want to do it I'll say so.' Then, with a lift of one of those expressive brows, 'Is there anything you'd like me to do for you?'

She had the uncomfortable feeling that they'd stopped talking about the campaign. But he couldn't possibly know about the shop. He'd have said something. Dave would have said something...

'Order pudding?' she offered.

He glanced up and a waiter appeared at her side instantly. She stopped him before he could begin to list what was available and said, 'Please just bring me something with chocolate.'

'Nothing for me,' McLeod said. Then, when the man had gone, 'So, tell me more about this brief relationship that caused you to bolt for home.'

'It was a relationship. It was brief.' He waited. 'He was a bastard,' she elaborated. 'Worse. I was a fool.'

'Since you're looking for another job, I assume you worked together.'

'You are way too bright to be an odd job man, do you know that?' He just smiled. 'You're right, of course. I made the fatal error of dating a colleague.' She shrugged. 'When it all goes pear-shaped, someone has to leave.'

'He was your boss?'

'Not *that* bright. I was his. Or at least I thought I was. When he ripped off my ideas and leap-frogged over me into the boardroom, I'm afraid I rather lost it. Now that really was a champagne moment.'

'You threw it in his face?'

'There,' she said, sitting back with a broad gesture. 'I knew it. It's just so predictable. A total classic. Put a glass of champagne in a woman's hand. Make a total fool of her in front of all her colleagues and, yes, it's Bolly all over the Armani and a swift departure with the contents of your desk in a box under your arm and seven years of hard work down the drain. He calculated my reaction, wound me up—'

'Juliet—'

'—and I performed to order. But my really big mistake was not stopping there. One glass of champagne was understandable. Grabbing a tray and flinging the

contents at the chairman, leaving him dripping with fizz
and treading the remains of the broken glasses into the
carpet, suggests you're heading for a nervous breakdown. Not just *persona non grata* at Markham and
Ridley, but an employment risk that no one in their
right mind will touch with a bargepole.'

'I'm sorry.'

'Why? It wasn't your fault.'

'I meant for ordering champagne. No wonder you
looked so horrified. I assumed it was because you
imagined I'd blown your entire budget before we'd
even looked at the menu.'

'No...' Then, 'I was afraid that after you'd gone to
so much trouble, so much expense, I might not be able
to get it past my lips without gagging. But once I'd
managed to get the shakes under control I actually
rather enjoyed it.'

'Maybe it's like riding a bicycle. You need to get
right back in there before it becomes a major problem.'

'How odd. My mother said much the same thing the
other day.'

'About champagne?'

'No, about—' She shook her head, but it was way
too late. He couldn't possibly have missed the meaning. 'What about you? There must have been some
significant other in your life besides Fiona?'

'She wasn't significant. Life changing, but not significant. But you're right, there have been lots of girls,
women. One, maybe two, that seemed important at the
time, but somehow didn't manage to clear the final
hurdle. Nothing recent. As you get older you get pick-
ier, I suppose.' He smiled. 'And I always had high
standards.'

She wondered if he was fooling himself. If the

mother of his child was the only person he could truly commit himself to, whether he realised it or not.

'What about the lunch date you ditched to come to my rescue?' she asked.

'I'm sorry to disillusion you, but I was planning to have lunch with someone who works with me. While Neil might appear to be a bit of an old woman at times, he does have a wife and small two children to prove otherwise.'

'Then why didn't you say so?'

As if she didn't know. How much more fun it must have been watching her tie herself up in knots...

He was saved from having to answer by the waiter arriving with an airy work of art created from spun sugar and chocolate.

'Good grief, I feel guilty even thinking about eating this,' she said, grasping any opportunity to move on, forget some of the things she'd said to him. Hope that he would too.

McLeod leaned forward, broke off an elegant filigree arch of dark chocolate and held it up to her lips. It crumbled as she tried to take it with her teeth to avoid touching him and, as she tried to catch it, her lips closed around his fingertips.

Time slowed down. Her heart, which usually went about its business without bothering her, thudded once, twice, three times against her ribs. Low in her abdomen, her womb contracted and every part of her felt soft, yielding, ready...

'There,' he said, putting his thumb to his mouth to capture a crumb she'd left, sucking it clean. 'It's easy.'

'Is it?' Her voice barely made it above a whisper. 'I've never found it so.'

And, as if answering a question she had scarcely

been aware of asking, he took her hand, holding it lightly between both of his. 'Life is too short to waste the simple pleasures, Juliet.'

Was it as simple as that? She'd spent all her life working. Pleasure had been for other people. And when she'd finally been tempted, her judgement—so lacking in practice—had completely failed her.

But she had nothing McLeod wanted other than the human warmth and pleasure of her body. Something that she knew he would give back in full measure.

A simple pleasure.

'Will you excuse me for a moment?'

He scarcely had time to do more than half rise before she'd walked swiftly across the restaurant. She left her credit card with a startled waiter.

'The bill,' she said. 'And will you please ask the receptionist to call a taxi to take us into Melchester.'

'But madam—'

'Now.' She didn't wait to see if he'd got the message but walked swiftly to the powder room, hoping that she'd find what she was looking for.

Her hands should have been shaking as she put the coins in the slot, but they were as steady as those of a heart surgeon. She really should have been embarrassed when a woman tidying her lipstick at the softly lit mirror caught her eye and smiled knowingly. Instead, as she dropped the foil packet into her bag, she smiled back.

She added an outrageous tip to the bill she signed, thanked the waiter for a wonderful evening and then dropped back into the seat opposite McLeod and picked up her spoon. 'I hope you don't mind passing on the coffee but we've got just five minutes before the taxi arrives,' she said.

'You've ordered a taxi?'

'Yes, Gregor,' she said. And looked up so that he couldn't possibly mistake what she was saying to him. 'I want you to take me home.'

CHAPTER NINE

GREG did not miss the significance of the deliberate way she'd used his given name for the first time. It seemed to purr off her tongue, soft as velvet, tugging at the hot desire he'd been doing his best to keep under control ever since she'd walked through the door of the restaurant.

He'd talked more than he had in years, telling her stuff that no one else knew, talking about the past to keep his mind from frying as he'd looked at her. This was not a date. It was just dinner. She'd dressed like that to punish him for behaving like a caveman and he wasn't offering any argument for the defence. At the end of the evening she was going to call a taxi and climb inside, leaving him with a last look at that sexy backside, those long legs, before waving him goodbye.

He'd spent the last four days with her continually on his mind. When had that happened before?

All his senses were working overtime. He didn't give a damn about the subtle taste of the food; it was the taste of her skin where he'd kissed her shoulder that was haunting him.

He could close his eyes and even listening to her talk about saving Prior's Lane—which right at this moment was his least favourite subject—was enough to make him hard. If he opened them the double whammy of seeing her soft mouth form the words made concentrating on what she was saying a tough call.

He had forced himself—he really did need to know

what she was thinking, planning—to the extent that he'd actually managed to drop in the occasional question so that he hadn't appeared a complete idiot, even while the combination of scents from her skin, her clothes, her hair had taken him close to meltdown.

Now she was sitting there, her liquid silver eyes regarding him so calmly that only her huge black irises betrayed what was going on inside her head and, with a single word, was offering him everything his overheated body craved.

But even while every cell was screaming 'Yes!' and 'Go for it!' something in his head warned him that this wasn't what she wanted. That it wasn't what he wanted, in his heart of hearts. When he buried himself in Miss Corporate Manager of the Year it would be because she was pleading with him for it, telling him she'd die if he didn't. Not because she'd coolly decided to take her mother's advice to get back on the bike before she lost her nerve and he was the lucky jerk she'd chosen for the ride.

He wanted her.

He couldn't believe how much he wanted her. But he wanted her boneless. Beyond reason. Out of control.

He refused to be just Any Other Business on the evening's agenda. She'd laid down the ground rules for this evening—dinner, not date—and now she wanted to break them. If he'd tried that he'd never have heard the last of it.

Easy to think, tougher to live with. He needed to cool down, give his body a chance to catch up with his head, and for that he had to put some distance between them.

'I won't be a moment,' he said, getting to his feet. 'Actually—'

He couldn't believe it. Was she really going to look him in the eye and tell him that he didn't need to visit the machine in the washroom because she'd already taken care of it?

As he waited hot colour streaked along her cheekbone and she shook her head. Whatever she'd been going to say, she'd clearly lost her nerve.

She wasn't quite as cool as she looked. And, as he stood on the steps of the restaurant, the chill air coming off the river the nearest thing he could manage to a cold shower, his heart lifted a beat.

When he returned she was still staring at the untouched dessert looking if not quite frozen with panic as near as made no difference. 'Shall we go?' he enquired, not bothering to sit down.

'But I haven't finished.'

'You're sweet enough,' he said, taking her arm and levering her to her feet without asking her whether she was ready to move or not. 'The taxi you ordered has arrived.'

'Has it? Won't he wait?'

She'd lost the bright flags in her cheeks, he noticed. In fact she had lost pretty much all her colour. Clearly she was having second thoughts. Back-pedalling that bicycle as hard as she knew how.

He recognised that, logically, he should have welcomed her change of heart. Just as he should have felt a whole lot safer as she wrapped her coat around her. It didn't work that way, he discovered.

With her long limbs, her pale skin, hidden away beneath ankle-length cashmere, his imagination went into overdrive as, somehow, what was veiled became infinitely more desirable.

And her sudden loss of confidence made him want

to take charge, make the decisions about where this was going. Toss her over his shoulder to carry her back to his cave and behave exactly like the caveman she thought him. All he needed was a chauffeur-driven limousine in which to carry her off...

As they emerged into the chill night he saw his car, safely dismissed and now out of reach, gliding away from the restaurant. His driver must think Gregor was mad. And as he'd handed him Juliet's cancelled credit card slip, disposed to pay the bill himself, it was obvious that the maître d' clearly thought one of them was; doubtless the size of the tip he'd received to compensate for complicating his bookwork would ensure that the man kept his opinion to himself.

He opened the taxi door so that Juliet could climb in. 'I don't want there to be any misunderstanding. When you say home,' he enquired, keeping his voice as cool, as expressionless as if he were negotiating a multi-million pound deal, 'do you mean your mother's house, or the bookshop?'

She hesitated a split second and for a moment he thought she was going to seize the escape route he'd offered her. Then, with an almost defiant lift of her chin, she said, 'The shop. I want to get an early start in the morning.'

He walked around the cab and gave the driver directions before climbing in beside her.

'Buckle up, Juliet,' he said, fastening the seat-belt that would keep a safe distance between them.

She wrapped the belt around her and drove the connection home with rather more than necessary force.

Did she imagine that he was going to make a grab for her the moment they were in the back seat? Sweep her off her feet so that she wouldn't have to listen to those second thoughts?

Tempted as he was, this was her game plan and she was going to have to call all the moves. He wasn't going to make it easy for her.

'Thanks for a great meal,' he said. 'The restaurant is lovely.'

'I'm glad you enjoyed it.'

Glad? Juliet could not believe she'd just said that. No, she couldn't believe he'd said that. She was a seething mass of conflicting desires and emotions and he was calmly saying that he'd enjoyed the meal.

'The duck was something else.'

How dare he be talking about food, *thinking* about food, when she couldn't actually remember a single thing that had passed her lips? All she could recall was the taste of chocolate. And his skin.

'You said,' was all she could manage in reply.

In a moment of bravado, of absolute certainty that she could carry this off, she'd said 'the word' and in doing so had all but offered herself to him on a plate. For dessert.

Gregor.

She was right, the word had felt good in her mouth. Soft as a Highland mist. Hard as granite. And now she was sitting beside him while the taxi sped them towards the city centre. She didn't care what he thought of the wretched duck. She just wanted his hands on her, his mouth doing unspeakable things. Her mouth…

And without warning the entire pretence that the evening was no more than a settling of debts collapsed like a house of cards.

Maybe it was the sudden shock of cold air as they'd walked from the restaurant to the car but that first I-can-do-this adrenalin rush had stalled somewhere between the chocolate and the chill of the taxi.

Or maybe it had just been his cool acceptance, almost as if he was doing her a favour. As if he didn't have to put in any effort to make her feel just a little bit special. It sent a chill through her. Did he imagine she did this regularly?

Did he have no idea how big a deal this was for her?

Damn him, he was sitting there, totally detached, looking out of the window, for Pete's sake, instead of at her. Touch me, she pleaded silently, begging him to read her thoughts. Just touch me. You're good with engines. Do something to jump-start my heart. Make it purr the way you did my mother's car.

He'd been flirting with her non-stop since she'd called Duke's number and he'd picked up the phone— and why had he done that if he was just buying a van?—but now he seemed more interested in the passing view of the river. The old warehouses.

What was the matter with him?

What was the matter with her?

She'd given him the green light, so why wasn't she wrapped in his arms right now, being kissed senseless before any niggles of doubt could set in? Wasn't that what men did?

Not Gregor McLeod, evidently, since they had enough clear air between them to allow not just a niggle but an entire phalanx of doubts to march between them.

How had she got so lucky?

In her dreams, this was the moment when he was supposed to look into her eyes and remember her, remember the day he'd truly been her knight and then...

No, even she wasn't that foolish.

She was bright enough to know that she was nothing more than a substitute for the woman he could never have. The St Mary's girl with the privileged background and the perfect vowels; his real 'princess.' She was simply a fake version, one whose mother had moulded her speech until it was indistinguishable from the real thing, assuring her that it would be worth it because she was going where the girls who mocked her would never be able to follow.

And she had been right. An ancient university, a first class degree, a career built on solid foundations. They had all been hers.

But those other girls had something else that she longed for. Men who loved them, children, the security of a proper family. All dreams that for her had somehow fallen on the 'downright impossible' side of the list because she'd never trusted anyone enough to let go of the safety rail.

But this was different. She wasn't asking for, expecting, a huge happy ever after, but just one night to fill the aching void. To hold close and cherish. Surely she was entitled to a tick beside one little dream?

Not in this life, apparently, and she said, 'So that's it, then. All debts paid.'

He glanced at her. 'Except for the coffee.'

'Coffee?'

'And the decorating. You are going to invite me in for coffee, aren't you? Show me how well Dave is doing fixing up the flat for you. I assumed that's why you rushed me out of the restaurant.'

Oh, good grief! She hadn't given a thought to the flat when she'd been whispering 'Gregor' across the table in a very bad imitation of some nineteen-thirties silver screen vamp. The flat actually looked worse than

when she'd first seen it. The hall carpet ripped up.
Blotches where Dave had made good the plaster. The
paintwork rubbed down and undercoated...

'That was so bad mannered of me. I didn't even ask
you if you wanted coffee or a brandy. I don't know
what I was thinking about.'

'Don't you?'

She swallowed. At least it was dark in the rear
of the taxi and this time he couldn't see her blush.
Then she thought about it. 'Hold on. Weren't you the
one who was in a tearing hurry, Mr "You're-sweet-
enough"?'

Greg managed a careless shrug. 'The meter was running on the taxi.'

He heard her shuddering sigh.

'Are you cold?'

'I'm fine.'

She was far from fine and it required every ounce
of will-power to stop himself from abandoning the
seat-belt, wrapping her up in his arms and warming her
to the point where spontaneous combustion was guaranteed. His only hope of behaving in a manner that
ensured he'd be able to look himself in the mirror in
the morning was to keep his distance. God bless whoever made back seat seat-belts compulsory.

'Maybe you should think about investing in some
thermals to go with that dress.'

'There isn't room for me and thermals in here,' she
pointed out, with just enough edge to let him know that
she was not amused. Better, he thought. Much better.

And much worse. He was now unable to think about
anything but the kind of skimpy underwear that *would*
fit in there with her.

A thong. It had to be a thong. A tiny black lacy

thong snuggled up tight against her body. Right where his hand should be.

And precious little else.

'I noticed,' he said, completely unable to stop himself. 'But since you shrink-wrapped yourself in lycra presumably that was the intention. I imagine you did want every man in that restaurant leering at you?'

'Every man?' she asked. And as they passed a street light he saw that her mouth was fighting a smile.

'Nearly every man,' he corrected. 'I wouldn't be that obvious. And there was a gay couple in the corner who didn't even notice you.'

'Rubbish,' she declared. 'This is a designer dress. They watched it every step of the way across the dining room as we left and I'm telling you that it wasn't the food they were drooling over.'

So it was the fact that he could actually remember what he'd eaten that bugged her, was it? Just as well that she didn't know the only reason he remembered the duck was because he'd watched her lips closing around his fork.

'Drooling? Oh, please…' And they'd seen it from the front. He'd been following her. There wasn't going to be enough cold water in the entire world… 'But then it is what they call a "result" dress, isn't it?'

'Excuse me?'

'A follow-me-home-and…'

'It's shoes, Gregor,' she said, before he could say the words. '"Result" shoes.' And, as he glanced down at her feet, 'And if you value your life, I suggest you keep whatever you're thinking to yourself.'

'I was merely going to remark that you're wearing very pretty shoes.' Then, because looking himself in the eye in the mirror in the morning was something he'd worry about tomorrow. 'And they worked. You've got a result. You're home. And I'm right behind you.'

Before Juliet could begin to think of a reply, the taxi stopped behind the shop. And what was she so outraged about? She had dressed to turn him on. Make him look. Make him want to touch. Damn it, she wanted to drive him so crazy that he wouldn't be able to help himself.

The driver opened the door for her and as she stepped on to the pavement she opened her bag to pay him. Gregor beat her to it and dismissed him.

'You might regret doing that, McLeod,' she said as the car eased quietly away down the narrow lane, leaving them alone in the tiny pool of light from above the door.

'I don't think so.' He held her gaze. 'Your key.'

She took it from her bag and handed it to him, a bundle of confused uncertainties, yearnings, muddled desires. If he would just touch her, put his arms around her and kiss her, everything would be so simple, so easy. But it was as if he was waiting, almost demanding that she make the first move.

Gregor unlocked the door, pushed it open, flipped off the alarm, before standing back to let her in ahead of him.

Juliet was instantly assailed by the smell of fresh paint.

About to reach for the light switch, she let her hand fall and, turning back to him said, 'Gregor... I have a confession to make.'

'Tell me later,' he said, and before she could explain about Dave, about how painting the shop was so much more important than her flat, about how she had been going to tell him just as soon as she was sure he'd be reasonable about it—well, okay, as soon as it was finished—he carried her back against the wall, pinning her there with his body. 'All I want to hear from you right now is one word.'

She went rigid with shock.

No! This wasn't how it was meant to be…

'It won't wait…'

His hands were inside her coat, pushing up the hem of her dress as they slid up her thighs.

Oh…oh…

'About the flat…' she persisted.

His palms slid over the silky stockings, encountered the lacy tops of the hold-ups she was wearing and he made a small guttural sound deep in his throat that tugged at something deep within her…

Oh, yes…

'About Dave…'

His mouth grazed the neckline of her dress, leaving a moist trail over the exposed cleavage and, instead of pushing him away, demanding to know what the heck he thought he was playing at, she whimpered for more, tipping her head back against the wall in an open invitation to help himself.

'About the shop…'

She was beginning to lose track of what she was saying as her insides began to dissolve—

'The painting…'

—settling into a low ache as, encountering no obstacle, he cupped her naked rear in his hands and lifted her against him, holding her there so that she could feel his arousal.

'You talk too much, princess,' he said, his voice a little ragged as he lifted his head to look down at her.

No man she'd dated had ever bypassed the opening

moves in such an outrageously brazen, utterly sexy manner. Her mouth was full and swollen and, without thinking, she licked it to try and cool it. She wanted him to peel off her dress, wanted him on his knees…

'Gregor,' she said, his name an unmistakable plea. The only light came from the window display at the far end of the shop, yet his eyes glittered like hot stars. 'Please…'

'Tell me what you want, Juliet.'

Greg knew he was crazy. She was saying 'please' in a way that no man could possibly misinterpret. He could feel her body yielding to him, feel it softening, opening, the soft little sounds she was making in the back of her throat. No doubt. All he had to do was kiss her and she'd dissolve, crumple up right here on the floor if that was what he wanted.

And still he held back, offering her a way out, giving her a chance to think again.

Why?

She wasn't some nervous virgin who didn't know whether she wanted this or not. He'd never been interested in those. He'd liked women who knew what they wanted and weren't afraid to show him. Juliet was a grown woman and they'd both known where this would end the minute they'd started baiting one another with verbal foreplay.

He had his hands full of hot, sexy womanhood. She knew exactly how he was feeling right now and she wasn't exactly pushing him away. This should have been so damned simple.

But it wasn't.

And he didn't know why.

Except, except…

'I need to know that this is what you want.'

Her response was to lift a hand, lay it along his cheek. She was trembling, he realised. Not with fear, because if she'd been afraid she would have been rigid in his arms, would not have been openly encouraging his mouth on her breasts. She was trembling with desire and knowing that made him feel ten times, a hundred times stronger, more powerful than he'd ever felt in his life. And still he waited, doing nothing to encourage her, nothing to discourage her.

He wanted her to know that despite his sudden lapse into the kind of machismo behaviour that he despised, that was an invitation to any self-respecting woman to show him the door, he was not so lost to his own needs that he wouldn't step back if that was what she wanted.

As if rewarding him for his patience, she lifted her other hand so that she was cradling his face. And then she lifted her mouth to his and kissed him very gently.

It was the sweetest kiss.

The kind that an innocent teenage girl might bestow on her first boyfriend. All soft, trembling lips. Uncertain longings. The kind that would be wasted on a hot, horny youth who had only one thing in mind. The kind that could steal a man's heart. She couldn't begin to imagine how much it cost him to hold back, allow her to take the lead, set the pace. Had no way of understanding that her tenderness was burning him up in a way that not even the hottest of kisses had ever achieved.

Then he realised that her face was wet, that tears were pouring down her cheeks and mingling with their lips. And at that point he knew that he was a fool. This wasn't a game. This was something beyond his imagining and if he couldn't have her, make her his—if not now, then one day when he'd earned her trust—he would surely die.

And remembering his earlier arrogance, his determination that he wasn't getting this close to the lady until she was the one who was pleading with him for fulfilment, he felt utter shame. Knew that at this moment he deserved nothing more than that she step back from her kiss and advise him to call a taxi because the evening was over.

CHAPTER TEN

'JULIET?'

Greg could no longer bear the silence. He was the one begging, on his knees inside his head, if not in reality.

Then in the faint glimmer of light seeping through to the rear of the shop he saw her smile and she said, 'Can you wait for coffee?'

Juliet opened her eyes. She felt reborn. New.

For once in her life she hadn't thought about anyone but herself. Her mother, her tutors, the company…

All her life she'd been trying to please someone else and last night she'd taken the risk, stepped off the edge and taken the decision to please no one but herself.

Above her the hideous black ceiling was blocked out by her beautiful, tender, unbelievably sexy knight, the slayer not just of her playground dragons but of her personal ones too. The low early morning sunlight shimmered off his naked shoulders and, unable to resist touching him, she trailed her fingers along the line of his collar-bone until she reached the little hoop of bone in the centre. Then she changed direction, moving down…

He caught her hand before she could do any serious damage. 'Princess, we have to talk.'

'Do we, McLeod?' she responded archly.

'Damn it, woman, don't start that again. I promise

163

you, I've never called another woman "princess" in my entire life.'

The sun edged behind a cloud.

Let it go, her subconscious warned. She was good at that. Not asking the important questions all her life. Avoiding hurt. Last night all that had changed.

'Never?' she challenged.

'Never,' he responded.

Only someone who knew it to be a lie would have recognised the millisecond pause before he replied for what it was. A man deciding whether to tell the truth or lie. And deciding on the latter.

Why was she surprised? Why did it even matter? It was just a little wriggle of a white lie to cover his slip. To make her feel special. He'd warned her that he wasn't Galahad.

What was the big deal?

He was just one more thing on the 'want/need/do' list of her life, after all. One perfect night in the arms of Gregor McLeod. All right, so that wasn't what she'd written in her notebook, but then she'd only been thirteen. A stupid, romantic, skinny kid who had known no better.

Whatever she'd written then, this was now. Last night had been no more than one more tick on her master plan, another brick in the wall of her ambitions.

So why was her heart crumbling into pieces?

'Juliet, Juliet, Juliet…' He repeated her name, lifting her hand to his lips, kissing her palm, and a quiver of hot desire rippled through her. 'Please—'

'Sorry, McLeod,' she said, never more grateful for the interruption of the shop doorbell. Nothing else would have saved her from the heat of desire burning in his eyes…that at least had been real. 'I'm afraid that's my mother.' And, reclaiming her hand, she flung back the bedclothes and began gathering his scattered clothes. 'She's helping me in the shop today.'

He rolled on to his side to watch her and suddenly she felt naked, exposed...

'I could help too. Then we could talk.'

Talk? Oh, sure, she really believed he wanted to talk.

She dropped his clothes beside him on the bed. 'The, um, debriefing will have to keep, I'm afraid. You're not on my to-do list today.'

He didn't move, watching her as she wrenched open a drawer in her hunt for clean underwear. She gave up on a bra and scrambled into a pair of jeans and a sweat-shirt.

'You've got the top on inside out,' he said.

She was half out of it before she realised that she hadn't. 'Oh, very funny...'

'You can't blame a man for wanting to keep you naked. Tell your mother that something more urgent came up.'

He wasn't even ashamed of himself. He was lying back, his hands behind his head, as if he was planning to stay in her bed all day. To just lie there waiting for her to come back so that they could continue where they'd left off and she felt the warm, heavy drag of desire respond to his arousal. That was the trouble with temptation. Once you'd surrendered to it, it was so much harder to say no. That was why she had to get away. Before she was irretrievably hooked.

'I thought you wanted to talk,' she said, looking away as she hunted for shoes. Anything to take her mind off what her body was telling her.

'I do. We'll fool around a little, talk a little, eat a little... We've got all day.'

'You may have. I've got work to do. Use the back stairs when you leave. They'll take you straight down to the street,' she said. 'Just watch out for Dave's ladders in the lobby. I'm already fully booked for hospital visiting.'

'What's she doing in the shop? Your mother.'

'Just giving me a hand to get it into shape for tomorrow.'

'If there's heavy lifting to be done you'll need me.'

'You're wearing a suit, McLeod.' A very expensive suit. Not that the designer's signature had come as much of a surprise. He rode a Harley, drove a vintage Jaguar, and while she'd never been to a party in a castle she was quite sure that they didn't come cheap. He might work for himself, but it certainly wasn't as an odd job man. Gregor McLeod was a lot more than that. She'd only kept taunting him with it in the hope that he'd tell her what he actually did.

But he hadn't. He'd told her the melt your heart story about his daughter and it had done the job. But he hadn't told her anything about himself. What he did now.

The omission told her everything she needed to know. Not that it mattered.

'I'll go home and change.'

'No!' Then, 'You don't understand. Mum will take one look at you and she'll know…' She swallowed.

'What? That we spent the night together? You're not a kid, Juliet.'

'It isn't that.' He frowned. 'It's just…'

'What?'

Why on earth did she have to explain? He'd got everything he wanted. In her admittedly limited experience hanging around to 'talk' after a night of hot sex was not on most men's agenda.

'I've already made a total mess of my life. She was the one who picked up the pieces and got me moving again. She'll take one look at you and see the kind of man that any sensible, level-headed woman—any *sane* woman—would run a mile from. She'll take one look at you and send for the men in white coats. Let's face it, McLeod, you're bad.'

He pretended to look offended. 'No, I'm not. I'm very, very good. You told me so any number of times last night.' He grinned and, putting on a feminine voice, he said, '*Oh, Gregor. Oh, yes! Oh, you're so goooooood…*'

Juliet blushed. '*Please…*'

'You are totally irresistible when you beg. Did I tell you that?'

'I didn't…'

'You're sure?' And the flash of mischief in his eyes suggested that he was considering a reprise of that too.

'Will you please *go?*' Then, 'This is begging, McLeod. You can't resist, remember?'

'Give me a kiss and I'll think about it.'

'Joo-o-o-ls…' Her mother's insistent call saved her from the temptation. She glanced out of the window and saw her mother standing back from the street door, looking up. 'Are you awake?'

She leaned out and called down, 'Hold on, I'll be right there.' She picked up her keys and avoiding looking at Gregor, she said, 'I've got to go.'

Greg was out of bed and blocking the door before she was halfway across the room.

He was the screw-up, not her, and he wanted her to know that. He'd thought he was so damned clever with his teasing. Thought this was just a sweet interlude with someone who, for once, wasn't looking at him as a meal ticket or wanting a job. He could just relax, enjoy himself. Help out an old friend and indulge a pretty woman…

Last night he'd recognised that he was fooling himself. From the first time he'd heard her speak, from the moment she'd brushed off his come-on with the derision it deserved, he'd known it was a whole lot more than that. This was not just another flirtation. This was different. Being with her, making her happy, was more important than anything else and he had to tell her that. Tell her everything.

He had thought he'd have all day to tell her the truth. Explain. Time between making love to her, sharing breakfast in bed, cramming once more into a shower so tiny that the water had barely room to seep between their bodies.

'Let me go, McLeod.'

Now she was calling him McLeod again. His mistake, calling her princess when she was alert enough to notice. She hadn't objected when she was so lost to desire that he'd thought they'd both go up in flames. In fact, he was sure she didn't mind at all, just enjoyed the verbal jousting. Was using it now just to distance herself from him and why would she do that?

'No, just hold on a damn second here. *Jools?*' If he could just make her laugh… 'I get earache for calling you ''princess'' and you allow your mother to call you ''*Jools*''?'

'She's earned the right to call me whatever she wants. Stand aside, McLeod.'

Not so much as a smile. 'That's it?' he said with a touch of desperation as he felt something precious slip-

ping away from him. 'Dismissed without so much as
a kiss?'

'No kiss,' she said, looking him straight in the face.
'I bought you dinner. All debts are settled in full. Don't
make a noise when you leave.'

Nothing had ever sounded more final. More like
goodbye.

Then she wasn't looking at him. She wasn't looking
anywhere and, as she fumbled for the door handle, she
lost her grip on the shoes, dropping one.

They both stooped to pick it up but he was margin-
ally faster and, as he handed it to her, she looked up,
her eyes glistening and said, 'Thank you.'

Juliet stumbled down the stairs and unlocked the door,
letting her mother in.

'Good grief, Jools, you look terrible.'

'Sorry, I overslept. It was a long night.' Long, beautiful and, inevitably, heartbreaking...

She had fooled herself into believing that a single
night would be enough. The temptation of a long, lazy
day had shown her just how wrong she had been. It
was going to be hard enough to cope with the fallout
from this, move on. If she allowed herself to indulge
in a whole day spent in Gregor McLeod's arms she
would never recover from the pain of losing him. She
cleared her throat.

'Do you want to put the kettle on while I go and
feed Archie?'

'You're overdoing it, Jools.'

'No, I need to keep busy. I was thinking about putting together a proposal for one of those self-help
books for women,' she rattled on quickly, whether to
distract her mother or herself she couldn't have said.

'You know, time management for your busy life.' She barely paused for breath. 'And maybe I could do some rather more basic articles for the women's magazines. I've been doing some research...' She would do some research... 'What do you think?'

Apparently reassured, her mother shrugged. 'Maybe you should think about writing a crime novel. One where the woman gets away with murdering a cheating, lying man and takes over the world. I bet that would be a bestseller.'

'Two good ideas in one morning.' She managed a smile. 'I'd better put them on the career-building list before I forget.' She glanced around for her notebook but, in her rush to escape, she'd left it upstairs. 'I'll do it later. Right now we have books to shelve, displays to erect and those two front windows to dress.'

If she wasn't quite busy enough to ignore the pain, at least she didn't have time to take it out and wallow in it.

It was like being hit with a sledgehammer.

Greg didn't move for what seemed an age. He'd known from the start that he'd seen her before. There had been something about her eyes, her voice, even her streaky fair hair—brighter than mouse but not quite blonde—that had tugged at some distant memory.

But she'd been a skinny little kid with hair in a plait that hadn't been pulled tight enough and was falling out around her face. She was being teased by a group of girls who were thirteen going on thirty, with their faces made up and their skirts up to their backsides. They had been all around her, mocking the way she spoke. Trying to escape them, she'd stumbled and fallen, spilling the contents of her bag, and he'd gone to her, had rescued a notebook before it was grabbed by one of the little cats who'd been giving her a hard time. Had helped her gather the rest of her things.

Her eyes had been swimming in tears and she was shaking like a leaf as he'd put the notebook into her hand, but she'd looked up and said, 'Thank you,' so sweetly, so softly.

And he'd said, 'Anytime, princess.'

He had never known her name, had just called her 'princess,' because she had sounded exactly like one. But he'd looked out for her after that, had made certain no one bullied her when he was around.

Dear God, she must have known who he was from the start. Why on earth hadn't she said anything? No, scrub that. Stupid question.

The answer was there in that moment when she'd opened the door. He'd just proclaimed himself her knight errant and had been standing there like a total idiot, pleased with himself, pleased with life, anticipating a warm welcome in return for his good deed; what he'd got had been a long silence. She'd recognised him the moment she'd seen him. And had waited for him to recognise her.

Damn it, but that was completely unreasonable and he'd tell her so right now. She'd had him at a disadvantage, he told himself, as he began to fling on his clothes. He hadn't changed that much. Put on a bit of weight, got a bit older, that was all. Nothing major. Damn it, he'd even been riding a motorbike. She'd have known him anywhere. But Juliet…

His little princess had changed out of all recognition. She was a woman. A beautiful, confident, sexy woman. How was he expected to know that she was that pathetic little kid in the charity shop clothes?

Except that he had known. Not on a conscious level, but somewhere deep inside where memories lurk to trip you up, give you a hard time when you least expect it, he'd known. And, without even thinking about it, he'd called her 'princess.'

She thought he'd lied to her about that. But he hadn't. She was the only one. Would always be the only one. He had to tell her, somehow make her believe it was true.

For that he needed her to listen to him and there was one sure way to grab her attention. He wasted no more time, but dressed, picking up his keys, wallet, notebook from the bedside table before using his phone to summon a taxi to pick him up at the end of the lane. He just hoped his architect had no other plans for the day...

Juliet was exhausted. She'd worked herself to a standstill in an attempt to stop herself from having to think. She was too tired to eat and the trip to the hospital had finished her. When she made it to the top floor flat, she only had the energy to fall into bed. The last thing she remembered thinking was that the sheets smelled of Gregor McLeod. That washing them would be the hardest thing she'd ever done.

'I'll be getting on with the flat now we're done down here, Miss Howard.'

Juliet was in something of a dilemma. Dave had told her that he'd been out of a job when Duke's went bankrupt. That at his age getting another job had been difficult. And clearly, for Maggie's sake, the flat needed decorating as much as the shop had.

But she didn't want to rack up any further 'debts' with McLeod.

There was one more thing he could do for Maggie, though. 'I'd rather you paint the outside of the shop, Dave. If that isn't taking too much advantage of your good nature.' She took him outside. 'Glossy black with gold lettering. Do you know a good sign-writer? Maggie and I have decided to rename the shop Kiss & Kill. It would be nice to have it done by the time she gets out of hospital.'

'Just tell me what you want, Miss Howard, and it'll be done.'

She thought of McLeod's expensive suit and tried not to feel too guilty as she explained.

'Greg? Where are you?'

'Neil, I can't talk right now.'

'Maybe not, but you'd better listen. Marty Duke might have fled the country but he didn't bother to take his wife with him and she's been talking to the press...'

Despite the obstacle of the ladders outside that deterred browsers, Juliet had plenty to do packing up the kind of books they were no longer going to sell in order to return them to the publishers. Packing up the orders that had come in the post. Talking about a Web site for the shop with a friend of Saffy's from the local college.

Putting a poster in the window inviting anyone interested in joining a crime readers group to contact her mother.

After lunch Saffy was despatched to the baker's to pick up the cakes that had been ordered for the romance readers group who were having their monthly meeting that afternoon—for the first time with refreshments.

'Juliet, did your mother once live in Milsom Street?' she asked when she returned.

'Years ago.' Before she'd been born. 'Why do you ask?'

'Someone was looking at the poster in the window and asked me.'

Juliet got up and went through to find a tallish, thinnish, rather elegant man and she offered her hand. 'I'm Juliet Howard. I understand you're asking about my mother.'

He went so pale that she thought he was going to faint, and she quickly ushered him into one of the roomy armchairs that she'd bought from a local second-hand dealer for the front of the shop.

'Saffy, get some water.'

'No, no, I'm fine, really, it's just such a shock. You're so like her.' He shook his head. 'I never thought of her married, with children.'

'I'm sorry?'

'Becky. Becky Howard. She is your mother?' He didn't wait for her answer. 'You carry this picture with you in your head, don't you, of things the way they were? For me she's always been that girl standing on the platform at Melchester Station wearing tight blue jeans and a white T-shirt as she waved me off.'

'You knew my mother?'

'We were both just teenagers. I…I moved away. I wrote with my address as soon as we were settled. She promised she'd write back…'

And that was when she realised that she was looking at her father. That he hadn't deserted her, run away. That he'd never even known she existed. That, far from being deserted by her young lover in her hour of need, her mother had never told him that he had a daughter.

'Where did you go?'

She asked rather more sharply than she'd intended and he looked up. 'Go?'

'When you left Melchester.'

'Oh. Well, Cornwall that time. My father worked for a bank and he was moved whenever he was promoted. I didn't want to go, but we were both still at school. I would have come back, but when she didn't write I thought, well, she's found someone else. It happens doesn't it? Of course we were ridiculously young—'

'Did you? Find someone else?'

'No one who could hold a candle to Becky. No one I could ever imagine being married to, living with...'

'Saffy,' she said, with an outward calmness that belied her inner turmoil. 'Will you please go and telephone my mother? Tell her to drop whatever she's doing and come here. Straight away. And then make some coffee. Or maybe you'd prefer tea...' She could hardly speak. 'I'm sorry, I don't know your name.'

'It's Walker. James Walker. And a cup of tea would be wonderful. Thank you.'

'Jools?' Her mother came through the door in a rush five minutes later. 'What's wrong?'

And then, as she saw the man slowly rising to his feet, she dropped everything she was carrying as her hands flew to her mouth. 'James...' She put out a hand, half withdrew it, and then he was holding it and they were in each other's arms.

Saffy said, 'What on earth is going on?'

'Romance, Saffy. Boy meets girl, boy loses girl, boy finds girl again.' With a broad sweep of her arm she encompassed the new dedicated romance section of the bookstore and said, 'Read all about it…'

Her gaze came to a halt on the newspaper her mother had dropped along with her handbag.

Mystery Developer Named

And beneath the headline was a photograph of Gregor McLeod.

Behind her the bell on the shop door pinged and she knew who it was even before she turned around.

'Juliet…'

'Mr McLeod. To what do we owe the pleasure? Have you come to view the site for your new car park?'

'I tried to get here before you saw that.'

'Why?' She felt extraordinarily calm, or maybe she was simply numb. Too much was happening and, like a computer when the buffer is full, her brain just couldn't handle any more… 'What difference would it have made?'

'I was going to tell you…' He hesitated, glancing at her mother and James who were staring at them both.

'Oh, please, don't be coy. You were going to tell me yesterday morning. Did you think that once you'd got me to bed I would be putty in your hands? That I'd forget all about Prior's Lane and the people who work here? Like your dear friend Maggie?'

The shop seemed very full all of a sudden, but that didn't matter, the more people who heard exactly what kind of a man he was, the better. 'You think you're so damned clever, Mr McLeod. Pretended you weren't interested in what we're doing to save Prior's Lane, but you didn't stop me talking about it, did you? You were always ready with a question if I drifted off topic. You even let me pay for the privilege, you cheapskate.'

'Juliet, please, let me explain…'

She was aware, on some level, that she was behaving very badly. But she'd spent her entire life behaving so very, very well while everyone around her had lied and lied and lied…

'What? Not your princess any more?'

Maybe he realised that there was nothing he could say or do that could begin to explain the depth of his betrayal because he didn't reply.

'No, obviously not. Well, you might think you've won. That I'll just crawl into a hole and stop bothering you, but you're wrong.' She took a step towards him. 'I am done with doing what other people want, done with running away from confrontation, done with being lied to. I will fight you every step of the way.' She jabbed at the soft cashmere overcoat he wearing. 'Do your worst. I will never let you destroy something people value.' She jabbed again because it felt so good to be fighting back.

He caught her hand before she could do it a third time. 'Juliet, I love you.'

She laughed. 'Oh, *please*. Now I know you're desperate.'

As she turned her back on him she realised that there were a dozen or so women standing open-mouthed behind her.

'Are you the romance readers group?' she asked. 'I'm sorry, we're having a really extraordinary day. My long lost father has turned up out of the blue and so has the man who wants to turn this area into a car park.

All it needs is the man who stole my career to turn up and we'll have a full set.'

'Juliet!'

This time it was her mother, but she ignored her too.

'Do you want to go through to the back, ladies? We've tried to make you as comfortable as possible and if you'll just let Saffy know when you want tea or coffee…' Then, because no one seemed to have anything to say, 'If you'll excuse me I just need to go somewhere so that I can scream.'

It didn't take her flight to the top floor to knock all desire to scream out of Juliet. It didn't take her that long to work out that one or all the people she was running from would come after her and she wasn't ready to face any of them.

Sooner, rather than later, she was going to have to apologise for her behaviour to them all—well, most of them—but not yet. Not until she'd had a chance to gather herself, come to terms with betrayal on an unimaginable scale.

She grabbed her coat and bag and took the back stairs that led straight down to the street but when she opened the door she discovered that Gregor had anticipated her flight and was standing on the doorstep, waiting for her. Her only retreat was back up the stairs.

'We need to talk,' he said.

'I haven't got anything to say—'

'But I have. Shall we go upstairs, or would you rather walk?'

'I—I…'

'Let's walk then,' he said, taking the coat she'd grabbed without stopping to put it on, holding it out so that she could slip her arms into the sleeves. 'It's cold,' he said when she resisted his invitation.

She silently submitted before banging the door behind her and striding out along the access alley in the direction of the river, leaving him to follow or not as he chose, saying nothing until she stopped to lean against the parapet of the bridge and catch her breath and blink back the tears that were nothing more than a reaction to the icy air.

Downstream the abandoned warehouses were reflected in the still water and she wished she'd gone in the opposite direction, up towards the cathedral. Something that McLeod could never own.

He caught up with her, handing her a cup of steaming tea he'd stopped to buy at a refreshment stall. 'That was your father? In the bookshop?'

'It would seem so.'

'How do you feel about that?'

She stared at him. He wanted to talk about the unexpected appearance of her father? 'How do you think I feel? My mother lied to me. She told me… let me believe…that he'd walked away. Abandoned her…me.'

'And he didn't?'

'He hadn't got the first clue I existed. When he saw me he thought she'd married someone else…that I was someone else's daughter.' No use pretending about the tears, or trying to hide them as she turned to him. 'Why would she do that?'

'You could ask her.' He shrugged. 'Or maybe use your imagination. They must have both been very young.'

'Still at school. Something you'd know all about.'

'Yes, well, maybe she wanted him to be free to

achieve all he was capable of. Maybe she loved him that much. If he'd known, nothing would have kept him away.'

'How do you know that?'

'Because if I'd been left in ignorance my daughter would feel the same way about me as you do about him.'

'And you think Fiona was thinking of your future when she kept silent?'

'I know that Fiona was thinking entirely about herself, but then we weren't in love.'

She sipped the tea and grimaced. 'You've put sugar in this.'

'I thought you could probably do with it.' Then, 'I didn't lie to you, Juliet.'

'You didn't tell me the truth.'

He stared down the river. 'When I called you "princess" it was purely instinctive.'

She frowned. That wasn't what she'd been talking about and he knew it...

'It's not an endearment I use casually, although I don't blame you for thinking it. The truth is that I have used it once before. There was this skinny little kid at school. Silver-grey eyes too big for her face...' As she shivered he took his scarf and wrapped it around her neck before wiping a thumb across her cheek. 'They were full of tears too.'

'Gregor...'

'She'd dropped her bag and I picked up some of her stuff.' He took something from his pocket and held up a scuffed black notebook. 'This notebook.'

Juliet swallowed. 'I wondered what had happened to that,' she said, not taking it.

'I picked it up yesterday morning by mistake,' he

said, placing it beside her on the stone parapet. 'I have one very like it.'

'I know. You wrote down the measurements for the glass in it.' Then, 'I—I suppose you've read it?'

'If I was a true knight errant, a perfect Galahad, I'd have resisted the temptation. I never pretended to be either.'

'No.'

'It's an impressive document. You had a very clear idea of what you wanted and you've achieved pretty much everything you set out to do.'

'I'm very disciplined. Shame about the directorship.'

'I'm far more concerned that most of the unticked ambitions are on the fun side of the list. I think you should spend some time filling in the gaps.'

On the contrary, she'd made a fairly impressive start when she'd spent the night with him, but this didn't seem the right moment to mention it so she said, 'Should I start with the spiky hairdo?'

'You have lovely hair…' Then, 'But if it's what you want, why not?'

'No, I never really wanted that. I just wanted to be like everyone else.'

'No reason to miss out on the trip to Disney in Paris, though. I've never been either.'

'I'm saving that up until I have at least four children of my own to take with me.'

'I noticed the four children on your master plan. If you don't mind me saying so, Juliet, you're not getting any younger. You need to start work on that in the very near future—'

'Thank you for that.'

'—and as the chosen father I'm happy to cooperate any time you say, although I'd have to insist that you make an honest man of me and marry me first.' Until then he'd been so serious, but without warning his eyes creased in the kind of smile that could get a woman into all kinds of trouble. 'That's not an offer I make lightly, Juliet. In fact it's a first for me.'

'The children, or the marriage?'

'Both.'

She tried to resist the softening of her mouth, to stop her eyes from betraying her feelings.

'Thanks, McLeod, but it'll take more than the promise of four children and a trip to Disney to make me forget about your plans for Prior's Lane.'

'Did anyone ever tell you that you set impossibly high standards in knights errant, princess?'

'Would you expect any less from the mother of your future children, McLeod?'

'Nothing less,' he admitted. 'Maybe if I showed you what I had in mind for that part of the city you'd reconsider my offer?'

He didn't wait for her to agree but reached into his coat and took a long envelope from the inside pocket, spreading out the contents for her to see. 'It's just an artist's impression, of course,' he said. 'Hilliard dashed it off for me yesterday. I've asked him to work with you on it.'

She stared at the sketch of Prior's Lane looking exactly as she'd imagined it, even down to the elegant wrought-iron roof protecting the shoppers from the elements.

'I don't know what to say, Gregor.'

'Yes?' he suggested as he folded up the drawing and handed it to her.

'Yes?'

'Well, if you say no, I might as well build a car park after all.'

'What? But that's blackmail.'

'You said it…I'm bad.'

And suddenly she couldn't stop the smile from breaking out all over her face. 'Maybe I was a little harsh, although…'

'There's more?'

'Well, I've been thinking about Duke's Yard. There are a lot of good men out of work and it seemed to me that if they had somewhere where they could set up as a sort of cooperative with an office manager to organise the paperwork…?'

'Only if you organise it.'

'I can do that.'

'I didn't doubt it for a moment, but there is just one more thing we need to settle.'

'Oh?'

He took a torn credit card slip from his pocket and handed it to her.

'What's this?'

'Just a little reassurance that if you say yes to all of the above you won't be marrying a cheapskate.'

She stared at the receipt, then at him, and as he gathered her into his arms there was no need for words. Her lips were saying yes, yes, yes more eloquently, more fervently than any affirmative listed in the dictionary. Which was maybe why neither of them heard the splash as a small black notebook fell from the parapet of the bridge, hit the water and then sank without trace.

'What's this? More fan mail for the new arrival?'

Juliet looked up at her husband as he gazed adoringly at the infant lying in the cradle beside her and bit back a smile at the sight of so much power laid low by such a tiny bundle of pink and white.

'There's a card from Chloe, full of heartfelt thanks for providing her with a baby sister at last. She's coming down at the weekend to drool in person...' She handed him the note so that he could read it for himself. 'There's a postcard from Mum and Dad too, presumably sent before they rushed back from their honeymoon. I feel so guilty about that.'

'There's nothing to stop them having another one any time they like. Is that a card from Maggie?'

'I do hope she's not overdoing it.'

'Jimmy's taking good care of her.'

'Um. I don't suppose it's a coincidence that the perfect job just happened to fall into his lap on the redevelopment project, is it?'

'It's what friends are for. What's that?'

'This?' She held up a letter written on heavy cream stationery. 'Just a note from Lord Markham asking me if I'd be prepared to join the board of Markham and Ridley. For some reason the shareholders seem to have been unimpressed with the nepotism of his last appointment.'

'Just another day in paradise then? How much are they offering?'

'Twice what they could have had me for if they'd been smart.'

'Tempted?'

'Not even remotely.' She let the letter fall to the floor as she lifted her baby girl from her cradle and tucked her into her father's arms. Then, leaning forward to kiss him, she said, 'I've got all I ever wanted right here.'

ORDINARY GIRL, SOCIETY GROOM

BY
NATASHA OAKLEY

Natasha Oakley told everyone at her primary school she wanted to be an author when she grew up. Her plan was to stay at home and have her mum bring her coffee at regular intervals—a drink she didn't like then. The coffee addiction became reality and the love of storytelling stayed with her. A professional actress, Natasha began writing when her fifth child started to sleep through the night. Born in London, she now lives in Bedfordshire with her husband and young family. When not writing, or needed for 'crowd control', she loves to escape to antiques fairs and auctions.

Find out more about Natasha and her books on her website www.natashaoakley.com

CHAPTER ONE

IT WAS true what people said—you were more alone in a crowd than any other place on earth. Eloise Lawton felt as lonely tonight as she ever had.

All she wanted to do was go home, run a bath and soak away her troubles. Instead she was here, making social small talk and avoiding the barbs of people who were fearful of what she might say about their dress sense. As well they might; she'd become more vitriolic of late. She couldn't seem to help it.

Eloise shifted her weight from one leg to the other, acutely aware of the way her Eduardo Munno sandals cut into the sides of her feet. Stunning to look at, but desperately uncomfortable when they were a size too small. Borrowed plumes for a woman who didn't fit in. Not with these people.

Everyone was vying for position, all judging the others on what they owned and who they were connected to. It was pitiful. Except it wasn't pity she felt. It was a deep, sickening sort of loathing. The kind that made her feel she needed to stand under the shower for half an hour to rid herself of the contamination.

But it was work. It paid the mortgage—and she didn't have the luxury of a handsome trust fund or an inherited ancestral pile. Unlike every second person here.

Eloise gave her wrist-watch a surreptitious glance and calculated how long she'd have to stick it out before she could make her excuses to Cassie. Not so long ago this kind of event would have filled her with excitement, but now...

Well, now things were different. A spontaneous decision to take her mother's belongings out of storage had changed everything.

It had seemed such a sensible thing to do. After six years it was certainly past time. She'd completed all the release paperwork without the slightest presentiment that she was opening a Pandora's box of emotions.

She'd known it was a mistake almost instantly. So many memories had rushed to crowd around her. Barely healed wounds had been ripped open and they felt as fresh and raw as when a lorry driver falling asleep at the wheel had altered everything.

She'd re-read the letter her mum had so carefully tucked inside her will and, six years on, she'd read it with a slightly different perspective.

Eloise let her eyes wander around the galleried grand hall. Enormous chandeliers hung down from the cavernous ceiling and huge displays of arum lilies, white orchids and tiny rosebuds had been tortured into works of art. No expense had been spared. Everything was perfectly beautiful.

A magical setting—but it felt like purgatory. How could it not? An ostentatious display of wealth for no apparent purpose. And her role in all this?

She no longer cared what colour anyone should be wearing or whether silk was the fabric of the season. When she sat at her keyboard tomorrow she'd summon up enough enthusiasm to get the article done but tonight it left her cold.

There was too much on her mind. Too much anger. Too much resentment.

'Mutton dressed as lamb,' Cassie hissed above the top of her champagne flute. 'Over there. At three o'clock.'

Eloise jerked to attention and swivelled round to look at the woman her boss was referring to in such disparaging terms.

'No, darling.' The editor of *Image* magazine tapped her arm. 'That's nine o'clock. I said three. Bernadette Ryland. By the alabaster pillar. Under that portrait of the hideously obese general.'

Obligingly, Eloise twisted the other way.

'In the yellow. Well, almost in the yellow. What was her stylist thinking of? The woman looks like some kind of strangulated chicken.'

Cassie wasn't kidding. It was a shame because the actress had been a strikingly beautiful woman before she'd succumbed to the lure of the surgeon's knife. It gave her face a perpetually surprised look. And that dress... It almost defied description. Certainly defied gravity.

Cassie took another sip of champagne. 'And Lady Amelia Monroe ought to rethink that haircut, don't you think? It makes her face look very jowly. Oh—' she broke off '—oh, my goodness... There's Jeremy Norland. And with Sophia Westbrooke. Now...that's the first interesting thing that's happened this evening. I wonder...'

'Jeremy Norland?' Eloise asked quickly, even as her eyes effortlessly fixed themselves on his tall, dark figure.

She'd seen a couple of photographs of him, one taken when he'd been playing polo and the other at a society wedding, but he was smoother-looking than she'd expected. Chocolate box handsome.

'By the door. Know him?'

'No.' Eloise's fingers closed convulsively round her

glass. 'I don't know him. I heard his name mentioned, that's all,' she managed, her voice a little flat.

'Haven't we all, darling?' Cassie Sinclair lifted one manicured hand and waved it at a lady in grey chiffon who'd been trying to attract her attention. 'That's the sister of the Duke of Odell,' she explained in a quiet undertone Eloise scarcely heard. 'Married a mere mister. Kept the title of Lady, of course, and makes sure everyone knows it.' She swung round to exchange her empty glass for a full one.

Eloise stood transfixed. Jeremy Norland. Here. Her mind didn't seem capable of processing any other thought.

Viscount Pulborough's stepson was here. In London. He was standing by the heavy oak door, his face alight with laughter. Not a care in the world.

But then why should he have? He was living a charmed life.

Cassie followed the line of her gaze. 'Gorgeous, isn't he? All that muscle's been honed by hours on horseback. And that suit is fabulous. Look at his bum in those trousers. The man's sexy...very sexy.'

'And doesn't he just know it?' Eloise returned dryly, watching the way he glinted down at Sophia Westbrooke.

'Can't blame the man for knowing the effect he has on women, darling. Looks. Money. Connections. Pretty lethal combination, I'd say.'

Eloise forced a smile. 'I thought he didn't like London.'

'He doesn't. He stays down in Sussex on his stepfather's estate. Makes tables, chairs, that kind of thing.'

'Fine cabinetry. Yes, I know.' Eloise sipped her own champagne. 'I read something about that.'

'You need a second mortgage to buy the leg of a footstool,' Cassie agreed. 'Sophia's dress too, I imagine. Do you know who made it?'

'Yusef Atta. Up-and-coming designer. Specialising in embroidery on chiffon,' Eloise answered automatically. 'Very romantic silhouettes. That kind of thing.'

'Worth a feature?'

'Perhaps,' Eloise agreed, watching the way the teenager gazed up adoringly. Sophia Westbrooke couldn't be older than nineteen. Could she? Whereas Jeremy was thirty-four. Thirty-five, perhaps—she couldn't quite remember from the Internet article she'd read two nights ago.

Cassie seemed in tune with her thoughts. 'Just back from Switzerland. Not a day over nineteen. And with a man like Jem Norland. Lucky cow.'

'There's no luck about it. It's all part of the in-breeding programme. Like marries like, don't you know?' she said in her best parody of an up-market accent.

Cassie gave a delighted chuckle, her acrylic-tipped nails clinking against her champagne flute. 'Wicked child. Now circulate, darling. Get me the gossip and no more ogling the natives. They bite.'

How true. It was a pity no one had mentioned that to her mother twenty-eight years ago when she'd first started work at Coldwaltham Abbey, not much older than Sophia Westbrooke—but Eloise would lay money on their fates being completely different.

Eloise watched her boss network her way back through the crowded room. Cassie didn't fit in any more than she did, but you'd never know it from her demeanour. She just owned the space, dared anyone to reject her.

Eloise had used to be like that, ambitious to the core—but things had changed in the past fourteen weeks. Fourteen weeks and three days, to be precise. The day she'd brought home those two crates. Who would ever have thought such a short space of time could make such an incalculable difference? Her eyes flicked back to Jeremy Norland, universally known as Jem.

He was the epitome of upper class living. His suit was fabulous. Hand-stitched, no doubt. Criminally expensive.

Money and opportunity had been poured on him from the hour of his birth. He'd the bone-deep confidence of a man who'd been to the best schools and who knew the old boy network would support him in comfort till the day he died.

And she resented him with a vehemence that surprised even her.

He reached across to kiss the cheek of the effervescent Sophia, who giggled appreciatively. He was so arrogant—it shone from the top of his dark expensively cut hair right down to his handmade Italian leather shoes. He knew exactly what he was doing—and the effect he was having on his youthful companion. Eloise just longed for her to rear up and tell him to get lost.

It didn't happen, though. Sophia smiled coquettishly and rested a hand on his shoulder. Eloise couldn't honestly blame her. She wasn't to know. It was years of sitting in a ringside seat seeing someone else's unhappiness that meant she would never be so stupid as to fall for a man like Jem Norland.

Anger and hatred had been building up inside her ever since she'd re-read her mother's letter and now she couldn't bear to be near these self-absorbed people who'd destroyed her mother's life so completely.

Her life.

With their grand houses, their horses and their public school accents. She hated them all.

A few short weeks ago she'd been fascinated by them. A detached and slightly amused observer. But now...

Now she had nothing but contempt for them.

For Jem Norland. The privileged stepson of the man she really loathed—Laurence Alexander Milton, Viscount Pulborough.

Her father.

Father!

That was a joke. He'd been no more than the sperm donor.

Six years ago, when she'd first read that letter, she'd been too numbed by shock to really take it all in. The sudden loss of her mum had been trauma enough and she almost hadn't had the emotional space to register what she now knew to be the identity of the man whose gene pool she shared.

Viscount Pulborough wasn't part of her life. He'd meant less than nothing to her. It was her mum missing her graduation ceremony that had filled her mind and twisted the screw of pain a little tighter.

So she'd packed all her mum's things away and scarcely thought about it...for six years.

Six years. Time had passed so fast. Life had been busy. There'd been so much to do—building her career, saving for her deposit, trying to pretend she didn't feel so incredibly alone in a big, frightening world.

There'd always been plenty of excuses as to why her mum's belongings should stay safely locked away. She'd had a small bedsit... She'd be moving on soon, so what was the point...?

The excuses stopped when she'd bought her flat. Her own home. It was time to finally sort out the last of her mum's possessions. All those things she'd put in box files and refused to think about.

The letter.

It had always been there. A time bomb ticking away—only she hadn't realised it.

Re-reading her mum's words six years later, she had found her emotions were different. She had a new, fresh perspective and, as she read, her antipathy had turned to anger.

It had been so easy to imagine what had happened that summer. Young, naïve, desperately in love, her mother had been swept up into a beautiful fairy tale—except for the fact that her prince had turned out to be married. More frog than prince. There'd even been a castle...of a kind. A brief spell of happiness and...what?

The rest of her short life alone. Struggling to bring up her daughter by herself. Crying over bills and juggling two badly paid jobs to make ends meet. A few hours' pleasure in exchange for a lifetime of pain and responsibility.

And did the esteemed Viscount ever think of that when he strolled about his great estate in Sussex? Did he?

All of a sudden she'd had to know. It had still taken weeks of soul-searching before she'd finally built up the courage to confront the man who had so bitterly betrayed her mum. And her.

And for what?

Nothing.

Eloise turned swiftly on her borrowed designer heels and walked over to stand by the open window. The buzz of traffic in the distance competed with the elegant strains of Beethoven.

A faint pulsing had started in her right temple and was shooting arrows of pain around her eye socket. She wanted to cry out at the injustice of it all. The total unfairness.

Jem Norland watched her, his eyes distracted by the flash of purple silk.

'Jem, are you listening to me?' Sophia asked, pulling on his arm. 'I'm going with Andrew to find somewhere to sit down.'

'Who's the blonde?' Jem cut straight to the question that interested him most.

Lord Andrew Harlington squinted across the room. 'In the purple? With the legs?'

'That's it.'

He concentrated. 'No idea,' he said, wrapping an arm around Sophia's waist. 'How about you, Sophy? Recognise her?'

'That's Eloise...' his girlfriend searched the deepest recesses of her mind '...you know, that woman off the television. Eloise...Leyton. No, Lawton. That's it. Eloise Lawton. The woman who does the clothes thing.'

Jem stilled. 'What?'

'She does that programme about style,' Sophia volunteered. 'Colours and so forth. Blue tones and red tones. It makes a difference to how great you look. She's really good at it. Writes for *Image* as well.'

'I'd heard that,' Jem said dryly, looking more closely at the woman who'd just pitched a missile into the midst of his family.

A blonde? Somehow he hadn't expected a blonde. Eloise Lawton—astringent, witty commentator on the fashion foibles of her contemporaries. This he knew. His mother and stepsister had told him.

But he hadn't expected the kind of cool, classy-looking blonde who might have stepped straight out of an Alfred Hitchcock movie.

'Champagne, sir.'

Jem pulled his gaze away. 'Thank you,' he said, reaching out and accepting a flute. He knew his mother would have counselled caution, but the opportunity was irresistible.

What he really wanted to know was why. Why now? Why Laurence? His stepfather was the gentlest of men. A deeply religious man, honourable and good. It was unthinkable...

'She is pretty, isn't she?' Sophia said at his elbow. 'Not your type, though.'

Jem looked down at her impish face. 'What?'

'Eloise Lawton. Very pretty.'

'Yes,' he stated baldly.

In fact, Eloise Lawton was beautiful. Beautiful, manipulative and dangerous. It was difficult to believe that anyone wrapped up inside such an appealing package could be guilty of such cold-blooded cruelty.

How could anyone dream up such a scam? And at such a painful, difficult time. Did she need the publicity so badly that she couldn't see the hurt she'd cause?

Oblivious of their amused glances, Jem made his excuses and threaded his way across to where she stood. He wasn't sure what he was going to say—not until the moment she looked up at him.

He saw the recognition in the depths of her dark brown eyes. He should have expected that. Someone like Eloise Lawton would have done her homework very thoroughly.

She'd certainly timed her letter perfectly. She'd selected the exact moment when the elderly Viscount was at his most vulnerable and the family would do practically anything to protect him.

He would do anything to protect the man who'd turned his life around. His anger crystallised into a steely coldness.

'Jem Norland,' he said, holding out his hand.

He watched the way her hands fluttered against her evening bag, the way she tried to smile before it faltered pitifully.

Eloise Lawton wasn't what he'd expected at all. It suddenly occurred to him how tired she looked. There were dark smudges beneath her eyes and they held the kind of expression he'd hoped never to see again. Such hurt. Almost hopelessness.

Slowly she placed her champagne flute on a side table. 'Eloise Lawton,' she said, placing her own hand inside his. It felt cold. Small.

He let his fingers close about it, suppressing every desire to comfort her. Whatever the appearances to the contrary, Eloise Lawton was one tough cookie. She had an agenda which would hurt the people he loved.

He knew, because he'd seen it, that the space for the father's name on her birth certificate had been left blank. Whoever her father had been, it certainly wasn't Viscount Pulborough.

Which meant?

His jaw hardened. It meant she was chancing her arm. Looking for publicity. He knew the kind of woman she must be. An 'it' girl. Looking for fame, for fame's sake. Famous for doing nothing.

And, God help him, he knew enough about that type of woman. They'd been the blight on his early childhood. The siren call his father had never been able to resist.

It was only... She didn't seem like that. She had more class than he'd expected. A gentle dignity...

She tried to smile again. He watched it start and then falter. 'I write for *Image*.'

'So I gather,' he said, releasing her hand. Her eyes flicked nervously towards the door. 'My friend, Sophy, tells me you're an expert on how other women should dress.'

'N-no. Well, I write about fashion, if that's what she means. It's all about opinion, after all.'

It was a diplomatic answer. She was clever. He had to give her that. And beautiful. Undeniably. A cool, serene beauty.

And beneath that...there would be...what? Passion? Fire?

And avarice. This had to be all about money, didn't it? About building a career. Using. Stepping on anyone to reach your goal.

Her goal, he reminded himself. She'd selected a vulnerable, ill, elderly man and claimed to be his daughter. With what proof?

None.

But she'd reckoned without him.

Jem forced himself to appear relaxed. 'And television? Sophy mentioned you'd been on television.'

'A little. I was asked to make a programme about the BAFTAs and I've done the occasional slot on morning television.'

Her hands moved endlessly over her evening bag. It didn't take a genius to recognise how nervous she was. She had good reason.

Laurence had stalwartly believed in Jem when he'd done everything he could to prove him wrong. He'd maintained a faithful belief in his stepson's innate goodness—despite all appearances to the contrary. And Jem had every intention of returning the compliment.

Laurence was not the kind of man to walk away from his responsibilities, whatever the personal cost. His sense of right and wrong was ingrained in the fibre of his personality. He could no more have rejected a daughter than he could have walked away from Coldwaltham Abbey. Both were sacred trusts, never to be abandoned.

'Do you want to do more TV?' he asked blandly.

'No.'

'No?'

Her fingers moved nervously. She placed her evening bag on the narrow table and picked up her champagne flute. 'Not really. It was exciting. Interesting. But no, I don't think so. I only really do it because it helps the magazine.'

'*Image*?'

'Yes.' She sipped her champagne. 'And it raises my profile.'

'That's important?'

Her eyes moved nervously. 'Very. Having a name people recognise is starting to open all kinds of doors.'

'Really?'

'Who you know is more important in this business than what you know.'

And Laurence was to be a casualty of that meteoric rise to the top.

But why Laurence?

Why try to use a man whose life had been beyond reproach? Someone who other people could look up to. Why be so cruel?

To his wife? To his family?

The answers came easily. She probably had a novel sitting in her bottom drawer she wanted publishing. All she needed was a 'name', a little scandal hanging about her, something that would persuade the big publishing houses to take a chance on her.

She sickened him.

'I'd like to write about other things. I love fashion but...' She broke off. Her gaze darted out of the window.

'You want more?' he finished for her. Of course she did. A high maintenance blonde, dressed in designer clothes.

She looked back, responding to the edge in his voice. 'Is there something wrong with that?'

'It depends what you're prepared to do to achieve it.'

Eloise frowned. 'Of course.'

Her fingers moved nervously on her champagne flute. His face was unreadable but she sensed he didn't like her. Perhaps it was for no other reason than he despised her profession. Many people did. But, perhaps....

Eloise quickly gulped another mouthful of champagne, the excellent vintage completely wasted. It could have been pure vinegar and she probably wouldn't have noticed.

She shouldn't have come. If she'd known Jem Norland had been on the guest list, she wouldn't have. Or any other member of Viscount Pulborough's family, for that matter. When she met them she wanted to be prepared, and for it to happen in her time and on her terms.

This wasn't the way it was meant to be. She wasn't ready. Jem Norland's startling blue eyes continued to watch her.

Did he know? Or didn't he? Had his stepfather spoken to him? The questions thumped through her head with the rhythm of a heartbeat.

'I understand from my mother that you're acquainted with my stepfather.'

Eloise tightened her grip on her glass. She could feel perspiration beading on her forehead, her hands become clammy. Her mouth moved soundlessly.

He knew.

It was a sensation akin to jumping off a cliff, the wind

roaring in her ears as she sped towards a fate she had no control over.

'Viscount Pulborough?' he prompted, as the silence stretched out between them. 'My mother's second husband.'

'We…we've never met.'

His right eyebrow moved in an exaggerated expression of surprise. His eyes travelled the length of her body, assessing and critical.

It was years and years of training that made it possible for a man to deliver such a non-verbal put down. Generations of believing you were somehow superior to every other member of the human race.

She really hated that he could make her feel so small and so worthless. If anyone should have been cowering with shame, it should have been him. It was his mother's husband who had abandoned a teenage girl carrying his baby.

'Really? I must have misunderstood what she told me.'

'My mum knew him. Years ago. I wrote to Viscount Pulborough to tell him she'd died.' Eloise carefully put her glass down on the side table and picked up her evening bag. 'He hasn't replied.'

Three weeks and there'd been no reply. Nothing. She hadn't expected that. She hadn't expected her father to welcome her with open arms—but nothing. No response at all. It seemed incredible. And with each passing day she felt more resentful.

How could anyone do that? How could he have created a life and care so little about it?

From the time she'd been old enough to ask questions about who her father was, her mother had said he was a good man. A man who couldn't be with them, however much he wanted to be.

His identity had always been a secret. But some part of Eloise had clung to the knowledge that he was a 'good man'. He would have wanted her in his life...if only it had been possible. He would have loved her. Loved her mother. He was a 'good man'.

Childish nonsense. He was a man who'd had too much of everything. A man who clearly rated people as worthy of notice or not worthy. A man who'd left a young girl to deal with the consequences of their affair alone and unsupported. A man who'd completely deleted the knowledge that he'd fathered a baby girl.

Her.

'He's been unwell.'

'Unwell?' Her eyes flicked up to his. She would swear his voice had become more menacing, beneath the suave veneer.

'But perhaps you know that already? He's been in hospital,' Jem continued smoothly.

'No. No...I didn't...I didn't know.'

Why would she have known that? She felt somehow that he blamed her. But for what?

'He's undergone heart surgery. A quadruple bypass.'

'Oh.' Eloise didn't know what to say. Considering Viscount Pulborough was a man she didn't know, had never met, it was strange to feel such an overwhelming reaction to the news of his operation.

'But at seventy-three it's taken its toll.'

She knew a moment of panic. He couldn't die. Not now. If he did she would never have the chance to speak to him. Would never know why he'd abandoned them.

'Could he die?' she asked, taking an involuntary step forward.

Jem held his ground. 'He had a stem cell bleed four years ago which made the procedure more risky than usual, but he came through the operation with only a small scare.'

'Scare?'

'His blood pressure shot up as he was coming round from the anaesthetic and they had to bring him round more slowly than they'd hoped. But he's making excellent progress now.'

'Th-that's good.'

'Yes, it is. The entire family has rallied round to support him.'

Eloise looked away, embarrassed. 'Of course. I'm sure… I…' She closed her eyes for a moment.

'Part of that is keeping him free of stress and making sure nothing's allowed to upset him.'

His words pooled in the silence. There was no possible way she could misconstrue what he was saying. From somewhere deep within her Eloise pulled out a quiet, 'I see.' And then, because she couldn't help it, 'You're protecting him from me. He hasn't seen my letter. Has he?'

'No.'

No. No apology, just an unequivocal 'no'. All these days, waiting for an answer that hadn't come. All the worry and nervous energy. The sick fear. The feeling of utter rejection. The anger.

And Viscount Pulborough didn't even know she'd written to him.

His precious 'new' family, his 'real' family, had closed ranks round him, lest he should be upset. Upset! It didn't occur to them to think how she might be feeling.

Of course it didn't. And if it had, they wouldn't have cared. She was beneath notice. An irritation. Someone born the wrong side of the blanket who was refusing to stay there.

And then there was a new thought. *Someone* had read

her letter. A feeling of coldness spread through her body. That someone had opened her letter. Read it. Dissected and discussed it.

It had been private. So difficult to write. She'd not imagined anyone reading the contents but her father.

She took a deep breath and met his eyes. 'Did you read it?'

'No.'

'Then who?'

'Does it matter?'

'They had no right to do it. It was a private letter. Personal. It doesn't concern anyone except...' She hesitated, uncertain how to refer to him. My father. She couldn't say that. The word 'father' stuck in her throat. 'Viscount Pulborough and myself. Not you, not anyone else.'

'Not even the Viscount's wife?'

Eloise met his critical gaze. 'No.'

She watched him check the retort he'd been about to make. A muscle pulsed at the side of his face. 'Why now?' he asked softly.

'Pardon?'

Jem smiled politely, his eyes flinty blue. 'I was wondering why now. Why make your claims now? Why not last year? Why this exact moment?'

Eloise drew a steadying breath. His words confused her. She didn't understand what he was trying to say, but she could hear the underlying criticism.

And then it hit her. Like a sledgehammer powering through the air, it hit her.

He didn't believe her.

The room around her felt hot, the air heavy with a mixture of cigarette smoke and perfume. Outside the open window the low hum of traffic and the occasional siren tore through the night sky.

Jem Norland didn't believe she was his stepfather's natural daughter. He was looking down his supercilious nose as though she was something he'd stepped in. It was none of his business, nothing to do with him but he dared…he dared…

She couldn't even begin to put words to what she was feeling. Her anger was incandescent. How dared he question her? Her mother? Did he think her mother hadn't known who'd fathered her baby?

He wanted to know why she'd made contact now. She'd tell him. She'd make him feel so small he'd want to crawl beneath the skirting board. 'Because I've only just realised how much it matters.'

She saw the frown snap across his forehead.

'When my mother died… There was a letter. Kept with her will.' Eloise found it difficult to speak. Her anger choked her and her grief was still raw. Even now. She couldn't do it. She couldn't go on.

Images of that day. The policewomen who'd come to tell her. The long drive back home. The shock and the emptiness. And the sense of disbelief as she'd read the words her mother had written in her distinctive italic hand. A letter from the grave. The truth. At last.

They'd been words her mum had hoped to say—one day. No dark premonition had made her put them down on paper. It was her usual, thoughtful care for the daughter she loved that had made her write it down and tuck it inside her will. Just in case.

At first Eloise had been too busy to think clearly. There'd been a funeral to arrange—and pay for. A home to empty. Her life had changed in a single second and she'd ached for things to return to the way they'd been before—even though she'd known they couldn't.

It was much later that the anger had set in. Six years later. When she'd collected her mother's meagre possessions from storage. A whole lifetime contained in two crates. When she'd really thought about the council-owned flat they'd called home. When she'd done that first Internet search and had seen a picture of Coldwaltham Abbey.

Her father had let them struggle with nothing. Nothing.

And then she'd re-read her mother's letter. Amazingly, there'd been no bitterness. Her mum had loved her father, had believed in him right up to the moment she'd tucked the letter inside her will. Probably until the day she'd died.

From that moment Eloise had felt a gnawing curiosity. That was *why now*. But how could a man like Jem Norland ever hope to understand even a tenth of what she was feeling? She wasn't entirely sure she understood it herself.

Eloise took a deep breath and tried again. 'My mother was involved in a head-on collision. Six years ago. A lorry…' Her voice faltered, tears blocking her throat. 'The driver fell asleep at the wheel. She d-died. Instantly.'

'I'm sorry.'

Eloise sensed Jem move towards her. She stepped back, her hand raised to shield her. 'It was a long time ago. You want to know why I waited until now?' She didn't wait for his answer, she continued relentlessly. 'She never told me who my father was. It was a secret. She told no one. She put a letter—'

'No one?'

The anger flickered back in her eyes. 'She must have

been a pushover for your stepfather. She just disappeared quietly. Went off to have her baby by herself. Never asked for anything. Never tried to make contact. Never...' Her voice broke on a sob. 'My mother was worth a million of him. It was his loss.'

CHAPTER TWO

SHE turned abruptly and pushed her way through the throng of silk and chiffon-clad women with their attendant dinner-jacketed swains, her heart pounding with an anger she'd never experienced before.

And sorrow. It had seeped into her bones. It permeated everything.

Her letter hadn't even reached the man her mother had loved. It had been passed around strangers. Her mother's secret had been shared with all the people she'd tried to keep it from.

Her own quiet, dignified request for answers, her need to understand what had happened, had been misconstrued. She felt violated and desperately hurt. Angry for herself—and for her mother.

Eloise found the ladies' cloakroom by pure instinct. She could hardly see for the tears burning behind her eyes. She pushed open the door and stepped down into the marble opulence.

Thankfully it was empty. She stumbled forward and let the tap run cold for a second or two before splashing her face.

He didn't believe her. She'd never expected that. She'd spent so much time imagining what kind of response her letter would receive. She'd never imagined for a single second it would be met with blatant disbelief and never reach the man she'd intended it for.

The door clicked open. Eloise glanced up at the two

middle-aged women who paused in their conversation the minute they saw her. She forced herself to stand straight and calmly turned off the cold tap. She didn't want their sympathy—or their questions.

As soon as they'd passed Eloise covered her eyes with her hand. She needed to go home. Decide what she was going to do now. Cry.

She needed to cry out the frustration and the anger. The sadness. The waste of it all.

Cassie wouldn't like it but she couldn't risk speaking to Jem Norland again. Why did he think her mother had lied? How dared he think that? She brushed away an angry tear.

The door at the end of the powder room clicked open. 'Are you feeling unwell?' one of ladies who'd passed earlier asked.

Eloise spun round. 'I'm fine. Sorry,' she answered briskly. 'I'm fine. Really.' She made a show of checking her make-up in the lighted mirrors and adjusted the narrow straps of her evening gown before leaving the ladies' room.

The babble of conversation immediately hit her as a wall of sound. The heat was stifling and the air was full of heavy perfume. Eloise pulled a tired hand across her forehead, easing out the tension, and crossed the room towards her employer.

'You look dreadful,' Cassie remarked as soon as she joined her.

Eloise let her breath out in a gentle, single stream. They were friends to a point, but Cassie wasn't the kind of woman you could confide in.

In fact, since her mother's death she'd discovered she really didn't have any friends she trusted in that way. Not for the things that were truly important, the things that touched your soul and defined your personality.

'It's nothing a good night's sleep won't cure,' she lied. 'I think I'll go home, though.'

Cassie's mouth thinned. She didn't like it. Eloise knew the signs of irritation well. Her employer ate and slept her job and expected everyone else to do the same. Nothing in Cassie's life was allowed to impinge on the really important business of running a magazine.

'Now?'

'I've got plenty of material.' Eloise glanced down at her watch and added, 'Which is more than can be said for Bernadette Ryland.'

Cassie's painted mouth relaxed into a half smile and she spun round to take another view of the actress's skimpy gown. 'True. But there are one or two people I'd still like to speak to, if I can.'

Failure wasn't in Cassie's vocabulary. She would speak to everyone she intended to—and stay until it was done. It was why she was as successful as she was.

Eloise followed Cassie's eyes as they searched out Monica Bennington, whose affair with a disgraced Member of Parliament had been headline news for the past week. A salacious story and Cassie wouldn't leave without some take on it.

'If you give me half an hour I'll come with you. We're all a bit jittery after Naomi's mugging.'

Naomi's recent attack had traumatised the entire office—but even that couldn't persuade Eloise to wait. Cassie's half an hour would become an hour, then maybe two. She had to leave now. Her temples had started to thud and she felt as if needles were being pushed into her eye sockets.

And she wanted to cry. Tough, sassy woman about town that she was—she wanted to cry like a baby. 'I don't want to rush you. I'll call a cab.'

Cassie's eyes flicked back to Monica. Eloise could see that she was torn as to what she should do. 'Alone? You're sure?'

'Positive. I'll be fine. It's not very late. I could even catch the tube but I'd look a bit daft dressed like this. Probably not the best idea for a fashion guru.'

Cassie laughed, as Eloise had intended she should. Her hard face softened slightly and she rested her hand lightly on Eloise's bare arm. 'Get them to call you a taxi from Reception. Bring the receipt in tomorrow. Keep safe.'

Eloise smiled her thanks and turned away. Thank God. Escape. Her eyes fixed on the double doors with the determination of a drowning man trying to reach shore. She'd never left an evening like this so early before. Had never felt such an overwhelming urge to run away.

But then she'd never met Jem Norland before.

The sudden cold blast of air was a relief. Eloise had never fainted in her life but she'd felt perilously close to it back in the ballroom. She took in a couple of steadying breaths, grateful for the comparative quiet.

Her fingers struggled with the stiff clasp on her evening bag before she managed to retrieve the small white ticket she needed to reclaim her wrap. With a nervous glance over her shoulder, she hurried down the wide-stepped staircase.

'Miss Lawton?'

She didn't need to turn round to recognise the voice of Jem Norland. Her fingers hesitated on the smooth mahogany banister rail and she stopped. 'Go away,' she managed. 'I don't want to speak to you.'

She carried on down the stairs, gathering up the fine silk of her skirt to keep it out of the way of her heels.

The marble-floored entrance hall was full of people and she had no choice but to take her place in a queue. He came to stand beside her. Tall and intimidating. 'I'm sorry.'

Eloise kept looking staunchly ahead. 'For what?'

'I've upset you.'

Bizarrely, he sounded genuine. Eloise couldn't quite understand that. He'd made a point of coming to speak to her when he'd known perfectly well who she was. He'd made it perfectly plain that he didn't believe her story. What exactly did he expect her to feel?

'I'm angry. Okay?' She turned to look at him. 'Not upset, angry. Very, very angry.'

'I'm sorry.' He kept his voice level and calm.

Eloise felt hot tears prick behind her eyes. 'Oh, go away.' Then, with a small break in her voice, 'Please, Leave me alone. Just go away.'

The queue moved forward and Eloise resolutely concentrated on handing over her ticket and reclaiming her wrap. She draped the soft folds about her shoulders, aware that Jem Norland had moved to stand near the reception desk.

Eloise looked back up the staircase to the oppressive portraits above. The sound of laughter and the general hum of conversation wafted down. She'd have been better off waiting for Cassie. If only he'd leave her alone.

She looked at the queue, which was five deep, all waiting patiently for the receptionist, and with sudden decisiveness she turned towards the exit.

Jem stopped her. 'We ought to talk.'

'About?' She pulled her wrap tightly about her shoulders. 'I've got nothing to say to you and I'm not interested in anything you've got to say to me. My mum was right when she decided to have nothing to do with my father.'

As exits went, it was pretty good. Head held high, she stepped out on the stone steps.

But it was dark.

And she'd meant to wait for a taxi. It was stupid to be walking about London at night, alone, in sandals with three-inch heels and wearing an expensive evening dress. She knew it.

But she couldn't go back. Stifling the panic she always felt about being alone at night, Eloise headed towards the main road. The street was deserted. Naomi had been unlucky. There was nothing to worry about, she told herself. This was a well-lit road in a good area and it would be easy to hail a taxi at Hyde Park Corner.

The wind whipped between the buildings and she pulled her deep purple wrap more closely about her shoulders as though it would offer protection. A shield against people who would do her wrong.

She pulled a wry smile. It wasn't even doing a particularly good job at keeping her warm. What was really needed on a night like this was thermal underwear and a duffel coat. Oh, and a pair of comfortable shoes. She'd kill for a pair of loafers right now.

A quick glance over her shoulder reassured her. There was no one. Not even Jem Norland. It was eerily quiet and, after the bright lights of Alburgh House, unpleasantly dark. It was strange how night made such a difference and made familiar places uncomfortable.

A sensible woman would have called for a cab from Reception; she wouldn't have let Jem Norland deflect her. She crossed the road and set out along the pavement at a brisk pace. Her skin seemed to prickle with an undisclosed danger. All the result of an overactive imagination, she chided herself immediately, but she still quickened her pace.

In the daylight this was a bustling affluent area. In the dark it seemed full of alleyways and litter. It was all fanciful nonsense, though, and the main road was only a short distance away. Lots of people. Lots of taxis. No problem, she muttered underneath her breath.

No problem at all. Keep walking, keep looking ahead, make it look like you know where you're going....

The wind picked up and Eloise sensed the first droplets of rain hanging in the air. Blast it. A drenching would really be a perfect ending to a miserable evening. She pulled her wrap tightly around her body.

It was getting colder and the wind stronger. Almost before she heard them she was aware of footsteps behind her. A sudden sound in the darkness. Her heart pounded uncomfortably against her ribcage and she quickened her pace, listening for the slightest sound behind her.

The footsteps seemed to keep pace with hers—although they were some way back. She took a deep breath to steady herself. She was jumping at shadows. A few more metres and she'd be on the main road. Plenty of people there, she reminded herself, but her heart continued to pound painfully against her chest.

With a furtive glance behind her to confirm there was someone coming up behind her, she saw a man still someway in the distance. Turning back, she did a few rapid calculations. How far from the main road was she? If she made a run for it, could he catch her? Probably. With her shoes off? Maybe not.

She let out another long slow breath. Time to discover whether not waiting in the Reception area had been one of the dumbest decisions she'd ever made. With a defiant toss of the head she crossed the road. And then she listened.

The footsteps stayed steady. For a moment Eloise allowed herself to relax. How stupid was she being? She was walking towards the main road; it was highly likely other people would decide to do the same. Then she noticed the footsteps behind her had quickened—and she heard the man cross the road.

Every nerve in her body was screaming as she resisted the overwhelming temptation to turn round and look. If she did that she'd be committed to flight and it wasn't much further. Not much further at all.

Eloise could see the corner approaching fast even as the footsteps sounded closer. The lights of the restaurants shone brightly. If this man got any closer she would kick off her heels and run for it. It was a question of timing.

Or she could turn and fight. Her mind struggled to remember what she'd learnt. Hand beneath the chin, knee in groin...

'Miss Lawton.'

She stopped and spun round to confront Jem Norland. Hot, molten anger rose even as relief flooded through her. 'Damn you. You stupid man! How dare you do this to me?'

Painful gulps of air shot into her lungs as she tried to control some of the anger bursting from her. 'Hasn't anyone ever told you that you shouldn't go following women, particularly at night, and even more particularly when they're on their own? It's an incredibly crass thing to do.'

'I didn't mean to frighten you,' Jem said, his footsteps slowing. 'I thought you'd seen me.'

'Just like you didn't mean to upset me? Why can't you leave me alone?' Eloise asked in a burst of anger before her chest contracted and she suddenly found she couldn't breathe. Her eyes opened in shock as she struggled to take in enough air, each shallow breath only serving to make her feel more frightened.

Jem took her face between his hands. 'Just breathe. In and out.' His blue eyes held her brown ones, the strength in them willing her to stay calm. 'It's okay. You're okay.'

Eloise didn't believe him but she kept looking up at him, the warmth from his hands giving her comfort. Her chest hurt and her breath was still coming in painful gasps. 'I'm sorry. I—'

'Don't try and speak,' he cut across her curtly. 'You're in shock. Just keep breathing steadily. In and out. If I had a paper bag I'd give you that to blow into.' He looked about him as though he might be able to conjure one up in the middle of a London street.

Eloise laughed, a hiccup and then a sob. 'I'm sorry.'

'What for? I'm the one that's frightened you. I should have called out earlier, made sure you knew I was there. I didn't think.'

As her breath steadied he let his hands fall down by his sides. There was silence for a moment as they looked at each other. Then Eloise shivered. Within seconds he'd slipped off his jacket and placed it around her shoulders.

'No. I can't—' she began but he stopped her.

'It's cold.' He looked up at the sky as the soft drops of rain continued to fall. 'And it's started to rain.'

He moved to place a hand in the small of her back and urged her towards the main road. After a few steps,

Eloise stopped. 'What are you doing? What do you want?'

'To talk to you,' he said, as though he were speaking to a child. 'We do need to talk.'

Eloise shook her head and her voice wavered. 'Why? You don't believe me.'

He put his hands in his pockets. 'But you believe it,' he said quietly.

His jacket hung heavy about her shoulders. She turned and walked towards the main road. He hadn't said he believed her, only that he believed she believed it.

And he wanted to talk. Why? But all at once she didn't really care. The most important thing was that she wasn't alone in a dark street. She hadn't been attacked. She was safe.

Still, after eight years, the memories of that night haunted her. She'd been one of the lucky ones, she'd got away unharmed, but in so many ways she was still a victim. Frightened of the dark, frightened of walking alone, frightened of being frightened.

Naomi's mugging had brought it all back. Had made that fear fresh. A large drop of rain fell on the fine wool of his jacket. Eloise glanced up and then across at Jem. 'You'll get wet.'

'I'll survive.' He gave a half smile and her stomach twisted in recognition of something. 'Where are we going?' he asked.

'To the main road. To hail a cab.'

'You could have got one from Reception.'

'I know.' She kept walking, her face turned away.

'But I was there,' he said slowly. 'Is that it?'

'Something like that.' She risked a glance across at

him. The rain had started in earnest and his crisp white shirt had begun to stick to his body.

It was a good body. Tautly muscled, as Cassie had noticed. She'd said he was sexy too, the tiny voice in her head reminded her.

And he was. Sexy. Strong. Safe.

Safe. Why had she thought that? Perhaps it was because of the way his eyes had held hers when she'd been panicked and fighting for breath. His hands had cradled her face.

Eloise looked down at her ruined sandals. 'I'll be fine now.'

'I'll find you a taxi.'

His voice brooked no argument and she was too relieved to protest. The lights of the main road ahead shone brightly, but she'd still prefer not to be alone. 'Thanks.'

'You're welcome. Having scared you witless, it's the least I can do.'

She looked up in time to see his blue eyes crinkling at the corners. Very sexy. But still the enemy.

He still thought she'd claimed to be Viscount Pulborough's daughter when she wasn't. What did he think she wanted? What could she possibly hope to gain?

'Why don't you believe me?' she asked suddenly.

Jem drew a deep breath and exhaled slowly. 'Laurence is a deeply religious man. He stayed married to his first wife for nearly thirty years, even when she was seriously ill with motor neurone disease. His opinions on the sanctity of marriage are very fixed.'

'So you think my mum was lying?'

'Laurence's name doesn't appear on your birth certificate—'

'How could it?' she responded swiftly. 'He didn't stay around that long.'

Jem turned towards her. His eyes were sad, compassionate, as though he didn't want to hurt her but believed he had no choice.

'I can't see Laurence ever turning his back on a child. It's out of character. He wouldn't do it.'

'But you didn't ask him. Did you?' Eloise hugged his jacket about her shoulders. 'You didn't show him my letter.'

'No. Not yet.' He stopped by the door of a lighted café. 'Do you want a coffee?'

Eloise glanced up and then through the window. The staff were clearing the tables. 'I want to go home. I'll be fine now, you go back to the gala.'

'I'm not going.' He slicked back his dark hair. 'I'm cold, drenched and I'm going to see you home.'

'What about Sophia Westbrooke? Won't she be looking for you?'

'Sophy will go home with Andrew.'

'Will she mind?'

'Why would she? They know I hate these kinds of events. I don't really like London. Too noisy. Too many people.'

They turned the final corner and stood beneath a street light, the rain glinting as it was illuminated in the soft beam.

'I'd read that.'

He glanced across at her. 'What else did you read?'

Eloise let her eyes scan the distance. She took a shallow breath. 'Your father is the late Rupert Norland. He died in a speedboat accident when you were fourteen and your mother married Viscount Pulborough eighteen months later. You were expelled from school. You design furniture and you're not married.'

'That's all?'

She glanced across at him. His hands were nonchalantly in his trouser pockets, his face mildly interested. 'You've a half-brother called Alexander who's at Harrow and who will ultimately inherit Coldwaltham Abbey. Rumour has it you were all but engaged to Brigitte Coulthard, heiress to the Coulthard retail empire. Since then, nothing particularly serious.' She raised an eyebrow. 'Do you want any more? I'm good at research.'

'So I see. I've no secrets then,' he said dryly.

Eloise pulled his jacket closely about her shoulders. 'Have I?'

'No.' He gave a half smile. 'I'm pretty good at research myself.'

There was a silence before Jem lunged forward and hailed a passing black cab. As the driver swerved over, switching off his 'for hire' light, Jem turned back. 'Where to?'

'Hammersmith.'

He nodded and Eloise noticed the way the rain was now dripping down the back of his neck, his shirt sticking to his back. His jacket around her shoulders was sodden, the bottom of her fine silk dress hung in miserable folds and her shoes were ruined.

She didn't care. About that or about anything. A strange fatalism seemed to rest upon her. Jem seemed inclined to make decisions and she didn't have the energy to stop him.

Settling back in the deep seat of the taxi, she didn't even comment when he took the seat next to her. It seemed natural he should. She didn't ask where he was going or whether this was taking him out of his way.

What if he were right? What if Viscount Pulborough wasn't her father? It was a small chink of doubt which made her feel like she was betraying her mother. But he was so certain. So very certain.

She turned her head away and watched the raindrops bead and weave their way across the window. Beyond it was all a blur of night.

Would her mother have lied? Eloise couldn't believe that. Wouldn't.

'Where to, luv?' The taxi driver half turned his head to talk through the open window.

Eloise jumped. 'Second on the left. Number fifteen.' She glanced across at Jem. His face was hidden in darkness but she knew he was watching her. She shrugged out of his jacket. 'You'd better have this back,' she said, passing it to him. 'Thank you.'

He took the jacket and felt inside the inner pocket for his wallet as the taxi pulled up outside her home. Jem opened the door and helped her out on to the pavement.

Eloise stood foolishly and watched him walk round to pay the driver. The rain had stopped but the pavements were dark and the air smelt damp.

Jem came back to join her as the taxi pulled away. As she watched the tail-lights disappear she glanced up at him. 'You'll never get another taxi round here.'

He shrugged. 'Then I'll walk.'

'That's silly.' Eloise shivered, her thin wrap doing nothing to keep her warm.

'Perhaps, but I'll be happier if I know you're safe.'

She turned and fitted her front door key into the lock. 'Do you want to come in for a coffee? You could ring for a taxi.' The words were out of her mouth before she even knew what she'd said.

'Coffee would be good.'

In the 'guide to all single women living alone in London' this was another foolish thing to do. You didn't ask a man you'd met that evening back to your flat. But even though Jem Norland was many things she loathed, she wasn't frightened of him.

She wasn't even sure she loathed him any more. It had burned itself out. It was the situation she hated and someone to talk to, anyone, was better than no one.

The traditional nineteen-thirties front door opened into a small lobby. 'My flat is upstairs,' she said unnecessarily. 'The house was divided ten years ago.'

'How long have you lived here?'

'Six months. I was lucky to get it.'

Jem followed her up the staircase and waited while she unlocked the second door.

'The lounge is through there. You'd better go in,' she said curtly. 'I'm just going to get changed.'

Eloise walked straight towards her bedroom, shutting the door behind her. She stood resting her back against the cold woodwork.

What was she doing? There had been no need to ask him in for coffee. No need at all.

There was no need for him to have accepted either, she reminded herself. No reason why he should have bothered to see her home. If he were so certain her mother was lying there'd be no reason for him to want to talk to her.

Eloise pulled out some dry underwear, jeans and a pale pink jumper from her chest of drawers, kicking off her Eduardo Munno sandals as she did so.

She slipped the narrow straps off her shoulders and let the damp fabric of her dress pool on the floor. Her skin felt cold and her hair was wet. It was so tempting to curl up beneath her duvet. To shut her eyes and let the day's problems melt into sleep. To forget all about Jem Norland waiting in her lounge.

Waiting. She pulled on her jeans and pulled the soft angora jumper over her head. He must be frozen—but she hadn't got anything for him to wear. She made a detour and grabbed a towel.

Why was he here?

She didn't want to talk about her mother. Not if he was going to criticise her and question her honesty.

In many ways it would have been better if she'd just folded up the letter again and forgotten all about it. Or burnt it, maybe. She should have trusted her mum's judgement. There must have been very real reasons why she'd decided to disappear quietly. Why she'd never tried to make contact.

Or had she? Perhaps she'd tried over the years but the Viscount hadn't wanted to know.

She walked nervously into the lounge. 'I'm sorry. I didn't think. You must be cold. Wet.'

Jem stood with his back to her, gazing down at the road below. He turned to look at her. 'It's quiet here.'

Eloise hugged the towel against her body. 'Yes.'

She had to pull herself together. To jump-start her brain in to some kind of working order.

What was the matter with her? She'd always had an answer for everything. Could cope with anything life threw at her. Just tonight it all seemed to have deserted her. She felt like a walking zombie. Like someone who'd had all their fire sucked out of them.

She tried again. 'That's why I bought it. That and the fact I could afford it. Plus it's only a short walk from the tube.' Eloise stopped. Total drivel. She was speaking total drivel.

He smiled. His blue eyes glinted down at her. Almost, Eloise thought as she was caught in their glare, she could almost forget he was the enemy. He had an uncanny knack of making you feel special. It was a rare gift.

Hesitantly she held out the towel. 'I've brought you a towel.'

'Thank you. Probably better to just lay it out on your sofa. Save the fabric. If I can sit down?'

Eloise shook her head. 'That doesn't matter.' Then, as she realised what he'd said, 'I'm sorry. Please do. Sit, I mean.' She rubbed a tired hand across her eyes. 'I can get you another towel, if you like.' She moved towards the door.

His voice stopped her. 'I'm fine.'

'Something to drink? I'm making a coffee.'

'Coffee would be lovely.'

His voice was rich and warm. A cultured voice. Safe. She watched him lay out the towel across her small green sofa before sitting down. Eloise closed her eyes for a second and forced herself to walk out of the room.

He made her small living-room seem tiny. He made her feel tiny, small enough to put in his pocket. She wasn't used to that sort of feeling. Eloise rubbed at her cold arms and shivered. Jem Norland was still the enemy, firmly on the side of the man who'd betrayed her mother's trust.

She had to remember that.

But Viscount Pulborough was fortunate in having someone so strong in his corner. There was no one looking out for her. No one to put their arms about her to hug her. She'd been strong for so long. Sometimes she just wanted...

Comfort.

She just wanted someone to tell her it would be all right. She missed her mum with an ache that was physical. It had been just the two of them for so long. She had always been supportive, loving and protective. And now...

Now she was alone. She'd been alone for such a long time. Six years.

For six years she'd fought her own battles and dried her own tears. There'd been no one to share the happy, triumphant moments of her life. She felt as if she was standing facing the sea and the tide was about to bear down upon her, an unstoppable force, and she would be swept away by the power of it.

CHAPTER THREE

ELOISE switched on the kettle and crouched down to search for the cafetière. It was tucked at the back of a bottom cupboard behind two large mixing bowls.

She sniffed the contents of an open packet of ground coffee, hoping it was still fresh. It didn't matter. None of this mattered.

Nothing Jem Norland could say would change anything. Her mum hadn't lied. Viscount Pulborough was her father—whether he wanted to accept that or not.

She glanced about aimlessly for a tray. She had one somewhere. Then she saw it. High on the top of the kitchen cupboards.

As she reached up with her fingertips it balanced precariously on the edge before tipping over, bringing with it a couple of bun tins and a baking sheet. Eloise closed her eyes and braced herself for the resounding crash.

She opened one eye gingerly.

'What the—?' Jem walked into the kitchen and began to pick everything off the floor. 'Not your day, is it?'

'I was looking for a tray.'

He held it up. 'You found it. Where do you want everything else?'

Eloise grabbed the tins off him and shoved them into the oven. Her mother would have had a fit if she'd seen her do it. It had been one of her pet hates.

Her hands shook as she rested the tray on the melamine work top. Why had she remembered that now? She closed her eyes and breathed deeply. When she opened them she saw Jem was watching her.

'All right?'

'I've been better.' She pulled out a couple of mugs from the top cupboard. Then she turned to look at him. 'Are you drying off?'

He smiled, the lines at the edges of his eyes fanning outwards. 'Steaming slowly.'

Eloise found her mouth curving in response. *Strange.* Awkwardly she turned and reached for a couple of cream mugs. 'Sugar?'

'No. No milk either.' He leant against the doorframe. Relaxed. Watchful.

Eloise tipped the last of a carton of milk into a jug and placed it on the tray.

'Perhaps you'd better let me carry it.' He stepped forward and picked it up. She stood back and let him do it, unusually passive.

Jem looked across at her. She looked absurdly youthful. Her chic bob lacked the sophisticated glamour it had had earlier. In bare feet she didn't reach his shoulder. Considering the damage she could do to the people he loved, he felt curiously protective of her.

And what if she was telling the truth?

More than that—what if it was the truth? What if she really was Laurence's daughter? It would mean Laurence wasn't the man of high ideals and personal integrity he'd always thought him. It would be a crack on the pedestal of the man who had done so much to restore his belief in others.

He followed her into the small lounge and watched her turn on the gas fire. The flames flickered up. She stood watching them for a moment and then turned to settle herself in the armchair, a cushion on her lap.

Jem carefully put the tray down on the old wooden trunk she used as a coffee table. It was on the tip of his tongue to ask if he should be mother. And then he remembered—her mother was dead.

That was what this was all about. He no longer questioned that her mother had left her a letter stating that Viscount Pulborough was her father. What he had to question, because he knew the man, was whether Eloise Lawton's mother had been lying.

And if she had been, the question was still why. Money was the obvious reason. Maybe it had been a clumsy attempt to provide security for her daughter.

Perhaps she'd even had an affair with the Viscount. Just two weeks ago he would have sworn it was impossible—but now…

It was possible. Maybe that was where the idea had come from.

But the idea that the Viscount would have turned his back on his child was unthinkable. No one who knew him would ever accept that as a possibility.

He was a man who placed huge importance on family. On duty and the care of others. It was what had persuaded his mother to take a chance on a second marriage.

And it had been a good marriage. His mother was settled and happy, a far cry from the woman he remembered from his early childhood.

Jem watched the way Eloise's hand nervously twitched at the tassel on her cushion, the burgundy threads stark against the pale blue of her jeans. 'Coffee?'

She jerked to life, every movement awkward. 'I'll do it. Sorry. I'm not thinking.' She cast the cushion aside. She pushed the plunger down and poured the dark liquid into his mug.

He pulled at the damp fabric of his shirt, then ran a

hand through his rapidly drying hair. This was crazy. He shouldn't be here. It certainly hadn't been his intention. He'd meant to warn her off, make it clear that Laurence wasn't alone.

Eloise poured milk into one of the mugs and gestured for him to pick up the other.

'Thank you.' He sat back on the sofa and watched her cradle her mug between two hands. She looked so tired. Beneath her eyes were dark shadows and there was a sorrow about her.

Not surprising, really. Life had obviously hit her hard. He sipped the liquid. 'Great coffee,' he said, a clumsy attempt to break the silence.

Her brown eyes briefly flitted up to meet his. 'Fair Trade. I buy it when I can. It guarantees the growers have received a fair price for their coffee beans.'

'I know.'

Her eyes flicked downwards. 'Yes. Sorry. I suppose you would.'

And then silence.

Jem had not felt so completely out of his depth for years. He'd forced this meeting. He'd followed her, frightened her. Had made the decision that it was something that had to be dealt with straight away... But now he was here he was reluctant to begin.

She was so fragile. Not the woman he'd imagined her to be. From her reputation on *Image* he'd expected to meet someone quite different. Not a broken butterfly.

He smiled and sipped his coffee. Butterfly was a good analogy for her. Particularly as she'd been earlier in the evening. Impossibly beautiful. Ethereal and fragile.

Jem glanced up. They had to begin somewhere and they might as well begin at the point of issue. 'When did your mother die?'

The hands on the mug moved convulsively. 'Six years ago.' Her voice was quiet. He had to concentrate to hear it. 'The twenty-eighth of November. I was away at university. They phoned.'

He didn't ask who 'they' were. He just watched her misery. Her body curved over her cream mug. Her face indescribably sad.

In the background was the sound of a clock, a steady ticking, marking the passing of time. And quiet. Jem set his mug down on the circular mat on the trunk, reluctant to break the silence. He watched the thoughts and memories pass over her beautiful face.

Because she was beautiful. The kind of woman men would happily have died for in centuries past. Had her mother been as beautiful? Had Laurence found himself irresistibly drawn to her?

'What was her name? Your mother?' he prompted. He knew the answer but he wanted her to talk to him. He wanted to understand what was going on.

'V-Vanessa. Vanessa Lawton.' She lifted a hand and wiped her eye.

Jem felt an overwhelming urge to walk across the room and hold her. The pale pink of her jumper, the soft texture of it. Everything conspired to make him feel protective.

Of course, she might be doing that deliberately, the logical side of his brain cautioned. But he couldn't believe it. Watching her, he had to accept that she believed Viscount Pulborough was her father.

And, moreover, that she believed he'd abandoned both her and her mother.

He shifted uncomfortably in his seat. 'How old was she?'

'Forty.'

Forty. No age at all. And then a new thought. Laurence was seventy-three. It would make an age difference of… He did a rapid calculation. An age difference of twenty-seven years.

Hell.

He frowned. 'Do you have your mother's letter?'

Eloise looked up, startled. 'Of course.' She stood up and placed her mug gently down on the tray.

He watched as she walked over to the bookcase and pulled down a plain box file. Opening it, she lifted the lever arch and picked out the top sheet. Wordlessly, she passed it across to him. 'It's her writing.'

Jem didn't doubt it. There was a quiet dignity about Eloise Lawton. Whatever was going on here, he was convinced it wasn't of her making. The sheet was closely written. He glanced up at her, suddenly unwilling to read her letter. 'May I?'

She gestured for him to continue. Jem lowered his eyes and read of a summer at Coldwaltham Abbey.

Every sentence, every paragraph, twisted the knife inside him a little deeper. He looked across at her. She sat back in her armchair, cradling her mug. 'This would make you twenty-eight?'

Eloise shook her head. 'Twenty-seven.'

Twenty-seven. He lowered his face to the sheet of paper and read on. All the descriptions of Coldwaltham Abbey, brief though they were, were accurate. And yet the records hadn't shown anyone called Vanessa Lawton working at the Abbey.

He wanted to say that, but one look at her face stopped him. Eloise had lost so much already. Carefully he folded her letter along the lines already there. 'Why do you think your mother refused to tell you earlier?'

She shrugged. 'Because he was married. I expect she was hurt by that, perhaps found it difficult to talk about.'

'And when his wife died?'

Eloise sagged visibly in her chair. 'I don't know.' Her hands clasped and unclasped the mug between her long fingers. Then she looked up. Her brown eyes were dark, soft like velvet. 'What's he like?'

Laurence? Like? Just a few hours earlier he wouldn't have hesitated to answer. He was a man of fearsome intelligence. Articulate. Loving. A great husband, father, stepfather...

Jem hesitated. How well did he know his stepfather? How well did one know anyone? You couldn't be privy to their every thought, feeling and action.

He placed the letter on the trunk, to the side of the tray. 'I'm sure he's everything you've read about him.'

His answer was pathetic. Eloise slumped back in her chair, obviously exhausted.

'Eloise...'

It was the first time he'd said her name. She glanced up.

'He's a good man.'

Something flickered in her eyes. He didn't understand it. Almost relief, as though what he'd said had given her immeasurable comfort. 'Will you trust this letter to me?'

Eloise shook her head. 'No.'

It was no more than he should have expected. The letter would have helped, but...

He couldn't blame her.

'I can't.'

'It doesn't matter. I'll speak to him.'

He passed it across the table. 'It doesn't say why she left.'

Eloise placed the letter carefully back into the box file and flicked the lever down. 'No.'

'Did she say whether Laurence knew she was expecting a baby?'

'She never *said* anything. All I know is in that letter.'

'That's it?'

She nodded.

'Had she talked about Coldwaltham Abbey before? Mentioned Laurence in passing?'

Eloise shook her head again.

'That's odd.'

'Why?' Her brown eyes were clear and bright as she looked at him.

'Never to have talked about a place that obviously meant so much to her.'

'Viscount Pulborough obviously meant a lot to her. She had his baby,' Eloise retorted swiftly, 'but she didn't mention him either. Some things are too painful to talk about.'

She stood up abruptly and walked over to replace the box file on the shelf.

Jem sat back on the sofa, his mind trying to meld what he knew of Laurence and what Eloise so obviously believed.

It just didn't fit. The man he knew would never have abandoned his child, however much he may have regretted the affair that had brought it into life. So, assuming Vanessa Lawton and Laurence had been lovers...

'Is it possible your mother left Coldwaltham without Laurence knowing she was carrying his baby?'

'No.'

He looked up. 'Why "no"?'

'She wouldn't have done that. No one would. Every

father has a right to know. She wouldn't... I know she wouldn't...'

A tear welled up and rolled down her cheek. Almost at once, Eloise looked down, the soft blonde strands of her bob swinging about her face.

Pain and loneliness rippled out from her as though she were the epicentre. Jem felt as though someone had punched him.

For the first time he wanted to kiss her. *Heaven help him.* Her face was so soft. So beautiful. The fine bone structure, the long arch of her neck... The curves of her body beneath the soft angora of a baby-pink sweater.

She was lovely.

And she was hurting.

'Do you have a photograph of your mother?' he asked abruptly.

Her brown eyes looked up again. She nodded. 'Of my mother when she was young?'

'Yes.'

'I think so.'

'May I see it?'

She stood up and crossed to a cupboard to the right of the fireplace. 'I retrieved a couple of crates from storage a few weeks ago. I'm sure there was a box of her photographs. I haven't looked at them. I didn't—'

Feel able to do it, Jem finished silently.

'I've still got piles of paperwork to sort through. Mum kept every Christmas card, every letter...' She opened the cupboard and pulled out a large cardboard box. 'Photographs are in here. I think.'

Jem squatted down beside her, lifting out the first of the albums. He opened the cover and looked at a young Eloise. She must have been about five. Her front tooth was missing, her eyes keen and bright.

He shut it quickly. 'Earlier than this.'

Eloise opened the next one down in the pile. 'I don't think it will be in any of the albums. There are some loose photographs at the bottom. I imagine they're more likely to be there.'

As she spoke Jem lifted out the next three albums and found a collection of photographs that hadn't made it into an album. Some had elastic bands wrapped round them. Others had been tucked into envelopes and bore inscriptions like 'Margate, August bank holiday'. Some were loose at the bottom.

He picked one up. It showed a young girl, not unlike Eloise. Her fair hair was loose and blown back in the wind. Her seat was an old tree stump. What astounded him was the oak tree behind that.

Jem's hand stilled and he peered closer. He knew that oak tree very well. He'd climbed it a couple of thousand times. It was the oak tree on the South Lawn. Now open to the public, but back then, when this photograph had been taken, it had been private land. Which meant…

What?

That Eloise was telling the truth?

That her mother's letter told no lies? That Laurence…was Eloise's father?

His fingers moved across the image. 'Is this your mother?' A stupid question, but he had to be certain.

Eloise glanced across. 'I don't know where it was taken. Before I was born. She was never as thin afterwards.'

'It's at the Abbey.'

'Is it?'

He nodded curtly, hating to see the hope that lit her eyes. It proved nothing more than that Vanessa Lawton had visited the Abbey. Hardly conclusive proof of paternity.

But it was enough to mean he'd talk to Laurence, sooner rather than later.

'May I borrow it?'

'The photograph?'

Jem nodded. 'I'm going back to Sussex tomorrow. I'll show him your letter. This photograph.'

'Thank you.' Eloise put the albums back in the box. Then she glanced back at him. 'Do you believe me?'

There was a part of him that wanted to say he did. But to say he believed Eloise would mean he had to accept that his stepfather had lied. And Laurence never lied. It was a pivotal belief.

'Honestly?'

She nodded.

'I don't know.'

He sensed her turn away, saw the flash of blonde hair swing across her face. Without thinking, he raised his hand and held her steady. He looked into her brown eyes. 'I'll show him your letter.'

Eloise nodded, her lips trembling, every emotion showing in her deep brown eyes. It was all he could do not to pull her closer. He wanted so desperately to take her face between his hands and kiss away the pain.

Instead he smiled and stood up, holding the photograph in his hand. 'And the photograph. I'll be in touch when I've spoken to him.'

She nodded.

Jem picked up his jacket and shrugged himself into the wet sleeves, placing the photograph in the inside pocket.

And he'd speak to his mother.

And his stepsister. If Laurence was Eloise's father he

could only have become so when he was married to Belinda's mother.

Hell! It was such a mess.

'Thank you.'

Jem looked back at her. She had precious little to thank him for. 'Go to bed. You look exhausted.'

And then he wished he hadn't said that. He could imagine her snuggled beneath her duvet, her blonde hair ruffled. His eyes drifted to her lips—full and sensuous.

'I'll be in contact.'

'Yes.'

She'd stood up. Her jeans hugged her thighs, her arms were wrapped about her body. He wanted to pull her close, rest her head on his chest and hold her.

Who was he kidding? He wanted to do more than that. He wanted to slowly undress her. He wanted to peel the soft fluff that passed as her top and cradle her naked in his arms. He wanted to drive that wounded, hurt expression from her eyes. He wanted...

So much—and yet it was impossible. This was the woman who was threatening the foundations of his mother's happiness.

Eloise followed him out of the room and down the narrow staircase. His clothes were nearly dry now. He didn't really notice.

'Thank you for the coffee.'

Eloise smiled. 'Thanks for the taxi.'

'You're welcome.'

If Vanessa had smiled like that it might have explained it. Jem pulled up the collar of his jacket and remembered he'd intended to call a taxi from Eloise's flat. There was no going back now. He'd head towards the main road and hope something would pass. If not, he was in for a long walk.

CHAPTER FOUR

JEM took the bend too fast and pressed down on the accelerator for the long straight before he realised what he was doing.

Laurence's tired face would haunt him until the day he died. The open remorse. The shake of his hand as he'd held the photograph. He would never be able to erase the image.

There was no room for doubt. Eloise Lawton was exactly who she said she was—Viscount Pulborough's natural daughter. One glance at the elderly man's face had confirmed everything. If he'd denied it, Jem wouldn't have believed him.

And in that moment something had died. He'd wanted to believe Laurence invincible, free of all human frailty. At fifteen he'd desperately needed that and somehow it had carried on into adulthood. He'd believed him to be a man above all others.

Laurence had always been a man to be trusted. A man to look up to. A man completely unlike his own father. He'd so needed that.

He pulled the Land Rover into a lay-by and sat. The sky darkened and tinted to a rich, dark red. And it was quiet.

Blissfully quiet. A few moments' respite before he telephoned Eloise Lawton. To say what?

To say that her father had at last been shown her letter. That Viscount Pulborough would be delighted to meet the daughter he'd neglected to tell his family about?

What would he say?

Should he tell her that his own mother had cried? Or that Belinda, her half-sister, had left the house refusing to talk about it?

It was as though the whole foundation of his adult life was suddenly unstable and in desperate need of under-pinning.

Secrets and lies. He hated it. Hated the sense of dis-illusionment that permeated everything.

Jem glanced down at his watch and jumped out of the Land Rover, eager to be doing something. Anything. He leant against the fence and rested his foot on the lowest bar.

In the distance he could see the old oak tree on the South Lawn. Tall, seemingly permanent, its branches spread out majestically, darkly menacing against the pink of the evening sky.

Impossible not to think of Vanessa Lawton who'd sat beneath it. Her face laughing up at the camera. A moment in time captured perfectly.

Laurence was a liar and a cheat. Had Belinda's mother known? Had she looked down from her bedroom window and seen her husband with Vanessa Lawton? Had Belinda known? He pieced together the dates and slammed a fist against the hard wood of the fence.

Belinda would have been thirteen. Old enough to have sensed something. Perhaps that explained the difficult re-lationship she had with her father.

Reluctantly he turned and walked back to the Land Rover. Telephoning Eloise was an inescapable duty. He'd promised and there was no one else to do it.

Truth be told, he wanted it to be him. He wanted to hear her voice—and that scared him. Eloise had the power to rip his family apart. His mother's carefully re-built life.

Eloise arriving at Coldwaltham Abbey could only cause pain to the people he loved. But what would this mean to her? Vindication, certainly. She was right to have had faith in her mother, whereas he...

He switched on the engine and took the road back home.

Eloise felt sick. It was the same kind of feeling she'd had on the day she'd gone to look at the notice board to discover her A Level results.

That day it had been good news, her place at Cambridge University confirmed, but it didn't seem possible there'd be a happy outcome today.

It was all too late. Twenty-seven years too late. Questions rolled around her mind in a ceaseless flow, but they could all be summarised in the one word—why?

Today she would get an answer. Summoned to meet the man who'd abandoned her mother—and her. What would she feel when she looked at him? Anger? Pain? Regret?

Love?

She had no way of knowing. Nothing in her life had prepared her for this. How could it? But the opportunity to come face to face with the man who'd helped create her was not something she could turn away from. However painful, it had to be faced.

She'd see Jem Norland again too. The man who'd made this meeting happen because he'd done what he said he would.

She hadn't expected that of him. Not really. The morning after the charity evening she'd have sworn he wouldn't bother. But he'd telephoned. The door to her father had swung open.

Even so, she wasn't a fool. His voice had been clipped, even angry. It wasn't difficult to understand why. He'd been so adamant that Viscount Pulborough couldn't be her father. He'd been wrong. Her mother had been right.

Her feet scrunched on the gravel of the drive as she forced herself to walk towards Jem's home. An estate cottage, he'd called it. But it was hardly a cottage. You had to have been brought up with his kind of privileges to describe it like that.

It was a solidly built, detached red-brick house with an impossibly pretty white gable. Everyone else's fantasy home. It reminded her of the gingerbread house in one of her childhood books. A far cry from the council estate in Birmingham she'd called home.

Viscount Pulborough probably had no idea what he'd consigned the young Vanessa to. He'd probably not given it a thought.

The familiar sense of injustice that had smouldered inside her over the past few weeks flickered angrily. She wanted Viscount Pulborough to know what her mother's life had been like. Ill or not, he had to know how much pain he'd caused.

And when she was sure he understood just what he'd done, she'd walk away. In no time at all she'd be back in London and he could continue his life unhindered. It was what he'd chosen, after all.

It didn't matter if Jem Norland didn't like it. He was obviously very protective of his stepfather, but it wasn't anything to do with him. Viscount Pulborough wasn't even his father.

Smoothing down her suede jacket, she reached up to ring the bell. The dark blue door was opened almost immediately by a man in his mid to late fifties, dressed in a red checked shirt and holding a steaming mug of coffee.

She was about to apologise for being in the wrong place when he said, 'You'll be looking for Jem?'

'J-Jem. Yes. Y-yes I am.'

'He's over in the workshop.'

She must have looked confused because he winked and said, 'I'll take you over. He'll be pleased to see you, I'll be guessing.'

He took a swig of the dark liquid and placed it on the small table by the door. 'Bess. Come here, girl.'

Eloise watched, stunned, as a brown Labrador padded down the hall and nuzzled the hand he held down to her. 'Do you mind dogs?' he asked, obviously seeing something in her face.

'No,' she replied carefully. 'Just not very used to them.' She glanced down at her cream trousers. 'Does she jump up?'

'Not this old lady.' Carefully shutting the door behind him, he nodded up towards a narrow path. 'The workshop's up there. No more than a couple of steps.'

Eloise glanced down at her soft leather shoes and stoically followed.

'I'm Matt, by the way,' He turned with a smile. 'Work on the estate.'

'Eloise Lawton.' Her feet struggled to manage the soft mud. 'Do many people work on the estate?'

'A fair few. There's thirteen thousand acres here. And the Abbey, of course. Always something that needs fixing.'

Eloise tried to nod intelligently.

'I'm the Estate Carpenter. Came as an apprentice to Pete and took over when he retired. Good few years back now.' They rounded a corner and Matt shouted out, 'Jem, lad. You've got a visitor.'

Eloise felt her shoe slip on the soft mud and she reached out for Matt to steady herself. The lines on his face contracted and he said, 'You'll need to get yourself some sensible shoes or you'll come a cropper.'

It was on the tip of her tongue to defend herself. When she'd set out that morning she hadn't imagined she'd be traipsing up a country footpath.

'You're early,' Jem said, walking out of the brick-built workshop. He shaded his eyes against the winter sun.

He looked very different from when she'd last seen him. Gone was the expensive suit and in its place was a pair of worn jeans and a T-shirt that looked as if it had seen better days. The effect on her was instantaneous. It began in the pit of her stomach and spread outwards.

Gorgeous.

Sex on legs, as Cassie had described. And completely out of bounds. She remembered the feeling of his hands on her face, the intent look in his eyes.

He walked towards her. 'I wasn't expecting you until ten.'

'It's half past,' Eloise shot back, her nerves as taut as a violin bow.

Jem glanced down at his wrist-watch. 'Damn, is it?'

'I'll be off then,' Matt said, tossing Jem a set of keys. 'Some of us have work to do. I'll take Bess with me. She's itching for a romp.'

Jem nodded. 'Thanks.' Then he looked at Eloise. 'I'll just grab my jacket and shut this place up.' He held out his hands to show her a pair of dusty palms. 'Better wash my hands too.'

Eloise neatly side-stepped a muddy puddle. 'Are we walking up to the Abbey?' she asked, following him, trying to ignore the way his denim jeans fitted snugly over a muscular rear.

What was the matter with her? Jem Norland was a representative of everything she disliked. He was a bona fide member of the moneyed upper class. She objected to him on principle.

Didn't she?

'Too far. We'll take the Land Rover.' Jem led her into the workshop, where the air was heavy with the smell of wood and dust.

Eloise looked round curiously. 'Do you work from here?'

He shook his head. 'This is purely my personal space. Everything I make here, I keep for myself.' He reached out and stroked the top of the enormous circular table in the centre of his workshop.

Eloise watched his tanned fingers splay out against the smooth wood. His touch was like a caress. He would touch the woman he loved like that. She forced herself to look away, suddenly aware of the burning heat in her cheeks.

Why had she thought that?

Perhaps because her emotions were heightened, her nerves pulled tight? It was nothing.

It would have made it so much easier if there'd been someone in her life who'd have held her hand through all this.

But not Jem.

His strength was appealing. There was something about him that would make it very easy to trust him, rely on him. She watched him turn away and walk over to a small basin at the far end of the workshop.

Jem glanced back over his shoulder. 'How are you feeling?'

An impossible question to answer. Nervous. Sick. Sad. Bitter. 'I don't know.' She tried to smile. 'Bit scared.'

Jem nodded, as though it had been the answer he'd expected.

She watched the way his muscles moved beneath the fabric of his T-shirt.

She rushed in, 'Th-thank you for arranging this.'

'There's nothing to thank me for. I merely did what I said I would.' He reached across and dried his hands on the taupe-coloured towel.

'I didn't think you would.'

'No? Well, that doesn't surprise me.' He folded the towel carefully into a long strip and threaded it through the loop of the towel ring. Then he reached up for a heavy sweatshirt and pulled it over his head, the blue picking out exactly a fleck in his eyes.

Eloise swallowed. *Gorgeous.*

'I owe you an apology.'

'Why?'

Jem crossed back to her. Eloise waited, finding it suddenly difficult to breathe. He stopped a short distance from her. 'I didn't believe you.'

'No,' she managed, nervously moistening her dry lips. 'I know.'

He pulled a hand across the back of his neck. 'Laurence…'

Eloise watched the self-deprecating smile, the weary expression that passed across his face. It told her more than he could have known.

She was stepping into a family that didn't want her. Of course they didn't. She'd known that. From the beginning—it was just that she hadn't thought about it from their perspective.

How naïve. She'd only thought about how she was

feeling. Her anger. Her resentment. But other people were involved too.

Viscount Pulborough…Laurence…was loved. Perhaps she'd cruelly made public his deepest, most shameful secret. Maybe he'd feared this day. Maybe her mum had known that and had loved him enough to keep silent…

She didn't know. And she hadn't taken time to think.

'Laurence,' Jem began again, 'was cross we hadn't shown him your letter immediately. He said we'd no right to withhold information from him. He recognised your mother's photograph immediately.'

Eloise felt her throat tighten and a burning sensation begin at the back of her eyes. 'R-Really?'

Jem glanced down. 'He called her Nessa.'

'Grandma called her that too.' Her heart jumped at the use of her mum's childhood name. Eloise hated the way she was so desperate for every snippet of information. She didn't want to hang on to every word Jem uttered, so needy.

He continued as though he hadn't noticed. He walked round his circular table, his voice bland. 'We hadn't been able to find a Vanessa Lawton on any employment records connected with the Abbey. Had I told you that? When your letter first arrived we spent some time looking.'

'She was a secretary,' she said stiffly.

'He told me. She came to type up his notes for a book he was writing.'

Eloise swallowed hard. She wouldn't cry. Wouldn't.

Jem stepped closer, his voice a deep rumble. His face seemed softer.

'It meant her name wasn't on the Abbey records.'

'Oh.' Eloise bit down on her lip.

Jem reached out and pushed back her hair, his knuckles

grazing her cheek. Eloise didn't move. She stood pinned to the spot as effectively as if she'd been nailed there.

It was a gentle, comforting touch. Eloise would have given a lot to be able to curl into it, to have him hold her. Just for comfort.

Or not. She felt as if she was in one of those daft turn of the century toys. The one you tipped upside down to make a snowy scene. Everything about her was shifting. Like being in a blizzard, with no point of reference anywhere.

She'd always been so certain of everything. And now…

Now she was certain she knew nothing.

'I'm sorry,' he said softly. 'Truly.'

He let his hand fall to his side and Eloise felt the soft brush of her hair on her cheek as it fell back into place. She sensed he was about to move away.

'What did he say about me?' she blurted out.

'I think he'd rather speak for himself.'

Eloise swallowed; it was almost impossible. A hard knot had settled in the middle of her throat. She'd never been as scared as she felt at this moment. She was completely prepared for total rejection, braced for it even. But desperately hoping for…

What?

She wasn't even sure what she wanted.

Acceptance? Some sense that she was not a 'mistake'? Not an accident of fate and bitterly regretted.

And where did Jem fit into all this? She didn't know. Didn't know at all.

'He said,' Jem said slowly, as though he couldn't resist giving her something, 'Alexander Pope wrote a poem called *Eloise to Abelard*.'

Eloise frowned, trying to understand the connection. 'I

know. In 1717 or thereabouts. It's one of the few things he ever wrote about love. My mum had a copy of it. It was where she...' She trailed off. *Got my name.*

Like a searchlight suddenly picking out something it had been hunting for—she understood.

'Laurence wrote a book on English poetry. Eighteenth century English poets, to be precise. It's his passion.' Jem turned away, but not before she registered the message in his eyes. 'We'd better get up to the Abbey. He's wanting to talk to you.'

He reached up to a hook on the wall for a large bunch of keys. Strangely, having come so far, she felt reluctant to leave. She'd have been happy if Jem had announced Viscount Pulborough had changed his mind and she wasn't going to meet him after all. She could cope with everything so far, but at the Abbey...

She didn't know whether she was strong enough for that.

'Will you be there?'

'If you need me.'

Her stomach flipped at his words. If she needed him. Did he have any idea of the turmoil surging through her veins? The uncharacteristic uncertainty.

'Will I meet anyone else?'

'No.'

It was the answer she'd wanted, but as soon as she heard it she wanted to know why. Did Viscount Pulborough want her to stay hidden in the background? Was he ashamed of her?

Or of himself?

'My mother intends to keep out of the way. There's no one else staying at the Abbey at the moment.'

Not Alexander. The fourteen-year-old who would be her half-brother. Jem's half-brother, too.

She glanced up at him. Strange. She hadn't thought about that before. Jem Norland was no blood relation of hers—but they would have a link between them. A shared brother. A connection between them. Always.

'Alex is away at school.' He steered her out of the workshop. 'And Belinda lives with her husband just outside Chichester.'

Belinda. Her half-sister. She'd seen a photograph of her on the Internet. There'd been a couple of short paragraphs. Very little to discover.

To her shame, she hadn't considered what Belinda might feel to be confronted with a half-sister. A half-sister whose existence meant her mother had been cheated on. Lied to.

She knew that Belinda was forty, married to the Hon. Piers Atherton and had no children. She knew the facts. She hadn't thought about the emotions.

'That's probably better,' she said, stepping out of the workshop.

'Laurence thought so.'

'Belinda's not going to like me, is she?'

Jem squinted up at the low winter sun. 'No.'

The single word hung starkly in the air. No. Of course she wasn't. Eloise had only thought about Belinda in terms of how unfair it was that her half-sister had received the best of everything, whereas she'd...

Whereas she'd had a mother who'd loved her.

And Belinda's mother had been ill and had died. With uncomfortable clarity Eloise suddenly saw the bigger picture. She might not have had an education at one of the best public schools, opportunities to travel and play a musical instrument like Belinda. She hadn't learnt to ride or owned her own pony. But she'd never felt unloved.

Never.

Her mum had always made her feel special. Had been completely behind everything she'd ever wanted to do with all the energy and support she could give.

'Does Belinda know about me?'

'Laurence told her.'

He'd told her. She could only begin to imagine how difficult a conversation that must have been. For them both.

They crossed the small courtyard, Eloise skirting around the uneven surface and small puddles. 'Why do you call him Laurence?' she asked suddenly.

Jem opened the door of the green Land Rover. He let his fingers rest on the doorframe. 'Nothing else to call him. He's not my father.'

He walked round and climbed in the other side of the car. He shut the door and settled himself in his seat before turning to look at her. 'My mother married him when—'

'You were fifteen,' she finished for him. 'I know. I read that.'

His smiled twisted. 'Your research. I forgot.'

'I was curious.'

'Of course.'

He twisted the key in the ignition and Eloise watched the movement of his fingers. 'Did you mind when your mother wanted to marry him?'

Jem turned his head to look down at her, surprised.

'Fifteen's a difficult age,' she apologised. 'I just wondered.'

'Honestly? I was as jealous as hell. In the beginning.' He looked back at the road. His hands moved smoothly over the steering wheel. 'I was away at school and came home for the Christmas holidays to find I wasn't as important any more. I didn't like it.'

'I can imagine.'

He smiled, the grooves in the sides of his cheeks deepening. 'I made life as difficult as possible for a few months. Got myself expelled from school.'

'You like him now, though?'

There was a momentary pause before he answered. 'He's been more of a father to me than my own ever was. I'm grateful for that.'

Eloise longed to ask what he meant. There was a wintry edge to his voice she couldn't miss. She hurried to fill the silence without really understanding why she felt she had to.

'I didn't want my mum to marry either. I liked it being just the two of us.'

'Was there never anyone?'

Eloise shrugged. 'There might have been a couple of possibilities…but I probably stopped any chance she had.' There was a short silence. 'I'd change that now if I could.'

'Would you?'

She'd not thought about how lonely her mum must have been. 'It can't have been the way she'd planned her life to be.'

It was all too late now. Her mum was long dead. Eloise turned slowly away. She looked down at her fingers, which were clasped in her lap. They were long, pale even against the cream of her trousers.

She saw the single tear drop down on her hand, a bubble of moisture which rested against her skin.

'I'm sure she understood,' Jem said brusquely.

Eloise swiped at her eyes. 'I'm not sure she'd have understood why I'm doing this. Contacting my father. Now. After all this time. It's only going to cause pain, isn't it?'

He said nothing. His hands moved against the steering wheel and his eyes stayed on the road ahead.

She understood why. She didn't need him to tell her the effect the sudden arrival of a mystery daughter would have.

'It's not my fault though,' she felt the need to say. 'You have to blame your stepfather for that.'

'And your mother.' He glanced across. 'It takes two to have an affair.'

'She wasn't married.'

'But she knew he was,' he replied. 'Don't try and apportion blame. You can't know what went on between them.'

Eloise pushed the palms of her hands tightly together until her knuckles glowed white. 'I know she was twenty-seven years younger than him. She was nineteen. Just nineteen.'

The same age as your Sophia Westbrooke, she added silently, forcing that memory between them. This connection she felt to Jem Norland was an illusion. She knew nothing about him. Didn't want to, either.

She looked back up at him, challenging. 'Who do you think carries the most blame?'

'Meet Laurence,' he said quietly. 'Talk to him.'

The flicker of anger smouldered and died. It was sensible advice. So much depended on what Viscount Pulborough said.

Eloise turned to look out of the window. The Coldwaltham estate stretched out to either side. Mature trees covered the grassland and a herd of deer grazed nearby.

And this belonged to her father. Had her mum been completely overawed by it all? So much wealth. Was that why…?

'When did the deer come?' Eloise asked suddenly.

'They're not just deer. It's a herd of dark-coated fallow deer.' Jem dropped down to second gear. 'And they appear in the records from 1624.'

Coldwaltham Abbey loomed up ahead. The pale stone façade looked both magical and intimidating.

They approached a set of large iron gates and drove over the cattle grid. Immediately the gardens became more formal. The lawns stretched out like a thick velvet carpet.

And her father owned this. It angered her.

She'd have loved a garden. Her own swing. A slide, maybe. She'd so envied school friends who'd had some kind of garden, particularly Isla who'd had a wooden Wendy house.

She glanced across at Jem's profile. 'Did you play here?' she asked, wanting to find something to fan her resentment.

'Not here. The Abbey is open to the public most days during the summer. There's a small fenced off area near the staff quarters reserved for the family.'

She sat back in her seat. Strange to own all this and not have the use of it. It was another world.

And she was about to enter it. An interloper. Unwanted.

'And there are the tennis courts. The stables are behind that. We have seven horses, four of which are mine.'

'Of course, you play polo,' Eloise interjected in a quiet, dead voice. The sport of the wealthy, she reminded herself.

He turned his head briefly to look at her. 'Most weekends.'

Jem pulled the Land Rover to a stop in a small courtyard. 'Laurence has commandeered a handful of rooms on the ground floor. The stairs are too exhausting at the moment.'

She was thankful for his matter-of-fact tone. She couldn't have coped with anything else.

Coldwaltham Abbey looked cold and forbidding in the grey February light. The windows stared blankly down and the whole thing reminded her of a museum.

This wasn't a home. Perhaps the current incumbent was as cold and forbidding?

Jem held open the car door. 'Ready?'

'Yes,' she lied, stepping down on to the gravel. Eloise had never felt less ready. How did you do this? How did anyone do this?

Jem shut the door behind her. 'I'll take you through to Laurence.'

Eloise nodded. Her knees felt weak and her stomach was churning. It was pure discipline that enabled her to keep walking behind Jem. Everything conspired to make her feel more uncomfortable, more hopelessly out of her depth: the high ceilings, the ornate doorways, the sweeping staircase.

She followed blindly, aware only of the rising panic inside her. Her shoes clicked on the limestone floor, occasionally muffled by the rich-coloured rugs. Walls of cabinets filled with beautiful china were interspersed by paintings.

Jem stopped at the end of a long corridor. 'He's through here. I'll introduce you and leave you alone. Is that what you want?'

'Aren't you staying?' She wanted to tell him she needed him. He'd said he'd stay if she needed him.

He thrust his hands into his jeans pockets. 'It would probably be better if I didn't.'

'I suppose so.' Eloise felt bereft. She glanced down at her cream trousers. 'Do I look all right?'

The muscle in his cheek pulsed but he answered smoothly. 'You look lovely.' And then, 'Don't worry. You'll like him.' A small pause. 'He'll love you.'

He turned the heavy brass handle and pushed open the door. Eloise could scarcely breathe, let alone command her feet to move. Somehow, though, she found herself following Jem into the cavernous room.

The furniture was of heavy oak but the room had a lived in feel. Fresh flowers were arranged in a vase on an oval table, a cheerful summer yellow.

Jem pointed at the far door. 'Laurence is still confined to bed. The operation is a very painful one and he's found it difficult.'

She looked where he indicated but said nothing. He strode out in front of her and Eloise had no choice but to follow. Her sense of fear was so real she could almost taste it.

Jem glanced back at her and smiled encouragingly. Eloise met his eyes and tried to smile.

'Ready?'

She nodded. For a minute they stood frozen, but to Eloise it seemed longer. It was as though time had become elastic and it stretched out between them.

Slowly his hand moved. He reached out and he touched the side of her face, his thumb slowly moving across her lips.

'Good luck,' he said softly.

Eloise stood bemused. She couldn't work out what was happening. All her emotions were swirling together in a vortex of conflicting sensations.

She knew he wanted to kiss her. She could feel his eyes follow the movement of his thumb. His hand fell away suddenly, as though he'd suddenly realised what he was doing.

He turned away, leaving her feeling bereft. She'd wanted him to kiss her. The realisation spread through her with a sense of shame. How could she want that?

The image of Sophia Westbrooke laughing up at him came up and bit her. So young. So beautiful.

Jem pushed open the door. 'Laurence, I've brought Eloise Lawton to see you.'

Eloise stepped through into the second room, her view of the bed shielded by Jem's body. She felt an overwhelming sense of panic and then a cold calmness.

This was what she'd been waiting for.

As Jem moved to one side, she looked at the elderly man sitting up in the bed. The expression on his face took away all fear.

This was the man her mother had loved.

Her father.

She stepped forward with a stumbling step. His hair was white and the lines on his face had fallen in pleasant places. A good man, her mum had said.

Over the past few weeks she'd vilified this man in her imagination but now she was faced with the reality of him. His eyes seemed to imply he expected her anger.

The angry red wound of his bypass operation showed livid against the paleness of his skin in the V of his pyjama top.

Viscount Pulborough looked steadily at her and then spoke softly. 'Eloise?'

His voice was hesitant and broken. She resolutely fanned the flames of her bitterness but they'd really disappeared, washed away in the wave of emotion.

Her father.

She heard the sound of the door behind her click shut and knew Jem had left her alone.

CHAPTER FIVE

DAMN it! He'd nearly kissed her.

Jem sat down on the Chippendale chair and leant his head back against the wall.

He'd meant to be kind. To be supportive of both Eloise and Laurence. Most of all he'd wanted to help his mother. If he'd refused the job of taking Eloise to Laurence she'd have had to take it on.

But he'd nearly kissed her. That hadn't been in his plan. He'd forgotten how beautiful she was. Had forgotten the shape of her face and the elegant curve of her neck.

Had forgotten, too, the vulnerability in her eyes. The sadness.

Jem brushed his hands across his face in a futile attempt to erase the image of Eloise.

Damn it!

This was a complication he could do without. He didn't want to feel any kind of attraction for the woman who'd had such a devastating effect on his family. Surely after everything he'd seen about love and marriage his cynicism should be protection enough?

'Has she gone?'

Jem looked up sharply at the sound of Belinda's voice.

'Has she gone?' she repeated with a nod at the door. 'Have I missed her? The not so dumb blonde?'

'If you mean Eloise, she's with him now,' he said, standing up. 'What are you doing here? We agreed—'

'You agreed. I don't think I said anything at all.'

Belinda pulled her jacket more closely around her pain-fully thin body. 'I want to see what she's like. Whether she's worth all this fuss.'

Jem moved towards her, his forehead pulled into a deep frown. 'Belinda, this isn't a good idea. You know it isn't. This isn't the time.'

Two spots of bright red burnt on her cheeks and he could smell the odour of stale alcohol. She'd been drink-ing. Automatically he glanced down at his wrist-watch and registered how early in the day it still was.

Her habitual resentment bubbled up. 'He's not your father. Even though he likes to pretend you are. He's mine. And he cheated on my mother. Mine.'

Jem reached out and took hold of her claw-like hand. 'This isn't the way to do it. Your argument is with Laurence, not Eloise. Tell him how you feel—'

'But not now! Wait until he's stronger. I heard you.' She snatched her hand away. 'But she can see him when-ever she wants. Ask all her bloody questions about her slutty mother.'

Jem saw her head flick round before he heard the door open. Everything slowed down as though it were an ac-tion replay, but he couldn't stop the inevitable.

He saw Eloise turn to him with a question in her wide brown eyes as Belinda strode forward, her movements agitated and jerky.

'So you're Nessa's daughter.' Her voice held all the contempt, the pent-up bitterness she must have held in-side for years and had never spoken about. 'You look like her. Are you a slut like her?'

The ugly word echoed in the large hallway, stark and hateful.

Eloise's mouth moved with some kind of denial, but

there wasn't time. Belinda's hand swung back and then forwards in a venomous arc.

'Belinda!' Jem shot forward, but not soon enough to stop the resounding slap across Eloise's left cheek. He saw her recoil, one hand holding the burning cheek and the other raised to protect herself from any further blows. 'Stop it. It's enough.'

Belinda turned to look at him, her eyes showing all the hatred she felt inside. 'It's not enough! It's not nearly enough.' She pulled her hand away from the hold he had on it. 'If you think I'm going to stand by and let her take over my father you've got another think coming.'

She drew herself up to her full five feet five inches. 'Your mother was a cow and everyone knows you're no better. Out for everything you can get. A hanger-on.'

Jem moved so he stood between the two women. He glanced back at Eloise. She said nothing and stood as though she'd been immobilised. Shock, he registered. He turned back to face Belinda.

'That's enough! Go home.'

Belinda sneered, her pretty face marred beyond anything Jem had ever seen. 'So she's got her claws into you, has she? Better watch out. Her kind only want money and you've got plenty of that. Perhaps she'd like to do a kiss and tell in that trashy magazine she works for.'

Jem heard Eloise's startled intake of breath behind him but kept his eyes resolutely facing Belinda. 'Go home,' he repeated firmly.

'I'm going. I've said everything I came to say anyway.' She spun round and started back along the hallway, her shoes clicking on the hard floors.

Jem waited until she had disappeared around the corner before he turned. 'I'm sorry, I...'

But he didn't know what to say. He watched Eloise's body sag as she crumpled with emotion, the tears falling softly over her pale cheeks. And he felt helpless.

There was nothing he could say that would take away the pain of that confrontation. She couldn't have missed the hatred in Belinda's eyes.

Her half-sister. The thought hit him like a bolt.

'She hates me.' Her voice sounded bemused. Lost, like a little girl in an enormous department store.

'She's angry.' He stepped forward and wrapped his arms around her body. Dangerous, he knew—but what was the alternative? The fine soft strands of her hair brushed against his chin as he pulled her close. And then closer.

He let his hand move to cradle her head, his fingers entwined in the gold of her hair. Her whole body seemed to judder and radiated with misery.

And all he could do was hold her.

He felt her sobs rack her body, the acute misery—and some of it echoed inside him. He knew she was crying about more than unkind words from a woman she'd expected to resent her.

It surprised him how angry he felt towards Laurence. The man he'd always revered. It was the lie he'd been living that repulsed him so much. With a secret in his past like this how could he take the moral high ground—ever?

Gradually Eloise's sobs quietened and her body relaxed. Her hair still touched his face. The soft suede of her jacket rested beneath his fingers. Jem pulled back and pushed the swinging blonde hair back from her face. 'All right?'

Her eyes were rimmed red and the mark of Belinda's fingers still stained her cheek. It was a stupid question.

He knew it the minute it left his lips but he felt so helpless.

And he didn't like to feel like that. It reminded him of how it had felt to stand by his mother, hear her racking sobs and know he could do nothing to help her. No one could, until she made the decision to help herself.

Eloise hiccuped and pulled back awkwardly. 'I've got a tissue somewhere.' She began to search her pockets. 'I'm sorry.'

'About?'

She swiped at her eyes. 'Crying all over you. Do you need to go after Belinda? I assume that was Belinda?'

'That was Belinda,' he concurred, looking up the empty hallway as though she might reappear.

Eloise bunched the tissue up into a tight ball and put it in her jacket pocket. 'She swings a hefty slap.'

'So I saw.' And then, 'I'm sorry.'

She shrugged, keeping her face turned away. 'It wasn't your fault.'

Jem reached out and touched the red mark on her cheek with his fingertip. He could see three fingers clearly marked on her skin.

'Has she left a mark?'

'For the moment. It'll fade.'

Eloise stepped back as though she couldn't cope with his touch any longer. 'It's turning out to be an unexpected day.'

'Is it?'

He watched the thoughts pass across her face. 'Not really,' she admitted quietly. 'I knew it was going to be difficult.'

Together they turned to walk down the long corridor, Jem slightly behind. Neither spoke. Eloise's mind was presumably taken up with everything Laurence had told her, and his with wanting to know what that had been.

Her whole body was held stiffly, the fingers on her right hand clutching at the strap on her handbag.

'When do you have to be back in London?' he asked neutrally, breaking the silence.

She turned to look at him, her blonde hair swinging back. 'Tonight.' And then, 'I'm driving back this afternoon.'

Eloise looked away and out through the large arched windows down an elegant vista. The whole aspect looked bare and wintry.

'I wondered if you had friends in the area.'

'No.' Again, that painful silence. Eloise couldn't seem to formulate any thoughts, let along put them into words. Everything she'd believed had been turned on its head.

She'd wanted to hate Viscount Pulborough—and yet she'd found him to be warm and compassionate. Hatred was impossible.

'Will you visit Laurence again?' Jem asked, interrupting her thoughts.

Yesterday she'd have been certain of her reply, but now she wasn't sure what she wanted. 'I don't know.'

They stepped out into the courtyard and headed back towards the Land Rover. Jem held open the door for her to climb up. 'Don't let Belinda influence your decision.' He walked round and sat in the driver's seat. He turned to look at her. 'Belinda is Laurence's responsibility.'

Eloise nodded, but Belinda's angry face sat at the forefront of her mind. She couldn't blame Belinda but she would never be able to forget the look of loathing in the other woman's eyes. How could she?

'They have a…difficult relationship. Ever since I've known her they've been…'

'L-Laurence told me,' Eloise cut in, her voice hesitating over the unfamiliar name. 'He blames himself. Wonders if she knew about his relationship with my mother.'

'It's possible.'

'That's what Laurence thinks.' She looked down as she felt the tears well up behind her eyes. For the first time she found she was blaming her mum. Had she known how unhappy Belinda had been? How scared and alone?

Perhaps she'd been too young, too infatuated with her new love, to realise how much hurt she was causing. Having met her father she couldn't believe the blame was entirely on his side and her mum completely innocent—despite the age difference.

Perhaps the most noble thing she could do would be to stop this now. To let this first visit to Coldwaltham be her last.

'Would you like to stop for lunch somewhere?'

Eloise brushed at the stray tears on her face. 'Pardon?'

'Are you hungry?' Jem asked. 'It's gone one. We could stop for a pub lunch.'

Part of her wanted to accept. The thought of returning to her London flat wasn't appealing. If only there was someone she could speak to about everything that was happening in her life. She felt so lonely.

So very lonely.

'You're busy. I don't—'

He shrugged. 'I have to eat. The Cricketers do some great food.'

Eloise hesitated. 'Are you sure?'

'I'm sure.' He swung the Land Rover down a narrow lane. 'It's not more than a couple of minutes from here and worth the slight detour.'

Bare branches overhung the lane, almost meeting in the middle. In summer it would be like a bower. Beautiful. Eloise let her eyes wander over the detail in the hedges even while her mind was questioning the wisdom of this.

But the alternative was a service station sandwich and too much time alone. Too much time to think.

'Did you like him?'

She didn't need to ask who he was talking about. 'Yes,' she answered quietly. 'I did. Very much.'

'And you're calling him Laurence now.'

'He asked me to.' Eloise turned her head and caught the edge of his smile.

His eyes remained on the road. She wasn't quite sure how he felt about her using his stepfather's name. Maybe he felt everything was moving too quickly.

Perhaps it was?

The Cricketers was a charming old English pub, the kind you found in faded sepia photographs of bygone days. The roof was a mass of different angles and the walls seemed to bow out, the architectural style a complete mish-mash of centuries.

Eloise stepped down from the Land Rover and sniffed the fresh air. It had been the right choice. There was space here. Beauty.

And there was Jem. She turned to look at him as he locked the door. Laurence had spoken so fondly of him, had hinted at the deep bond of affection between them. It made sense of his initial attitude to her.

'Ready?'

She turned and nodded.

'This way then,' he said, indicating the low doorway. 'You might need to duck your head. The lintel's very low.'

Eloise's eyes took a moment to adjust to the darkness. Light came from the small panes of glass in the tiny windows and from the open fire at the far end of the room.

'It's beautiful,' she remarked, walking towards the fireplace. Around the mantel were the almost obligatory horse brasses, shining as though they'd been lovingly polished very recently.

She made a show of warming her hands in front of the flames—but it was only for show. Something to do.

Jem came to stand behind her. 'What would you like to eat?' he asked, handing her a menu.

She took it and gave it a cursory glance. It was difficult to think of anything as mundane as food. 'I'll just have soup.'

'Anything to drink?'

'A coffee. Please,' she added as an afterthought.

She was grateful that Jem hadn't asked her any questions. She wasn't ready to talk and wouldn't have known how to answer them.

The fire was warm so she slipped off her jacket and folded it with meticulous care before sitting down on the curved seat by the bay window. In the hearth the logs spat more than crackled.

Her head felt fuzzy as though too much information was swimming about in her brain. And she wanted to sleep. The effect of tension, she supposed. It would be so easy to take to her bed and refuse to emerge until this was all over.

Except it wasn't going to be over. It was the rest of her life. *Who* she was.

'One coffee,' Jem said, placing a white cup and saucer in front of her. Then, reaching into his pocket, he pulled out a small wooden cube with a number on the side and placed it on the table. 'They'll bring our food over in a moment.'

Eloise made an effort to snap out of her languid mood. 'This is nice.'

His fingers curved around the tall beer glass but he said nothing. His blue eyes flicked up and he watched her face, as though he were reading her mind.

'D-do you often come here?' she said hurriedly, and then winced at the clichéd question.

'Occasionally.' His fingers moved on the glass and she found her eyes were drawn to the movement. 'There's a pretty garden at the back. In summer it's a nice place to sit after a hard day in the workshop.'

'I suppose so,' she answered blandly.

'And, of course, it's haunted.'

Eloise looked up. 'Is it?'

'So the story goes.' He lifted his pint glass and took another sip. 'In 1760 the barmaid, Sukey Williams, fell in love with a wealthy traveller.'

'Did he love her?'

'Sukey presumably thought so. At any rate, she became his mistress...much to the chagrin of the local youths. One night she received a letter purporting to be from her lover, asking her to meet him in the spinney.'

Eloise sat forward. 'Did she go?'

'Oh, yes.' He nodded. 'She went. No one knows exactly what happened in that spinney, but Sukey returned to the inn with a nasty gash on her head and died in her sleep. Ever since it's been said that Sukey walks at night, still waiting for her lover to return.'

She gave a short laugh. 'Do you believe all that?'

'Me? No.'

'Nice story, though.'

He smiled. 'You ought to get Laurence to tell you some of the tales he told me about the Abbey when I first arrived. I doubt they're all true but they make good listening.'

Her face shadowed. 'Perhaps.' She tore open the top of the demerara sugar and tipped the brown crystals into her coffee.

Jem was a nice man. Whatever way you looked at it, he was a man to admire. This couldn't be easy for him, but he was…incredible, really. When you considered what she was doing to the people he loved.

The hatred in Belinda's face had been shocking. All her earlier conjectures about how her half-sister would feel had paled into insignificance before the real thing. Her half-sister hated her.

And what about Laurence's wife? Jem's mother? How did she feel about her husband's illegitimate love-child suddenly appearing on the scene?

It would be better for everyone if she just went away…

But there was such a temptation to stay. There was so much more she wanted to know about her father.

'I particularly liked to hear about the Civil War,' Jem continued, unaware of her thoughts. 'I'm convinced Laurence made up story after story to satisfy my cravings for adventure and honour.'

He broke off as the waitress brought across their food. Eloise smiled her thanks before trying a spoonful of her leek and potato soup. It was comfortingly warm and deliciously seasoned.

'Good?'

'Fantastic. I think…' she broke off and let the flavours swirl about her mouth '…I think it's got soy sauce in it. It's lovely.'

'Richard Camford is a genius. He took over this place a couple of years back. A refugee from city life.'

'You really don't like London, do you?'

'Not much.' Jem cut into his beef and kidney pie. 'Pleasant enough to visit, but I've got no yen to live there. I'd rather come to a country pub like this than follow the pack to the next up-and-coming restaurant. I don't like the big society parties either.'

'Why?'

His strong mouth twisted as though it were some kind of private joke. 'Because I prefer to have more say over whom I spend my time with. London parties are full of people I'd be quite happy never to see again. They bore me.'

Eloise thought back to the sumptuous events she'd attended for *Image* magazine. True enough, there were the same people over and over again. Different dresses, different themes, different venues—but essentially the same.

'But surely the polo set is pretty much the same people over and over?'

Jem raised his glass and drank before placing it back down in the exact centre of the coaster. He looked up, his eyes a vibrant blue with a hint of mischief. 'True enough, but the horses are interesting.'

She found an answering smile. Somewhere in the past half an hour she'd relaxed; her body no longer felt stiff and unyielding. She took another scoop of soup.

Jem had made a point of talking about other things. Anything. The cold sense of panic and fear had started to recede. Even the memory of Belinda's slap had softened.

'You haven't asked me what Laurence said,' she observed, her spoon poised mid-air.

'You'll tell me if you want to.' Eloise threw him a sceptical glance and he added, 'And if you don't, Laurence will.'

'Will he?'

His mouth twisted into a smile. 'That's his habit.'

'It must be nice to have that kind of relationship with someone.' She hated the wistful edge she heard in her voice.

There was no one, absolutely no one, she could tell her secrets to. It had never really bothered her before, but now, with so much going on in her life, she found that it did.

'You're in the wrong line of work,' Jem observed.

Eloise looked up at him.

'A journalist,' he clarified.

She smiled. 'A fashion journalist. Quite different. I'm just the girl no one wants to be at a party with.'

'I doubt that.'

His words hung in the air and Eloise found it difficult to breathe. There was a pain in her chest. His voice had deepened; his eyes seemed to be resting on her lips and all she could think of was how it had felt when he'd touched her face.

She looked down hurriedly.

'How did you get into it?' Jem asked smoothly.

'Work experience. During my A Levels I managed to talk myself into a two-week placement at a small magazine. I made coffee, answered the telephone and shadowed the stylist.'

'Then Cambridge and a first in English Literature.'

'Then Cambridge,' she echoed. 'Your research is good.'

Jem smiled and Eloise pulled her eyes away. What was happening to her? Why was it happening to her?

She struggled to bring her mind back to what she was saying. 'After university I went to work on the magazine, again for no money. I worked in a bar four evenings a week to pay the rent.'

'You must have been determined.'

'Oh, I was. There was no way I was going to have a life like my mum…' She broke off.

Jem paused and then asked, 'Was it so hard?'

'Miserable.' Eloise felt tears well up behind her eyes. 'You can't know what it's like—'

'I know miserable,' he cut in. 'Miserable doesn't necessarily have anything to do with lack of money.'

Eloise looked up, stunned. The anger in his voice was such an abrupt change, his words so unexpected. 'I thought…I thought you loved living at Coldwaltham Abbey.'

'The Abbey became my sanctuary,' he said, spearing a piece of broccoli. 'But by the age of fifteen there can be a lot of damage already done.'

'I suppose.' Eloise frowned. By the age of fifteen she'd known what it was like to go without. She'd never been on an aeroplane, she'd not been able to go to France on the school visit, she'd not been able to play a musical instrument because her mum couldn't afford the lessons.

But Jem? What had he had to do without?

And then she remembered he'd been expelled from school. A disturbed child, perhaps? Traumatised by his father's death?

And Belinda? If she had known about her father's affair she'd have known what miserable was.

Eloise felt vaguely ashamed. It was easy to forget that other people had their burdens; everyone seemed to have their own secret sorrow.

'My mum went to work at Coldwaltham Abbey when she was nineteen.'

Jem kept his eyes focused on his meal. Eloise watched for some kind of reaction, some flicker of interest, but he kept his face turned away.

'Laurence says it was like a thunderbolt. Like two halves of a puzzle.' She picked up her coffee cup and wrapped her fingers round it. The warmth spread into her cold hands. 'His wife…' She choked on the words, tears starting in her eyes. 'I'm sorry… Damn, I'm not usually like this.'

She put down her cup with shaking hands and shielded her face.

Jem reached out and laid his hand over hers. Her fingers moved convulsively beneath his. He sat there in silence, waiting. There was nothing he could say. Nothing that would make this an easier story to tell.

'I'm sorry.' Eloise pulled her hand away and brushed at the tear streaks on her face. 'I always seem to be saying that to you.'

She seemed embarrassed. Her cool, elegant façade had snapped and he would never be able to feel the same about Eloise Lawton again. She was no longer the icy blonde he'd first thought her. She would always be a woman of emotion, of compassion…

'I don't know why I'm crying.'

Jem felt the smile as it tugged at his lips. He watched as she bravely fought for control.

She made one last brush across her eyes. 'He told me about his wife. Sylvia. About her illness.'

'They were married for twenty-nine years,' he stated baldly.

Eloise looked up, her brown eyes soft and hurting. It twisted something inside him. He'd imagined she'd be cold and hard, but watching her now he knew she understood every nuance of emotion.

He wanted to make it easier for her, but the facts were difficult to tell. Sylvia had died of motor neurone disease, a cruel way for anyone to die but particularly hateful for the charming, educated woman that had been Sylvia.

For a man like Laurence it would have been agonising to watch. Jem drained the last of his beer. 'It was a long illness.'

She nodded, her blonde hair swinging. 'Laurence told me. He said how much he'd loved her and how difficult he found watching her suffer. He said he didn't cope very well and tried to ignore what was happening. He spent long evenings in his library and consoled himself by buying in the best help money could buy.'

This part of the story wasn't new to him. Laurence himself had explained how much he regretted the way he'd managed Sylvia's last few months. But an affair?

And to send his child away? It was still unthinkable.

'My mum arrived that summer. He said she was very young…and very lovely. And kind…' she sniffed '…he said she was very kind.'

Her eyes became distant and she seemed to be remembering things from far away.

'And they began an affair?' Jem prompted as the silence stretched on.

'Eventually. Laurence says he'd never intended it to happen…or imagined my mum would feel anything for him. Nessa, he calls her.'

Jem watched the way her fingers twisted together, an outward manifestation of the turmoil inside. 'But she did?'

'Yes.' Eloise drew a shaky breath. 'He said a hundred small decisions led up to their love affair. He said it began with something as harmless as a cup of tea on the terrace and became something as important to him as breathing.'

Jem could almost hear his stepfather saying the words.

He'd said, many times, that big decisions were made up of many little ones. He'd said it was important to keep a guard on the small decisions so the big ones were right...honourable.

For the first time he wondered whether Laurence's philosophy on life had been born out of turmoil.

'How long were they lovers?' he asked.

'Not long. At least not physically lovers.' Her hands began to twist again. 'Laurence said he'd loved my mum from the first few days of her being here. He thought he'd be safe because she wouldn't be interested in an old man like him.'

'He was only forty-five.'

'And she was nineteen. He described her as fresh and lovely, like a May morning.'

Tears welled up once more in Eloise's eyes. One single bead rolled down her cheek, leaving a silvery trail. Jem reached forward and wiped it away, almost without thought.

It was a mistake. His cynicism wasn't doing a good job of protecting him from anything.

Eloise was like a May morning. At twenty-seven she had more poise, more maturity about her face than the photograph he'd seen of Vanessa Lawton—but the similarity was marked.

He heard the small catch of her breath. Jem could easily imagine how a man would fall for such a woman. He sat back in his chair and waited.

'They read poetry together. Talked. They drank whisky on the terrace—' Eloise smiled '—and he almost forgot he was married. That his wife was ill and dying. That everything about his life was bleak...'

She looked up, clearly asking for understanding—and, amazingly, he found he could give it. He'd have thought that impossible. Affairs to him were inexcusable. They meant lies and deceit. They were an act of ultimate selfishness.

And perhaps they were. But he couldn't ignore the feeling of empathy and compassion building inside him. A forgiveness.

'It changed when he kissed her.'

Those brown eyes looked across at him and he felt his own gaze move across the angular planes of her face, coming to rest on the soft fullness of her lips.

'Before that they hadn't felt guilty. He says it was the moment they had to decide to walk away. But they didn't make that choice. Not then. The thought of not being together was too painful.' Eloise smiled, hesitant and nervous. 'Is it very wrong of me to be glad he loved her? Even a little?'

Jem didn't feel qualified to answer. His instinct prompted him to answer that anything that made Eloise feel better was good, but…

But he had other images in his head too. He could picture Sylvia, trapped inside a body that was refusing to work. Scared and lonely.

And he could see his own mother, confused and hurting when his father was alive. So many lies. So many new starts and desperate disappointments.

It wasn't Laurence. With the rational part of his mind, he knew it wasn't Laurence—but it was all knotted up together and he wasn't ready to untangle it.

'He didn't know she was pregnant.' She said the words almost triumphantly. 'He didn't know about me.'

Jem felt an answering surge of euphoria. 'Why didn't she tell him?'

'I don't know. He says he wishes she had.' Eloise smiled sadly, soft pain colouring her eyes. 'I don't suppose that's true, though. What would he have done if he'd known? His wife was dying.'

Jem moved through the different options. Laurence would have found the moral dilemma impossible to solve. Whatever decision he'd made, it would have been imperfect. 'What happened to Vanessa?' he asked quietly.

'Mum went home. Had me.' She looked up as the waitress came to remove their plates.

'Would you like anything else?' Jem asked. 'Dessert? Another coffee?'

Eloise shook her head and glanced down at her watch. 'I ought to get back to London. I don't like driving in the dark.'

'That was beautiful, Penny. Thank you,' he said with a swift smile at the brunette before turning back to Eloise. 'Shall we go?'

She nodded again and picked up her suede jacket.

'I'll settle the bill and drive you back to your car.'

'I ought to give you some money…' She trailed off as he stared at her as though she'd spoken in Portuguese.

Perhaps not. Maybe there was an unspoken rule among the rich and famous that the person who had suggested the outing paid the bill. Or maybe the concept of equality hadn't reached the upper echelons of society.

Either way, she wasn't going to let it bother her. Soup and a coffee wasn't going to break the bank or her feminist principles.

She watched him flick open his soft leather wallet. Expensive. He owned these things without giving them a thought. Part of his life—always.

He would never really understand what it had been like to roll over the sleeve of your school jumper in an attempt to hide the darn on the elbow. The embarrassment of knowing you were wearing the cast-off coat from Alison McEwen at number fifteen.

But he was kind.

'Ready?' He turned back to her.

'Yes.' She led the way back through the low doorway, pulling her arms through the sleeves of her jacket as she walked.

'Did you live with your grandparents?'

Eloise turned and laughed, the sound emotional and brittle. 'My grandma thought it shaming to have an unmarried daughter having a baby. She told everyone her daughter had got a marvellous job away somewhere and sent mum to live with her cousin in Birmingham.'

'Did you tell Laurence that?'

It had been unavoidable. Laurence's questions about Nessa's fate had been unceasing—and the answers obviously painful.

'I've told him the truth. I can't change what happened.'

'No.' Jem shut the door of the Land Rover and walked slowly round to the driver's seat. 'How did he take it?'

He cried, Eloise answered silently. It had robbed her of her need for vengeance. There was nothing she could do or say that would inflict more pain on her biological father than he would place on himself.

She forced a smile. 'It wasn't all bad. I had one fantastic parent, who loved me very much. That's more than some.'

'And you stayed in Birmingham?'

'Mum could have gone back home if she'd had me adopted, but she refused.' Eloise kept her voice devoid of emotion. 'Grandma came to visit us but we never went to her.'

'Never?'

Eloise shook her head. 'She was embarrassed. It ruined the image she had of having a perfect family.'

Jem glanced across, his eyebrows drawn together. 'That's terrible.'

'Perhaps.' She shrugged. 'People can only do what they're capable of. Lots of people are paralysed by the thought of what other people are thinking of them.'

There was a short pause. 'Is she still alive?'

Eloise shook her head and looked away. She'd died peacefully a couple of years ago. No one had grieved over-much; she hadn't been the kind of woman who'd inspired much love.

But his words reminded her how alone she was. There was no one left in the world who was there for her. No one for whom her presence was important. Not really.

It made Laurence's parting words more poignant. More important.

They followed the lane round and turned into the small courtyard where her Astra was waiting.

Eloise reached down for the door handle and was out of the Land Rover before the engine had stopped humming. She pulled her jacket closely round her body and waited until he'd walked round to join her.

She shivered as the wind whipped through the break in the hedge. 'Thank you for waiting.'

Jem slammed the door of the Land Rover shut, his hands resting for a moment on the metal. 'You're welcome.' And then, suddenly, 'Are you coming back?'

'I don't know.'

He turned round slowly and looked at her, his blue eyes startling against the grey of the February sky.

Eloise looked down at her shoes. 'It's complicated. I've said I'll think about it.'

His shadow moved across her body and his hands

reached out to hold her arms. Even through the thickness of her suede jacket his touch jerked her eyes upwards.

'Come back,' he said softly.

And then he kissed her. Gently on the top of her head, almost like a benediction. Eloise felt the tears smart behind her eyes. She stepped back, her smile wavering.

'I…I'd better go.'

'Yes.' His hands were thrust deeply in his jeans pockets.

She lifted her hand in a small half-hearted wave before climbing into her car and driving away.

CHAPTER SIX

ELOISE glanced down at the softly swinging ivory skirt of her dress with a sense of guilt. Classically elegant and beautifully understated, it had cost a fortune. She would suit the environs of Coldwaltham Abbey perfectly, but it had cost more money than she had to spare.

And just who was she trying to impress? And why? She would like to have believed it was her father, but...

She couldn't fool herself. There would be other people to impress today. Her father's second wife, her half-brother, her half-sister...

Jem.

Jem. Eloise clutched at the small gift she held in her hand. She didn't like the way Jem Norland had started to fill her mind. It was inevitable she would think of him to some degree—he'd been so involved in her first meeting with her father, but...

Did she really have to behave like a nervous teenager whenever he phoned? Or wonder whether he was pleased she'd decided to accept a second invitation to the Abbey? She couldn't tell from his voice or from what he said. There was always the suspicion that he was charming simply because he couldn't be anything else.

As she headed for the central steps, she took a moment to steady her breathing. This time she'd have to walk in the main entrance. Alone.

It was so difficult. Walking into Coldwaltham Abbey alone was like removing your armour without knowing whether you were going to be killed. She'd always been so self-sufficient, so confident, but the potential for being hurt was immense.

Outwardly Eloise appeared calm, her habitual poise completely intact. Her hair hung in a smooth curtain, her make-up flawless, and the shape and colour of her dress a testament to her skill as a style guru.

She could do this. Of course she could. Her stomach churned unpleasantly as she forced herself to walk forwards. The main entrance to the Abbey was so imposing. So grand.

It had probably been a mistake to come. She wouldn't be wanted. How could she be? Countless times over the past few days she'd decided to make a telephone call to her father and cancel, but something had always held her back.

And here she was. A guest at her father's seventy-fourth birthday. A small, select gathering. Just the family.

The wide door swung open before she'd climbed the first of the steps.

'Hello,' she began foolishly, 'I—I'm Eloise Lawton.'

The butler smiled. It was professional perfection. Just the right mix of confidence, warmth and servility.

'The family are expecting you, Miss Lawton. They're in the Winter Sitting Room. If you'll follow me?'

Divested of her soft wool coat she followed, desperately conscious of the opulence and the intimidating formality. The entrance hall had been designed to impress and it entirely met all the expectations of that long-ago architect.

Eloise stepped through the doorway into the Winter Sitting Room, the butler's understated announcement ringing in her ears. Her fingers convulsively gripped the present and her smile was over-bright.

The immediate impression was of warmth. Along one

wall heavy curtains in a paisley pattern hung at the four floor-to-ceiling windows. Large sofas in a rich burgundy were arranged symmetrically around the open fireplace.

Then her eyes took in the people. Just the four of them, all turned towards her. Jem winked, almost imperceptibly, but Eloise noticed and her stomach fluttered.

It seemed such a long time ago she'd thought him just chocolate box handsome. Now his presence seemed to electrify the room. Resolutely she turned away, the mere knowledge he was there, watching her, supporting her, gave her strength.

The Viscount—her father—immediately came forward to greet her. He looked so much better than at their first meeting. His pleasantly lined face was smiling with genuine pleasure at her arrival.

'Eloise, my dear, I'm so glad you were able to come,' he said, drawing her into the centre of the room. 'It's ridiculous to celebrate birthdays at my age, but this year I felt I really had to.'

'Happy birthday,' she murmured. 'I brought you…a gift. I wasn't sure what you would like. It's only a token, I…' Eloise let the words trail off as she held out the oblong package tied up with deep burgundy ribbon.

This felt so strange. In her mind she played over the years when she hadn't had a father to buy presents for. Was he thinking of that?

The Viscount squeezed her hand as he took the parcel from her. 'I'm delighted you're here. Now,' he said, turning away, 'let me introduce you to my wife.'

He led Eloise towards a woman she recognised instantly as being Jem's mother. Standing side by side the similarity between the two was startling. Mostly it was because of the eyes, a startling blue, Eloise thought as she accepted the hand offered her.

'You must call me Marie,' she said with the faintest trace of a French accent. Eloise had forgotten that she'd read that. Somewhere in all her research there'd been mention that the Viscountess was French by birth.

'Marie,' she repeated obediently.

Marie stood gracefully and smiled. 'This must be very difficult for you, but you must know we are all delighted to have you to join us for Laurence's birthday.'

'Thank you.'

'My son, Jeremy, you already know.' Her voice with its husky accent gave his name a sexy uplift.

Eloise turned briefly and acknowledged him with a smile, unaccountably embarrassed. 'He's been very kind.'

'And this is Alexander. The son Laurence and I share together.' She indicated the one remaining person in the room, a coltishly handsome boy of about fourteen.

Her half-brother.

Eloise looked at him curiously, wanting to see some similarities between them. Alexander looked back at her with equal interest.

'How do you do?' he said with the unmistakeable accent of one of Britain's top public schools.

'Lovely to meet you,' she murmured.

His mother interrupted. 'Sit beside me, Eloise. That is such a beautiful name.'

'It's from a poem,' Eloise said carefully.

Marie smiled, a merry twinkle in the depths of her blue eyes. 'So I know. It was inspired by one of France's greatest love stories, but so tragic.' Her hands spread out expressively. 'Your mother shared Laurence's love of eighteenth century English poets?'

'I—I don't think so. Not really.'

The Viscount interrupted. 'You were born on the anniversary of Pope's birthday. Nessa would have known that.'

'The twenty-first of May?' Eloise turned to look at him.

'1688.' He nodded. 'Quite a remarkable coincidence.'

His wife smiled, turning back to Eloise. 'I'm so sorry I didn't show Laurence your letter immediately. If I had known of my husband's relationship with your mother, I would have done so.' She reached out and took hold of her hand. 'I hope you will be able to forgive me.'

Eloise cleared her throat. 'Of course.'

'I thought he had no secrets from me, but I have found him to be more...surprising than I thought,' she said, releasing her hand.

The Viscount moved to stand behind his wife and laid a gentle hand on her shoulder. Marie reached up and placed her own on top of it. 'Open your present, Laurence.'

Jem stood up and walked over to a circular table with cut-glass decanters on it. Eloise immediately glanced across at him.

'What would you like to drink?' he asked.

'Nothing. Thank you.'

'You're sure?'

Eloise nodded. She was too nervous to drink.

Jem poured out a small glass of sherry and handed it to his mother. He looked completely comfortable and at home in this environment—which, of course, he was. A world apart from the one she'd known.

What would it have been like to have grown up in a place like this? She felt a small dart of envy. For the first time in her life she understood what people meant when they talked about it being a privilege and a sacred trust.

The Viscount untied the ribbon and revealed a biography of Samuel Johnson. 'It's written by a friend of mine,' Eloise said, almost apologetically. 'We were at university together.'

'Cambridge,' Jem cut in. 'English Literature.'

The Viscount looked up, his eyes suspiciously moist. 'My own university.' And then, 'I see you share my passion for books. Dr Johnson was a remarkable man.'

'Wasn't he the man who wrote the *Dictionary of the English Language*?' Jem asked, strolling over to peer down at the book.

'1755,' his stepfather said, flicking his eyes over the bibliography. 'Brilliantly clever and very witty. I love his definition of angling as "a stick and a string with a worm on one end and a fool on the other".' He looked up at Jem's crack of laughter. 'Can't abide that sport. Total waste of time.'

'Have you seen a copy of Laurence's book?' Marie asked softly, watching Eloise's face.

'No.'

'Oh, Laurence,' she said, turning to her husband. 'You should have shown her.' She looked back at Eloise. 'Your father dedicated it to "Nessa". Your mother. *Oui*?'

Laurence shut the biography. 'I will fetch it from the library after lunch.'

'Jeremy—' Marie turned to her elder son '—why don't you show Eloise now? I'm sure she'd love to see it…and we are still waiting for Belinda and Piers.'

'No. Really,' Eloise began. 'It doesn't matter. I—'

Marie stopped her. 'Until very recently I had no idea who Nessa was.' She smiled at her husband and said softly, 'Or how important.'

She must have caught something of Eloise's surprise because she added, 'I see no point in pretending we do not know what we all know. It is quite ridiculous,' she said with a dismissive wave of her hand, 'particularly when Eloise is such a delightful addition to our family. Would you like to see the book, *petite*? It's the start of your story.'

Jem stood up. 'Come and see the book.'

She looked up questioningly and he held out his hand to her.

Eloise let her fingers slide inside his, intensely aware of the feeling of his hand wrapped around hers. 'I'd like to see it.'

'The library is through here.' He pointed to the double doors.

Eloise was vaguely aware of the nineteenth century mouldings, but mostly she was conscious of being with Jem.

A nice man—doing well by the people he loved. In the back she could hear the soft murmur of conversation, the words blurred.

'Laurence has a study off here,' Jem said, releasing her hand and pulling open the heavy doors. 'If he hadn't been born to this inheritance I'm sure he'd have lost himself in academia.'

'His work is well thought of,' Eloise said, hating herself for the controlled primness of her remark. And then, 'I looked it up. It's considered a definitive study.'

She looked up to find him smiling at her. 'He gets pretty little respect for it within the family.'

'Why didn't he write anything else?'

'Lack of time, I suspect. Keeping Coldwaltham Abbey solvent is a full-time job, and something of a thankless one. I don't envy him it. Or Alex.'

'He'll inherit?'

'Unless the law is changed and Belinda gets the honours.' He reached up and pulled down a hardback volume. 'Here it is. It has pride of place among original editions of Dickens and Keats.'

Eloise reached out and opened the first page.

To Nessa. With love.

There in black and white. It wasn't a wedding ring but it was a public avowal nonetheless. Proof that her mother had been loved.

She'd been the product of love.

'Did his wife—his first wife—mind it being dedicated like this?' she asked, smoothing her fingers over the words.

'I don't think she knew. By the time this was printed Sylvia was past caring about anything.'

But his daughter would have known. 'Poor Belinda,' Eloise remarked, closing the book and handing it back to him.

He turned it over in his hands. 'I have a copy at home. I'll lend it to you.'

She shook her head. 'No need. I've found a secondhand copy on the Internet. It should arrive any day.'

Jem reached up and put the slim volume back in its slot. She was glad now that she'd taken the trouble to find a copy for herself. The words of the inscription would always be proof that her mum had been loved.

That mattered so much. She'd never been comfortable with the idea of being an accident. Unwanted. A problem to be managed. Her grandma's crippling embarrassment at her daughter's lack of a husband had registered somewhere.

However much it was possible to rationalise one's childhood, it didn't change the emotional scarring. She would always be the product of her upbringing.

As would Belinda. It must hurt her to read an inscription like that. Laurence's precious book dedicated not to her mother, not to her—but to the woman her father had loved.

'Does Belinda still hate me?'

'We haven't spoken about it.'

'But…?'

'I imagine she'll find you difficult.' He reached out and took hold of her hands. 'It's not you, it's not personal. Surely you can imagine how she'd feel?' His thumb moved across the palm of her hand.

'I—I shouldn't have come.'

'I'm glad you did.'

She looked up. 'Really?'

Jem let go of her hands. 'Of course. Truth is never something to be afraid of.'

'Sometimes it hurts, though.'

'Sometimes it does,' he agreed.

Eloise looked out of the near window, along the long vista to the pond. 'I nearly didn't come.'

'Why?'

She turned slowly. 'I thought your mother would hate me. That—' She broke off, her words choked.

'She's not like that.'

And she wasn't. Marie had been warm and lovely, seemingly able to accept her arrival in her husband's life with no great trauma—and yet Jem had felt the need to protect her. She was sure of it.

'But,' Eloise began, confused, 'you hated the idea of me. You were so certain…' Her voice wavered.

Jem moved forward and gently wrapped his arms around her. Her head rested against the steady beat of his heart. 'It has nothing to do with you.'

'No?'

He pulled away and tilted her face so he could see into her eyes. 'It has far more to do with me,' he said at last. 'I don't understand.'

And Jem didn't want to explain. She'd been right when she'd said some things were too painful to be spoken of. Putting into words how he felt about his father made it all seem more real somehow.

From the moment he'd read her letter he'd had a sense that history was repeating itself. It had been a sharp reminder of all the deceit and lies that had been so much a part of his childhood.

It was him who couldn't cope with Laurence's betrayal of his sick wife and daughter. His mother had shed a few tears, more out of shock than anything else, but it was him who found Laurence's frailty difficult to come to terms with.

None of it was Eloise's fault. He knew that. But the fact of her, that she existed, had taken away the blind faith he'd always had in his stepfather.

And yet she was a victim too. Eloise had grown up without a father. Without any knowledge of who her father was.

His arms tightened around her. The feel of her hair was soft on his hands, her body warm—and he wanted to kiss her. Her beautiful face was etched with emotion and he wanted to smooth away the wrinkle on her forehead and kiss away the pain.

Jem stepped back. It was too soon. And she was too vulnerable. Too preoccupied with everything else going on in her life.

Besides, he wasn't sure what he wanted—or what her reaction would be. He pulled a hand across the back of his neck, easing out the tension.

His reaction to Eloise confused him. Outwardly she

was so cool, so controlled, and yet she didn't seem that way to him. He had an overwhelming desire to protect her, to shield her from the bitter winds of life and make everything sweet for her.

He watched as she wrapped her arms around her waist, her body stiff and nervous. He knew how difficult this was for her, how much courage she'd needed to come to Coldwaltham Abbey again.

Laurence's delight in his unexpected child was obvious, but Eloise was no fool. She'd know how difficult that would be for Belinda. Her behaviour in striking Eloise had been inexcusable but he understood the motivation. The anger.

Presumably so did Eloise, because she hadn't told Laurence. The older man obviously had no knowledge of his elder daughter's outburst.

He glanced down at his Rolex watch. 'We'd better go back. Belinda and Piers must have arrived by now.'

'Yes.' She looked nervously back at the bookshelves as though she hoped there'd be something to detain them.

'She's had more time to become accustomed to the idea of you.'

Eloise turned back and looked at him, her brown eyes luminous. 'You mean she won't slap me this time?'

'I think that's unlikely,' he answered with a small smile.

He held out his hand and she took it. Jem carefully threaded his fingers through hers. Her skin was so pale against his own, her nails perfect ovals. He pulled his gaze up to her eyes. 'If she does, I promise to leap across the scallops and rescue you.'

She gave a small giggle of laughter. 'Would you do that?'

'Absolutely.'

He led her towards the door, before releasing her hand and guiding her in front of him. Eloise hesitated in the doorway. A cursory glance around the room told her that Belinda had arrived. She was seated on a high-backed chair, her face flushed and angry.

Unconsciously, Eloise lifted her chin and she walked a little taller. She felt Jem place his hand in the middle of her back, the warmth from his fingers spreading through her body. She was glad he was there. Strong. Supportive.

'Eloise.' The Viscount came to meet her. 'I'd like you to meet my daughter, Belinda.'

Belinda's eyes looked up, a mixture of scorn and fear in their greeny-blue depths.

Eloise knew why and felt a wave of empathy, real and tangible. The kind that binds you to another soul for as long as you live.

Belinda might be forty now, but inside she was the frightened teenager she'd been all those years before.

Back then it must have felt as if her world was ending. Her mother was dying, her father had fallen in love with someone else. Belinda had been alone. Very, very alone.

It made Eloise glad she'd said nothing to her father about meeting Belinda. On their second telephone conversation he'd said how much he hoped his daughters would become friends in time and Eloise had said nothing.

That would be their secret. Eloise held out her hand with a composed smile. 'It's lovely to meet you.'

There was a flash of something. Gratitude, perhaps? She wasn't entirely certain, but Belinda took the outstretched hand in her own cold one. 'Hello.' Then her expression changed. It was like a sheet of steel coming down between them. 'I remember your mother.'

Eloise sensed Jem move closer.

'You look very like her.'

'Thank you,' Eloise replied, although she knew it hadn't been intended as a compliment.

Laurence interrupted, drawing her attention to the handsome man standing beside the mantelpiece. 'And this is Belinda's husband, Piers Atherton.'

'How do you do?' Eloise said politely, disliking the man instinctively. She couldn't say precisely why, but there was a sliminess about him that made her uneasy.

Piers took her hand in both his. 'It's a pleasure to meet you.'

His eyes said far more. They were lascivious and openly sexual. It made her feel she'd have been more comfortable if she'd chosen to wear a dress with a much higher neckline in an unbecoming shade of fuchsia.

Eloise itched to pull her hand away. She glanced back at Belinda and wondered why she had married a man like Piers. If her father's affair had caused her pain, it was strange that she'd married a man who clearly was open to suggestions.

'Shall we go through to lunch?' Marie said in her gentle French accent. 'Now we are all together.'

Belinda stood up abruptly as though she wanted the whole thing to be over. Eloise hung back until she felt Piers's fingers stroke along the length of her arm.

Under normal circumstances she would have slapped him off and told him exactly where to go, but these were hardly normal circumstances.

'I'll show you the way to the Dining Room.' Jem spoke at her elbow.

Gratefully, she turned and followed him out into the long corridor. One glance at Jem's face told her his intervention hadn't been accidental. He didn't like Piers.

For a moment they were alone and she whispered, 'Thank you.'

As the others joined them she was almost certain she heard him say, 'You're welcome.'

The Dining Room was less intimidating than she'd imagined it would be. Instead of a long formal table it was a more intimate circle. Although it still sat an easy twelve it had a homely feel.

'Eloise, if you sit beside Laurence,' Marie said with an expressive wave of her hand, 'and Jeremy beside you...you will have the two people you know best near you.'

Eloise smiled with real gratitude and sat where she'd been directed. While everyone else arranged themselves she took in the muted decorations, the heavily starched linen tablecloth and the tasteful arrangement of blood-red roses in the centre of the table. It was a far cry from her childhood.

She couldn't imagine her mum in a place like this. Had she been desperately overawed or had she loved the luxury and beauty? Was that why she'd begun an affair with a much older married man? She must have known it was wrong.

She didn't like to think about that. It was easier...more comfortable...to think of her mum as being the wronged woman, but actually that position could only fairly be occupied by Belinda's mother.

Eloise suddenly became aware that she'd been spoken to. 'I'm sorry? I was daydreaming.'

Marie smiled. 'It wasn't anything important. I was merely saying I hope you like scallops. They are Laurence's favourite and have become something of a birthday tradition.'

'Yes. Yes, I do.'

The meal dragged on interminably. It passed in a blur of Scallops with Black Peppered Tangerines, Duck with Juniper Onions and Pears and finished with a triumphant Chocolate and Date Tiramisu.

The food was exquisite, but Eloise couldn't help but think wistfully back to her family tradition of a mountain of chocolate brownies lit with candles. The formality was oppressive and the conversation laboured.

She sipped her Kahlua, perfectly chosen to accompany the dessert, and willed the meal to be over. Laurence appeared to be oblivious to the undercurrents around his table. He smiled benignly at them all, choosing to ignore the silence of his elder daughter, the inappropriate remarks made by his son-in-law and the discomfort of his son.

Alex seemed a nice young man. He was slightly diffident and certainly quiet. Marie was a superb hostess. She was elegant, intelligent and a genuinely lovely person. Often she would look to Jem for support and with innate good breeding he supported her.

It was interesting. She let the conversation, stilted though it was, happen around her. She learnt of Laurence's concerns about the damage to the Abbey's roof during the Christmas storms, about Alexander's difficulty with French, about Jem's autumn launch of directional furniture…

Marie smiled her thanks at the uniformed woman who took away her plate. 'I think coffee in the Sitting Room?'

There was a general murmur of assent and within minutes Eloise found herself back in the Winter Sitting Room, the ornate clock on the mantelpiece ticking the silence.

Belinda had brought her wineglass with her. She sat

on the left-hand sofa and fixed Eloise with a look of dislike. 'You've not said much.'

'Belinda!' her father interjected.

Her husband's mouth curled. 'She's had too much to drink.'

'What would you like to know?' Eloise answered quietly. Belinda had been steadily drinking throughout the meal, her unhappiness obvious. It didn't matter how much she told herself she wasn't to blame, she still felt guilty. Responsible for the other woman's unhappiness.

Belinda shrugged. 'I don't know. Perhaps something about your life. You live in London, don't you?'

'In Hammersmith.'

'And, before that, Birmingham? I'm sure that's what Daddy told us.'

Eloise nodded.

'You don't have the accent.'

'No.' It didn't seem worth explaining much about her childhood, the elocution lessons her mum had insisted upon, the public speaking trophies that had sat on the shelf in the lounge. Belinda wasn't genuinely interested and her questions were only making everyone else uncomfortable.

Belinda crossed her legs and swirled the wine in her glass. 'Did your mother work?'

'She was a secretary.'

'Really? I'd heard she was a cleaner.'

Eloise didn't flinch. 'That, too, if money was tight. Sometimes I went to help and earned myself some pocket money.'

'Ah, coffee,' Marie said with relief as the tray was brought in and set before her. 'How do you like your coffee, Eloise?'

'White. One sugar.' She accepted her cup with grateful

thanks and spooned out the sugar crystals with a spoon she felt certain was silver. The interruption led the conversation off in different innocuous directions.

Belinda spoke about people and places she'd never heard of. Eloise felt sure it was a deliberate ploy to demonstrate how much the outsider she was, but the most painful thing was the way the older woman refused to make eye contact. She could have been invisible.

All at once Eloise felt as though a twig had snapped inside her and she knew she'd reached the point where she couldn't cope with being here any longer. Everything about Coldwaltham Abbey was a strain: the house, the furniture, the paintings, the people.

She didn't belong here. Perhaps this was how her mum had felt in the end? Maybe that was why she'd thought it better not to try and make contact?

Jem was there to take away her empty cup, his fingers lightly brushing against hers.

'I'd better go,' she said, watching as he placed it carefully on the tray.

Marie looked at her son and back at Eloise. 'Are you driving back to London tonight?'

Eloise deliberately didn't answer. The truth was that she'd booked herself into a nearby hotel, but the prospect of being offered a bed at Coldwaltham Abbey terrified her. She wasn't ready for that—either for herself or for Belinda.

She glanced across at the other woman. It was strange to feel so much compassion for someone who so obviously didn't like her. But then they were sisters. It was an idea that was gong to take some getting used to.

In her peripheral vision, Eloise saw Marie speak quietly to her elder son and noticed his slight nod of agreement. Then the older woman turned back to her and asked, 'Perhaps Jeremy could show you something of the Abbey grounds before you have to leave Sussex?'

Jem looked across at her. 'I could do with some fresh air. Would you like a walk?'

'I—I'm not…' Eloise floundered. Then, 'Yes, I'd like that.' There was no reason to refuse. 'A walk would be lovely.'

Within seconds she was standing on the steps, her goodbyes said. The wind whipped round the front of the Abbey and Eloise pulled her lambswool coat closely round her body.

Jem looked up at the sky. 'It's going to be cold.'

'Yes.'

'My mother was concerned that Belinda might have upset you. She doesn't want you to leave Coldwaltham unhappy.'

Eloise forced a smile. 'I'm not.'

He looked across at her. 'Do you want this walk?'

The air contracted around her. She did. The prospect of walking with Jem was immediately appealing. She might try and tell herself it was because she didn't want to be alone in a hotel room, but she knew better.

Being with Jem wasn't wise. She didn't belong here and she ought to leave.

'Is it too much trouble?'

He smiled, deep grooves appearing beside his mouth. 'It's no trouble at all.'

CHAPTER SEVEN

THEY walked down the steps and started to follow the long path. Jem pushed his hands deep in his overcoat pockets, then lifted his face and studied the grey sky. 'Belinda was very rude.'

'I was expecting it. I probably shouldn't have come,' she said, her smile twisting, 'but I couldn't resist it. I've never had a father before.'

'Laurence was glad you came.'

'Was he?'

Jem's face softened and he turned to look at her. 'You've been his ray of sunlight. His bypass operation has really taken it out of him. He says it's the most painful thing he's ever had to endure.'

'Oh.'

'My mother's been very scared.' They walked through the courtyard and Jem steered her towards an archway on the right. 'You've not got the right footwear for heavy walking. We'd better stick to the main tourist route.'

In her three-inch high stilettos Eloise was grateful for the wide flagged path. The wind caught at the hem of her dress and blew it against her legs. 'When did Coldwaltham Abbey open to the public?'

'1948. Like many big houses it's struggled for survival since the Second World War.'

'That doesn't seem right.' And then, suddenly, 'Does Belinda have a drink problem?'

'She has a drink problem. A self-esteem problem.' Jem

glanced across at her, gauging her reaction. 'A husband problem.'

'Piers is a bit of a slime ball.'

Jem gave a crack of laughter. 'You noticed.'

'Difficult to miss. Cassie, my editor-in-chief, would describe him as a ''stroker''. Why does she stay married to him?'

He shrugged. 'Who knows? She was brought up under Laurence's aegis; perhaps she thinks marriage is insoluble?' A silence stretched between them, and then he added, 'I'm sorry, that was insensitive of me. I shouldn't have said that to you. I—'

'He clearly did think marriage was for keeps,' Eloise interrupted. She turned and looked back at the house, the mellow walls covered with roses and wisteria. 'I wish Mum had told me. I don't know why she didn't. We had such a good relationship…'

Eloise fumbled in her pocket, searching for a tissue. She brought one out and dabbed at her eyes.

Jem looked away, his eyes still focused on the house. 'She died very suddenly. She might have intended to tell you…later.'

'How much later? I was twenty-one when she died, for heaven's sake. It's not as though it's such a shameful secret, is it?' She balled the tissue up angrily. 'Or perhaps it is. Damn! What they did to Belinda is pretty shameful. I wonder if anyone was thinking about her.'

'You're a very unusual woman,' he said, turning towards her with his slow smile.

'Why? I'm only telling the truth.'

His smile deepened. 'I'd say that was fairly unusual. Not many people can face reality without filtering the glare somehow.'

Together they turned and passed through wrought iron

gates framed by vast leaves. 'I wish she'd told me. There are so many things I want to know, but I don't know Laurence well enough to ask.'

'Like?'

'Like what did they say to each other on that last day. They must have known his wife was dying. Why didn't they plan on meeting up later? Why didn't Mum tell Laurence she was expecting me? Why didn't she contact him after his wife died? It doesn't make sense, does it?'

It didn't. But then neither did the affair in the first place. Everything Jem had ever known about Laurence would have suggested such a thing was impossible. His stepfather's opinions were fixed and unalterable.

He was aware of Eloise turning to look at him. 'Don't you think it's odd they didn't keep in contact? They didn't seem to have had a row. Nothing. So why?'

'You never really know what's going on in other people's lives,' Jem replied carefully.

'That sounds personal.'

'It is.' They turned and approached the South Lawn. It was incredibly personal. His mother had lived a lie to the outside world. His father. He'd watched the lies and the deceit play out until his father's death. He'd witnessed the incredible hurt one human being could inflict on another.

Nothing much surprised him any more. Piers's treatment of Belinda was despicable and yet she seemed powerless to walk away. Her personality had been ground down, much like his own mother's had been. He'd seen it before. Two people who'd promised to love each other and yet did everything they could to hurt and to wound.

But Laurence…

That had cut him where it hurt. Almost, almost he'd believed it was possible to live life on a higher plane.

'There's the tree,' he said, with a nod at an old oak tree in the centre of a sprawling lawn.

Eloise looked up questioningly.

'The tree in the photograph you gave me. Of your mother. That's the tree in the background.'

Ignoring the softness of the grass and the way her heels dipped in the mud, Eloise walked towards it. Her hands reached out and touched the craggy bark. 'Here?'

'Don't you recognise it?'

Eloise let her eyes follow a path back to the house. The South Front of the house had large symmetrical windows all along its length, making the most of the long vista down to the Church. 'They certainly weren't skulking in corners, were they? Do you think people knew?'

'With staff around…Belinda…I can't imagine their affair went undetected.'

'Did her mother?'

'It's possible. Perhaps Sylvia was too ill to notice.'

That didn't seem likely. Eloise leant back against the broad trunk and closed her eyes, shutting out the intrusive image of a dying woman watching. Hurting.

It was uncomfortable to have to think of her mum as less than perfect. She had such a sanctified image of her. She'd been so loving, so supportive…such a wonderful person.

She desperately wanted to cling to all of that. To remember all the good times, treasure up every precious memory. Of course, all of that was still true. It was just that there were other facets of her mum's life she hadn't known about.

It changed things. Shifted her perspective slightly. With new information she had to filter all her perceptions a little differently.

Her mum no longer seemed a pawn in a rich man's

game. No passive participant in her misfortune. She'd made wrong choices. She had been human with her share of human frailty. Eloise wished she'd been given the chance to say she understood.

She opened her eyes and turned to look at Jem. He hadn't moved; his blue eyes were watching her. Slowly he reached out and touched the bark of the tree, his fingers almost reverent.

Eloise watched as they spread out. He wasn't at all the way she'd imagined he'd be. There was an innate strength about him. He made you believe he could be trusted.

'If you want to see any more of the garden we ought to get going. The light is fading.'

They turned and walked back to the path, following it as far as the espaliered apple trees. The scale of the place was mind-blowing.

Jem followed the line of her gaze and remarked, 'Those two beds are used for growing cut flowers. There's a band of ladies who produce all the arrangements through the house. Every Friday.'

'That's quite a commitment.'

'Coldwaltham inspires great love.' Jem pulled a face at the steadily darkening sky. 'We can't be much longer.'

Eloise took her mobile phone out of her handbag. 'I'd better ring for a taxi. I'm staying overnight in Arundel.'

'With friends?'

She stopped searching through the pre-programmed numbers and looked up. 'Actually, no.' She hesitated. 'I don't like driving at night.' Jem's eyebrows shot up. 'Stupid, I know. I've never liked it much, but since mum's accident…' She shrugged and continued searching for the number of the local taxi firm.

He laid a hand over hers. 'It doesn't sound stupid at all.'

Her fingers stilled and she looked directly into his blue eyes. Nice eyes. Nice man.

It had been such a long time since she'd thought that about a man. So many games, so many hidden agendas, but with Jem it was different. He really was genuine.

He let his hand fall away. 'If you're not rushing back to London... I've got something to show you.'

'What?'

'Wait and see.'

Eloise put her mobile back in the side pocket of her handbag and they cut through the herb garden and back out to the long central path.

Coldwaltham Abbey rose up majestically from behind the high yew hedge. It was all so beautiful, steeped in history. It felt so permanent. Something to belong to.

Eloise turned back to look at it and caught sight of Jem's expression. It was a mixture of pride and content-ment. He really loved this place.

His words echoed in her head. *Coldwaltham inspires great love.*

The thought came as a shock. She'd always imagined the people who lived in these kinds of houses loved them as a possession, but Jem seemed to be really connected to the house. It showed on his face and reverberated in his voice. Perhaps that was why he stayed?

Would she have felt like that if she'd been brought up in Coldwaltham Abbey? It would be wonderful to feel connected to a place. To feel your roots firmly established with friends and family about you.

It seemed very unlikely that would ever be her lot. She'd discovered that today. You couldn't just adopt a family. It came from years of belonging, of knowing you were working together for the good of each other. She would always be the outsider here. Her presence would always cause Belinda huge pain.

Eloise turned away from the house and scanned Jem's profile. He had a quiet, intelligent face. It was difficult to imagine him as a rebellious teenager, kicking out against the world.

'What are you going to show me?' she asked quickly as he caught her staring.

'My pet project. I think you'll like it.'

She frowned but he wouldn't say any more. He led her to the small gravelled courtyard where he'd left his Land Rover.

'Where are we going?'

Jem smiled. 'It's not far, but too long a walk in heels like that.'

She glanced down at her feet. Shoes were such a weakness. She loved the soft creamy leather, the high twisted heels. It was almost as though he could read her mind because his blue eyes were laughing when she looked up. A sinful glint that stopped her breath in her throat and made the air freeze around her.

'You should read my column. They give a great shape to calves.'

'Who needs heels?' he shot back.

Eloise felt as if she was in free fall. The air swirled around her, colours blurred and Cassie's words reverberated in her head. *Sexy. So very sexy.*

His eyes caressed her. Teased her. *This was a mistake.* She ought to plead a headache and leave now.

'Shall we go?' He stood with the Land Rover door held open.

Eloise jerked into life. She climbed up into the worn seat, aware of the way her skirt rode up, displaying a length of creamy thigh. Without looking at him, she quickly slid the soft folds of her dress back into place. Outwardly she was the picture of cool control, but internally she was a whirling inferno.

She'd never been so confused by a man. Had never been so uncertain what she wanted from him. Did she want him to kiss her? Hold her? Make love to her?

Had this been how her mum had felt about Laurence? Maybe it was Coldwaltham Abbey itself that wove the magic?

Jem settled himself in the driver's seat, his movements smooth and unflustered. But she'd seen the flash of desire in his eyes. Whatever he said, whatever he did, she knew their attraction was mutual.

And unexpected. How could two people from such dissimilar backgrounds find any common ground?

And impossible. They weren't merely two strangers, free to like each other or not at will. She was the illegitimate daughter of his mother's husband. It was an invisible barrier between them; neither would risk crossing it. The stakes were too high.

It was all so wrong. She would see what Jem wanted to show her—and then she'd leave. Not just now, but leave for good. She didn't belong with these people. If she stayed she would only get hurt.

Jem drove past all the landmarks she recognised. She turned away from the window. 'Where are we?'

'Still on the Coldwaltham estate,' he answered, shifting gear for a tight bend. 'And this…is my baby.'

He stopped outside a converted barn. Large glass windows dominated the front and Eloise turned to stare down at the view.

'It's incredible, isn't it?' he murmured at her elbow.

'There's Windmill Hill, which takes you back to the Abbey, and all around are the Downs.'

'It's breathtaking.'

'As soon as I saw this place I knew I had to do something with it. It's taken years for the planning department to agree.'

Eloise tore her eyes away from the view. 'It's yours?'

'All mine. Laurence gave it to me on my twenty-first birthday, but I only got permission to convert it to a dwelling last year. I'm eight months in and it's just about habitable.'

As he spoke he led her through the heavy front doors and into a high, galleried entrance hall. The scale of it was immense but the central area was dominated by a large, circular table.

Eloise stepped forward and stroked her hand across the fine grain of the wood. The movement echoed a memory and she turned back to look at him. 'This is the table you were making? In your workshop?'

'That's my Arthurian Table. I wanted something that would really make a statement. It's a demanding space.'

Eloise let her eyes scan the incredible beauty of the piece, the exquisite craftsmanship. The wide, circular top had been divided into segments. In each segment was a word—a virtue—picked out in contrasting woods.

She traced a finger across the word 'Honour'. 'What do they call this technique? Is it marquetry?'

'That's right. It's never going to catch on as a commercially produced piece, far too expensive to make, but it was a real labour of love.'

They were all there. 'Faith', 'Hope', 'Peace', 'Love', 'Valour'…

'How did you think of this?'

Jem coaxed her further inside. 'Put it down to too

many fantasy novels as a child. I loved all the tales of King Arthur and the Knights of the Round Table. It's just a grown-up version.'

It was more than that. Just a few short months ago she would have written him off as a parasite. Someone who'd got where he was purely by dint of being connected to the right people.

But Jem Norland had talent. Real, discernible brilliance in his chosen field. He couldn't help the circumstances of his birth any more than she could hers.

Her mum had always said a person's responsibility was to use their talents and opportunities as well as they possibly could. He had done just that. How irritating it must be to him to have his achievements disregarded merely because he was born to money.

'What are you thinking?' he asked.

Eloise spun round. 'You're really good at this.'

'And you're surprised?'

Yes. No.

He smiled at her hesitation. 'Yes, I'm good at this. But without my father's money I might never have got started.'

'How did you know I was thinking that?'

His feet echoed on the wooden floors. 'You and everyone else. I've always been battling to prove myself.'

'I'm sorry.'

He shrugged. 'Come and see the kitchen. It's not quite finished. I've still to make some of the cupboards, but you can see the idea.'

The kitchen was a pale maple, startling against the dark granite worktops.

'What do you think?'

'It's incredible. The whole place. No wonder you dislike being in London.'

Jem set a kettle to boil on the Aga. 'Tea? Coffee?'

'Tea, please.' Eloise spun round to take in the full impact of the huge open-plan living-kitchen-informal dining room. It was spectacular. The floor was an endless expanse of wide floorboards with a rich patina.

'I admit the floor was a bit of a find,' he said, following the line of her eyes. 'I managed to source it from an old hospital that was being demolished in Aberdeenshire. Then I had to arrange for it to be transported down here.'

'It's reclaimed?'

Jem poured water into a hand-thrown teapot. 'A new floor wouldn't have worked here. Sourcing old materials is a time-consuming business, but this place is a labour of love.'

'Your pet project,' Eloise echoed, smiling even though she felt herself falling deeper under his spell. It was impossible not to.

'Nothing's allowed here if I don't love it. The mugs,' he said, holding up a pottery mug in a cobalt blue, 'were made by Saskia Kemsley.'

'I've heard of her.'

Jem poured in the tea. 'Her pieces sell in Harrods, but she's a local girl with a pottery a couple of miles outside of Chichester.' He handed her a mug and indicated one of the large modernist sofas in a pale cream.

She sat down and wrapped her hands round the pottery mug. Through the large picture window she could see the light dip and fade until the view became lost in blackness. There was a curious peace about it.

Even their silence was companionable. Eloise looked across at Jem, his head resting against the back of the sofa. He looked tired, as though the day had been as stressful to him as it had been to her.

She noticed the small lines fanning out at the edges of

his eyes, the small slivers of silver in his hair. He opened one eye.

'I—I ought to be going,' Eloise said, hurriedly looking away and putting her mug down on the maple coffee table in front of her.

'Why?'

There was no reason she cared to explain. Nothing and no one to go back to. 'It's late,' she managed lamely.

'Not very. I don't have much food in the house but I can probably rustle us up an omelette.'

'But—'

'I can drive you into Arundel later. When I go home myself.'

Eloise frowned. 'Don't you live here?'

'Not yet.' Jem stood up and reached down for her mug. 'I'm still at the cottage. There are no beds here yet and the bathrooms only went in last week.'

He wandered across to the fridge. 'Omelettes are a definite possibility. I can even manage cheese. Plus,' he said pulling a bottle of white wine from the wine cooler, 'I've got a nice bottle of Chardonnay. What do you say?'

Eloise glanced down at her watch. It was still so early, the evening stretched out before her. And the alternative was so tempting. *Would it really matter?*

'I'll certainly stay for the Chardonnay.'

'Good girl!'

She watched as he broke the eggs into a bowl and lightly beat them with a fork.

'How long have you lived in London?' he asked.

'Since I finished at uni. That's over six years now.'

'You didn't go back home?'

'I didn't have a home to go back to.'

Jem glanced across at her. 'I suppose not. Nice you and Laurence both went to Cambridge.'

Eloise looked down at the colours in the granite, touches of blue and grey mixed in with the black. 'It must be so strange for him to suddenly find he has a daughter he's known nothing about.'

Jem poured the eggs into a hot frying pan and tilted it so the eggs covered the base of the pan. His eyes watched for the optimum moment before he drew a palette knife through the soft mixture, making a channel.

He looked across at her intently watching him. 'Do you cook?'

'Never.'

'Why?'

'It's never occurred to me to try, I suppose,' she said slowly.

He flipped the omelette out on to a plate, before pouring out a large glass of wine. 'We'll have to eat on our laps; I've not made the chairs yet.'

Foolish it might be, but Eloise had never felt so happy. She felt comfortable, settled and completely at home. She took her plate and wine across to the place she'd sat before and slipped off her shoes.

A minute later, Jem walked over to join her.

'Aren't you drinking?' she asked, noticing his iced water.

'I've got to drive home.'

'You shouldn't have opened the bottle for me.'

'Why ever not?' He sat down opposite her, precariously placing his glass at his feet. 'I can't decide what I want to do with the chairs. Do I go for something timeless or something dramatic?'

'Dramatic. No doubt about it,' Eloise replied, giving up and sipping her wine. 'With a room like that, you've not got any choice about it.'

Jem laughed and put his plate down on the floor.

'You'd better have a look at these.' He walked over and pulled open one of the kitchen drawers. Tucked inside a black folder were sheets of design ideas, some no more than outline sketches, others had been shaded and construction points noted.

'I like this one,' Eloise said after a moment. 'That one's too Gothic, but this one has the height and I love the asymmetric back rest.'

He took the paper from her hand. 'Difficult to get the curve, but...'

'How did you start?' Eloise asked curiously, watching the intent look on his face as he studied his design.

Jem carefully placed the drawing back on the top of the papers in his file. 'I began shortly after I came to live here. At Coldwaltham. I was allowed to use off-cuts of wood from projects that were going on around the Abbey. Given the space to do it.'

'But you're not self-taught?'

'Wasn't that in your research?'

Eloise had almost forgotten about her Internet searches. They'd given the merest outline, the facts, but they'd actually told her nothing about the man in any real sense.

She frowned, concentrating. 'You've got a degree in design.'

'Very good.' His blue eyes glinted over the top of his water glass.

'A first. I can't remember from where.'

His mouth twitched.

'You weren't the primary focus of my research!'

Jem gave a crack of laughter. 'I suppose not. After I graduated, I found myself a top rate apprenticeship and really learnt how to work with wood.'

He smiled. 'There are some advantages in not having

to earn a living. I had nothing to do but follow my own inclinations.'

'That's lovely.'

He shook his head. 'I was lucky to find something I love doing. It could all have been very different. When I arrived at Coldwaltham I was set to go very wrong. I'd the money to finance it too.'

Eloise sipped her chilled alcohol, letting the flavours fill her mouth. 'What changed things?'

'Laurence.'

The silence pooled softly. Eloise finished her omelette and carefully placed her knife and fork together.

'Do you want to know why I resented you so much? When I first met you?' he asked suddenly.

Eloise nodded.

'Because it meant Laurence isn't better than any other man.' Jem walked over and refilled his water glass. 'Do you need a refill?'

Eloise shook her head, her blonde hair swinging.

He'd no idea why he wanted to tell her; he only knew that he did. She was so restful, her graceful fingers linked loosely round the stem of her wineglass.

'My father was a bully.' He saw the slight widening of her brown eyes. It gave him some satisfaction to know that he'd shocked her.

It gave him even more to actually say the words out loud. For years he'd kept his feelings locked inside him. It had seemed wrong to denigrate a man who was no longer alive to defend himself and with complete cowardice he preferred to shutter the past firmly away, pretend it had all been part of another lifetime.

But his father's legacy lived on—not just the financial one but the emotional one too.

'A cheat, a liar and a bully,' he said with controlled deliberation.

'Rupert Norland?' Eloise's voice held the faintest trace of a question.

He couldn't blame her for that. The whole world had a completely different image of the successful, charming entrepreneur. Women had loved him and men had admired him. They'd had no idea how the man had transformed once he'd been at home.

As soon as the front door shut his charming visage had vanished and you'd been left with a brute of a man. A man who, when the pressure rose, had vented his spleen with his fists.

He'd grown up seeing his mother cowering in the corner and carefully concealing the bruises on her arms and legs. His father had been careful never to leave a mark where it could be seen.

He'd watched as his mother's personality had slowly been eroded until she was too fearful to do anything but stay. And Jem had grown up knowing what it was to feel completely powerless.

'Things aren't always what they seem,' he said quietly. 'When Laurence fell in love with my mother he was so gentle with her. So patient. I admired him for it, even though it frightened me.'

'And with you?' she said softly, her words travelling on a breath.

He felt a smile tug at the corner of his mouth, the dark images of his past vanishing. 'He'd the patience of a saint. I was a tearaway. More ready to use my fists than my tongue.'

'I've never understood that.'

Jem looked up. Two short lines were creasing the smooth skin on her forehead.

'Why do children of bullies become bullies? That was what you were saying, wasn't it?' she asked hesitantly, suddenly uncertain.

'I think,' Jem said slowly, sitting back on the sofa, 'it's because it's the only thing you've seen. You don't rationalise it, of course, you just respond to the anger inside. It's all there, bubbling away. Then it suddenly erupts uncontrollably.'

'Was that why you got expelled?'

Jem nodded. 'For that, and for bringing into school an illegal stash of cigarettes.'

'Was that after you were living at Coldwaltham?'

'The expulsion was. Everyone had really reached the end of their tether with me by then. My father's death had been sudden, so people tended to make allowances, but then I broke another boy's front tooth and they couldn't ignore my behaviour any longer.'

Eloise moved slightly and her hair shone in the light like softly spun gold. She was almost not human. Perhaps that was why he felt able to open up his soul to her.

Maybe it was because he knew she understood something of loss.

'What did Laurence do?'

Do? He'd never put that in words before. He'd done everything and nothing. 'He listened,' Jem said at last. 'He seemed to like me and he believed in me.'

Eloise smiled and the effect was incandescent. It lit her face as though she were divine. 'My mum did that for me. I could talk to her about anything...'

She trailed off, her face shadowed.

'Which is why it hurts so much that she didn't tell you about Laurence?' he suggested.

She gently bowed her head, her hair shielding her face.

'They're not perfect,' he said softly. 'Not Laurence. Not your mum.'

'No.' She looked up. 'I do know that. I just wish…'

The air crackled between them, whatever she'd been about to say forgotten. Jem felt as if he was being drawn across the room by an invisible thread.

Somehow he was next to her and it was so easy. So very easy. He let his hand slide into the rich gold of her hair. It was soft and fine.

He felt the shape of her skull beneath his fingers as he drew her closer. And closer. She didn't resist him. Eloise seemed to melt beneath his fingers in a way she'd only done in his dreams.

She came to him as naturally as if there was no other place in the world she wanted to be. Her body curved towards him and her lips parted. Blood surged in his ears and he forgot how foolish this was. Forgot every resolution he'd made.

Her lips moved beneath his. Impossibly sweet. Her hands snaked round his neck and her fingers buried themselves in his hair. He heard the soft murmur in her throat, felt her body relax against his.

There was a sense of inevitability about it. The small voice of caution had long since been silenced. There was only her and his great need of her.

Love?

All his life he'd avoided this intensity of feeling. The need to be in control was paramount. He would never, could never, trust another human being with his happiness. He'd seen too much. Hurt too much.

But, with Eloise, it felt right.

The paralysing fear was gone and in its place was a sense of wonder. A feeling that the world was no longer out of kilter, but in perfect alignment.

'Eloise,' he murmured helplessly against her throat.

Jem felt her hands still and then uncurl from his hair. It was a moment of utter despair. She was pulling away from him, not just physically but emotionally.

'This isn't...it isn't a good idea.'

His hands fell to his sides as though they were made of lead.

'I can't do this. I'm so sorry.' She turned away in agitation.

Her hair was ruffled, her lips swollen from his kisses—and Jem felt as if his world had ended. 'Why?'

Eloise looked up at him, her eyes gleaming with unshed tears. 'I shouldn't...we shouldn't...' She turned round and searched for her shoes. 'I'll ring for a taxi.'

'I'll drive you.'

'I can't—'

Jem reached out and held her by the shoulders, forcing her to meet his eyes. 'I don't pretend to understand why we can't, but I respect your decision.' Even though it killed him to say it. 'I'll drive you to Arundel.'

'Thank you,' she said, backing away. 'It's just not a good idea. With Laurence. Belinda.'

He watched as she slipped her stilettos on and reached for her long cream coat. Slowly he picked up his own jacket and felt in the pockets for the keys to his Land Rover.

Her lips trembled as she tried to produce a smile. 'Shall we go?'

Jem nodded, feeling as though a knife had been twisted in his gut.

He shut the door of the barn firmly behind him, aware of the way Eloise shivered in the night air. It would have been the perfect opportunity to wrap his arms around her, tilt her face upwards and kiss her.

Instead he forced a smile. 'Let's go.'

CHAPTER EIGHT

ELOISE shut this month's issue of *Image* and sneezed into her tissue. She felt so sick. Her head felt as if it had been stuffed with cotton wool and her throat felt as if it had been shredded with razor blades.

It didn't help that Jem had just won a prestigious award for innovative design and his photograph had been featured in this month's *Image*. His personality seemed to leap directly off the page. It meant she remembered how it had felt when he'd held her. *Kissed her.*

There was no escaping it. His face even stared down from the coffee room wall at the *Image* offices because some bright spark had put it there 'because of his bedroom eyes'. And she didn't want to remember.

It had all been a terrible mistake.

She'd kissed him.

Or he'd kissed her. She couldn't remember who'd actually crossed that invisible line. The fact remained, they'd kissed.

And things would never be the same again. She would always know what it was like to be in his arms. To hear her name murmured softly against her throat.

Eloise reached for another tissue and curled up on her sofa. Laurence had been right. He'd been speaking of himself and her mum, but it all pertained to her as well. There had been so many little decisions which had led up to that life-changing moment.

She could have turned down the invitation to her father's birthday lunch. She could have left immediately afterwards and not gone on a walk around the gardens.

She could have refused Jem's offer of a lift to Arundel. She should never have gone into his house, or allowed him to make her an omelette and drink his wine.

They had seemed such little things. Each one leading naturally on to the next.

Laurence had said everything changed when he'd kissed her mum. He'd said it was the point at which they could have chosen to walk away...

They hadn't made that choice—but she had. She'd walked away.

It had been the right decision. The only decision. Eloise knew how Jem's world operated in a way her mum couldn't possibly have known.

It was a closed shop. People knew other people who knew people. It mattered who your father was, your grandfather. People networked and built dynasties.

They did *not* marry girls from Birmingham council estates or even nice suburbs. They might sleep with them, use them, but that was as far as it went.

And she didn't want that. If she'd wanted to be a rich man's plaything there had been plenty of opportunities in the past couple of years.

Jem Norland was an attractive man. Sexy. *Very, very sexy.* But she didn't want what he could offer her. She couldn't afford to let herself love him. So the only thing she could have done was walk away.

Wasn't it?

What was the matter with her? There'd been no choice. She didn't want a life like her mother's. She'd seen what that had looked like—and rejected it. It was a tough, hard road to travel. And it wasn't for her.

Jem Norland wasn't the right man for her. Everything

about his beautiful barn conversion had told her that. She didn't belong there. She *never* would belong there. And she wasn't going to think about it any more.

Eloise adjusted the cushion to make it more comfortable before abandoning the attempt and sitting up, tissue in hand, her head foggy and her nose blocked. She felt dreadful and decidedly sorry for herself.

Twenty-eight today and all she had to show for it was a particularly nasty head cold and a voucher to have her legs waxed from her colleagues at *Image*.

The buzzer to her flat managed to pierce her befuddled brain. With an inner groan Eloise picked up her roll of toilet tissue in one hand and padded across to the intercom. 'Hello?'

'Eloise?'

Even through the hazy fog of cold, Jem's voice echoed in her head. Jem was here. Now. She leant against the door frame and closed her eyes.

Oh, no. Please, no. What did he want? Why was he here?

She took a moment for the shock to subside and then pushed the button that enabled her to speak. 'Go away. I'm ill.'

'Laurence sent me.'

Eloise banged her head gently on the wall. *Laurence had sent him.* Of course; he was here because of Laurence and her birthday. It was nothing to do with her. For one moment she'd allowed herself to hope. How stupid was that?

Damn, damn and damn.

She tried again. 'I'm sick.'

'He's got you a present.' Jem's voice sounded muffled through the intercom. There was a pause and then, 'Eloise, open the door.' He sounded weary. 'It's raining.'

Reluctantly, she pushed the button to let him up. Then she looked about her lounge with growing horror. Piles of her mother's papers lay strewn about the room where she'd been making a futile attempt to go through them. Empty coffee cups sat on the side and an old worn blanket sprawled across her minimalist sofa.

She made a mad dash for the pile of tissues down the back of the sofa and gasped as she caught sight of her wan face in the mirror. There was no time to do anything. Jem rapped on the door.

Eloise clutched at her gaping dressing gown and went to open the door, stopping only to tuck the toilet roll out of sight under a cushion. She opened the door a few centimetres. 'I'm sick. Go away.'

Jem had his collar turned up against the rain and he looked irritated. 'Is it catching?'

'Yes.'

'Then don't breathe on me,' he said, pushing the door open. 'Hurry up and let me in. I'm not about to push Laurence's present through the gap.'

Eloise gave in to the inevitable. She stood back and let him come in.

'You look terrible.'

'Believe me, I feel worse.' She sunk down on the sofa and clutched a tissue to her nose.

Jem frowned. 'Who's looking after you?'

'I'm looking after myself. That's what big girls do.' She sneezed.

'Are you drinking plenty of fluids?'

Eloise looked up over the top of her tissue. 'What is this?'

It was scarily good to see him. He looked so much better than his photograph in *Image*. It had not been that long since she'd seen him, but she'd forgotten quite how tall he was, how blue his eyes were…

And last time she'd seen him she'd kissed him. Her fingers had curved into the thick black hair, her body had pressed up against his.

She watched as he unbuttoned his jacket and threw it over the chair. He didn't behave like the phenomenally rich man he was. Perhaps because he was so used to it, it didn't occur to him to think about it? Jem seemed as comfortable in her small lounge as he had in Coldwaltham Abbey's great rooms.

He hunkered down in front of her and laid a cold hand on her forehead. 'Have you got a temperature?'

'I've got a cold. It's nothing.' She pulled her dressing gown more closely round her body and tucked her feet beneath her. 'If you want a drink you'll have to make it yourself.'

'Fair enough,' he said, starting for the kitchen.

Eloise gave a squawk. 'I'll do it. What do you want?' she said, scrambling from the sofa as she remembered the state she'd left the kitchen in.

'A coffee would be great. If it's no trouble.'

She pushed past him and flicked on the kettle switch. 'I'm going to make myself a hot lemon drink anyway,' she said ungraciously. 'It'll have to be instant coffee, though. It's all I've got.'

Jem stood in the doorway and watched as she ripped open the packet of cold remedy and poured the powder into a mug.

'Go through to the lounge,' he said. 'I'll bring it through.'

For a minute she looked as if she might protest, but then she shrugged and padded back to the lounge. 'I'm too ill to argue.'

If she'd thought about it she would have expected Jem to be in London this week for the presentation of his award. She could hear the sounds of him moving about in her tiny kitchen, the sound of her fridge door being shut.

Eloise curled up in the corner of her sofa and closed her eyes. She hadn't got the energy to fight it.

Jem placed the tray on the wooden trunk. 'Be careful with the lemon; it's still very hot.'

Eloise cast him a scornful look and picked it up, cradling the mug between her hands. 'Congratulations on your award.'

'Thank you.'

'We featured it,' she said lamely, a half nod at the magazine on the trunk.

'I know.'

His eyes seemed to skim over her body as though he'd actually touched her. She felt a trailing blaze of heat alert every nerve-ending to the fact that he was here. Now. Standing in front of her. No longer a figment of her imagination.

'Why didn't you answer my calls?'

Eloise hesitated and sipped her lemon drink. Why did he think? Everything about him terrified her. Everything about love and loss and rejection terrified her too. It wasn't worth the pain. At least she knew where she was with what she'd got now. She could cope with that.

'I've been busy.'

'But not too busy to talk to Laurence.'

No, not too busy to do that.

Jem sat down opposite her and picked up his coffee. 'Or Belinda.'

Her fingers moved against the warmth of her mug.

'She telephoned me. She came up to London and we had lunch.'

'How was it?'

'What did she say?' Eloise hedged.

Jem's mouth twisted into a reluctant smile. 'She's booked into rehab.'

'Really?' Eloise looked up, her eyes finding a new sparkle. 'That's good. Really good. I'm so glad.'

She'd wondered whether Belinda would do what she'd said she would. Amazingly, she'd liked the other woman. *Her half-sister.* Would there ever be a time when that seemed a natural thought?

'Laurence is delighted.'

Eloise smiled across at him, forgetting everything else but her pleasure at the news. 'I hoped she would.'

'How have you been?' he asked softly.

Her smile faded. 'Great.' She fidgeted with the fabric of her dressing gown. 'Apart from this cold, of course.'

Jem watched the movement of her fingers. He'd almost forgotten how beguiling she was.

He hadn't thought there could be anything more alluring than the Eloise he'd already met, but he'd been wrong. Her hair was ruffled, her skin pale and her eyes bloodshot, but she still exuded a sexuality that astounded him.

Frightened him too, if he was honest. All his adult life he'd avoided intimacy. Laurence had done a lot to repair the damage of his early childhood, but even he hadn't been able to remove the fear of betrayal.

Eloise shifted slightly on the sofa and he caught a glimpse of those long—impossibly long—legs. Jem turned away and walked over to his jacket.

He no longer wondered at why Laurence had fallen in love with Nessa. It would have been like a siren's call, impossible to resist. Every time he was with Eloise he heard the same call. Piercingly beautiful.

All he had to do was hand over Laurence's present—and his own—then he could leave. It could all be done in moments and he could be on his way. He didn't even need to stay and drink his coffee.

If that was what she wanted.

It would probably be for the best. Even Laurence hadn't been able to remain faithful to the things he believed in. He'd been lured away by something beyond his control.

Why should it be any different for him?

His fingers closed round the oblong package Laurence had asked him to bring. 'Happy Birthday,' he said, turning round. 'Laurence said if you couldn't come to Sussex I had to be his messenger and give you this.'

Eloise put the lemon drink back down on the trunk. 'For me? A present for me?'

Jem passed over the parcel, watching the shadows pass over her face. Disbelief and then pleasure. Was she really so alone in the world that a present was a surprise to her?

'What is it?'

'Open it.'

Eloise slid her fingers under the sticky tape and pulled back the shiny silver paper.

'Do you speak French?' he asked, watching the bemused expression pass over her face as she saw the title of the book Laurence had sent.

She looked up. 'Not well. At least,' she said, brushing her hand through her hair, 'not well enough to manage this.'

Jem deliberately chose a seat opposite her. 'It's the story of Eloise and Abelard. Actually Heloise,' he said in a perfect French accent. 'They were real people, apparently.'

Eloise sat with her hand resting on top of the book as though it were the most precious thing she owned. Her face took on a softness he hadn't seen before and, for the first time, he really understood how much this mattered to her.

It was about *family*. About acceptance. No one knew better than him how healing that could be. To suddenly find oneself swept up into a warm, supportive community. To belong.

Eloise needed that. Just as he'd needed it.

'Who was she?' she asked.

Jem picked up his black coffee and sipped slowly. 'Heloise was the eighteen-year-old niece and ward of a powerful churchman in eleventh century Paris. His name was Fulbert.'

'And Abelard?'

'Peter Abelard was her tutor and a philosophy scholar. Much older. That account,' he said with a nod at the book, 'places him in his forties.'

Eloise picked up the book and turned it over. 'My mum really named me with a vengeance, didn't she?'

'I don't think Laurence sees it quite like that. He sees you more like a bequest.'

A bequest? Could that really have been her mum's intention in putting that letter in with her will? Had she wanted her to get in contact with her father?

It was a beautiful theory, but Eloise couldn't quite believe it. Her mum hadn't expected to die and Laurence was…well, he was much older. She must have expected to outlive him.

Eloise knew the poem verbatim; she'd read it so often since her first visit to Sussex. The Eloise of Pope's poem lived with a lifelong regret and a yearning for the man she'd been forcibly parted from. Had that been reality for her mum?

It had been a waste of a life. And it was too late to really know. Eloise had never imagined that their time together was going to be cut short so suddenly. There were still so many answers she wanted, so many questions to ask.

The pain of it rose up and threatened to engulf her. She felt the first shuddering of grief, regret for everything that might have been. Eloise looked helplessly across at Jem as the first tear started to fall.

She didn't know when he moved to sit beside her. All she felt was the moment when his arms wrapped around her and held her close against the muscular strength of his body. She clutched at him helplessly, as though he were her anchor in a stormy sea.

His fingers moved to stroke her hair. Soft and rhythmic. Eloise lay still, curled within the circle of his arms. It was rather like she imagined it must feel to be washed ashore after a storm. Suddenly safe and at peace.

She knew the moment when he sensed she'd stopped crying, because his hand stilled against her hair. Then he moved, but only to settle her more comfortably in his arms, her back resting on his chest, her head laid back on his shoulder.

The small voice of caution warned that the sensible thing to do would be to move away. Instead she relaxed into the cocooning safety of being held by him.

'How are you feeling?'

Eloise had almost forgotten her cold. Had forgotten everything but the sensation of hearing the soft, regular beat of his heart. 'I'm sorry—' she began, but he interrupted swiftly.

'Don't.'

It held her silent. She knew exactly what he meant. They'd come too far together for any apology to be necessary. He knew so much of her journey…because he'd walked it with her.

A deeply compassionate, empathetic man. From the very first he'd made her feel safe. He did that now. She felt safe. Protected. Loved.

Loved. The truth imploded in her head. Laurence's words echoed in her head: 'a hundred small decisions' and then 'as important as breathing'.

How had that happened to her? Was it really too late?

Each tiny step had been taken completely unawares— almost. Focused primarily on her father, she hadn't paid enough attention to the man standing at her side.

Jem.

She loved him.

Eloise lay against his chest, not daring to move. It was an exquisite agony. As long as she remained silent his arms would stay about her. She would have this moment.

Later he would leave and she would be alone again. It had to be that way because she couldn't cross the divide into his world. She couldn't risk the rejection.

'I haven't given you my present yet,' Jem said softly.

'You haven't?'

He shifted her slightly and leant across for his jacket. 'I nearly didn't…but when I saw it I thought of you.' He handed her a square parcel.

Reluctantly Eloise sat up and faced him. She felt so vulnerable, as though by looking into his eyes he would be able to see what she was feeling.

'It was made by a friend of mine.'

Eloise lifted the lid and stared down at an intricate twisting of platinum vine leaves shaped into a narrow bangle. 'I can't. I—' She felt as though the carpet had been pulled out from under her.

It was exquisitely beautiful—and it was from him. But it was obviously expensive. The kind of jewellery you would see specially lighted in a window in Bond Street.

'Put it on. It's nothing.'

Hundreds of pounds of nothing. Eloise let him fit the bangle around her wrist. Was this how her mum had felt? Completely intoxicated. Overcome by an emotion she'd never experienced before.

'Happy Birthday.'

'Thank you,' she said quietly. No one had ever given her anything as beautiful. No one had been able to afford to.

She twisted the bangle round her arm. It was a physical manifestation of the gulf between them. Jem had a personal fortune that ran into millions and a Viscount for a stepfather. It wasn't possible even if he wanted it to be otherwise.

Had her mum felt the same sense of hopelessness? Was she destined for the same lifelong heartbreak?

Jem pulled her back to rest against his chest. She went, unresisting. It was where she wanted to be.

The light faded around them until they sat in murky darkness. Every sense was heightened. She was aware of every shadow, the feel of his jumper, soft cashmere against her cheek. Her ear was attuned to the sound of his breath and her nose to the scent of his musky aftershave. Too scared to move in case the magical bubble was burst.

How could anything wrong feel so right? Had her mum felt that? Had that been the reason why she'd forgotten Laurence's wife, ill and dying? And Belinda, scared and lonely.

And what was Jem feeling? He said nothing. His arms were wrapped around her but he simply held her. Perhaps he felt nothing for her but sympathy.

His rich voice broke the silence. 'How are you feeling now?'

'Better. Better, much better.' She probably always would feel better when he was near.

'You probably need to get some sleep.'

'Yes.'

Jem lightly kissed the top of her head. Perhaps he thought she wouldn't feel it. 'I'd better go.'

His voice implied the opposite. Even with a cold, it would have been easy to ask him to stay.

And what then? What would become of her then?

Eloise wrapped her dressing gown more closely round her legs and sat up. 'My head does feel a bit foggy. I'll go back to bed.'

'Not a good way to spend a birthday.' Jem accepted her rebuff without question. He stood up and picked up his jacket. 'You'll be all right?'

'I'll be fine.' Eloise stood up and her hand touched her bangle. 'Thank you for my present. It's beautiful.'

He hesitated, as though he had been about to say something else. 'You're welcome.'

'Thank Laurence for me, if you speak to him. I'll telephone him, but…' She trailed off, her eyes falling before the intensity of his.

'Perhaps we could meet for lunch some time?'

She looked up. 'Some time would be good,' she said with a slight stress on the 'some time'.

'I've got to fly out to Milan tomorrow, but after that… We could have dinner.'

'That would be…great.' Except it wouldn't be. In real life Cinderella would have been miserable in her palace with Prince Charming. She wouldn't have known how his world worked. It was no different for her.

But if he really loved her?

But no, the rational part of her brain cautioned. She would always be his stepfather's illegitimate daughter—never quite good enough.

Jem reached out and pushed back the hair across her face. He smiled. 'You look totally washed up. Get some sleep.'

She nodded.

'I'll see myself out.'

CHAPTER NINE

ELOISE woke when the morning sunlight streamed through the narrow chink in the curtains. It could all have been a dream, but it wasn't. The book her father had given her lay on the wooden chest and Jem's bangle was still clasped around her arm.

She rolled over and looked at her bedside clock. She'd slept for over twelve hours. She couldn't believe it. For the first time in days her throat didn't feel lacerated and her head had cleared. She might not feel like she could climb Mount Everest, but she did at least feel as though she might live.

Eloise got out of bed and went to the kitchen. She turned her nose up at her usual muesli and settled for some hot buttered toast and a cup of tea.

Jem was in Milan. Or about to go to Milan. She remembered that much from the day before. And she'd agreed to have lunch with him. Or dinner? Either way she'd taken another small step in a direction she wasn't at all sure she wanted to go.

Actually, that wasn't true. She did know she wanted to be with Jem. It was almost like an addiction. He filled her mind completely. It would be easy to pretend the outside world didn't exist. For a time.

And there was the problem. It could only be for a time. Laurence and her mum had discovered that. Real life would always be there, just brushing at the edge of their consciousness. So what was the point of beginning something that could have no future?

She felt as if she was a tiny fish hooked on a line. Slowly but surely she was being reeled in—and there was nothing she could do about it.

All her protestations were as effective as a little fish thrashing about. Totally futile. The end result would be exactly the same. She was going to get hurt.

She knew it with the same certainty she knew her name. He might look at her as though she kept his world turning, but that didn't mean he loved her.

Not as she loved him. Eloise curled up at the end of her sofa and picked up a pile of her mother's papers. She'd not wanted to fall in love.

But with Jem that had all changed. She knew exactly how her mum had felt, all those years before. It was destiny. Some alignment of the stars had predetermined this would happen. There was nothing she could do but give in to the wave of emotion that was Jem.

Her fingers flicked through the top few sheets on the first pile. *How could one person have generated so much paperwork?* Her mum had even made lists of jobs she had to do. There was a sheet costing out a four-day break to Barcelona. Eloise hadn't known her mum had even wanted to visit Barcelona.

In all her forty years her mum hadn't parted with anything. She'd kept her own school reports, her swimming badges and her RSA III typing certificate, passed with a distinction. It was going to be difficult to discard any of them. No wonder she hadn't been able to face sorting it all out six years earlier.

Further into the box Eloise found piles of letters. Correspondence from long ago, all sorted with meticulous care and held together with elastic bands.

Her grandma's handwriting, immediately recognisable,

was on the envelopes of the first pile. The date stamps showed they'd been posted while her mum had been pregnant with her. Eloise laid her letters to one side. She didn't want to read about her grandma's disappointment.

The next pile was in a hand she didn't recognise. Eloise slipped off the elastic band and opened the first letter. It had been written a little earlier, during her mum's stay at Coldwaltham Abbey, and was from a girl called Janice.

A friend?

She couldn't place anyone called Janice. Presumably their friendship had died a natural death. Perhaps when her mum had decided to stay in Birmingham and keep her baby?

The letters were light and chatty. Full of the kind of details that would interest a girl of nineteen. There was a description of a party and a new dress.

Eloise took a sip of tea and picked up the next letter in the pile. No mention at all of Laurence, so she could only assume her mum had kept her own counsel. Probably wise. Janice had met a mechanic called Steve and they were going to the cinema.

The letters were addictive. Like reading someone's diary. You knew you shouldn't, but…

Eloise read on through the pile. Her hand hesitated on a letter where the address changed. Her mum had moved to Birmingham.

Which meant her mum had discovered she was pregnant. Eloise pulled out the thin sheet of paper. Janice's tone had changed. Her writing was more stilted, as though she hadn't been sure what to write.

And then Eloise read a line that tore the bottom out of

her world and sent her into free fall. A single line, but it
had the destructive power of a napalm bomb.

You must know who the father of your baby is.

The words didn't seem to make sense. Eloise ripped
open the next letter. Her mum's side of the conversation
was missing. She read a stream of dates as Janice tried
to work out who had been where and when. And then
there was Patrick McMahon. A sailor whom no one knew
how to trace.

Oh God, no. She felt the blood drain from her face
and her body become icily cold as she understood what
she was reading.

Her mum had left Coldwaltham Abbey on the nineteenth and she had met Patrick on the twenty-second.
Was that possible? Had her mum really taken two lovers
in the middle of her monthly cycle? Was it really possible
she hadn't *known* who the father of her child was?

It was clear from Janice's words that she'd known who
she *wanted* to be her baby's father. Perhaps that was why
she'd never told her daughter who her father was? And
why she'd not made contact with Laurence after his wife
had died?

It might even explain the letter she'd left with her will.
In the natural course of things Laurence should have pre-
deceased her. Maybe she'd thought it would be safe to
tell her daughter about the father she hoped she had.

Thoughts, questions, memories all flitted through her
head like an old time slide show.

And then Eloise realised just how much she'd lost.
How much it had mattered to her that she had a father.
It had been so important to know *who* she was. That her
father was the 'good man' her mum had described. To

feel she had a place in the world and know what that place was.

Now she'd been cast adrift. She belonged nowhere. She didn't know who she was. Or who her father was—possibly Laurence, possibly not.

As the initial shock passed she felt the pain. It felt as if acid was running through her veins. Every new thought brought a fresh realisation—and then the one that brought the tears coursing down her face.

Laurence. Somehow she'd come to love him like a father. She *wanted* him to be her father as much as her mum had obviously done. It felt as if she was being torn from the family she so desperately wanted to belong to.

Until this moment she hadn't known she'd felt like that. She'd thought it was all still in her control. In reality it wasn't like that. As Laurence had opened up the inner sanctum of his family she'd slipped inside. She couldn't explain how it felt to know she was going to have to stand back on the outside. To have no half-sister. No half-brother.

To have no one.

Eloise sat in stunned silence, her tea cold beside her and her face streaming with tears. She'd thought she knew all about loss, knew every possible ramification it brought.

But this…

This was beyond anything she'd ever experienced. This was the kind of blow you would never recover from and it hadn't run its course yet.

She had to tell Laurence. She couldn't let him go on thinking he had a second daughter when it was quite possible he didn't. She had to ring him and thank him for her present and tell him…

Dear God, she couldn't do it. But there was no alternative. To hide this new knowledge would be wrong. *Her mum hadn't known for sure.* She had to tell him.

Did Laurence know anything about Patrick McMahon? Somehow Eloise doubted it. Patrick had happened after Nessa had left Coldwaltham. After she and Laurence had decided they couldn't continue with their affair.

Had her mum been so distraught she'd stumbled into another man's bed? Eloise didn't dare to make any assumptions. She couldn't know.

Eloise stood up shakily and stuffed the letters into her handbag. She mustn't give herself time to think. She had to act now. Quickly. She had to get down to Sussex immediately. She had to tell Laurence face to face.

Eloise looked every inch the professional. Her hair had been swept up into a neat chignon and her make-up was flawless. Inside she might feel like she was dying but outwardly everything was as it should be.

'Gullivers supplied the tiara for Lilly Bamber's wedding to that rock star. What was his name?' Cassie asked, drawing on a cigarette.

'Garth Ryman.'

'That's it! Can't stand his music.' She stubbed out her cigarette on the pavement. 'I wish smoking wasn't banned inside. Are you coming?'

Eloise nodded. This was business. Work. Somehow she'd managed to go through the motions for the past two weeks.

'Every diamond in the tiara was flawless. Must have been worth thousands. Personally I don't know how you tell. Still, everyone who's anyone should be here…which is all excellent fodder for the magazine.'

Which was all that mattered, Eloise reminded herself as she followed in her boss's wake. The magazine. Her career. Her future.

Cassie was right. Anyone who was anyone had made a beeline for Gullivers tonight. The paparazzi were out in force and there were easy pickings.

Caleb, the photographer *Image* had sent to cover the opening of Gullivers' flagship store, seemed more than happy. She watched as he snapped a cruel shot of some society hanger-on.

Same people, same venues. Almost. Last month it had been a new fashion store, but the feel was the same. It was all faintly ridiculous. Eloise walked along the red carpet and avoided the mini-skirted girl who had been hired to sprinkle rose petals.

It was then that she saw him.

Jem.

Back from Milan. She'd missed him. She hadn't realised how much until she saw him.

His face was turned away for the moment, and then he spun round. His blue eyes sought her out as though they were programmed to find her among the heaving throng.

She'd wondered how she'd feel when she saw him again. Now she knew. Suddenly the world was a brighter place simply because he was in it. She'd expected the evening to be dull, and suddenly it wasn't.

He looked amazing. For someone who professed to dislike society life so much he managed to fit in effortlessly. Which, of course, he did. He'd been born to this.

Whereas she'd clawed her way into this life. Her white trouser suit was borrowed and would be returned in the morning. The long diamond earrings that brushed her shoulders would be returned before she left Gullivers.

She belonged nowhere.

'Hello.' His blue eyes glinted shamelessly down at her.

'Hello,' Eloise echoed foolishly, her heart pounding painfully against her ribcage. Her eyes took in the trendy stubble on his chin, the threads of grey buried deep in his black hair.

She had so much to tell him. About her discovery of the letters. About Laurence. About her abortive attempt to find out information about Patrick McMahon. So much. And yet the words she needed didn't come.

It was enough that he was here. There would be time to explain everything. Talk through all the emotions of that long conversation with Laurence. Perhaps Jem already knew.

Jem leant forward to kiss her cheek. It was the kind of kiss complete strangers were sharing all around the room, but Eloise felt as though she'd been struck by lightning.

She loved him.

And she suddenly realised she wouldn't change that even if she could. Knowing him and loving him was worth the risk.

Perhaps that was what her mum had thought. Her mum's relationship with Laurence had caught fire and crashed spectacularly, and her mum had paid a high price—but that didn't mean her fate would be the same.

Her mum had made a poor choice and there'd been consequences to that. If she'd chosen differently she could have contacted Laurence when his wife died, just a few months after she'd left Coldwaltham Abbey. Maybe, just maybe, her life would have been completely different.

'I need to talk to you,' Jem said.

'I know.' There was so much to say. It would be painful to express her feelings about her mum, but it was necessary.

Belinda passed across her peripheral vision. Eloise turned to look at the woman who might possibly not be her half-sister after all. Laurence was right; in so many ways it didn't matter. There would always be a bond between them.

Belinda looked incredible. Her hair was newly cut in a skull-hugging modern style and her clothes were cutting edge. She was barely recognisable from the woman she'd been when Eloise had first met her.

Jem let out a slow whistle. 'You look marvellous.'

She reached out and held Eloise's hand. 'I had help. This woman's a genius.'

'An easy project. Belinda's got a bone structure models would kill for.'

'And the clinic?' Jem asked.

Belinda again glanced at Eloise. 'One day at a time, one day after the other.' She smiled, a new confidence in her face. 'I'm an out-patient.'

'And Piers?'

A slight shadow passed over her face. 'Is with Corinne Risborough.' She held up a hand to stop the comment forming on his lips. 'I've always known; it's just time I stopped pretending.'

Jem cast an amazed glance across at Eloise.

'You must have known it,' Belinda said, smiling bravely. 'I think everyone knew. He wasn't very discreet.' She waved a hand at a woman at the far side of the shop. 'I'll see you both later. I've just seen someone I know.'

'I couldn't believe it when Laurence told me,' Jem said, watching his step-sister thread her way across the room.

'She's done really well.'

Jem turned back to look at her and Eloise held her breath, waiting for what he'd say next.

So much rested on what he said. Did he blame her for

not checking her mum's paperwork thoroughly before contacting Laurence? She blamed herself, although she couldn't regret the outcome.

Nevertheless, she had to admit she'd caused a great deal of pain and soul-searching.

Cassie had told her not to be so foolish when she'd finally confided in her. Her worldly counsel had been a soothing balm, but she needed to hear from Jem.

It was still a fact that Laurence and her mum had been lovers. It was still possible that she was his daughter...

'You're Eloise Lawton,' a female voice said at her elbow.

Eloise pulled her gaze away from Jem and looked down at...Sophia Westbrooke. It took no more than a moment to identify the petite blonde, even though she'd only seen her at a distance.

The teenager's outfit was as expensive as before. If she judged it correctly, it was another Yusef Atta creation. The peacock embroidered on her kaftan-style top showed all the hallmarks of his exquisite work.

This time she'd teamed it with a pair of well-cut jeans. It was an effortlessly stylish creation and she wouldn't have had change out of a couple of thousand pounds.

'Yes, I am.'

'I thought you must be. I love your column.' Sophy tucked her arm inside Jem's, glancing up at him. 'I was wondering where you'd got to, darling,' she said in a voice that was surprisingly husky.

The familiarity in her voice and the way she threaded her fingers through his made Eloise feel as if a branding iron had been pushed into her heart.

Sophia Westbrooke had the right kind of pedigree. She was *exactly* the kind of woman someone of Jem Norland's background required. She was young, beautiful, malleable and clearly adored Jem. What more could he want?

It wouldn't be someone like her. Only in fairy tales did the stepson of a Viscount fall in love with a member of the proletariat. For a moment she'd allowed herself to forget that.

Blithely unaware of how Eloise was feeling, Sophia turned back to her. 'I buy *Image* all the time. This is a Yusef Atta,' she said, holding out the hem of her floaty top.

Eloise knew she said everything that was appropriate. She somehow shifted into professional mode and Eloise, the ambitious career girl, took over.

Sophia Westbrooke's father was the principle shareholder of Westbrooke and Dyer. She could almost hear Cassie's hissed instructions as though her boss had been by her side to say them. *Worth millions, darling. The Westbrookes know everyone. Tread carefully.*

Eloise, consummate professional, smiled. 'I'd better circulate. I hope you both have a lovely evening.'

She made it as far as the door before Jem caught up with her. 'Where are you going?'

'Out.'

'Why?'

Eloise looked up at him speechlessly. He probably didn't know. He'd been living in his ivory tower so long he probably didn't know that other people lived by different standards, a different moral code. He might have kissed her, but it probably meant nothing to him.

'Go back to Sophia.'

'Sophy is Andrew's girlfriend,' he said, catching her arm. 'Lord Andrew Harlington. He's a friend of mine.'

'He is?'

Jem's smile slowly twisted and his eyes lit with sinful laughter. 'You thought Sophy and I...'

'It's possible,' Eloise said stiffly.

'It isn't,' he shot back. 'I kissed you. What did you think that was about?'

'Men do that, particularly from your class.'

'Class, my...' He stopped just in time. 'That's the most arrant piece of inverted snobbery I've heard in my entire life.'

Eloise looked down at her white trousers, feeling strangely ashamed. Jem reached out and lifted up her face to look at him. 'Interesting, though.'

'Is it?'

'Despite what you may have heard, the days of catching the parlour maid unawares have long gone.'

The laughter in his voice brought a pinkish colour to her usually pale cheeks. She looked self-consciously over one shoulder.

Jem moved his thumb across her cheek. 'We'll develop this later.'

Eloise risked a shy glance up at him. 'I'd better circulate.'

He stepped back. 'Just don't try and escape without me.'

She wouldn't do that. Eloise watched him thread his way back into the throng. Her stomach was churning with nervous excitement... and happiness. She was almost daring to believe the dream. That maybe, just maybe, it was possible.

Eloise passed the next half an hour with a glorious sense of optimism. She felt like a rosebud slowly unfurling in the hot sun of a summer's day.

She earned Cassie's approval by managing to talk for

at least ten minutes to the current face of Lancôme. It was all going so well.

And then she saw Piers Atherton. It had been a kind of sixth sense that made her look up at exactly the right moment to see him slither into Gullivers, a stunning-looking woman hanging off his arm.

Eloise instinctively sought out Belinda. She saw an expression of acute misery pass over her face as she immediately made excuses to the man she was talking to. Suppressing the desire to tell Piers exactly what she thought of him bringing Corinne to a place he knew his wife would be, she quickly negotiated a way through the small chatting groups.

Belinda had stood still for a moment and then gulped as though she'd been slapped. Eloise watched helplessly as the other woman headed for the exit.

Her instinct was to follow, but she had several thousand pounds worth of Gulliver diamonds hanging from her ears. It took a minute or two to find a security guard, unclip them and sign the appropriate forms. A few more seconds to hand Cassie her handbag for safe-keeping. Only then was she free to follow Belinda out into the night.

There were groups of people all round the entrance, some sipping champagne, others having followed Cassie's example and popped out for a cigarette break. The petal-strewing nymphet had long gone.

Eloise looked up and down the pavement, deciding finally to turn left as it was the quickest way to the tube station. It seemed improbable that Belinda would head for public transport, but where else had she gone?

She made a couple of tentative enquiries but no one had noticed her pass. There was no sign of her at all. Eloise headed back to Gullivers.

It was the merest chance that made her look up a side alley. She recognised Belinda's dress before she saw what was happening to her. Three youths, two male and one female, were standing around her. All wore tracksuit tops and had the hoods pulled up around their heads.

'Belinda,' she began, breaking into a run as she saw one youth push his victim hard against the wall. 'Belinda,' she said again more loudly. 'Help. Someone.'

It was the impulse of a moment. A mixture of anger and friendship, certainly a need to protect. Eloise didn't think of the danger or the possible consequences to herself.

She only thought of Belinda. How far she'd come in such a short time and how frightened she must be now.

'Help,' Eloise shouted again, as two of the attackers ran off in the opposite direction. The other sprinted towards her.

As he passed he grabbed at her shoulders and thrust her hard against the wall. His hand went for the platinum bangle on her wrist.

It all clicked in her head. All the evenings she'd spent at her self-defence class. Everything she'd learnt to try and rid herself of that insidious feeling of vulnerability.

Her tutor's words echoed in her ears. *The only wrong move is no move at all.*

He pushed her face up against the rough surface of the brickwork as he struggled to remove her bangle.

'No,' she shouted with an energy that was rooted deep within her. At the same time she rammed down with her heel.

She heard his yelp of pain, followed by a string of swear words, many she'd never heard used in that particular combination before.

And then she was free. He took off in the direction of

the main road. Eloise spared the merest second to look after him before she ran over to where Belinda was slumped on the ground.

She had a nasty cut under one eye and her lip was already swollen.

'Belinda?' Eloise knelt down beside her, heedless of her white suit.

Slowly the tears began to fall down Belinda's battered face. She looked up at Eloise with a pitiful, 'You were so brave. Why can't I do that?'

'Nonsense. Have they broken anything?'

Belinda shook her head, 'I don't think so.' She hiccuped. 'They wanted my engagement ring.'

Eloise heard the sound of voices and feet running. She twisted her head, first in alarm and then in relief as she saw Jem.

He was beside them in a moment. Jem glanced quickly across at Eloise and then concentrated on Belinda. He took in the vacant expression in her eyes, the cuts on her face. 'Can you stand?'

'I don't think so.' Her tears were falling steadily.

Shock, Eloise recognised. She stood back, but Belinda called her nearer.

'What happened?' Jem asked, looking across at Eloise.

'She was being mugged. Two of them ran away when I arrived.'

'And the other?' he asked quickly.

'Eloise kicked him.'

He looked down at Belinda and then up at Eloise. 'You were mad.'

'What did you expect me to do?'

His voice became clipped. 'Use your mobile, like everyone else.'

Eloise held out her empty hands mockingly. 'Funnily enough, I forgot to bring it with me.'

Jem reached into his pocket and brought out his own cellphone. She heard him give clear, concise instructions as to where they were. An ambulance would be here in minutes.

Now that the incident was over, Eloise felt her energy levels start to sag. For a time the adrenalin had kept her going, but now she felt the start of a reaction.

It was good that an ambulance was coming. Belinda's face had become paler and there was little doubt she had some sort of concussion.

It was also good that Jem was in charge. His steady voice kept Belinda focused on him. It reminded her of how he'd held her face when she'd had difficulty breathing.

What a terribly long time ago that now seemed. But, in reality it was only a few months.

She watched as the ambulance crew arrived, followed shortly after by the police. Belinda had drifted into semi-consciousness, so there wasn't much she could tell them.

They turned their attention to Eloise and she gave them her contact details and agreed to make a statement at the police station the following morning.

Jem came to stand at her elbow. 'You ought to go to hospital too. Be checked over.'

'I'm fine,' she said, ignoring the throbbing of the graze on her cheek.

'Eloise—'

'I'm fine,' she repeated more sharply. 'I just want to go home. You go with Belinda.'

Jem didn't answer her immediately. He flicked open his cellphone and made a short call.

One of the ambulance men, a portly man who had said

his name was John, came over. 'If you've had any sort of head injury, miss, you ought to come with us.'

Eloise shook her head, suddenly wishing that they would all go away and leave her alone. Jem came over to stand by her side.

The ambulance man looked across in a mute appeal.

'I only got pushed against the wall. It's a graze,' she said, feeling her face.

'She oughtn't be left alone. Just in case.'

'I'll stay with her,' Jem said curtly.

'What about Belinda? She shouldn't be on her own.'

Jem slipped off his jacket and placed it round her shoulders. It was only then that Eloise realised she'd started to shake.

It was another reminder of that first day. When she'd first met Jem. She'd never dreamt then how much she'd come to love him.

'My mother's in London. I've rung her and she's going to meet Belinda at the hospital.'

'Oh,' Eloise managed. There was nothing else for her to worry about.

'Do you need anything from Gullivers?'

Eloise struggled to bring her mind back into focus. 'I've got a bag. It's small. White.' She blinked, trying to remember. 'I gave it to Cassie.'

Jem placed a hand in the small of her back and led her out on to the main road. Her foot was sore where she'd rammed it down hard on her assailant.

Cassie was standing outside Gullivers, cigarette in hand. She let out a loud expletive when she saw Eloise. 'What happened to you?'

'You should see the other guy,' Eloise replied, with a brave attempt at humour.

'She went to the rescue of someone who was being

mugged,' Jem cut in on the pleasantries. 'I'm taking her home.'

'Shouldn't someone have a look at the gash on your face?' Cassie said, dropping her cigarette to the ground and stamping on it. 'It looks nasty.'

'It's just a graze.'

'You haven't seen it,' Cassie objected. 'You might be concussed.'

'I'm not, I—'

Jem cut in. 'I've said I'll stay with her. We've just come back for her bag. It's white…'

Mutely Cassie handed the clutch bag over. Eloise could see the speculation light up the other woman's grey eyes, but she was too weary to do anything about it.

And it was just possibly true.

Jem had arranged for Marie to go to the hospital so he could stay with her. A small glow of optimism settled deep inside her, its gentle warmth spreading out through her veins.

It made it possible to forget the anger and the fear she'd felt earlier. In its place she felt a calm sort of contentment. A certainty that somehow everything would work out for the best.

CHAPTER TEN

JEM had never felt such a conflicting set of emotions. There was a sense of gratitude and pride that Eloise's actions had saved Belinda from greater hurt, but there was fear at what might have happened.

His ice maiden had become a fiery tiger. Now the incident was over she'd reverted to a serene blonde beauty. Her chignon remained almost intact. It was only the graze on her face and the dirt on her trouser suit that showed any sign of what had been.

He hailed a taxi. His one aim was to get her home as quickly as possible.

'You don't have to stay. I've not got concussion.'

'I promised.'

He saw the faint tilt of her lips and he felt a sense of relief. 'What happened? How did you know Belinda was in trouble?'

Eloise glanced across. 'I saw Piers arrive. Did you see him?'

'Yes,' he answered shortly.

'I assume that was Corinne?'

He nodded.

'Anyway, I looked across at Belinda and saw her face. I couldn't let her go on her own. It was a good job I followed her.'

Part of him agreed. The other part wished she'd stayed where she was—safe. 'What made you go down that side road?'

Eloise shifted in her seat. 'Oh, that was pure luck. By

the time I'd signed off the diamonds I'd lost sight of which way she'd gone.'

Eloise had looked for Belinda. And then she'd gone into battle for her. His stepsister had been lucky.

'You could have been hurt,' Jem observed quietly.

The taxi stopped outside Eloise's flat. Jem didn't ask whether he could come in; he rather assumed he would.

There was so much unspoken between them, but if there was any chance Eloise might have sustained concussion he was going to be there. Whether she liked it or not.

Her small lounge had been restored to pristine order since his last visit. Flowers sat on a side table, obviously chosen for their sculptural quality.

Eloise kicked off her shoes and picked the left one up to study the heel. 'I've rather ruined this,' she said, holding it up with a wry smile. 'I hope I damaged his foot as well.'

'Is that what you did? Stamp on his foot?'

'Absolutely. Did you know the heel is the toughest bone of the foot? A metal-tipped stiletto was an added advantage.'

Jem took in the angry tilt of her chin, the determination on her face.

'Anyway, he let go of me.'

'I imagine he did.'

Eloise turned towards the mirror and began to remove the hairpins that held her chignon in place. 'Good job, too. You don't want to know what I'd have done next.'

She pulled her fingers through her hair and turned round, her smile triumphant. 'I'm really proud of myself. I actually remembered what I'd learnt. You never quite know how you're going to react when you're in the situation.'

No, you don't. Jem could say the same for this moment. He suddenly felt as gauche as any teenager. There was so much he wanted to say to this woman. To explain.

But he felt tongue-tied and uncertain, painfully unsure of how to begin. How to express all the feelings that were beginning to take shape inside him.

He wasn't even sure whether he entirely understood what they were. It might be love. Possibly.

Who knew exactly what that emotion was anyway? As he'd seen it modelled by his father, it had all been about control and power.

And, by his stepfather, it had been about friendship and acceptance.

Where did he fall in that spectrum? Until he was sure, it was safer to stay in neutral territory. Once he said the words they'd be said for ever.

She helped him. 'I'd better have a shower. Make yourself at home, if you're determined to stay.'

Eloise turned and padded along the narrow hallway, leaving him alone in her lounge. He drew the curtains shut and switched on the side lamps.

He could hear the sound of running water and his imagination hit overdrive as he pictured her standing beneath it.

There was nothing to do but wait for her to return. The room seemed so much clearer. Her mum's boxes had disappeared from the corner. She must have finished going through them all.

He turned at the sound of her voice, muffled from the shower. 'There's some wine in the fridge. Glasses in the cupboard.'

Jem opened the fridge and pulled out the dry white wine she had there. Glasses took more effort, but he found them. 'Do you want me to open it?'

'Corkscrew in the top drawer on the left.'

He rummaged through the contents and triumphantly pulled out a serviceable corkscrew.

'Find it?' she asked, appearing in the doorway, wrapped in a short kimono.

Her hair was wet, darker than he'd ever seen it. Her face, devoid of make-up, showed the graze livid on her cheek.

And there was nothing neutral about how he was feeling. Any control he thought he had was an illusion. He wanted her with a passion that was primeval.

She must have read the spark in his eyes because she turned away with a quick, 'I'd better get some clothes on.'

'I'll pour the wine,' he mumbled.

He was drowning, and going down for the third time.

She reappeared in a soft jersey dress which wrapped around her body. He noticed, because he couldn't help it, that it appeared to be held together by one simple bow. All it would take was one easy pull...

Jem handed her a glass.

'Thank you.'

Her eyes looked luminous above the rim of her glass. Her hair had already begun to dry to a corn-gold around the edges of her forehead.

'I feel so much better after that shower.'

'I imagine you do,' he said, following her back into the lounge. 'How is it you're such an expert on self-defence?'

'I did a course.' Eloise settled herself on the sofa. 'When I was at university.'

'Very sensible.' He sat in the opposite corner.

'I was nearly attacked once. Or perhaps I was. I don't

know how you classify these things.' She sipped her wine. 'Anyway, I had a near miss.'

Jem said nothing. He waited, letting her decide when to continue.

'I was walking home from a party.' She looked up over the rim of her glass. 'Far too late, of course. It was dark and the roads were completely deserted.

'I decided it was safe enough so I kept to the main road and started to walk back to my flat. I wasn't particularly worried when I heard someone behind me. I just kept walking.

'Then I heard the footsteps speed up. I think it was the change of pace that made me anxious. So I crossed the road.'

She looked up, her eyes full of wry laughter. It was as though she wanted to soften her tale with some sort of humour.

'I'd read the book, you know. Thought I was invincible.'

As she was speaking, Jem could picture it all in his mind's eye. What surprised him was how he was feeling. It was a surging anger that anyone could treat Eloise in this way. *His Eloise.*

His feeling of possessiveness scared him. It reminded him of so much. Played to that long held, deep-seated fear that he might be like his father.

And then he looked at her face. He minded for *her.* It was the soft, faraway look in her brown eyes that prompted every instinct he had to keep her safe. *For her.*

He wanted what was best for her. He wanted her to have the fullest life possible and to reach her potential. He wanted her to be happy.

That wasn't about control, was it? Or ownership?

'What happened?' he prompted.

'I was lucky. We were running down the pavement, but at the point at which I knew I couldn't outdistance him a bus turned the corner.'

'A bus?'

She nodded. 'A night-time bus. They must have seen me because they slowed down and one of the passengers pulled me up. Very lucky.'

Jem reached out and took hold of her hand. He threaded his fingers through hers. They were starkly pale against the tanned skin of his own.

'Very lucky.' He looked deep into her brown eyes. So deep he could see the tiny amber flecks that fanned out around her jet-black pupils, now dilated to the size of saucers. 'You should have taken a taxi.'

'No money.' Her answer sounded breathless.

Jem would have given his last penny if it would have kept her safe. *Was that what love was?*

All his life he'd known that women were attracted to his money as much as him. Brigitte Coulthard would have married a changeling if he'd had access to the millions at Jem's disposal.

His eyes flicked to Eloise's soft full lips, he noticed the tiny tremble and finally understood. It was as though huge cogs in his brain had suddenly slotted together.

Eloise wanted *him*. Despite all the fears that held her back.

And God help him, he wanted her.

None of it mattered. Not Laurence. Not Nessa. Not Belinda. All that mattered was that he'd found a woman who could see past his money to the real him.

And, he could see the real her.

Finally, he understood why he'd wanted to show Eloise his home. He wanted to share the vision he had of the barn. Share the spectacular views.

He wanted to be able to picture her in it because by being able to do that it made it feel more like a home.

Slowly he drew her closer. There was nothing casual about this. It was what made it so frightening. If he made love to her now, he would never be free of her. It was all a question of trust.

His of her, and hers of him.

Jem looked deep into her soft brown eyes and read the fear in her own. 'Trust me,' he said softly.

And he knew he was saying it as much for himself as her.

'Trust me.'

Eloise looked up at him, her eyes desperately searching for something. Some reassurance. And then she smiled. 'I do.'

With slow deliberation she reached out and pulled his head towards hers. The feel of his lips touching hers blew his mind.

He knew the moment when he felt for that tiny bow at the side of her dress. The feel of the material beneath his fingers. The soft tug as the knot held.

He felt the small resistance within Eloise, felt the slight tension and then her surrender.

It was a moment of complete euphoria. A prize won.

And then he stopped thinking at all. His lips hungrily devoured hers. His hands moved across her body, needing to touch her.

His fingers unclipped the lacy bra and he saw the soft rosy peaks of her breasts, more beautiful than he could ever have imagined.

And finally he knew what love was. There was no risk—because this was Eloise. There was no hidden agenda. No secrets. No lies.

Just the two of them. Together.

Eloise opened her eyes and looked at the sleeping man beside her. His handsome face looked scrunched against her pillow and his hair was tousled.

He'd never looked sexier, she thought, pushing back a heavy lock of hair.

And he was hers.

Was that possible?

He'd told her to trust him, and she did. For the first time since her mother had died she really believed she could trust another person.

It all felt so new and tentative, but she'd woken with a feeling of complete peace. Of rightness. Her heart felt so full it was near bursting.

There was so much that needed to be sorted if they were going to be together: he hated London, she worked there—but none of it mattered.

He'd said to trust him and she did. She trusted him to make things right for them.

Jem opened one eye and then a slow smile spread over his face. 'You're here,' he said with a note of wonder.

She felt the answering glimmer. 'I live here.'

'Then what are you doing with a man in your bed?'

Eloise appeared to consider. 'Well, he didn't seem to want to be alone last night and I thought it would be a kindness to give him a bed.'

'I don't want to be alone any night.'

'Really?'

He reached out and pulled her naked body up against his. 'Hmm, really.'

Eloise gasped in pleasure as he pressed a kiss against the small sensitive spot at the base of her neck. His hands moved to skim across her buttocks.

'I don't generally have a vacancy,' she teased.

Jem answered with a playful pinch, his blue eyes glinting mischievously.

She squirmed against him and caught sight of the clock by the bed. 'Do you know what the time is?'

'No.'

'It's gone ten o'clock.'

He rolled over and checked. 'So it is,' and made to snuggle back down.

'We ought to check on Belinda.'

Jem groaned but said, 'I'll grab a shower.'

'Towels in the cupboard and I'll make a cup of tea.' Eloise flicked her long legs and got out of bed.

Jem found he had the most amazing view. He watched as she picked up her kimono from the chair and wrapped it round her slender body.

She looked back across her shoulder like some old-time seductress. 'Get up.'

It was difficult to make his body respond. His limbs felt heavy and his heart was completely at peace. He never wanted to leave this moment.

And then he realised he didn't have to. This moment was his for all time. And there would be other moments. A lifetime of moments.

'Are you going to ring the hospital?' Eloise asked as he appeared after his shower.

'We may as well turn up on spec. She was only admitted as a precaution, so I doubt they'll keep her in.'

Eloise nodded.

'Besides, if we're barred entrance, I'll take you for a greasy fry-up in a café I know.'

She handed him a mug of tea. 'I thought you didn't know London.'

'You'll be surprised what I know.' He winked.

She left, laughing, and Jem sat down on the sofa. It

felt like a weight had been lifted from him. His life had a purpose and meaning he hadn't thought possible.

The telephone rang on the side table and Jem glanced across at it, wondering whether he should answer it. Three rings and the answering machine clicked into action.

'Eloise, pick up. Are you there?' A silence and then, 'It's Cassie.' Another silence. 'Ring me, the minute you get in. I want to know about the sex god.'

Jem picked up his tea and sipped.

'You've got twenty-four hours to ring me before I tell the team. Oh, and,' she added after a short pause, 'what about the letters?'

Jem could almost see her drawing on a cigarette.

'Eloise? Have you told him your father's name is Patrick McMahon? Ring me.'

Cassie ended the call and Jem sat in stunned silence. He couldn't process what he'd heard. It made no sense. No sense at all.

Eloise came into the lounge. She looked exactly the same. Like an angel. Her hair swung in a bright curtain of sunshine, her deep aubergine dress hugged every curve of her body.

'Was that the phone? I thought I heard someone speaking.'

Jem put his tea down on the table and reached out to rewind the message. His eyes never left her face as the machine replayed every word Cassie had said.

He watched the blood drain from her face, her eyes enormous in her pale face.

'Jem, I...' she began.

'It seems there's something you should have told me,' he said in a voice he hardly recognised as his own. His words grated in a hard metallic sound.

She didn't move towards him. She stood by the door, frozen in that one spot. 'I—I was going to tell you. There wasn't a right moment. It happened while you were in Milan—'

Jem couldn't bear to hear any more. He held up his hand to silence her.

He'd been played for a fool. He allowed himself one last look at the elegant visage that was Eloise Lawton, scam artist. There had to be no other explanation.

She'd almost succeeded. He'd been completely taken in by her. As had Laurence. He looked at her and felt complete revulsion.

Love and hate were so very close. He had no difficulty in deciding on which side of the equation he stood.

But it didn't stop the disappointment. Or the slow sense of disillusionment, followed by the searing pain of total betrayal.

Jem said nothing. He stood up, walked to the door...and shut it. He heard her shout his name, but he didn't pause or look back.

Eloise had never felt pain like it. Not her mum's death or the news of her parentage had been anywhere on the scale of agony she now experienced. Each of those times she thought she'd reached the lowest possible point but now she discovered there were further depths to plummet.

She was being forcibly wrenched from a place of such happiness. Torn asunder.

If it was true that the physical act of making love joined two souls together, this feeling made perfect sense. It felt as if she was being ripped in half.

She went to the window and watched Jem walk away. He didn't look back. No hesitation, just a clear determination to leave her.

She watched him turn the corner and that last tiny flicker of hope died.

He hadn't waited to listen to her explanation.

He'd told her to trust him, but at the first test he'd refused to trust her.

She walked over to the answering machine and played back Cassie's message. And then again.

It sounded so damning.

But he should have waited, listened to what she had to say.

There were no tears. She couldn't feel anything. She sat in stunned disbelief.

He'd left her. It was over.

Eloise left her own tea on the table. The two full mugs were a visual mockery. It was the only sign Jem had ever been there.

She'd survive. Of course she would. People didn't really die from a broken heart. Even her erstwhile namesake had gone on to carve a successful career as an Abbess, even if life in a nunnery hadn't been freely chosen.

Eloise pulled on her aubergine boots and let herself out of the flat. The early June air held the promise of spring. Such optimism.

She went to the police station and left a detailed statement. The graze on her cheek was photographed and she heard that two of the youths had been apprehended. They'd been caught running away on CCTV. The police sergeant said there was 'no honour among thieves' and he was confident they'd catch the third.

Eloise smiled and nodded and pledged whatever support they needed. Then she took the tube to the hospital Belinda had been taken to.

Whatever Jem said, and however he felt, she still had

a responsibility to the woman who *might* still be her sister. She had to know how she was. Whether Piers had been in contact. Whether her fragile confidence remained intact.

She made it with only fifteen minutes to spare before the end of visiting hours. The nurse at the desk indicated a private room at the end of the corridor.

Eloise pinned a smile to her face, which froze the minute she saw Jem sitting by Belinda's bed.

He looked up and a bleakness passed across his face. He stood up. 'I'm just leaving.'

'You don't—'

'It's time I was going.' Jem quickly kissed Belinda's cheek and escaped.

Eloise turned in time to see the door swing shut and then looked back at Belinda, now several interesting shades of brown and yellow.

Belinda patted the chair Jem had just vacated. 'Your wounds don't look too bad,' she observed.

'They're not.' *At least not the ones people could see.* The most painful wound was the one Belinda's stepbrother had just inflicted.

'I've been to the police station. Made a statement,' Eloise continued, with an attempt at brightness. 'They photographed my face.'

'They've been here to do mine.' Belinda nodded. 'You didn't tell him.'

Eloise looked up.

'About the letters.'

Eloise put her handbag down on the floor and played for time. 'I was going to. But you were attacked… Then, well, one thing led to another.'

'Jem didn't tell me that,' Belinda said, holding her bruised face as she started to smile.

'He wouldn't listen to me. I'm sure he thinks it's all some kind of elaborate con. But I don't understand. Just what does he think I'm going to get out of it?'

'Money,' Belinda answered succinctly.

Eloise looked at her, aghast. 'I don't want his money.'

'I know that. He does too, I think.' Belinda's fingers pleated the stiff fabric of the hospital sheet. 'Give him a chance, Eloise. He'll come round.'

She'd started shaking her head even before Belinda had finished speaking. 'It's too late.'

'Only if you let it be. You didn't know Jem when he first came to Coldwaltham. He was an obnoxious boy.'

Eloise found she was listening in spite of herself.

'Has he spoken about his father?'

'A little. He said he was a bully and a cheat.'

Belinda gave a scornful laugh. 'That's an understatement. Rupert Norland was a nasty piece of work. He would make my Piers look like Mother Teresa.

'Jem is almost unrecognisable from the boy he was when he first arrived. But,' Belinda said slowly, searching for words, 'the thing is…Jem doesn't trust easily. He was lied to too often.'

'Daddy and Marie have been amazed at the ease with which you've got under his defences. He loves a few people very deeply. You threatened them, but still he couldn't help but fall in love with you.'

Eloise shook her head in mute denial. A man who truly loved her wouldn't have left her like he had this morning.

'He loves you very deeply,' Belinda said stoutly. 'I wish there was someone who felt that way about me. It's because he loves you he's hurting so much now.'

Eloise frowned. Against her will a small glimmer of hope had started to take shape.

'But I'm still not likely to be Laurence's daughter.'

'That doesn't matter.' Belinda reached out and touched her hand. 'Daddy's right. He said if you're not his biological daughter, you should have been.'

Eloise felt the tears well up behind her eyes.

'And if you're not really my sister, you should have been. Daddy told me—' she gripped Eloise's hand in a painful grasp '—he said he'd only ever loved three women. My mother. He'd loved her until the day she died. Marie.' Her voice softened. 'And your mother. But, he told me, it was your mother he let down.'

Eloise felt the tears trickle over her face and she quickly brushed them away.

'So it doesn't matter any more. I'm sure you could have a DNA test or something. But why? It won't change anything. He loves you as a daughter. So that's what you are.'

'Th-thank you.'

Belinda released her hand. 'Give Jem a chance.'

It didn't seem likely he'd want one. 'I'd better go. Visiting time is nearly over.' Eloise picked up her handbag and headed for the door. She felt as if she'd been wrung out and fed through a mangle.

She couldn't cope with all the emotions surging through her body. Her head hurt with trying to process them all and understand how she was feeling.

The signs to the exit were clearly marked. Eloise blindly followed the arrows, not really noticing anything about her surroundings.

'Eloise?' Jem's voice. Half command, half plea.

She stopped, not daring to turn round.

'I should have listened.'

She felt the tears rise up and trickle down her face. She didn't want to turn round. She didn't want him to see them.

And she heard Belinda's voice. *'Give Jem a chance.'*

She wanted to. More than anything else in the world.

But he'd let her down. He'd failed her. Just as Laurence had failed her mum. Was that inevitable? Did loving someone always mean you were going to be hurt?

'I thought you'd been deceiving Laurence. Making him believe something was true…when it wasn't.'

Eloise closed her eyes against the pain. 'I—I haven't.'

'No.'

She heard him step closer. She could almost feel his breath on her hair.

'I'm sorry.'

Her tears continued to fall, scalding on her cheeks. Sorry wasn't enough. She couldn't do it. She couldn't make herself trust him again.

'I don't know who my father is,' she managed. 'I suppose it might not even be Patrick McMahon, whoever he might have been.'

For one moment she thought Jem was going to touch her, but he didn't. He was standing so close.

She made one desperate swipe at her face, clearing away the betraying trails of moisture. Then she stepped forward, putting some distance between them before she turned round.

'I don't even know who my mum is any more. I've lost everyone…and it isn't my fault. I—It isn't my fault.' Her voice broke, her face awash with tears she no longer cared about.

'I love you.'

His words were quiet, but very distinct.

Eloise wrapped her arms around her body, as though she could shield herself from hurt.

'I love you,' he repeated, moving closer.

She let out a sob and his arms wrapped around her. 'I'm sorry. So sorry,' he whispered against her hair.

Eloise felt his fingers stroke her hair.

'I will always love you.'

She pulled away and immediately he released her. But she'd only moved far enough away to look up into his face.

It was there in his eyes. All the love in the world. For her.

Slowly she smiled. 'I love you too. I should have told you about—'

'The first part is all I need to hear.' He reached across and cradled her head, bringing her towards him for a kiss of commitment.

He leant back and looked deep into her eyes. 'Marry me.'

Her smile widened.

Jem's own smile sprang into life and his voice became more confident. 'Marry me. Stay with me until the day I die.'

Eloise nodded. She couldn't speak; the words just wouldn't come. It didn't seem to matter because he gathered her close and held her there.

She had no idea how long they stood like that, or whether anyone passed them. She felt as if she'd passed through fire and had suddenly found safety.

It was the start of a new love story. Theirs.

EPILOGUE

ELOISE missed her mum. A girl would always need her mother on her wedding day.

She would have loved all this. An August wedding with all the trimmings. Something she'd never had for herself.

Eloise picked up her bouquet, carefully chosen to symbolise all her hopes for the future. Apple blossom which spoke of better things to come. The sprig of myrtle for love.

'Ready?' Belinda asked, elegant in a stunningly cut dress the colour of a summer sky.

Eloise nodded.

'Scared?'

'No.' There had never been anything in her life she'd been more certain of. She was going down the long staircase of Coldwaltham Abbey to meet Jem.

There was nothing to be scared of. There would never be anything to be scared of.

They'd both suffered too much in the past to ever risk losing what they'd found together. They knew how precious it was.

Laurence was waiting at the foot of the stairs, his kind face shining with father-like pride. 'I remember Marie wearing that dress,' he said, reaching up to catch her hand.

Eloise looked down at her 'something borrowed'. It had been the loveliest gesture when Jem's mother had offered the use of her dress and veil. The classical cut and princess sleeves were timeless, and she loved it.

'You look beautiful.'

'Thank you.'

'Marie is already at the church.'

Eloise felt a sudden surge of excitement which didn't leave her. A bubble of happiness that fizzed like the best champagne.

At the door of the church she paused to kiss Belinda and covered her face with the veil. Then she took her father's arm.

Whatever the truth of it, Laurence would always be her father in every way that mattered. Through the misty whiteness of her veil, she set off down the aisle.

On her side of the church sat her colleagues from *Image*. Cassie, resplendent in a dramatic hat, and no doubt still sulking because they'd refused to allow their wedding to be featured.

And at the altar there was Jem. Her heart swelled with love for him. As she drew near, he reached out and took hold of her hand.

It was a perfect day. His deep voice spoke the vows she knew he intended to keep. His strong hand pushed on the narrow platinum band they'd chosen to symbolise their love.

And then the vicar pronounced them 'husband and wife'. For ever.

To the sound of the 'Wedding March' Jem led her out into the bright August sunshine. Eloise looked up at him and smiled, complete trust in her beautiful face.

There was just a moment before their guests joined them. Jem pulled out a single flower from her bouquet. He placed it in the palm of her hand and closed her fingers round it, crushing the petals.

She looked up at him questioningly.

'It's something I read,' he said, opening her hand so she could see the bruised petals. 'It's a Danish saying.'

'Which is?'

His voice deepened. 'Love is like a precious flower. It is not enough to admire it. You must also cherish and protect it.' He brushed the petals out of her hand. 'And be prepared to devote your life to it.'

Eloise needed no more. She understood everything he was trying to tell her. The promise he was making. It was a promise her heart echoed.

His expression lightened and he pulled her close to kiss her. 'I love you, Mrs Norland.'

'I love you too,' she whispered softly, as their family and friends began to gather round them.